Feb. 2017

LAUREN,

For All you do

The Best

Always

TS

THE POET
THE COUNT
AND
THE PEDDLER

ALSO BY ANTHONY BOTTAGARO

To Create a World More Human and More Divine

Revolution: a Challenge of Love

THE POET THE COUNT AND THE PEDDLER

A NOVEL BY
ANTHONY BOTTAGARO

Rockaway
Press

Longmont, Colorado

Published by Rockaway Press
Longmont, CO 80502
www.rockawaypress.com

This novel is a work of historical fiction. It contains certain historical events and characters, as well as actual businesses and well-known places. In some instances, however, the incidents portrayed as occurring at these businesses and places are entirely fictitious. Any resemblance of a fictional character portrayed herein to a person, living or dead, is purely coincidental.

Sicilian dialects may vary from city to city and town to town. Therefore, what you will encounter in reading the Sicilian words and passages in this book are the result of a best-efforts attempt to reach a reasonably reliable phonetic representation of common pronunciations.

A reading group guide is available at www.rockawaypress.com.

First edition 2006

Printed in the United States of America

10 09 08 07 06

ISBN-13: 978-1-933696-78-2
ISBN-10: 1-933696-78-8
LCCN: 2005936089

⊚The paper used in this book meets the minimum requirements of the American National Standard for Information Sciences—Permanence of Paper for Printed Library materials, ANSI Z39.48-1992.

This book is printed on acid-free recycled paper.

For THE WHITE ROSE OF LOVE . . . always.

Acknowledgments

My deep gratitude goes to my editor Joyce Miller, who defines the word committed, and to Dan Miller for his sound management and technical direction.

To those friends, who unselfishly gave their time and creative insight: Moe Albanese, Garry Appel, Tony Bonacci, Carol Colombo, Harry Flynn, Larry Green, Don Humphrey, Louis Kirby, Julius La Rosa, Tomaso Maggiore, Joe Martori, Rose Perry, Laurie Roush, Mark Roy, Michael Vera, and Jill Weber.

I would be remiss if I did not express my sincere appreciation to friends in the religious communities for their generosity of spirit. They had the courage to stand with me, open doors, and live love in the quest for justice and peace.

Also, to the many people I have met along the way who have someway and somehow, influenced the writing of *The Poet, The Count, and The Peddler.*

Last and foremost, to *la famiglia,* who give their unflagging love and support. They inspire me, always. Thanks to my precious children and their spouses: Kathleen; Tom and Christine; Andy and Tina; Monica and Aaron; and David and Paige. Thanks to my glorious grandchildren Caitlin, Alexandra, Anthony, and Joey. And thanks especially, to my wonderful wife, Cathy. Without her endless support and love, this novel would not have happened.

Dear Reader,

I wrote The Poet, The Count, and The Peddler with one thought in mind: what we need most today is to recognize we can each be a force for good. I was energized in my writing by the strong conviction that there is a way we can mend, with Divine Love, the rips and tears in the fabric of our world.

Much like the peddler, all my life experiences, good and bad, have molded me into who I am—a peddler of words. I live every day knowing without a doubt that Mario's dream of liberty is not just a future possibility. It is attainable now, in the oneness of humanity, through love!

The tale of The Poet, The Count, and The Peddler is something of a personal tapestry. It is my desire that this story will speak to you in your life's journey. It is my hope that you embrace the peddler and his words of change with the love with which they are shared and only in your Truth.

So, if you dare, go ahead, and with the courage and the curiosity of a great explorer and adventurer, turn the pages, travel with Mario on his exciting and bold journey. Discover how and why he became a peddler.

With unconditional love, I am,

Tony

Anthony Bottagaro

Prologue

Sicilia . . . a timeline

Sicilia . . . thousands of years of occupation . . . the Greeks, Romans, Byzantines, Arabs, Normans, French, and Spanish . . . together, their influence created a diverse people unified in Sicilian blood.

Sicilia . . . a fascinating island shaped by three different seas, and extreme climatic conditions; and possessing kaleidoscopic topography full of beauty and charm.

Sicilia . . . in the hands of a potter,
reshaped by the Inquisition and Renaissance,
reshaped by rebellion and turmoil,
reshaped by corruption and poverty,
reshaped by war and scoundrels,
and reshaped . . .

Sicilia . . . where the Ferrara and Pizzo families, for generations upon generations, had lived in Conca d'Oro, "the Golden Shell" of Palermo.

In 1860, Giuseppe Garibaldi and his bold band of volunteers, in one full sweep, invaded and conquered Sicily, crossed the Strait of Messina onto the mainland, and pressed on toward Naples to achieve his unstoppable goal—the liberation and unification of Italy. This incredible accomplishment may have unified a country; but to the dismay of the revolutionary Garibaldi, the South, known as the Mezzogiorno, continued to suffer in hopelessness. As a result, it became increasingly difficult to subsist, let alone build a life in oppressed and poverty-stricken southern Italy.

By the 1900s, Sicily was reeling in despair: inadequate or non-existent housing, poor medical care, and unemployment as well as general chaos pushed men and women of all ages to follow a path to the sea and break the shackles of yesterday. The result of this massive exodus caused the South to lose many courageous souls to a New World.

Although this move meant they were faced with the sorrow of saying what was possibly their last good-bye to parents, siblings, friends, and homeland, off they went to live the dream of Garibaldi.

Immigrating to a foreign land somewhere on the other side of the vast Atlantic Ocean was only the beginning of many challenges to come.

In anticipation, America lay waiting for her newly adopted and downtrodden children to arrive. Between 1880 and 1924, more than four million Italian immigrants crossed the Atlantic Ocean in search of the American dream.

BOOK I

Chapter 1

In Florence, Italy, in 1321 a young man sat silently on a grassy bank at the edge of the Arno River. A white rose with its tender petals perfectly in place floated by in the gentle waters. His heart leaped in ecstasy. As he reached for the rose, a shadow loomed at his side. Startled, he turned and looked directly into the dark eyes of the poet Dante Alighieri who whispered, "Always remember the darkest places in hell are reserved for those who maintain their neutrality in times of moral crisis." The young man nodded knowingly. Then, his eyes blurred. Suddenly, he was standing on a cobblestone street in a mist so thick he could see only a few feet ahead. He turned, tripped, and fell over Dante's epic poem that lay beside him. The young man cut himself on its tattered cover and began to bleed. He hurriedly picked himself up and began to run. As he fled through the medieval city of Palermo in 1785, he could hear *Conte Alessandro di Cagliostro* shouting from the rooftop, "To really know a thing you must become that thing."

Inadvertently slapping his taped-up alarm clock to the floor, the peddler was jolted out of his haunting dream. Sitting on the edge of his rumpled bed, he wiped away beads of sweat and recalled how the Poet and the Count profoundly influenced his life.

9:00 AM
MONDAY, SEPTEMBER 10, 2001
LITTLE ITALY, NEW YORK CITY

Beneath a faded red, green, and white canvas awning at 231 Elizabeth Street, a stoop-shouldered old man smiled and gently closed the front door to Ferrara's Grocery and Bakery.

Moments later, weighed down by a cracked and torn, brown leather bag, he paused and then sighed as he struggled with a rickety Sicilian pushcart.

Despite increased arthritic pain, the peddler was determined to press on and complete the journey to Battery Park at the south end of Manhattan Island.

Slowly pushing his peddler's cart, he wove his way through the narrow, brick and mortar, jam-packed streets of colorful Little Italy.

Walking the cobblestone pavement step-by-step, block-by-block, he inhaled—to his delight—the bountiful aroma of basil, garlic, and imported cheeses wafting from kitchens and delicatessens.

Along the way, the peddler enjoyed listening to the hum of endless chatter coming from the diversity of people, some rushing, some strolling to their destination.

Laughter, weeping, and shouting filled the air only to be interrupted now and then by wailing sirens of fire, police, and other emergency vehicles.

Just as he passed Gaetano's Delicatessen on Grand Street, his *paesanu*, animated as ever, rushed to the open storefront, wiped his huge, hairy hands on his stained, white apron, and shouted, "Mario, let me know the next time you go into the inferno with Dante. I need a favor." With arms flailing, the grocer continued, "Please take my mother-in-law with you and drop her off in the pain-in-the-ass section."

Mario's smile lit up his weathered face. Gaetano's robust body shook with laughter as he slapped the side of his balding head and tossed Mario an apple.

The peddler nodded his appreciation.

Along the way, tears of joy blurred his crinkled, blue eyes as children rushed to greet him with giggles and hugs. As always, they anxiously looked forward to hearing one of his fascinating tales.

Their favorite story was of Mario's journey into the Village of Soul that began at Mascotti's Fruit and Vegetable Stand.

Now, strange as it may seem, adults were also captivated by this mystical story. As a result, more and more families were buying their produce at Mascotti's, and that's why it was not unusual to see boys, girls, women, and men walking along Spring Street tenderly holding a beautiful red tomato with both hands.

On the Lower East Side, countless sidewalks were littered with makeshift wooden and cardboard stands holding a wide variety of fresh produce, meat, poultry, fish, cheese and other products ranging from buttons to electronics. But nowhere else, not even on the sidewalks of New York, could you find the trinkets of sorts Mario carried on his peddler's cart.

Opera, Sicilian folksongs, dogs barking, people talking, children laughing, horns blowing, sirens shrieking, or carpenters hammering—it just didn't matter to the peddler.

All that noise was part of the ever-present sounds of life, and in his slight Sicilian accent, Mario proclaimed, "Life—what a glorious sound!"

Chapter 2

10:15 a.m.

Most every day, a bit of the peddler's topsy-turvy past found its way to his conscious mind.

Traveling south past Little Italy, he crisscrossed through an encroaching, hectic, vibrant Chinatown and marveled as always at the casbah of shops along Canal Street.

It was no surprise that the peddler, raised in New York City, was extremely adept at avoiding the never-ending, horn-blaring, pothole-thumping, brake-squeaking stream of cars, trucks, buses, and taxicabs.

When passing Thomas Paine Park, he shuddered at the sight of the beautifully wooded, postage-stamp patch of green that had turned red with blood during a regrettable moment in 1970.

It didn't matter what time of day, weather, or route, his trek to Battery Park always took him by the city's romantic skyway, the Brooklyn Bridge. Mario's heart pounded with fond memories every time he glanced at the majestic bridge with its massive, stone gothic arches and wooden promenade. In homage, he respectfully tipped his dark brown fedora.

Gingerly dodging traffic, he crossed Park Row to City Hall Park. Assortments of greenery harmonized by a medley of flowers adorned the entrance, providing a welcoming atmosphere and a marvelous place for him to sit and relax.

Taking a deep breath, he dropped his tattered bag from his shoulder and plopped down on a splintered park bench opposite the park's centerpiece, a Victorian fountain surrounded by ornate gas lamps. Mario was spellbound by the sound of spouting water cascading off its charming circular sculpture and by the rising mist.

As usual, City Hall Park was occupied by those looking for a respite from the grinding life of Lower Downtown. There, in a timeless moment, young, old, male, and female sat, sunned, read, slept, talked and people-watched.

After he carefully opened his satchel, a huge grin softened his lined face. Mario unveiled a mangled paper bag, spread its content of seed on a fractured walkway, and called out to awaiting families of birds and squirrels, *"Mangia!"*

A short time later, the peddler continued south along a boisterous, swarming Broadway, its confusion and noise magnified by construction barriers and torn-up roads under repair. As his tired legs inched by the soaring Twin Towers of the World Trade Center, his eyes sparkled in amazement at the extraordinary engineering accomplishment.

Crossing Liberty Street, Mario shouted out an obscenity in Italian when he nearly had the front end of his cart taken off by a speeding delivery truck running a red light. Despite the near mishap, he cheerfully flagged down a taxi for a frustrated young family of five on vacation from Montana.

A few blocks later, at Broadway and Rector Street, he found himself at the moss-enshrouded, well-kept Trinity Church graveyard. As he held on tightly to a black iron post, Mario's mind drifted back to a heated conversation with Father Tim Gallagher that had taken place among headstones dating back to the 1700s. Mario often wondered whether he should have taken his childhood friend's advice.

Pushing forward, he managed to maneuver his cart around double-parked trucks and through the winding steel and concrete forest of the financial district. But before exiting the first canyon, he decided it was time for an interlude.

Under a fiery sun, Mario stood on a beat-up, wooden milk crate in front of Federal Hall. The building stood opposite the New York Stock Exchange, America's bastion of capitalism.

With mixed emotions, the peddler gazed at the flag-draped Exchange Building at 18 Broad Street. The building's six massive Corinthian columns spaced across its façade symbolized stability and prosperity. Although fortunes had been made at the epic trading center, lives had also been shattered there.

While handing out bottles of *Count Alessandro's Healing Tonic of Love*, with confidence and in a strong voice, he said, "Out of a cocoon is born a most beautiful butterfly. So, always look within the ashes to find a hidden treasure. There is no death—just life. So live and do not grieve."

A twenty-six-year veteran of the New York City Police Department who had patrolled the financial district for years gradually made his way toward Mario. The slightly overweight policeman raised his hand and motioned for him to step down. The peddler, grinned, nodded in acknowledgment, stepped down, picked up his crate, tossed it into the peddler's cart, and began to push off.

But being suddenly distracted, he abruptly stopped to look directly into the eyes of a man from his checkered past.

The pudgy-faced man was spitting and screaming at the peddler. "They should have tarred and feathered you when they had the chance," yelled the man.

Tugging on his scruffy fedora, Mario calmly said, "Those who partake in senseless and harmful acts have sunk lower than the worms that fertilize our soil. Their place in history is secured alongside the barbarous." He paused, rubbed his forehead, shrugged, and added, "And oh, in the meantime, I ask all hate groups to disappear into the sewers from which they came."

The man snickered, gave him a one-finger salute, and stomped off.

Tipping his fedora, Mario smiled.

A thirty-something woman in jeans and red turtleneck blurted, "Nut! The old man is delusional."

With a twinkle in his eyes, the seasoned policeman said, "Don't let his worn clothes and manner fool you. This man is daring!"

As she removed her oversized Calvin Klein sunglasses, blustery winds whipped through the canyons of Lower Downtown.

The last leg of Mario's trip took him by the same art deco buildings that had graced the streets of Lower Manhattan at the time he and his family had arrived from Palermo, Sicily, in 1923.

Chapter 3

11:45 a.m.

The peddler finally reached the south end of Manhattan Island just before the noon hour and entered Battery Park.

He headed toward the Castle Clinton National Monument, formerly called Castle Garden. It had been the predecessor to Ellis Island, a processing plant for arriving immigrants from the 1830s to 1924.

Along the way, Mario paused to reflect on a masterfully crafted bronze sculpture representing immigrant strangers who had shared an overwhelming experience upon entering the United States. Their faces were contorted; their expressions were intense with emotions ranging from elation to anxiety, and their bodies were connected by touch. The sculpture was aptly entitled *The Immigrants*.

Mario moved forward; his eyes glanced in the direction of the Statue of Liberty. The ecstasy of sailing into New York Harbor on the steamship *Dante Alighieri* and catching a glimpse of *la Statua della Libertà* for the first time had been a breathtaking experience for Mario; his parents, Antonio and Vincenza; his younger brother, Giovanni; and his sister, Carmela.

The place he chose to set up his peddler's cart was situated by the very first series of steps to a winding promenade alongside the East River and within a stone's throw from the Liberty and Ellis Island ferries. It was a magnificent site to behold, seagulls perched on piers or hovered overhead while cruise ships and leisure craft moved in and out of the harbor. Further, it provided a key vantage point to peer at the resting place of his *papà's* admired Lady Liberty.

Mario shared Battery Park with other peddlers, street musicians, artists, tourists, pickpockets, joggers, writers, readers, card and checker players—plus city dwellers meditating or sitting on the scattered benches placed throughout the glorious park.

Always enthusiastic despite jeers or ethnic slurs, Mario met and greeted all people of diversity: those of any color, race, language, social status, nationality, or religion.

Daily, they rushed on and poured off ferries from tours of Liberty and Ellis Island. This smiling old man opened his heart to anyone whose curiosity he aroused. With arms raised, he told intriguing tales that sparked the imagination and touched upon issues, problems, ailments, and solutions.

Before preparing to hawk trinkets of sorts and *Count Alessandro's Healing Tonic of Love*, he retrieved from his cart a white rose with its tender petals perfectly in place. He strolled to the water's edge, knelt down, and gently tossed the fragile rose onto the rippling waters.

The peddler mindlessly removed his fedora to allow the soft bay breeze to blow through his unruly gray hair. Hearing a whisper in the breeze, Mario smiled and gazed upward.

Back at the cart, he looked over flowering gardens and recalled the words of his papà.

"*La famigha è sacra!* Family . . . all families everywhere are the paste, the glue that keeps the universe together. Family is first and last . . . Number one! That is the family."

The peddler thundered, "Be bold. Live love. Experiment in living life to the fullest and proclaim your liberty."

And so, Mario Ferrara, the peddler, began another day at Battery Park.

BOOK II

Chapter 4

Wednesday, April 25, 1923
Conca d'Oro, Palermo, Sicily

It was a moment in time never to be forgotten.

Monte Pellegrino's enchanting summit, rising above the morning mist, appeared to be floating in glowing sunshine. It was as though nature captured the heart and tearing eyes of Mario and his *famigha*. After much nervous anticipation, they were to leave their beloved home and the medieval city of Palermo.

Palermo, bounded by hills, sea, and fertile land and rooted in diverse cultures and traditions was to soon become a memory.

With the blessings of their respective families, Antonio Ferrara, age thirty; his wife, Vincenza Pizzo, twenty-nine; and their children, nine-year-old Mario, seven-year-old Carmela, and six-year-old Giovanni, were prepared to leave the only home they ever knew.

The family would no longer have the comfort and warmth of their primitive one-room stone house.

Antonio's weather-beaten body would no longer labor in groves harvesting oranges, lemons, and tangerines; work at the fish market in the harbor district; or care for his livestock.

Vincenza, her olive skin darkened by a burning sun, would no longer work in the fields next to Antonio, prepare meals on a blackened wood-burning stove, or wash clothes by pounding them with rocks.

Carmela and Giovanni, older than their years, would no longer collect water from the village to help their *mamma*, climb a ladder to sleep in a loft, or feed the chickens that shared the first floor of their home.

Mario would no longer gather twigs to burn, tend to his mule, Francesca, help his *papà* in the fields, or bake bread in their wood-fired oven to sell on the *piazza*.

Thanks to Vincenza's tireless hands, the family was dressed in their finest handmade clothes. They were hoping to make a good impression on the inspectors who would carefully scrutinize them upon their arrival in America.

Antonio was out of character in his black coat, brown vest, white shirt, and black tie. Vincenza looked stunning in her favorite rose-colored dress and crocheted white shawl. Carmela, whose features resembled her *mamma's,* was giggly in her long, lacy white dress. Mario and Giovanni, dressed in white shirts buttoned tight around the neck, gasped for air.

Mario's hands trembled as he wrapped his old bandana around Francesca's neck, cuddled her, and then quickly ran to join Carmela and Giovanni.

Outside their home, they stood in eerie silence with their parents, grandparents, and extended family. The children's roving eyes darted across the memorable white, yellow, and pink wild flowers gracing the terrain of the Ferrara homestead.

Although it seemed like an eternity, it was only moments later that the silence was broken by sobs accompanied by hugs and kisses. Unfortunately, many of those hugs and kisses would have to last a lifetime. It was a living funeral if there ever was one.

With the help of their *paesani,* the Ferraras loaded all the baggage they could carry on donkeys and carts for their pilgrimage. Antonio reluctantly rounded up his weeping family and began their difficult journey to the deep-blue waters of the Tyrrhenian Sea.

By virtue of Sicily's crushing economic and social atmosphere, a family support system was about to be shattered. A portion of the Ferrara and Pizzo bloodline would be lost to a New World.

The evening before, the dark, narrow streets of Palermo were bustling with villagers. Many assembled at the welcoming *Piazza Verdi* that embraced Antonio's favorite building, the glorious *Teatro Massimo*, to greet and wish the family an emotional farewell.

Hours later Mario, standing on the vast cobblestone *piazza* where he daily sold his fresh hard-crusted bread, said with his voice breaking, *"Picchi´ papà?"*

Antonio wrapped his strong arms around his son, kissed him on the cheek, and whispered, "Instead of asking why, think memories. Just like the opera house will be for me—memories: they are yours forever. In your heart you will hold your *nanna e nannu* and all of *la famigha*. You will never forget. And that includes the land of your birth." He hesitated a moment, took one last look at the noble opera house, smiled sadly, and said, "Come, my son; it's time to go."

The Ferraras left the *piazza* for the long walk home and another restless night of tossing and turning in their beds. Alberto, a long time *paesanu*, felt a knot of pain forming in the pit of his stomach as he began strumming melancholy cords on his mandolin, seemingly in tune with the low-spirited steps of the family.

Tomorrow would arrive soon enough.

Nestled in the wide Bay of Palermo under a blazing Sicilian sun, the transatlantic steamship *Dante Alighieri* waited patiently. In contrast, the dock, jam-packed with a sea of humanity, was tumultuous. Voyagers were immersed in noise and confusion. Trunks, suitcases, and makeshift bags were strewn along the splintered pier while hordes of people, including those who had climbed aboard in Naples, milled about the landing.

Once the Ferraras arrived at the seaport, reality quickly set in. Vincenza's slender body shivered as her light blue eyes, filled with fear, met Antonio's dark bright eyes, filled with adventure.

They embraced.

Moments later, to the delight of the children, their parents were laughing loudly as Antonio twirled Vincenza around and around.

As the sun was dipping low in the sky, the call for departure snaked its way along the pier. The family warily began climbing the rugged gangplank. After taking only a few steps, Mario broke free, fled down the plank, threw his arms around Francesca, kissed her goodbye, and then raced back toward his family. Vincenza, her eyes clouded by tears, looked back at their *paesani* who were waving wildly and shouting, *"Addiu! Addiu!"*

Once on deck, Antonio tipped his mangled hat. Vincenza brushed back her curly black hair and forced a smile. Carmela and Giovanni giggled in excitement and wonderment. Mario, tears rolling down his cheeks, stood in silence as his eyes glanced upward toward *Monte Pellegrino.*

Soon they would set sail for America.

Life would never be the same.

Chapter 5

Crossing the Atlantic on a loud, rolling, cramped transatlantic steamship full of human cargo and their ragged luggage was a trip into purgatory, if not the inferno itself. The family's belongings became their beds, chairs, and tables.

A vicious storm hit the *Dante Alighieri* after she passed through the Strait of Gibraltar. It would have been difficult enough at any time eating paltry portions of macaroni and herring; but it was nearly impossible when riding massive swells. Pounding waves slammed into the ship often creating huge geysers.

Vincenza thought the ship was cursed by the evil eye.

The Ferrara's minimal funds forced them to travel third class or, as it was called, "steerage passage." Antonio was unaware that his family would be packed like sardines in windowless quarters. In their overstuffed area, the simple task of breathing became a chore. To add to the distress, they had to endure a horrible stench and were subjected to relentless pounding sounds that emanated from the ship's steering mechanism and engines.

When possible, in order to gasp a breath of fresh air, the family would make their way to a fragment of upper deck that was allocated for those traveling steerage. This, however, was not exactly euphoria. Each time, the children watched in horror as passengers collapsed in misery or stretched themselves over the railing, vomiting at the upheaving movement of an ocean that never seemed to end.

Many immigrants, Vincenza included, carried a bag of guilt for leaving their homeland, evidenced by the long, tearful *viaggio*. Most would agree that among the millions who traveled the rough seas, there was an enormous number that found hardship and suffering commonplace. They called the excursion *"a via dolorosa,"* the sorrowful way.

From the time they left the harbor in Palermo, neither seasickness nor vomit nor foul air dampened Sicilian and Italian determination in their dream of hope and liberty. The Ferrara's desire to laugh, sing, and dance with their countrymen, though it sometimes waned, was never entirely lost along the arduous journey.

On the voyage to America, those from the northern provinces of Italy no longer looked down on those from the South. They were keenly aware that aloofness or snobby attitudes towards those in steerage would not be tolerated. And although dialects were as different as night and day, the space so overflowed with humanity that separation was not a choice. Consequently, they found comfort and support in each other.

It was a wonderful opportunity for Antonio to instill in young Mario the strange phenomenon of unity. They would, however, soon discover an equally strange occurrence in the New World. Though America was a nation of immigrants, Italians would again see a difference of perception between North and South, and in this new world other ethnic groups added a difference—a difference in color.

Following two excruciating weeks of travel, Antonio suddenly took hold of his family, quickly guiding them from the darkness of steerage to daylight on the cramped forward deck. They watched in awe, wiping away tears of ecstasy, as the *Dante Alighieri* slowly traveled the Hudson River and entered New York Harbor.

Despite the fact that they were bathed in soot from the belching smokestacks, those gathered on deck gleefully shouted, *"L'America! L'America!"*

The rugged old ship seemed to lift out of the water in respect as it passed *a la Statua della Libertà*. There she stood in her magnificent glory, a beacon of hope for all immigrants and the reigning symbol of American liberty.

Antonio's body quivered in celebration. Overwhelmed, he pointed and bellowed, "Look, there she is. She holds the torch high to welcome us to a land of liberty and opportunity."

"Ra signura a libertà è bedda," added a watery-eyed, seasick Vincenza, holding tight onto Carmela and Giovanni.

Mario's smile was frozen on his face as he stood in homage to Lady Liberty.

The friendly waters of the Tyrrhenian Sea were a long way off.

Chapter 6

....

The morning of May 9, 1923
ELLIS ISLAND, NEW YORK

Those who traveled to America on first- and second-class passage underwent a cursory inspection aboard ship before the *Dante Alighieri* docked at Pier 13 in Manhattan. Afterward, they were free to enter the United States. All remaining passengers, along with their baggage, would be herded to a waiting area on the packed New York pier.

"*L'America,* so close and yet so far," said Vincenza, tightening her shawl around her chilled body.

Mario chimed in, "*Papà,* you said we are in the land of liberty. Why can't we go?"

Antonio, straining his broad shoulders, picked him up, smiled, and said, "*Pacienza fighiu mia . . . Pacienza.*"

An hour later, the family was moved to the other side of the dock and tagged with manifest numbers that designated their ship of arrival. Soon afterward, they boarded crowded ferries and navigated the choppy waters of the East River to Ellis Island, "*a isula d' immagrant,*" the immigrants' island.

As the ferry approached Ellis, fear and anxiety, coupled with a grapevine of rumors, spread quickly among its passengers.

Immigration would be tough.

Though physically, mentally, and emotionally exhausted, Antonio tried to ease the fears of his family. Holding Carmela in his arms, he softly said, "Soon, my dear, your tears will turn to smiles. No more crying in America." He kissed Vincenza on her cheek and told Mario and Giovanni, "If you treat this land with respect, liberty will be yours forever."

Vincenza was eternally grateful for having survived the crossing, and she was mentally prepared for whatever hurdles lay ahead. So she thought.

Under a huge canopy in front of the main building, the family waited patiently for the immigration process to begin. Except for Vincenza who's stomach twisted in knots every time she heard men screaming out commands in a strange tongue. Seeing her fearful look, Antonio smiled, reached out, and held her hand.

A large, imposing man sporting a full salt-and-pepper beard met the family with a robotic greeting. Carmela spun around to hide behind Giovanni who an instant before had covered his big brown eyes with his hands. A smile broke on the interpreter's hardened face.

The Ferraras arrived with only six pieces of ragtag canvas luggage holding their clothes and bare essentials. Due to the steamship's space restrictions, the rest of their possessions were left on Palermo's dock.

The interpreter first escorted the family to a mammoth baggage room to check their belongings.

Mario slowly backed away. His tattered bag flung over his small yet strong shoulder. He was most reluctant to leave his prized belongings with a stranger dressed in military attire. Only with the assurance of his *papà* did he grudgingly let go. Antonio knew the bag held a treasured gift from his *nannu*. It was Dante Alighieri's *Divine Comedy*.

As soon as the baggage was secure, the interpreter directed the bewildered family up a steep stairway leading to the second-floor Registry Room. The room was outfitted with tall metal dividers that resembled cattle pens. The Great Hall, as it was called, adorned a high majestic ceiling, huge, half-moon-shaped windows, and an upper circular balcony. Although imposing, it was a welcome breath of fresh air for those had been crunched together in steerage.

Mario nervously observed men and woman dressed in white as they peered at his family's every step and movement. The efficient, keen-eyed medical staff was quick to determine obvious as well as subtle infirmities.

Antonio was deeply concerned as the family endured an unnerving eye examine for a disease known as trachoma. A metal instrument used to button gloves performed the painful "buttonhook" examination. The examiner would pull the eyelid back and look for signs of infection.

The inspection process included a humiliating medical examination, especially for the women who were asked to strip naked in front of strangers.

To compound their trauma, families were separated until the medical examinations were concluded. Any medical rejection was identified with a dreaded chalk mark that led to deportation, possible family separation, and heartbreak.

Finally, moving through the inspection area, waiting rooms, and prison-like corridors, the immigrants were reunited with their fumigated clothes. Much to her displeasure, Vincenza's handcrafted work, which they had worn since leaving their home in Palermo, was returned in a heap.

As difficult as it was passing the intrusive medical tests, immigrants now faced a final obstacle to enter America. An intimidating question and answer session conducted by an interpreter often set nerves on edge and brought many to the brink of imploding.

Taking advantage of advice given by returning immigrants aboard ship, Antonio was prepared for the concise, rapid, probing questions. Topics included prison record, literacy, relatives living in America, history related to anarchy, and the amount of money possessed. When asked about potential employment, he told the interpreter in broken English, "My *paesanu*, Mike Borelli, in New York helps me find work."

Distracted by a huge American flag hanging from the balcony, Antonio looked away for a moment and turned back just in time to see the stranger give a curt nod of approval, flick his wrist, and hand him a "landing card." He leaped at the startled man, hugged him, and blurted, "*Grazie . . . Grazie!*"

Antonio, in a state of euphoria, collected their possessions and his family and excitedly rushed out of the main building. With their customs, traditions, and memories intact, the Ferraras boarded the ferry *Columbia* and prepared to begin a new life with daring optimism in what they believed was the Promised Land.

Thus, the family's first major hurdle in the new land was met with awe, fear, courage, and elation.

Mario, tears welling in his eyes, said, "*Papà,* I thought you said there was no crying in America."

"*Sì . . . fighiu mia.*"

The entire family wore tears of celebration.

However, not all sweetness and gold awaited them in a city called New York.

In Italy, steamship companies had spread the word that streets in America were paved with gold. Much to their chagrin, the immigrants found no streets paved with gold. In actuality, some were not paved at all.

The immigrants would pave them with their sweat.

In most cases, Italian immigrant wages were at the bottom rung of the accepted pay scale of other ethnic groups. Nonetheless, the Italian work ethic did not diminish in the face of adversity. They always chose work over charity.

Heightening the misery of the workforce was the *padrone.* He was labeled as the immigrant's agent, sponsor, and loan broker. Instead, most *padroni* were slave peddlers and leeches who charged exorbitant fees and took advantage of bewildered immigrants.

Eventually, the *padroni* system faded into the wake of assimilation.

Chapter 7

Standing at the railing, Antonio cried out, *"Bedda! Bedda!"* as the ferry *Columbia* approached the glistening towers of New York City's skyline. Vincenza jumped up and down in celebration while she watched Mario, Carmela, and Giovanni joyfully sing and dance with other immigrant children.

Moments after docking at Battery Park, Mario was the first one off the bobbing boat, plunging into the confusion that greeted the family.

Antonio glanced at Mike Borelli's crude hand-drawn map, gathered his family together, and moments later, holding their unwieldy baggage, tentatively began walking the short distance to Little Italy. As they passed by the towering canyons of concrete and steel, Antonio tilted back his hat, ignored the mass of humanity, and pointed to the gracious, gothic-style Woolworth building.

"Vincenza, look how high; it reaches to the heavens," he said, spreading his arms wide in amazement at the tallest building in the world. "There are more buildings here than in all of Italy. It's too hard to believe." His eyes got wider, and he slapped the side of his head, declaring, "Look at all these people rushing to nowhere: the streetcars, automobiles, horse wagons, and—"

Vincenza interrupted. "Don't worry about the buildings and don't worry about the people or horses; instead, worry about our clothes. The disinfectant they used for lice was terrible. The odor remains. How are we going to look, meeting the Borellis?" she asked.

He laughed and replied, "Don't worry how you look. Just worry how you smell."

Mario, his eyes popping at the swirling activity, cried out, "*Papà* . . . I *am* worried about the horses."

Along the way, under the close edgy scrutiny of Vincenza, the children were freely skipping, running, and walking, and not in any particular order.

After dodging trolleys, traffic, and people, Antonio turned the corner at Prince and Elizabeth Street and cracked a huge smile of relief as he spotted the Borellis and their son, Joe.

Mike Borelli, a childhood friend of Antonio, and his wife, Angelina, were Mario's *parrino e parrina.*

They rushed to greet their *paesani.*

The Borellis had arrived in New York's Little Italy three years earlier and had somewhat adjusted to the unimaginable noise, congestion, and confusion of the American way. Finally, after years of correspondence and anticipation, with tears of joy, hugs, and kisses, they welcomed the Ferraras into their modest home on Elizabeth Street.

Angelina, a small, yet robust woman with long, dark brown hair took Vincenza aside, gently held her hands, and said, "Don't worry about anything. Stay with us until you settle. We will help you find a safe place of your own."

Embracing her, Vincenza humbly replied, "*Grazie . . . Grazie . . . Grazie.*"

Mario, Carmela, Giovanni, and Joe played on the fire escape.

Mike, a tall and wiry man, was tough yet tender. He not only opened his home to the Ferraras, but his contacts and wallet as well. The Borellis graciously provided Antonio Ferrara and his family what they needed—support and encouragement during their struggles while adapting to a strange new way of life.

Even though hundreds of thousands came to *Italia Nica* to find a new and better way, countless Italians found an unfriendly country.

Crossing streets meant crossing territories and encountering varying standards established by already settled Lower East Side residents, mainly Jews, Irish, Germans, and a small community of Chinese.

The American dream became tarnished.

Many immigrants lived in cold-water, firetrap tenement buildings. Moreover, as hard as it was to live in Sicily, the slums of lower downtown took their breath away.

However, the Italians were not dismayed by congested apartments. At times, ten to twenty people squeezed into a space barely large enough for a family of four. Amazingly enough, there was always room for one more. Close living resulted in close ties. From *buon giorno* to *buona sira*, extended families found open doors and open hearts that never closed. Sicilian respect and loyalty to one another never needed to be spoken. It was embedded in the blood running through their veins.

It would soon become apparent to the Ferraras that the gateway to liberty was through Little Italy, a community bonded by a common language and Old World customs and ideals. Early Italian immigrants found adjusting to new surroundings was easier than understanding or speaking the English language.

Therefore, an Italian blueprint, in the process of assimilation, was to remain intact, animated, and upbeat in the hullabaloo of their new neighborhood.

Italian immigrants, desperate for work, were grateful for any opportunity that provided employment. Subsequently, they became a major labor force in New York City, leaving a legacy by building roads, cutting stone for the Grand Central Terminal, digging tunnels, laying track for a developing subway system, connecting steel cables on towering bridges, and walking the plank as hod carriers in the construction of skyscrapers.

Few were fortunate enough to enter the professions.

Some became longshoremen on the New York waterfront; others became seamstresses in sweatshops and factory workers.

The more enterprising opened barbershops, restaurants, and stores selling a multitude of products in the emerging marketplace.

Then, there was the jovial peddler with his pushcart who from dawn to dark offered services or merchandise for sale.

A colorful, noisy bazaar of pushcarts and makeshift stands flooded sidewalks and streets on the Lower East Side. Peddlers, each with their distinct shrieking cry, hawked their goods of fish, vegetables, and fruits. Actually, anything you could imagine was bargained for, sold for, or bartered for services or other merchandise.

Organ grinders and hurdy-gurdy players added a musical atmosphere to the moving open-air market.

So, whether they were unskilled laborers, professionals, neighborhood merchants, or pushcart peddlers, all in one way or another were part of the family.

They knew the neighborhood and the neighborhood knew them.

1923

Since their arrival, a tar of misery permeated the air in the Ferrara household. Yet Antonio and Vincenza were determined to overcome the staggering odds of mental depression, ethnic discrimination, and actual poverty that faced most immigrants.

With the help of the Borellis, the Ferraras located and moved into an apartment on the corner of Prince and Elizabeth Street in the Sicilian stronghold of Little Italy.

Vincenza miraculously managed to transform a sterile apartment, barely outfitted with necessities for living, into a warm, welcoming home.

Antonio faced hardship with daring optimism and resiliency.

He told Mario, "Here we live in liberty. And remember the great liberator Garibaldi and what he risked his life for—it is here in America. Be not afraid and experiment with your life in this extraordinary journey."

On a daily basis, the family linked the Old World to the New and slowly began to assimilate into their city and country of choice.

> *Here, there were*
> *People, people, and more people;*
> *Buildings, buildings, and more buildings;*
> *Stores, stores, and more stores;*
> *Pushcarts, pushcarts, and more pushcarts.*

Whatever the Ferraras witnessed, there was always more and more of it.

An indelible image for Mario was of horse-drawn wagons gingerly making their way through a multitude of people and pushcarts occupying most of Mulberry Street. What seemed impossible turned to reality.

In the midst of their trials and tribulations, all was good, especially when everyone convened around the dinner table for a celebration of family.

Little Italy was a microcosm of Italian provinces and Sicilian cities, villages, and towns: Palermo, Polizzi Generosa, Siacca, Messina, Catania, and Taormina—and the list went on. Most of the time it didn't matter where your loyalty rested. When you left the comfort of your cold-water flat, there on the streets waiting to greet you were Italians with warm hearts.

Little Italy was a neighborhood embraced by a medley of Italian emotions that resonated from inside their love-filled homes, and when they were joined by the rhythmic noise from the street an opera of life was composed.

Status was exposed to the curious by improvised clotheslines that showed off an entire family's wardrobe.

Backyards were the size of pool tables; still, they sufficed for holding family gatherings.

As there was no main *piazza* in Little Italy, the immigrants improvised. Weather permitting, tables and chairs covered the neighborhood sidewalks, inviting interaction with the community-at-large. Together, they listened to music, played cards, laughed, gossiped, argued, and talked about anything and everything.

The neighborhood was a true sight to behold.

When Mario was free of work, he took advantage of his youth. Summertime was his favorite.

Children were everywhere, playing street games of stickball, kick the can, hide and seek, or whatever their creative imagination contrived.

Mario and his *amici* would run through ice-cold water that spewed from fire hydrants or chase one another up and down alleys and fire escapes, tease the not-so-kind peddlers and test his *mamma's* patience by snatching apples from street-stands.

The "wild bunch" as Vincenza called them, loved the challenge of convincing Salvatore, the iceman, to break off a small piece of his huge ice block, an Italian prelude to the Popsicle.

As a young boy, Mario anxiously waited to hear the raucous "yell" of the fruit and vegetable peddler Enrico Mascotti.

In anticipation, he would stand and watch from the fire escape as Enrico and his overworked, aging horse, Pasquale, sluggishly clip-clopped down Prince Street toward his home.

Enrico, an unlit *DiNobili* cigar hanging from his sun-cracked lips, would play catch with Mario. No balls, just bags filled with eggplants, peppers, zucchini, garlic, tomatoes, and onions, all tossed up to the second floor in exchange for a few coins.

Mascotti later opened a fruit and vegetable shop on Spring Street between Elizabeth and Mulberry. Shopping at his store was a challenging experience, as customers weaved their way on the saw-dust floor between crates, bushels, boxes, and shelves that overflowed with Sicilian delights, all priced right.

In 1924 the federal government, worried about communists and other "potential" threats, changed immigration law to a quota system. The discriminatory purpose of the change was to restrict mainly immigrants from southern and eastern Europe. They were considered different. For the hardworking Italians, it was a slap in the face.

1925

From the time he had arrived in America, Antonio, now called Tony, clawed his way up. He worked as a common laborer the first year using a pick and shovel and had earned a degree from the "University of Scars."

In his second year, he saved enough money to become a push-cart peddler with a "call" resembling the sound made by Mario's Sicilian donkey, Francesca. Pushing his rough and tumble cart from sunrise to sundown, he crisscrossed the streets of Little Italy selling imported olive oil, cheeses, and Mario's fresh, hard-crusted bread.

Tony signified immigrant toughness at its best.

During the '20s, intimidation of shopkeepers and those working the streets by thugs or the infamous "Black Hand" was prevalent.

As far as Tony was concerned, he would never back down to the strong-arm tactics of those trying to extort "protection money" from his sweat earnings. He was well aware that issues related to terror-ization of "family members" by outsiders would be settled by *la famigha* . . . just as disputes within the family were settled by *la famigha*.

While his pushcart provided living wages, Tony envisioned the possibilities that existed in America. His goal was to provide a safe haven for Vincenza, create opportunities for his children, and own his own home and grocery and bakery store. To that end, he stretched his mental and physical resources to the limit to earn extra money.

Tony sacrificed leisure time, toiled at odd jobs, and worked the night shift at the sprawling Fulton Street Fish Market. The market was dark, dirty, and chaotic.

"You can smell my *papà* from blocks away," Mario would say with a slight grin.

To supplement the family's income, Vincenza found underpaid work in a Lower East Side, slave-driving sweatshop. A short time later, she decided enough was enough and took in piecework garments.

Mario, besides baking bread in his *mamma's* oven and selling it on the corner of Mulberry and Grand Street, also became the pick-up and delivery boy for Vincenza.

Carmela and Giovanni, in addition to keeping the home spotlessly clean, took part in their *mamma's* work endeavor. Actually, the children were quite good in the art of piecing garments together and crocheting.

In between it all, Vincenza shopped, cooked, cleaned, and washed. Tired or not, she was always there for her family. Sacrifice was Vincenza's roadway to contentment.

In spite of the fact that the family struggled financially, Tony was no stranger to *Banca Italiana* located on Mulberry Street. He and Vincenza frequently made arrangements to send money back to their families in Palermo.

Years later when Tony and Vincenza finally acquired enough money to return to Sicily to visit *la famigha*, their parents had passed on. This untimely turn of events left a lasting mark of sadness on both their hearts.

Trains, trolleys, and legs transported the Ferrara family to visit their *paesani* who had moved out to the Upper East Side of Manhattan and the outlying suburbs of Brooklyn and Queens.

According to Vincenza, the excursion to Bensonhurst, Brooklyn, to visit the Borellis in their new home had its share of road hazards, especially in crossing the Brooklyn Bridge. The sights and sounds of moving traffic unnerved her. She always worried that a trolley may somehow recklessly hit one of her children or that one of the three would fall off the wooden walkway and wind up in the murky East River below.

Although only five feet tall, Vincenza possessed a shrill voice that could rattle the steel-webbed cables traversing the bridge.

"Please stop! Mario, you're the oldest and should know better. How many times have I told you not to run? You children are making me crazy." Raising her overworked arms while looking upward to the heavens, she pleaded, "Please, . . . God, help me . . . please!"

Tony, shaking his head, and with a twinkle in his piercing, dark eyes, fired back, "God, by now, is in a rest camp. Nobody, not even God, would have the patience to listen to you over and over again. Give Him a break."

"God willed us together. So be nice; we deserve each other," said Vincenza, holding back a smile.

From that moment, the adventurous trip continued with a vow of silence, at least between Vincenza and Tony. Mario, Carmela, and Giovanni, ignoring the situation, played tag.

The Ferrara family was not without their share of disagreements. They would argue over the necessity of the children buttoning up their coats before leaving for school, the rules regarding eating what was on their plate, or the logic of the criteria for determining how late they could stay out. There was, however, one cardinal rule that was not open for discussion: never let the sun set on your anger.

One evening, the boys got into a rip-roaring fight with Carmela who stomped off to her room. That altercation prompted their *mamma* to give a dissertation on anger.

Vincenza, rubbing her frowning forehead in frustration, said, "Why don't you ever listen to me? If I die in the middle of the night, I will never forgive myself for letting you go to sleep angry."

The children smiled and hugged her.

Tony and Vincenza viewed Palermo as a patchwork quilt of family. As a result, they carried that mindset to America and considered relatives and friends as extended family. One such friend was Frank Nunzi.

Frank arrived from Polizzi Generosa, Sicily, in December of 1924. He was only in New York a few months before he became the victim of a territorial mugging.

At the time, Tony was still working the night shift at the Fulton Fish Market. He was on his way to work when he spotted a man being pummeled in an alley.

"What the hell is going on?" Tony shouted angrily and rushed into the ruckus.

The man didn't answer.

It was Frank, under attack by a gang of Irish thugs who despised the Italians for a number of reasons, one of which was their entry into the American workplace.

Without giving any thought for his own safety, Tony jumped into the fray. The thugs quickly turned their attention to Tony and began to beat him. It was Sicilian luck that saved him from serious harm. The sounds of approaching sirens scattered the hoodlums into the night.

Taking advantage of the distraction, Tony dragged Frank deeper into the alley, tossed his burly body into a pile of garbage, and dove head first on top of him.

When the crowd of gawkers dispersed and the last police car with its flashing lights faded into the distance, both men emerged from their hiding place and headed for Tony's home.

Frank's white T-shirt, barely fitting his barrel chest, was soaked with blood from a knife wound. Tony's hands and arms were scraped and bleeding. Both men's clothes were filthy, torn, and smelled foul.

Vincenza cried out, "Look, both of you are a mess!"

Sitting upright at the kitchen table with a hot cup of coffee in his hand, Tony smiled and said nothing.

His beefy hands rubbing his thick neck, Frank shrugged meekly and in his gravelly voice said, "Mrs. Ferrara, thank you so much. I will never forget what you and Tony have done for me."

She cleaned their wounds and nursed them with the basic Italian treatment of iodine. Antiseptic iodine was not perfect. It removed the present pain only to replace it with the king of pain, the sting of stings of pukey-smelling, red iodine.

After the infirmary stop, Tony, his hand bandaged, left to finish the remaining part of his night shift at the fish market.

Frank, with a patched knife wound and broken nose, went directly back to his cold-water flat on Houston Street.

The following Saturday, Tony invited Frank to play *bocce* and introduced him to Mike Borelli. It was the beginning of a long friendship among the three men.

Two years later, with the financial help of Mike, Frank Nunzi opened a check-cashing facility in another Italian stronghold. This one was in Corona, Queens.

Tony was a wonderful storyteller of Sicilian folklore, especially when telling a tale of *Conte Alessandro di Cagliostro*. Mario, Carmela, and Giovanni, now called John, would sit on the floor in the living room and listen in wonderment to their *papà*.

Sitting on the edge of the sofa, looking down at them with a gleam in his eye, he would begin . . .

Long, long ago somewhere in the land of mountains, villages, cities, and valleys . . . in the Kingdom of the Two Sicilies, lived Giuseppe Balsamo, known to some as Conte Alessandro di Cagliostro and to others simply as "the peddler."

This man was born to poor and humble parents who lived in the slums of the Albergheria district of Palermo.

Soon after his papà died, the unruly young boy joined a band of vagabonds and wandered the maze of narrow cobblestone streets and alleys, causing mischief in the beautiful medieval city.

His mamma, in her frustration, sent the urchin away to a Benedictine monastery school. During the years he spent there, he became fascinated with chemistry and medicine, but his restless spirit caused him to finally escape and return to the city of his birth.

Months later, seeking to find himself, the young man set off across the Madonie mountains where eagles led him to the Mediterranean Sea.

Three days later, at midnight on a hot and steamy summer evening, spirits lured him to an enchanted forest and mysterious cave deep inside Monte Etna. There, in the midst of wonderful colorful caverns, he discovered a crystal spring spewing hot vapors. Exhausted, he sat down by water's edge, fell into a deep sleep, and in a dream-state, heard the musical, magical whispers of nature tell him the process of transformation.

When Giuseppe awoke, before his very eyes was a granite wall full of cryptic writing describing the process of turning the crystal waters into a healing potion, just as the whispers had spoken it. With the help of air, earth, water, and fire, he applied the secret rite over the bubbling spring. His eyes opened wide and almost fell out of his head as, one by one, the poetic words embedded in the wall turned to gold dust, and like a halo, floated in the air above his head.

Without delay, he poured the mystical water over his swollen, bloody, gnarled feet. It was but a moment later that he gazed in amazement. First the left foot, then the right . . . poof . . . just like that . . . they became instantly healed. The young man leaped in excitement.

Giuseppe swiftly made his way out of the mountain and down to a church in the nearby city of Catania. He wanted to share his discovery, but no one wanted to listen, and no one wanted to believe the young man. Saddened, the adventurer returned to the cave inside Monte Etna.

With nature's secret safe inside his mind, heart, and soul, he bottled the mystical water and ran far, far away.

Three years later, after traveling to Egypt to explore the mysterious Great Pyramids, he came to a crossroad in his upside-down life. After much thought, he decided to change his name to Conte Alessandro di Cagliostro and set out on a journey to heal the peoples.

Now this peddler, the likes of which there never was, but "is," traveling short and long, close and far, found himself in the midst of royalty and religious hierarchy, as well as of the poor.

The Conte, though not too big in stature, had the heart of a giant. He carried a purple wooden staff and wore a spectacular black cloak draped over his deep red robe. Each day he would don his flamboyant dark brown hat, complete with a gold band that held a pure-white feather in place, and adjust it so that it sat on his head slightly to the right of center.

This marvel of a man with shaggy hair sold trinkets of sorts and bottles of healing potion that he claimed was a cure for all diseases and problems.

Many said he was also a wizard who could transform metals into gold; others declared he was a saint who helped the poorest of the poor; and still others were certain that he was a magician, prophet, soothsayer, psychic, healer, or an immortal from China who migrated to Sicily.

But the Conte, in his many years of travels, also had many enemies who thought him a charlatan, scoundrel, and sinner. So . . . the charismatic peddler was arrested and sent to the Bastille in France. Then came the most horrible event . . . The Holy Inquisition accused him of being a heretic and sentenced him to be executed. But Pope Pius VI, instead, sent him to San Leo to die in a rat-infested prison.

Hearing news of the Conte's death, Napoleon went to visit his tomb and discovered that there was none. While Napoleon declared that Conte Alessandro di Cagliostro was dead, no one really knew for sure.

Some say he returned to Sicily and lives inside Monte Etna.

Others maintain that he hangs in Catacombe dei Cappuccini among the noblemen, priests, and poor, where, at midnight, he makes the rounds among the mummies. Still many others say that he still travels the earth as a peddler of healing tonic.

The children would plead, "Tell us more, *Papà*."

He would merely smile and answer, "Not now. Maybe tomorrow, I will tell you about the magic of healing."

1926

Tony Ferrara, ruler, master, and commander, ran the family with an iron fist. At least that was the impression left on outsiders. The children had a suspicion it was Vincenza, their loving *mamma*, who was the ultimate manager and matriarch of the family; and in fact, that was the reality.

In addition to working long hours, Tony studied hard to advance his understanding of the English language and American history. This was important to achieving his other goal of becoming a citizen of the country he had grown to love so much.

Still, to him, the most important thing was his *famigha* . . . first and last. In the middle, were his homegrown tomatoes, *bocce*, country, and, of course, his cherished fig tree which he carefully covered with linoleum every winter to protect it from the New York cold.

Mario, Carmela, and John were raised understanding that the family mattered most. It was their rock of stability, the one constant they could rely on, loyal to the death. A by-product of family was self-sufficiency. There was no need to look elsewhere for support, including the government or outside agencies, regarding conflict of any kind.

At every opportunity, Tony, in Sicilian dialect commingled with broken English, would remind the children, "Never forget, your blood is my blood . . . and your *mamma's* blood."

Bottom line was that love, honor, loyalty, and respect for the family was paramount—the supreme code of ethics and ideals. Everyone contributed to the common good of *la famigha*.

One moonlit evening, Tony sat at the dinner table over a huge plate of *linguine aglioe olio,* and with his eyes focused on the children, calmly said, "I struggle with the English language, but you must learn better than I in order to fulfill the opportunity that America gives freely."

He wiped the lingering olive oil from his mouth and continued, "Another thing. For the rest of your life, when it comes to people, you need to be colorblind and judgment free. Always remember, accept and extend your hand to all. Be available. Follow through on your promises and commitments to one another. I tell you again to respect everyone, listen to them, and when you do . . . you will have an understanding heart and you will know how to act."

"Please, you kids, listen to your *papà*," said Vincenza. "Right here in our city is division and hostility. The people from the North who settled here years ago still think of us as peasants who know nothing."

"*Mamma* is right," Mario cried out. "Yesterday, some man on Mulberry Street looked down at me, laughed, and yelled, '*un siciliano cafuni.*'"

Tony, his mouth full of bread, blurted, "Pay him no mind!" He slammed his fist down on the table, causing the flatware to rattle against the plates. "What he said doesn't matter. It's what you say and do; that's what matters. Always believe in yourself and trust your intuition. Each day you will be asked to make choices. So, you need to use your head, but never forget your heart."

The children, anxious to leave the dinner table, started to fidget. Yet all it took was one look from a fiery Vincenza, waving her wooden spoon, and they settled down.

Never short on words, Tony placed his macaroni-filled fork down and rolled on. "Someday you will truly understand that I speak from experience, the experience of coming to a new land we thought to be filled with promise."

Gesturing with his hands, he continued, "Instead, we found poverty and prejudice, not only from northern Italians, but from *l'Americani* as well. Not to worry. I tell you when you believe and act out of love, like your *mamma* does, the world and all its goodness is yours, now and forevermore. It's the only reality that no one can take away from you."

The children stopped eating.

Pausing, he rubbed his forehead, smiled confidently, and said, "Let me tell you something that happened before we came to *l'America*. Strikers at the Lawrence Textile Mills, who worked in outrageous conditions, asked for bread. Instead . . . what did they get? They got bayonets. But the Italian women with their strong hearts and determination and the children with faces of anguish touched the hearts of the people. What happened? The strike was settled."

With a heavy sigh, he said, "And another thing; *always* respect a woman. They act from their heart." Placing his fork down, he said, "Oh, one more thing; choose a direction that makes life exciting."

Vincenza pushed back her hair and said, "Yes. Look at beautiful Amelia Earhart and brave Charles Lindberg. They did exactly what your *papà* just said." She hesitated a moment, smiled, and said, "Except . . . maybe with too much excitement."

The next morning Mario asked. "*Papà*, tell me more about the brave people."

"That's good. That's a good thing for you to know. Come sit down, and I'll tell you about this courageous General George Washington, a wonderful revolutionary man."

Then Tony took Mario on an intriguing journey. He didn't stop with Washington, but went on to tell of other courageous men: Jefferson, Paine, Franklin, and Hale.

The Ferrara children each were distinct in their makeup. Carmela, concerned and caring, mimicked her *mamma* in taking control of household responsibilities. John was mild-mannered, nervous, and gifted with a presence of warmth, gentleness, and love. Just like Vincenza, he avoided conflict at all costs.

On the other hand, Mario, much like his *papà*, was known to lose his temper when pushed to the edge. He watched over his younger brother and sister like a hawk. One hot summer day, while children were playing stickball on the local playground, an overgrown Irish kid twice Mario's size brutally hassled John. Standing by, egging the bully on, were two other Irish kids from the neighborhood who were growing up in an atmosphere of deep-seated prejudice.

Ignoring the other two, Mario picked up his broom-handle bat and smacked the belligerent older boy over the head. The boy let out an earsplitting scream and ran down the street as blood oozed from his scalp. Having seen the horror that just took place, the other two boys took flight. Mario, his arm around John, slowly, very slowly, walked home in silence.

Tony and Vincenza were embarrassed and furious. In reality, they were more furious than embarrassed. They insisted Mario go to the boy's home and apologize. And they were adamant that he pay any medical bills out of his allowance, even if it took forever.

Mario obeyed. He knew that because it had been his decision and action that caused the damage, he would have to suffer the consequences. In any event, the bully never bothered John again.

On occasions, sweet little Carmela also would take to the streets to defend her brothers in a brawl. One time she came to Mario's rescue when he was getting a sound thumping by a local nemesis.

Carmela, a skinny little girl, simply bit the boy on the ass and sent him off crying. Only she and Mario knew what took place, and that's the way it stayed.

Chapter 8

1929

Because of their marvelous work ethic, it took only six years for Tony and Vincenza to save enough money to purchase a picturesque four-story, deep-red brick building located at 231 Elizabeth Street, just south of Houston Street. A wonderful addition to the structure was an elaborate ironwork fire escape that could serve as an extra icebox when needed or cool bedroom on hot summer nights.

It was a perfect building and location to fulfill part of the American dream, as Tony perceived it. The new purchase would house his family and his business.

Ferrara's Grocery and Bakery was no longer just a dream. Bakery ovens installed in the basement were capable of producing a variety of breads in every shape and size. They would all be displayed in the store's window.

A variety of cheeses and salamis hung inside and outside the store.

Shelves were stacked with pastas, olive oil, and an assortment of canned and boxed goods.

Sitting on the floor were barrels of fava beans, garlic, onions, and nuts.

With Vincenza's support and the inventory in place, they opened Ferrara's Grocery and Bakery. At every opportunity Mario would be by his *papà's* side, working in the store and baking bread, the finest hard-crusted bread in Little Italy.

During his breaks, Mario immersed himself in reading Dante's epic poem, *The Divine Comedy.*

The Ferrara's home had a revolving door at all times of the day.

Paesani dropped in at will, bringing pastries and food that would permeate the kitchen with pleasant aromas. Food, an Italian passion, was the neighborhood's sacred passage.

While Vincenza's warm smile greeted all with open arms, Tony made sure his wine cellar was on ready alert.

Vincenza's meals defined Sicilian cooking. Tomato sauce, meatballs, and sausage set on a slow flame to simmer all day, homemade macaroni, garlic, and imported olive oil—these were her delights.

Dinnertime was precious, a celebration of sharing mouth-watering food: and God forbid if you said you were full!

Whether relatives or friends came for lunch, dinner, or just to say hello, talk would go on and on, and then on and on. In order to make it through the gathering, you had to have a quick mind, thick skin, and sharp tongue. More often than not, Tony's mandolin strumming would turn the talk to music, and those gathered would sing. They would sing and laugh until it hurt, and then, would sing and laugh some more.

After church on Sunday, the gathering was beyond special. The family would lose count after the first fifteen arrived for the marathon dinner.

The table overflowed with food, family, and friends.

Women, preparing the feast, overtook the kitchen. Children played everywhere, inside and outside, before and after dinner. Tony led the men to the living room, where they talked or argued about work, politics, the Old Country, or the state of the Italian struggle. Mario would sit and listen in earnest.

Mario embraced his *papà's* enthusiasm and became an extension of Tony's thoughts and actions. In Tony's opinion, the lessons of life were found on the streets. He would say, "Experience the people, the sounds—everything around you—and you will master life."

During mealtime, a chorus of *"mangia, mangia, mangia"* led by Vincenza reverberated in the room.

When dinner was over, the men played pinochle or poker and the women gossiped and talked, as always, about the family and the neighborhood. Hence, if a derriere was able to grow calluses, this was a perfect time for it to begin.

Every waking moment of family life for the Ferraras was filled with gusto. They would sing, dance, cry or laugh, and sometimes all that took place before breakfast.

The Ferrara's timing in opening the store could not have been worse. They opened on March 1, 1929. On October 29, 1929, Black Tuesday hit and the Stock Market collapsed. The Great Depression began, and the economic disaster lasted three long years.

To calm his mind, Tony would recall the conditions he left behind in Sicily and the "boat ride" to America.

Mario, an impressionable fifteen-year-old, became aware that his *papà's* reaction to adversity was not to stutter step but to meet it head on.

During this time of crisis, the family worked harder and, with the backing of Mike Borelli and Frank Nunzi, none of the suffering unemployed *paesani* ever left Ferrara's Grocery and Bakery needy for food.

Mario's Sicilian code of conduct merged with the law of the streets and grew in proportion to his age. His closest friends were Joe Borelli, Tim Gallagher, and Sam Castellano.

Joe, possibly because of his muscular frame, could get in trouble just looking the wrong way. His dark brown hair matched his devilish brown eyes. Joe was wild, fun loving, and tough as nails; and he had inherited a great work ethic from his father, Mike. Ever since Mario arrived in Little Italy, he and Joe had been the best of friends.

At least once a year, Mike would take the boys for a weekend respite to his summer bungalow in Port Washington on the north shore of Long Island. It was not Palermo, but it made do. Mario enjoyed the quiet sound of nature as he and Joe walked the tree-lined dirt streets that led to the welcoming, white sandy beach on Manhasset Bay.

Sam "Peep" Castellano was quiet, serious, and outfitted with horn-rimmed glasses that fit his nickname perfectly. He excelled in school by staying focused and obedient. His goal was to become filthy rich. For such a little person, he sure could stuff down Angelina Borelli's *cannolis*. At any opportunity to devour this heavenly pastry, he would always eat until he was ready to burst. Sam was considered the resident brain.

His Uncle Nick owned Castellano's Ristorante, a popular Italian restaurant in Bensonhurst, Brooklyn, frequented by Tony Ferrara, Mike Borelli, and Frank Nunzi.

Tim Gallagher, a redheaded, freckle-faced, perennial altar boy at Our Lady of Loreto's Church, could have been Ireland's poster child. Tony would tease and call him Galla, making him an honorary Sicilian.

Tim, an all-around guy, always made himself available to the needy of the neighborhood and, at his parents' urging, eventually studied for the priesthood.

Every now and then, James Hennessy—cocky, bright, aggressive, and smartly dressed—would show up at the Ferrara's and attempt to meld into the group. This attempt rarely worked. Self-centered and slightly prejudiced, James had a heart that was entrenched in James. Besides, he remembered all too well Mario's temper that sizzling hot day in the schoolyard when he had watched one of his older friends wind up with a split skull.

Tony viewed James as a show-off and warned Mario to be careful of his motives. He commented to Mario one day, "If James keeps running his slimy fingers through his hair, he'll go bald before he's twenty."

Richard Barrett, an outsider who wore high-water pants, occasionally joined the younger group of friends. Though Richard's ruddy, red-cheeked face had the look of benevolence, he would run over his mother or cut your heart out for a nickel.

Barrett had an oral fixation; he was always sucking on an unlit cigar, pen, lollipop, or whatever. Joe called him an egg-sucking weasel.

Vincenza, besides being a caring wife, loving mother, unbelievable cook, and meticulous housekeeper, was also a surrogate mom to her children's friends who came and went as they pleased in and out of the Ferrara household. The neighborhood children knew they always had the warmth and safe haven of another home.

One evening after playing street stickball, Mario got "the look" from his *mamma* but was spared a scolding for ripping his pants by sliding across home plate, a manhole cover.

The way Mario, Tim, Joe, and Sam were eating Vincenza's leftover *ravioli* you could never guess they were down in the dumps after having lost to the Houston Street kids. But Tim, his nostrils filled with the crisp aroma of freshly baked bread, was the only one with a smile. He was always quick to trade in his "American bread," the white, pasty, dough-boy type, for Ferrara's hard, thick-crusted Italian bread.

Tony, enjoying the interaction among the boys, decided to speak under the ever-watchful eye of Vincenza. In a light-hearted tone he said, "In life, no one should be afraid of failure. It's simple: if you screw up . . . so what. Admit it and move on. What's a boot in the ass among friends?"

Vincenza, beside herself, gave him "the look."

"I understand what you mean, Mr. Ferrara. Like last winter when we made money pushing cars out of snow banks," Joe Borelli said, chuckling.

"What's wrong with that?" asked Tony in astonishment.

"Oh, I'm thinking about the cars we first pushed into the snow banks."

"Now that's not failure: that's ingenuity and deserves a kiss on the cheek . . . but, no matter what, you did screw up by being deceitful, and, so now, you deserve a boot in the ass," Tony said, gently smacking him on the side of the head.

Joe grinned.

Never taking "I'm full" as a statement of fact, Vincenza encouraged everyone, in her most delightful and nagging way, to *"mangia!"* And eat they did.

Tony was full of passion. So it was understood that when he became enraged every obscenity in the Italian language would fly about.

In the midst of the verbal bedlam, Vincenza would say, "Go get the mandolin for your *papà.*" Then she would break into her infectious laughter and say, "That will sooth the beast in him."

She forewarned her children. "If you ever repeat your *papà's* curse words, I will wash your mouth out with soap."

Her ominous warning was accompanied by light smacks to the side of Mario and John's heads.

For Carmela, a gentle pinch on the cheek was harsh enough treatment.

The children would do anything for their *mamma,* and their deep love for her was written on their faces.

Everyone in the immediate family, as well as the extended family, called Vincenza a living saint. She always played the role of peacemaker, servant, and sometime martyr. No, maybe she was more than a sometime martyr. Vincenza lived a life of self-sacrifice. She was always there when anyone needed her and, at times, when no one needed her.

In 1932 with the financial assistance of Tony and Vincenza, Vincenza's siblings, Lucia, nineteen, and brother Tomasso, twenty-three, arrived from Sicily.

One afternoon, Lucia, who was known to seize any opportunity to be ornery, said indignantly, "You're the patron saint of meddlers."

Tony stuck his nose into the melee and said, "Lucia, your sister is a saint because of you. If you were my sister, I would be in an insane asylum. Because you're *stunata,* a nut!"

Lucia fired back, "You live with my sister, so you must be *stunato*. So there, . . . one nut to another!"

Tony shrugged his shoulders and walked away smiling.

In spite of it all and at whatever the cost, Vincenza always strived to keep the entire household together. Her love was unconditional.

Vincenza was strong spirited and a first-class worrier. She worried about everything from the wailing sounds of fire engines screaming down Little Italy's streets to the amount of food her children ate before going swimming. The children never did figure out why they had to wait longer to go into the ocean after eating a hotdog than after eating a meat-ball sandwich.

Tony told anyone willing to listen: "Worry is part of Vincenza's cross. She would worry more if she didn't worry. So, let her worry in peace. Please!"

Mario enjoyed work, whether in the solitude of stacking shelves or in the camaraderie of interacting with customers. Best of all, he loved the "miracle" of baking bread. No matter the task, he usually did what he had to do and would rise to the occasion in doing it.

However, there was one instance during his teen years when he was confronted with a choice: he could either work for his father on a Saturday or join his friends on a trip to Coney Island, Brooklyn.

Coney Island, a wonderful seaside amusement park with its famous boardwalk, terrifying wooden Cyclone Roller Coaster, and clean sandy beach, was close, yet far enough away. Joe Borelli wanted to raise hell and be out of sight of the roving eyes of Little Italy's *paesani*.

Tim Gallagher, Joe, and Sam Castellano were enjoying pizza at Lombardi's on Spring Street when they discussed Mario's problem. Even though he was only four days older than Mario, Tim was considered by

the guys to be in possession of the wisdom of the ages and, therefore, he
was appointed spokesman.

Tim talked with Mario that same evening while Mario was working
at the bakery, kneading dough, forming loaves, and fitting them into
pans. In a serious tone, Tim said, "You need to do what you said you
would do; it's that simple. However, if you didn't commit, then you're
free to make your own decision." He leaned toward Mario, smiled, and
whispered, "But, if you *did* commit, then you need to cover your ass
someway, somehow, and come to Coney Island."

"Very funny. But I don't know. Tim, you know *Papà*. He's always
reminding me about how road blocks and choices are each a turning
point." He thought for a moment, scratched his head with his flour-dust-
ed hand, chuckled, and said, "Hey, tell Joe and Sam I'll be there."

Mario stood his *papà* up.

Tony ignored the situation for two days. On the third day, it hit
the fan.

"Mario!" Tony yelled, staring at him with a look of a crazed lion.

Mario's face turned white as snow, and his nervous laughter further
infuriated his *papà*.

Pulling down on his worn fedora, Tony bellowed, "You have no idea
how much you upset me. I'm disappointed. You forgot to think like a
Sicilian! So, rather than go into some huge lecture, let's just agree . . . this
will never happen again." His dark eyes filled with anger. "*Capiscu?*"

Mario meekly nodded his head in agreement.

"Let's forget it; come on, *mangia*," said Tony, hugging him.

Mario's stomach was in so much turmoil that he was unable to eat
his favorite dinner, *pasta e fugioli*.

At breakfast the following day, Tony, looking directly at Mario,
bluntly said, "So . . . for not showing up on the job Saturday, you're fired
. . . except for baking bread. But don't worry. I'll keep track of your
wages on the ice."

"*Papà*, you said you would forget it."

"I did. But then I remembered!"

"But—"

"*Sta zittu*, . . . be quiet. You talk too much already."

Mario learned the lesson of responsibility. He had no job and no money, translating to no fun. Two weeks later, he was hired back.

Tony fired every one of his *paesani* at least once during his or her term of employment at Ferrara's Grocery and Bakery.

Chapter 9

Mike Borelli owned and operated Borelli's Sicilian Import and Export, located in Queens near New York Municipal Airport #2, later called LaGuardia. His company was noted for delivering the finest wine, olive oil, and cheeses from throughout Italy and Sicily. He was a risk taker and always the optimist. He frequently reminded his son Joe, "Contacts, . . . that's how you dig up gold in the streets. It's not what you know; it's who you know. Period."

Angelina Borelli, a cheerful woman and great cook, adhered to the standard of preparing enough food for an entire village, even if there were only three at the dinner table. Her specialty was making rich, cream-filled *cannolis.* They lasted barely long enough to reach the kitchen table.

Tony and Mike often spoke of Mayor Fiorello LaGuardia. They both admired him for his no-nonsense, fiery demeanor.

Mike, while packing his own groceries, once said, "They call LaGuardia the 'little flower.' To me, he's a giant. As a former interpreter at Ellis Island, he understands the Italian immigrant and carries in his heart their desire to embrace liberty."

Tony leaned against the countertop and said enthusiastically, "You're right. Fiorello works his ass off. The man is everywhere. It's almost as if there's two of him. Without him, we would still be in the Depression."

No doubt, Tony was opinionated.

Topics, running the gamut from baseball to politics, could send him into orbit. On the other hand, when discussion turned to religion or the plight of the Italian immigrant in America, he would rise to greater heights.

Unfortunately, organized crime also traveled across the Atlantic Ocean, leaving a scar across the face of the Italian community—especially in Little Italy.

Mike Borelli's prosperity, coupled with the fact he migrated from Palermo, Sicily, caused those who had stereotypical minds to link him to the Mafia.

On a rainy April day, Tony, joined by Mario, Mike, and Frank Nunzi, had lunch at Umberto's Clam House on Mulberry Street.

Tony, as usual, sat with his back to the wall. He lamented, "It was bad enough that in the old country we were exploited and considered stupid. Now, there are *l'Americani* who call us *wops*, *ghinis*, or *dagos* and look upon us as less than human." Clapping his hands together once and then holding them open, palms up, to dramatize his point, he continued, "We did all the dirty work and broke our asses. For what? This prejudice and bigotry thing is disgusting." He shifted in his chair and somberly said, "It's a shame that we have to live in the shadow of the *Mafia*. Many think these big shots do good. But in the end . . . it comes back and bites us in the ass."

Mike, his eyes getting bigger, nodded his head in agreement.

Frank, waving his knife, snapped, "Bigots are those who think only where the sun doesn't shine."

"You realize that there are still some from northern Italy who look upon us with disdain. Their arrogance and innuendoes infuriate me." In a calmer voice, Tony continued, "Thank God for this kid Joe DiMaggio. He is a breath of fresh air and holds up the Sicilian name and heritage with honor."

Mike tilted his head back and swallowed the last of his espresso. "Take it easy. It's not worth getting sick about. Besides, patience is the key. I'm telling you, things will change."

"*Take it easy*?" Tony barked. He pounded his fist on the table. The cups rattled. "Look what happened to Sacco and Vanzetti: innocent, yet found guilty. And what about the *Siciliani* that were massacred in New Orleans? Their crime? They were *Siciliani*. Tell *them* about patience. They're all dead. Murdered. Government or vigilante, the same ruthless injustice." He dabbed clam sauce off his mouth and shook his head sadly. "This is the land of liberty. But I worry. I'm beginning not to trust anything or anybody, including the government. All everyone wants is power."

Mike, watching Tony's expanding neck veins, pleaded, "Please stop, you're going to get a heart attack."

Frank threw his napkin down in disgust and in a loud whisper said, "Government! Look at that bastard Mussolini. To distract the people from squalor, he invaded Ethiopia."

Tony and Mike nodded knowingly.

Mario, a young man of twenty-two, sat between Frank and Mike and listened intently to the three men. The seeds of rebellion were sown deep in his soul.

The next evening after dinner, Mario approached Tony. "Please tell me more about Sacco and Vanzetti."

Before responding, Tony thought about it for a moment and then, in a voice filled with frustration said, "It's a terrible story. It began in 1920. Two men robbed and killed a paymaster. Weeks later they arrested Nicola Sacco and Bartolomeo Vanzetti, two hardworking immigrants, not criminals. But no matter; the powers that be accused them of the crime."

Unable to control his pent up emotions, Tony began pacing the living room. Raising his voice a bit, he continued, "In *l'America*, after the Russian Revolution, it was a time when people had a great fear and hatred for the Reds . . . they called it the *Red Scare*. Sacco and Vanzetti, two poor men with strong views opposed to authority, were known as anarchists. They became the perfect suspects to feed the frenzy of ignorance, distrust, and prejudice.

"What made it worse was a climate of fear that was injected into a biased jury and ruthless judge. These two men were tried and convicted for who they were, not on the evidence. People all over the world made their voices heard and demonstrated for their freedom. But . . . no justice. The presiding, prejudiced Judge Webster Thayer had no conscience. He sentenced them to death.

"Six years later, after many failed appeals, sitting in his jail cell, Vanzetti boldly said, *'I'm suffering because I am a radical and indeed, I am radical. I have suffered because I was Italian and indeed, I am Italian.'*"

Tony left the room and returned with a neatly folded piece of paper. "When I think of what Nicola wrote four days before he died, I shudder with sadness. Let me read what he wrote to his son.

> *In this struggle of life you will find more love and you will be loved. Yes, Dante, they can crucify our bodies today as they are doing, but they cannot destroy the ideas that will remain for the youth of the future to come.*

Nicola and Bartolomeo, with no tears shed for themselves, were executed in the electric chair on August 23, 1927."

Mario's eyes welled up. "Why, *Papà?*"
Breathing hard, he said sadly, "Fear. And those who fear multiply fear, . . . and when fear multiplies, mob mentality rules. Remember, my son, the system may have crucified their bodies but not their spirit."
Looking his *papà* straight in the eyes, he replied in a firm voice, "I will never forget."

The next day at Caffé Roma on Broome and Mulberry Street, Mario spent hours writing his reflections.

Tony Ferrara guided his children with Sicilian street wisdom. One evening, on a walk through the neighborhood, he said to Mario, "Listen carefully to what I have to say. Always react to the ups and downs of life, not in the shadows, but in the light. Never hide your feelings and never give up. Along with great expectations of accomplishments, you will experience disappointments."

He hesitated, tugged on his worn black vest, and in a confident tone, said, "But it's far better to experience disappointment, than to live in mediocrity."

"I understand, *Papà*," said Mario, with his hand on Tony's shoulder.

"What about injustice? Do you think Dante's perception of the inferno is true?"

He stopped and gently took hold of Mario's arm. He couldn't help but smile. "If you think liberty, you will rise above any injustice. And don't worry . . . Dante's hell is in the mind of humanity. And another thing, only trust yourself or your *famigha*." He paused and said, "And another thing, *watch* your back with two-faced friends."

Mario, as the oldest, had an inherent sense of responsibility to help his *papà* whenever and wherever.

Tony was confident that the knowledge Mario would absorb from the streets and his basic public school education would be enough to guide him through life.

Moreover, Mario found books pertaining to America's fight for independence, the Italian plight, and of course, Dante, more interesting than school.

At the opposite end of the spectrum, Carmela broke the stereotype of an Italian stay-at-home daughter and, with the blessings of her parents, attended New York University.

John, at the insistence of Tony, had no choice but to attend college and chose Fordham.

Chapter 10

When anyone in the Ferrara household was sick, Vincenza turned to superstition with a Sicilian twist.

Her sure cure for most illnesses was to place a string of garlic around the neck. She also considered this a preventive medicine. When her children repeatedly asked, *"picchi´?"*

Vincenza would exclaim: "You ask *why?* Who would dare come near you . . . including germs?" Then she would smile and say, "Believe in the garlic and you will be healed."

Then again, if envy was on the loose causing problems or unexplained maladies, she had the ultimate cure, *malocchiu,* an old Sicilian remedy.

She would carefully finger a few drops of oil into a bowl of water, wait a moment, and then observe the result. If the drops remain . . . no problem. But if they scatter, the dreaded evil eye is present, which would require an additional delicate maneuver. As her finger methodically cut through the oil and water to remove the evil eye, Vincenza would raise her eyes to the ceiling and with a resolute voice recite a special incantation.

Young Mario didn't know exactly how the magic worked, yet he, Carmela, or John always felt better following the ritual.

Nevertheless, in order to remove the spell in severe instances, you had to engage that extraordinary old lady from the neighborhood.

The lady in black had the power and knew the mystical, magical words for the ultimate cure. Yet, this sometimes required a knife or scissors to cut through the curse. And if you believed, the wizardry worked and the spell was gone.

The Ferrara's sorceress lived above Gramolini's butcher shop, owned by a family from Messina, Sicily, who in 1909 had migrated to New York. It was rumored that she gained her special powers after the 1908 earthquake that brought Messina to its knees.

Mario wrote a poem for his *mamma* that she framed and hung in the kitchen.

MALOCCHIU

If you Believe,
Apply Faith, Hope, and Love;
Add Water, Oil, and Prayer;
And Cut through the Darkness
In an Absolute Healing process
Of Body, Mind, and Spirit.

On a blustery spring day, Vincenza's anxiety reached a breaking point.

Tony came to the rescue.

"Imagine, if you mix garlic with *malocchiu* you would put the drug companies out of business," he said, laughing.

"God help me! Why me, why always me?" she cried out. She held her head between her hands and pulled slightly on her hair in an act of exasperation.

"Vincenza, please, you need to calm down. You're making yourself crazy; everything will be alright."

Hearing his feeble attempt to comfort her, she clammed up for maybe two minutes before her demeanor changed. Instead of *God help me*, her phrase changed dramatically, at least to her own ears, and her plea took on new meaning. She shouted out in despair, "Oh my God! Why?"

Tony, in answer to her agonizing plea, gave her a bear hug and kiss on the cheek.

Vincenza giggled.

In the more serious cases, she varied her cure. Sometimes she applied leeches to blood-let poison buried in a wound. Vincenza used the method very successfully on her sister's fractured leg. Nevertheless, no one could tell that to Lucia who never forgave her.

Over a steaming hot cup of coffee, Lucia, frantically waving her finger, said, "Look at my leg. What did I do to deserve this? It looks like chopped meat. You should write a book about witchcraft and superstition."

"If yesterday morning, you didn't walk under a ladder . . . and in the afternoon fall in the gutter and break your leg, I wouldn't have had to use leeches. And for your information, using leeches is not witchcraft. It's a Sicilian remedy," said Vincenza smugly.

Mario often wondered why his *mamma* never used *Conte Alessandro di Cagliostro's* miraculous healing water from his *papà's* enchanted tale.

At times Vincenza had to resort to her backups. To provide special blessings and grace, she called upon those she honored.

The saints.

A specific saint for a specific difficulty.

And, if necessary she would enforce a barter system between the children and the chosen saint that worked most effectively.

Then, of course, there were the guardian angels. She assured the children if they prayed and believed the angels would be with them at all times.

Still, the ultimate call for help was to Mary. Vincenza paid special tribute to her and was quite certain that the Blessed Mother of Jesus was Sicilian.

With its peaks and valleys, Italian life was meant to be experienced—at times bursting with turbulent emotion. And that's whether you were living or dying.

A comforting thought graced every Italian's consciousness that when they were no longer among the living, which was commonly called *dead*, they could be assured that whenever their name was mentioned, it would be accompanied by *God rest his, or her, soul*. These words guaranteed peace forevermore. And if you listened carefully while lying in state, you would hear that you never looked so good.

The celebration of death was another way of keeping the family together.

One snowy evening twelve days before Christmas, Lucia and Tomasso, who were then living on the floor directly above Ferrara's Grocery and Bakery, went upstairs to visit their sister.

Lucia, always seeking perfection, drove her older brother crazy trying to determine the perfect spot for the family's Christmas tree. After moving the tree for the third time, Tomasso finally settled the indecision.

As calm as a bath of warm water, he walked over to the window, flung it open, and tossed the tree, decorated with lights, ornaments and tinsel, to the street below.

Vincenza saved Christmas that year. After shedding tears of torment, she asked Mario to haul the tree back to the top floor. She then creatively redecorated the mangled tree with silverware. Afterward, she pleaded with everyone to "be nice" and admonished her brother and sister for their childlike behavior.

No one listened because Lucia and Tomasso had already forgotten the incident.

"Vincenza, you are making something out of nothing. For God's sake, it's only a tree," said Tomasso impatiently, while eating a *cannoli*.

"He's right," added Lucia, hugging her brother.

Tony, rolling his eyes, walked away smiling.

Mario, *biscotti* in hand, was elated that all was well.

Eventually Lucia and Tomasso moved to 108th Street in Corona, Queens. Tomasso found employment as a chef. On the weekend, they would follow Vincenza's command; *Don't make any plans for Sunday*. They would drive into the city to join the family for dinner.

On one particular gorgeous June Sunday, their car suddenly stalled in the middle of a railroad crossing, dead center on the tracks.

Although there was no train in sight, Lucia screamed, "We're going to die! My God, help me! Vincenza, please forgive me! We're going to die!"

Tomasso, staring at her in amazement, opened the car door, hailed down a passing motorist and together with him they pushed the vehicle off the tracks. As he pushed, his ears burned with Lucia's wailing pleas: "Save me. Please God, I'll never argue with Vincenza again."

Once the car was safely out of traffic flow, Tomasso got back into the automobile and minutes later was able to restart the engine. Except for his occasional fits of laughter, which he attempted to muffle as best he could, they rode to the city in silence.

As they parked the car on Elizabeth Street, Lucia, slapping her hands together, bellowed, "Vincenza makes me crazy!"

He laughed long and loud.

On March 30, 1938, Lucia married Carmine Russo, a carpenter from Catania, Sicily. Tragedy hit when six months later he was fatally injured, falling off a roof during construction of a pavilion at the New York World's Fair. Soon after, Lucia contracted tuberculosis. Her untimely death at age twenty-five left the family in absolute desolation. Consequently, a deeply saddened Tomasso moved back to Palermo the following year.

Chapter 11

"La festa" was a feast in honor of a patron saint, and for many Italians, it was a celebratory lifeline to structured religion carried forward from the Old Country. It was a perfect time for friends to visit and to renew the community.

Little Italy's annual religious festivals honored its saints: *San Gennaro* of Naples, *San Rosalia* of Palermo, and *San Gandolfo* of Polizzi Generosa, to name a few. Their statues were held high in the air and carried by celebrators making their way through crammed streets of the neighborhood, from Mulberry to Houston to Elizabeth to Grand. As the statue was paraded through Little Italy, it was the embodiment of the old spiritual "The Saints Go Marching In."

In preparation for visiting *paesani*, new lacy curtains went up and extra mattresses were spread on the floor to accommodate visiting family and friends.

Italian and American flags hung from windows and fire escapes and, of course, there was an abundance of food.

A dedicated marching band, decorative floats, and the barefooted faithful walked in a colorful procession.

Women dressed in their finest holiday clothes and men in dark suits, ties, and hats stood in storefronts and doorways, watching proudly as the parade passed their way.

Frank and Mike, wearing red, white, and green sashes were among the men holding high the honored saint's statue dressed in ornamental robes and smothered with pinned offertory dollars.

Evening turned extraordinarily special as multicolored lights strung high and low, crisscrossed and illuminated streets that were overcrowded by fun-loving locals and outsiders. In addition to hawking cries from merchants selling a wide variety of products and blaring music emanating from glistening booths, there were tantalizing smells of pepper, onion, and sausage sandwiches; pizza; baked pastries; and more—many more—delicacies.

Mario viewed *la festa* as a magical celebration where Italian Americans and other ethnic groups found common ground in irresistible, love-laced *Italia Nica*.

For a quick get-a-way from the noisy, swarming neighborhood of Little Italy, Mario enjoyed Greenwich Village and its famed Arch, hidden alleys, charming townhouses, quaint courtyards, and interesting shops.

The Village had its own identity. Its inhabitants were, among other things, writers, artists, and anarchists; and all of them welcomed everyone. The word *conformity* was not in their dictionary.

One late Monday afternoon in August of 1938, after meandering the heart of the village, Washington Square Park, and New York University's library, Mario entered Pinocchio's Books on MacDougal Street.

Distracted by a stunning store clerk, much to his embarrassment, he walked straight into a bookcase, scattering books over the tiled floor. She smiled shyly while her face flushed cherry-red.

Mario stumbled up to the counter holding the evidence of his bumbling mishap. He placed the books on the counter and smiled. "I'm sorry about that. Could you please tell me where the American Revolution section is? I'm looking for Thomas Paine's independence pamphlet, *Common Sense*."

"Sounds like the right title for you," she said. She grinned and pointed to the back wall.

Quickly finding the book, he very slowly wandered through the small store and, while checking out titles, he took furtive glances at the attractive auburn-haired lady with sparkling blue eyes and radiant smile. At the end of the third lap, he approached the counter. His heart pounding, he froze and stared. Mario stood in silence fumbling with the coins in his pocket, when out of nowhere he found the courage to speak what was on his mind.

In a slightly shaky voice he said, "Please . . . excuse me. My name is Mario . . . Mario Ferrara. I live in Little Italy. Now, if I could be so bold to ask . . . if you will . . . uh . . . after work, join me for a cup of espresso at Caffe Reggio. I would be most honored."

Hesitatingly she said, "Alright. My name is Catherine—Catherine McGuire."

"That's only if you would like to go . . . I mean for espresso. Uh, wait . . . did you say OK?" he asked in a surprised tone.

"Why not, . . . I have always been fascinated by rebels and radicals. Not that you look like one. Uh, I mean . . . I was talking about Thomas Paine . . . not you—other revolutionaries. Did you know he lived in Greenwich Village? So did Mark Twain and Edgar Allen Poe," she said, flustered. Her cheeks flushed and the red in them moved downward, coloring her neck as well.

Mario smiled. "What time shall I come back?"

"I'll be closing the store at five o'clock. We can go then."

"Wonderful!" he exclaimed and tipped his fedora.

THAT WAS THE BEGINNING.

The following Friday night over pizza at Capri's on Bleeker Street, they continued to share their idealism and concern for humanity. The topics ranged from the newly formed German, Italian, and Japanese "Axis" to Irish and Italian immigration and injustice.

Mario put down his piece of pepperoni pizza, looked into her eyes, and said, "My *papà* is most upset with people like Capone and other notorious thugs that exploit the innocent and give Italians a bad image. Someday, I'm going to write about all the injustice, including government actions that quell liberty. Remember what they did to Sacco and Vanzetti?"

She reached for his hand. "Make sure it's your heart that speaks and not your anger."

It was late when he walked her home under a marvelous starlit sky. He shook her hand, tipped his fedora, and with a lump in his throat said, "Do you think that maybe we can see each other again . . . sometime?"

"I would love that," Catherine answered with a wide smile and squeezed his hand.

One week later on a stroll through Washington Square Park with Catherine, Mario sighed and said, "For some unexplained reason, this park reminds me of Garibaldi Park in Palermo."

"I'm listening."

"My *mamma* would drag us to Saint Catherine of Siena Church to attend Sunday mass. Afterward we would go to play in the beautiful gardens. The park was laced with fig and palm trees and what we called the ancient tree. It was a gray, gnarled banyan tree with moss-laden branches that spread widely and seemed to form a protective haven for me, my brother, and my sister."

Pausing, he grinned and added with his arms extended, "We played on its huge, mysterious protruding roots as big as tree trunks. It gave me comfort much like this park."

"Mario, there are no banyan trees in Washington Square Park."

"I know. I know." He nodded in a friendly greeting to a family walking past them. "So maybe the mystery I encounter here that reminds me of Garibaldi Park and the wonderful banyan tree is within *these people* who come to the park."

She smiled.

And so it went. They had been dating for three months when, after walking across the Brooklyn Bridge, taking in the brilliant display of thousands and thousands of lights beaming from the New York skyline, Mario took Catherine home to have dinner with *la famigha*.

The family had no trouble accepting her. In the comforting words of Vincenza, she was "not Italian," but she was "nice."

"Please, don't say that to anybody," said Tony, shaking his head in disbelief.

"Why? All of sudden you're embarrassed of me. Let me remind you of all the things you said about the Irish," she retorted glaringly.

"Maybe I should go to church and pray for patience."

"Aha! So you're saying I'm making you crazy."

Tony bit his lip.

The night Catherine's family had their first dinner at the Ferraras was classic Sicilian. Catherine's mother, Margaret, a sweet lady with a slight Irish brogue, and her husband, Owen, an Irish immigrant and New York City policeman, had looked forward to the evening.

The only glitch was going to be their stomach capacity.

After drinking Tony's wine and eating a bountiful antipasto of cheese, salami, olives, tomatoes, peppers, and Mario's thick-crusted Italian bread, they were prepared to leave the table, believing that dinner had already been served. Just then, Vincenza brought in a big platter of macaroni with meatballs and sausage. It was soon followed by the arrival of a third course of veal cutlets, zucchini, broccoli, and asparagus.

The food kept coming and never seemed to end. Next, came dessert. Once the dinner plates were cleared, the table was filled with every imaginable fruit, a variety of nuts, a heaping plate of *cannolis,* and, of course, the espresso.

That's when the McGuires knew the rumor was true: Italians do have a passion for food.

The Italians were as passionate about religion as they were about food. Once when Vincenza questioned Tony about going to church, he went into a tirade.

"I'm not going to be a one-timer, those who go to church at Easter or Christmas. I'll make an exception for funerals . . . and weddings or maybe baptisms . . . or, for that matter, whenever I feel like going!" Not attempting to control his emotions, his voice rising, he said, "Church is nothing more than a prison run by tyrants. The Pope gives you his orders and you obey; if not, you go straight to hell."

Holding her head in frustration, Vincenza said, "*You* are going straight to purgatory, if not hell itself."

Tony, ignoring her, kept on talking. "Church, it's not for me. Remember how the Irish controlled 'old' Saint Patrick's? There they were, the high and mighty. I remember this one Irish priest at the door. What does he say? '*Ghinis* downstairs.' That stinks. Faith. Faith's good. That's something different. No one can take that away from you *or* me *or* my family *or*—"

Vincenza, frantically sweeping the floor, cried out, "Please, please, stop! Do you want to send me to the crazy house?"

Tony threw his arms up as he walked away smiling.

Vincenza viewed religion differently. Throughout the Ferrara home, there were statues of saints everywhere, in particular the Virgin Mary. Displayed in a place of prominence was a picture of Jesus's bleeding heart. She daily prayed her rosary for her family and those in need of help anywhere in the world. And on special occasions, she would raise her level of dedication to a new height. For instance, on Saint Anthony's Day, the glow of candles would flicker throughout the house. The children would wait for Tony to close the store, come upstairs, and start the fireworks.

"Vincenza, you have lit enough candles in honor of Saint Anthony that I called the fire department and placed them on ready alert," Tony would complain.

Vincenza would cry, "Why? Oh God, please help me!"

And then, Tony would counter with a sarcastic remark. "OK . . . never mind; I'll call Con Edison and tell them they can shut down the power plant. You have generated enough candlepower to light up the Brooklyn Bridge."

"If it weren't for me, you would be in hell already," she would say, throwing her hands up in despair.

Carmela and John would giggle. Mario would smile.

Tony was never enamored with Archbishop Arthur Stanley. When visiting a parish in Little Italy, the archbishop would invariably talk down to youth. His pompous style was always accompanied by finger pointing at no one in particular, just the whole congregation.

After attending John's confirmation, Tony stood outside Our Lady of Loreto's Church, winked at Mario, and much to Vincenza's embarrassment, urged Father Giuseppe Carelli, "Giuseppe, between you and me, maybe you should tell the archbishop what he really should do with his finger."

Father Carelli, Pastor of Our Lady of Loreto's Church, covered his face to prevent the children from seeing a huge smile that showed his cigarette-stained teeth.

AND SO IT WENT UNTIL SPRINGTIME IN 1941.

A slight problem arose in the Ferrara family. Carmela, now a gracious, petite, blue-eyed Italian woman with long, black, glistening hair and Thomas Travino, her husband-to-be, decided to get married at Battery Park.

Rose Gramoli, her childhood friend and choice for maid of honor, had introduced the two while walking along the park's wonderful waterside esplanade.

Carmela had accomplished the unthinkable and had become a New York City schoolteacher. Tony, unlike many Sicilian fathers who discouraged their daughters from working or pursuing an education, went against the grain and encouraged Carmela to pursue her love of education.

Mario teased his sister and told her he thought it was their *mamma's malocchiu* that cleared the way for her. When she received her teaching degree from New York University, Tony was concerned he would have to widen the doorways so Vincenza's head would fit through the opening.

Inspired by Carmela, her friend Rose ultimately became an attorney. Rose, tall, slender, and very attractive, held herself and set her chin in a manner that reflected her determination. She wore her dark hair pulled back. Being from a family with four boys and only one girl, she had learned the art of verbal sparring with men and, when they were younger, always won out by turning the tables in conversations where the guys tried to make her the brunt of their jokes. Carmela thought this sparring ability stood her in good stead to become a litigator.

Vincenza, perplexed, asked, "How could you get married in Battery Park? It's bad enough the Irish think we're pagans."

Carmela, in a conciliatory tone, replied, "*Mamma*, I know it's not inside the church. So what? It's what we want. It's God's earth."

"Your *papà* is not going to be happy. What are people going to say? What about Father Carelli and Timmy Gallagher? What are they going to think of us?"

"Mario is right. *Mamma*, you worry too much."

"Alright! Talk to your *papà*!"

Carmela and Tom nervously waited for Tony to arrive home. As soon as he crossed the threshold, she greeted him with a big hug and smile that would melt an ice block.

Tom, panic-filled, stood immobilized by the door. He remembered well the interrogations and warnings from Tony the night he told him of his intention to marry Carmela.

"What's going on? What did *Mamma* tell you to ask me?"

"I love you! Since when can't I give you a big hug without asking for something?"

"I love you too." Tony laughed as he put his hands on his hips and stared at her. "What's the question?"

Without further hesitation, she said, "Tom and I wish to get married in Battery Park."

First, there was silence; then Tony raised his arms in celebration. "That's wonderful!"

"You're *all* making me crazy," Vincenza bellowed. She had been pretending to be too busy preparing dinner to listen to their conversation, but she couldn't resist announcing her displeasure at its direction.

Tony, hugging Carmela, enthusiastically said, "It's going to be wonderful. The park . . . the birds . . . the Statue of Liberty. It's going to be extraordinary."

Wiping sweat from his round face, Tom still stood at the door. Tony motioned for him to come over and join the conversation. His face flushed. He moved slowly toward them.

"*Mamma*, *Papà* is right. We're going to have a great time."

"Of course! But what will everyone think? What are they going to say?" asked Vincenza in a fretful tone.

"Whoever doesn't like it, . . . they can go to hell," Tony said. He put his arms around Carmela and Tom.

They sighed in relief.

Vincenza prayed to the Virgin Mary.

Vincenza's hesitation proved to be right. Father Carelli had to clear the marriage location with the archbishop.

The archdiocese, run by the iron fist of Archbishop Stanley, refused to bend. Battery Park was not sanctified ground and therefore was out of the question. Furthermore, he perceived the Italian population as a major problem for his disciplined archdiocese. Tony cared little for Archbishop Stanley's stringent rules. Consequently, Carmela's wedding location created a standoff between Tony and the archdiocese, widening the gap in his already strained relationship with the Church. He believed his daughter's wishes superseded that of the Church.

"This makes no sense," he said sadly.

Mario hugged him.

While he accepted the upcoming marriage of his only daughter, Tony's smoldering worry was Carmela's choice of a husband. It was secretly unnerving to him. Tom was agreeable, intelligent, and even had an architectural degree from Columbia. However when it came to gainful employment, he had a poor track record.

"Vincenza, I know Carmela will be able to support herself. I like Tom, but he needs to settle down. I'm getting like you . . . I'm worried."

"What's the matter with you? Are you crazy? Tom's a wonderful man! He's nice looking, comes from a good family, and will make a good husband. Just look at his father, Pietro. The poor man works everyday, sometimes 16 hours, in the dark hole they call a subway to support his family."

"That's my point. If Tom worked, he could help his *papà* get out of the dark hole."

"Please stop. Please!"

One evening while Vincenza and Carmela were out shopping for her trousseau, Tony was alone with Tom for the first time since he asked permission to marry his daughter. Tony, standing, read him the Sicilian code of work ethic. His dark eyes glaring at the young man, he determinedly said, "If you do not pull your load or if my daughter ever calls me complaining, I will make your life miserable."

"Yes sir!" he said, feeling his cheeks tremble.

Tony kept talking.

The valuable lesson Tom learned that night was this *la famigha* was now his *famigha*.

Chapter 12

Catherine often tried to temper Mario's emotions and actions with solid reasoning and rationalization. Sometimes it worked and sometimes it didn't.

One afternoon, Mario and Catherine were at their favorite place in Central Park, Bethesda Terrace, which had an outstanding view of "The Lake," beautiful woods, and a boathouse. Their conversation grew into a somewhat heated discussion about Carmela's upcoming marriage.

While holding his hand, she spoke, her tone and expression revealing her discomfort at broaching the subject, "Mario, stay out of the fracas. Let your father work out Carmela's wedding arrangement with Father Carelli."

"Why would I do that? It's upsetting Carmela. John's being distracted and can't concentrate on his studies. My mother is worried and my father doesn't need this aggravation. It's her wedding and—"

She interrupted. "Mario, for once in your life, mind your own business."

"Please! *Sta zittu.*"

She fired back how-dare-you darts with her blazing blue eyes and then went silent.

Not deterred by Catherine's plea, a couple of days later, Mario decided a phone call to Archbishop Stanley was in order. Each and every time he telephoned, the staff stonewalled him. Call number nine proved lucky when by happenstance the archbishop answered.

Mario plunged in: "Hello, this is Mario Ferrara. Your Excellency, with all due respect, I think your decision about Carmela's wedding is dead wrong. You upset my sister who loves Battery Park almost as much as she loves Tom. You upset my father who wanted Father Carelli to perform the ceremony. You upset my mother; she's upset because my father's upset. Further, you worried my brother because he worries easily. Lastly, you caused a fight between my girlfriend and me. For what? For nothing! All for nothing."

"Who is this?" asked the archbishop coldly.

Mario took a breath, pushed back the hair from his eyes, and said, "Mario. Mario Ferrara." Without hesitation he continued in a forceful manner. "Let me ask you something. How in the world can the Catholic Church be called the *Universal Church* and ignore earth's beauty? It's plain stupid that a Catholic marriage would be sanctioned if it were performed inside a building someone called a *church* and not be honored if it takes place, instead, on God's green earth."

The archbishop responded in his usual condescending style: "Young man, you need to learn manners. Rather than explain the theological reasoning for sanctified ground, which would be above your understanding, let me say you need to accept the law of the Church. Period!"

Mario snapped, "Give me a break . . . please! You're making me sick!"

The archbishop slammed the receiver down and sat motionless.

In the midst of Carmela's crisis, James Hennessy hit on Catherine. It was an attempt to take advantage of what his warped mind perceived to be a little bump in the road in the relationship between Mario and Catherine. And at a party at Castellano's Ristorante, hit on her, he did.

The next day, Joe, wisely or not, decided to tell Mario what he had overheard.

Though Catherine never gave him a detailed description of what had happened, Mario, more than a little irritated, tracked James down.

With his jaw clenched tightly, Mario was barely able to spit out words. He decided to skip a cordial hello and instead, in a low voice, said, "We're friends, right? So, do me a favor. Stop hitting on Catherine, or I'll break your face."

"I don't know what you're talking about," James replied stone-faced.

Mario's tone became nasty, "Don't give me any of your bullshit. Lay off or we have major problems."

"I still don't know what you're talking about," he replied meekly.

"Tell you what," Mario said, raising his voice a couple of decibels, "if you don't know what I'm talking about, then you have nothing to worry about. But if you understand what I'm talking about, then lay off, or I'm going to kick your ass."

Mario swiftly flung up his arm. Hennessy flinched, and Mario leaned forward and coldly said, "Don't you ever, ever lie to me again."

The following week, Father Carelli had a ferocious argument with Archbishop Stanley regarding Carmela's wedding. In the end, he had no choice but to decline to celebrate the service. Otherwise, he would be removed from Our Lady of Loreto's Church.

Tim Gallagher, by then an ordained priest, visited the Ferraras three days later.

"Mr. Ferrara, don't worry; I just received special permission to offi-ciate the sacred ceremony," said Tim excitedly, adjusting his stiff white collar.

Tony raised his eyebrows and asked, "You're fooling me . . . right?"

Tim replied confidently, "Don't you or Mrs. Ferrara worry. Let Carmela know that this is going to be a terrific wedding. Battery Park will never be the same."

Mario walked Tim outside the store.

Standing in a brisk breeze with his burly arm resting on Tim's shoul-der, Mario grinned and said, "I know you're full of crap. So tell me what really happened."

"You know Stanley is king of control and rigid. He doesn't care which way you do something, as long as it's his way."

"That, I understand! But how did you get him to agree to the wedding in the park?"

"I didn't! I figured the worse that can happen is that I get a reprimand and the archbishop sends me to Staten Island." With his hands clasped behind his back, he shrugged and said, "I'm not worried."

Despite the fact that Tim was Irish, the neighborhood thought of him as one of them, making him an Italian by osmosis. He had an uncanny knack for raising money, which enabled him to deliver substantial funds to the archbishop's programs. Tim thought he had the edge—*money*. He anticipated the archbishop would turn his head rather than punish him.

Tim guessed wrong.

The archbishop got wind of Tim's plan and called him about it. When Tim asked him to reconsider his position he replied, "No! Absolutely not."

Tim came up with an alternate plan.

Tony arranged for horse drawn carriages to take his daughter and entourage to Battery Park following the "real wedding" at Our Lady of Loreto's Church, complete with seven bridesmaids and grooms.

The "do it again" wedding service, officiated by Tim on the park promenade was glorious. As *"Ave Maria"* played, Tony motioned Mario aside, smiled, and said, "Now let go. It's over. No vendetta! Leave the archbishop alone to wallow in his own rhetoric. Getting even is plain stupid and will get you nowhere. Do you understand?"

"Yes, *Papà*," said Mario, looking straight at his father.

"Good!" Tony said, taking hold of him in a bear hug.

As Tony, Mario, and Catherine entered the reception celebration held at the overflowing Sicilian Social Club on Prince Street, the band was in full swing. Tony stood grinning as he watched Vincenza happily dancing to the *tarantella* with Tom.

Tony was right. Carmela's marriage in Battery Park on June 21, 1941, was wonderful, and he celebrated it with a bottle of Chianti.

LIKE EVERYTHING ELSE IN LIFE, ALL THINGS PASS.

The stress of the wedding dissipated and life went on.

Carmela was elated with her teaching job at PS 41.

Tom never wavered in his respect for the family, and he secured a position with the established architectural firm of Nelson-Turner in Manhattan.

Vincenza became close friends with a woman from Milano as northerners and southerners were coming together to form a new identity, Italian American.

John had received his business degree from Fordham and was working with Joe Borelli on a housing development in Corona, Queens.

Tony, as usual, kept one eye on the family and the other on the store.

Mario embarked on the next stage in his life. In August of 1941, in a rented rowboat in the middle of "The Lake" at Central Park, he began, "Every time we visit this incredible park I admire the beautiful bronze angel that stands on top of Bethesda Fountain." Taking Catherine's hand in his, he continued, "And here, in this rowboat, with all my heart, I love a living angel. Please, will you marry me?"

Catherine rose suddenly from her seat, almost tipping the boat, kissed him, and gleefully shouted, "Yes!"

For a change, everything seemed to be going smoothly and everyone in the Ferrara family seemed to be doing well.

Chapter 13

The Great American Depression that had given rise to poor economic conditions throughout Europe left a huge void for Hitler and Mussolini to exploit. And in Japan, the military warlords were stirring.

On October 31, 1941, Mario was in his father's office reviewing a Ronzoni macaroni order when he received a phone call from a somewhat frantic Joe Borelli.

Evidently, someone was under the Williamsburg Bridge with a truckload of furniture, refrigerators, and an assortment of other appliances. The price was better than right, ten dollars each, and your choice.

Calling from his father's office in Queens, Joe said hastily, "Mario, please call Carmela. She may need some of this stuff; you know it's hard getting started."

"I think you've lost your mind," Mario shot back. "It's hot!"

With the radio blaring Louie Prima's "Angelina," Joe pleaded his case, "No, listen to me. The guy swears it was merchandise rejected by the receiver. He was told to unload it anywhere he could."

"Please turn the radio down so I can think."

"The hell with the radio, for God's sake! The guy is parked under a bridge, and it's raining like crazy. He needs to do something, and he needs to do it now."

"Joe, it stinks! The guy's an idiot!"

"Look, if not Carmela, what about Mr. Artuso? That poor bastard was robbed two times this year. Maybe he could sell some of this stuff at the store."

"Now I know you've lost your mind," Mario said, starting to lose his patience. "First of all, Artuso's store is a candy store. So what in the hell does he need with appliances? Second of all, the last guy who robbed him wound up with a bullet in his ass. Don't you remember?" asked Mario. He laughed.

Waiting for a response that didn't come, he continued, "Mr. Artuso begged the scum for his life, telling the thief to lock him in the closet. The old man was smarter than the crook. He had a rifle hidden in the closet, and the door had a peephole. When the crook turned his back, bang; he got shot in the ass. I love it! True justice, firsthand. Or, should I say *first ass!*" said Mario, still laughing.

"Great story," Joe said flatly. He did not see the humor in such a remark at a time when a quick and serious response was needed. "In the meantime, what do I tell this poor bastard with all the stuff on his truck?"

"It's not worth it. I say 'no go.' Tell him to forget about it. Joe, tell him *tough!*"

"We're missing a great opportunity here," Joe said, fingering the *corno* necklace given to him by Mario. The necklace's attached red horn was for perpetual protection from the evil eye. But just in case, Joe knew he could always resort to Mrs. Ferrara's *malocchiu*.

"Hey, I have to go; Peep's coming over to help me with my father's accounts. *Papà* just loaned Nick Castellano money for, . . . uh, I really don't know what for—"

"That's just great," Joe said, showing no interest. "Mario, maybe I should call James," he said, not ready to give up.

"I don't know. I'm still not happy with the sneaky bastard, and besides, he's gotten worse since becoming a lawyer and getting all buddy-buddy with Barrett, the shylock."

"You mean *weasel?*"

There was a loud knock on the door.
"Hold on a second," Mario bellowed.
"It's me, Sam."

"Keep your shirt on, I'm coming. Hold on, Joe, I need to let Sam in." He opened the door, shrugged in desperation, and gave Sam a ten-second briefing before handing over the phone.

Mario urged, "Talk to him."

"Joe, it's me, Peep. If you want my advice, forget it. Do you even know this guy?"

There was a long pause, and then Joe blurted, "You're right. I can't believe it . . . I don't even know how this guy got my name and number. I'm in construction, not appliances."

"Wait a second; I just got a great idea. Call Tim Gallagher. Tim knows people all over the neighborhood who can probably use the stuff," Sam said eagerly.

"Brilliant!"

"Let me know." Sam ended the bizarre conversation, took off his horn-rimmed glasses, and wiped them clean. Chuckling, he asked Mario, "What can you say about Joe?"

Father Tim Gallagher was grateful for the appliance opportunity, and within a matter of hours, Halloween turned into a real treat, as it resulted in making a bunch of people on the Lower East Side very happy.

Mario and Catherine were married in a simple ceremony on December 6, 1941, at Our Lady of Loreto Church. Tim officiated the sacred ceremony.

Again, the Sicilian Social Club on Prince Street housed an unbelievable celebration of love and marriage.

Chapter 14

December 8, 1941

A headline in the *World Tribune*
JAPAN ATTACKS PEARL HARBOR

World War II broke out with a vengeance on December 7, 1941, as the Japanese attacked Pearl Harbor and all but destroyed the United States naval fleet. Loss of life was beyond comprehension.

That night at dinner, Tony openly cried. Vincenza was trembling, while Mario and Catherine sat in stunned silence tightly holding on to each other.

Life quickly changed for all Americans. Food and gas were rationed, and although Tony supported President Roosevelt, much to his dismay all Italian immigrants had to register as enemy aliens. It was the beginning of global conflict as a way of life.

The draft changed life for everyone. Even though Carmela was pregnant at the time, Tom was drafted in January 1942. Mario and Joe were drafted in November and John in December. Tim volunteered and served as a chaplain in the Navy. James Hennessy received a deferment by using every method available to him. Sam and Richard Barrett were 4F, medically unfit.

Every time one of the boys shipped out, Elizabeth Street overflowed with music and well-wishers, as streamers and American flags flew from windows and railings.

The evening before Mario had to leave for basic training, he and Catherine cuddled on the fire escape. Mario, holding her in his arms, tenderly said, "Look, the brightest star of all . . . Venus . . . the star of love. Every time you look up, I'll be by your side, looking up with you."

Tony and Vincenza prayed together.

Carmela held on tightly to Angelo, her now one-month-old baby boy.

A true Italian American, Mario at age twenty-seven was prepared to fight for his adopted country. Although he was ready to accept his assignment of deployment, he was hoping he would not get deployed to Sicily. The thought of fighting against his cousins, extended family, and most of all, Uncle Tomasso, was incomprehensible. No such luck: he was assigned to General George Patton's Seventh Army.

Mario lay awake nights running his father's words over and over in his mind: *u sangu ra famigha è sangu tua,* the blood of the family was his blood.

In July 1943 Patton's Seventh Army invaded Sicily.

Sicily recoiled under the thumping rain of allied bombs as both soldiers and civilians suffered in the nonstop assault. Mussolini's promises of paradise had turned sour, and by 1943, fascism in Sicily was crumbling. The Allied armies, led by General Patton, took Palermo by storm and headed straight to Messina. Though many Sicilian troops surrendered without a fight, there was a tremendous loss of life and wounded on both sides.

When the Americans crossed the Strait of Messina into the mainland, Mario couldn't help but think of Garibaldi and his red-shirts in the quest for the liberation of Italy.

Allied forces were greeted and embraced by thankful men, women, and children.

Sicily was about to be reshaped and transformed again.

It was January 20, 1944, almost two years to the date after Tom was drafted, when a military officer stood at Carmela's doorstep holding a neatly folded American flag. In a somber voice, he informed her that Tom had been killed in a fierce firefight with German troops during the American landing at Anzio beach in Italy.

Carmela gave out an anguished cry and collapsed.

Catherine, shaking violently, rushed to her.

Angelo would never get to know his father.

Vincenza wailed.

Tony wrapped his arms around the three sobbing women.

Months later when he finally received a letter giving him the news, Mario wrote one word to General Dwight Eisenhower: "Please!"

JUNE 7, 1944

A headline in the *Daily Mirror*
ALLIED ARMIES LAND IN FRANCE

June 6, 1944, D-Day, was the beginning of the end as Allied divisions with almost 3 million men landed on Normandy Beach in France. Three months later, Paris was liberated as Allied forces kept pushing toward Germany.

On May 8, 1945, Germany surrendered and with it the gruesomeness of the Holocaust at Auschwitz, Dachau, and Buchenwald began unfolding, shocking humanity to its core. In the wake of the atomic bombings and fiery destruction of the cities of Hiroshima and Nagasaki in August, Japan surrendered.

Tony, with his head down, said to Mike Borelli, "Truman is one tough son of a bitch to make a decision like that."

AUGUST 15, 1945

A headline in the *New York Journal American*
WAR ENDS
2,000,000 PACK TIMES SQUARE

On August 14, 1945, the streets of Times Square disappeared under the feet of two million people who were crying and laughing joyfully as lights again blazed from movie marquees and signs. Everyone loved someone that glorious night in Midtown Manhattan. The wave of exuberance quickly reached Little Italy and moments later, northern and southern Italians burst onto the streets, dancing, kissing, and hugging one another. A celebration of family exploded.

SEPTEMBER 29

September was a month made in heaven for the Ferrara and Borelli families.

Mario, John, and Joe came home to a jubilant street celebration that rocked Little Italy with an outpouring of food, flowers, music, and love lasting well into the next day. Tim Gallagher, who had returned a month earlier, joined the lavish feast with Sam Castellano.

A month later, Mario and Catherine moved to the fourth floor of Tony and Vincenza's home.

Tony and Vincenza moved down to the third floor and Carmela and Angelo were living on the second floor.

Life had changed for the normally jovial Mario. When he needed to get away from his recurring nightmares of war and its horrors, he and

Catherine found Central Park to be the perfect escape, a place to discover some semblance of peace.

When talk turned to the war, all it took was one look at the anguish in Mario's face for Catherine to intuitively understand his need for isolation. The result was that if Mario wasn't working or baking in the store, he was at Caffé Roma, either writing about injustice or dissecting every piece of Dante's epic poem.

One morning, soon after the store opened, Tony, holding a huge roll of provolone cheese in his hand, said, "While you were gone, something terrible happened. It was in July. In the fog, somehow, I don't know how, a pilot made a big mistake and crashed his army plane smack into the seventy-ninth floor of the Empire State Building. It looked as though the whole top of the building was on fire." He stopped slicing cheese and sadly said, "Fourteen people died; dozens hurt. It was a nightmare."

"I can tell you, *Papà*, as sad as that may have been, Palermo is crippled and in shambles. The cities of Berlin and Tokyo are all but gone. London is still digging out of rubble, and the people in Moscow are starving. War should never happen again." Mario sat and wiped away tears. "We talk about liberty but for six million Jews it came too late. Where the hell was the Pope?"

"My son, war is worse than hell. I know." He rubbed his forehead and continued, "I never told you that my best *paesanu* died in my arms in World War I. Me, like you, never wanted to talk about it."

"Sorry."

"I can't answer where was the Pope, but I can tell you this: your *nannu* told me sometimes talk is good. So I told him all about it. To you, my son, I say the same thing—I listen good."

Mario took a deep breath and the words flew out. "It didn't matter, Germans or Italians, they were shooting at us. They were the enemy. It was horribly simple. Kill or be killed, and kill I did."

Tony shook his head slowly.

"Seeing limbs being blown off and walking through body parts strewn on the battlefield are enough to destroy your mind. My buddy was blinded by an exploding artillery shell. The gut-wrenching cries of *medic, medic* still rings in my ears."

Tony wrapped his arm around Mario's shoulder.

"General Patton was indestructible. A man possessed. He drove us relentlessly. He was focused on one thing. Use overwhelming force to destroy the enemy and liberate Sicily. And that we did, just like Garibaldi. Sicily was free." Mario paused his voice choking. "Every time I think of the smiles that spread across the faces of the Sicilian people, I cry for joy for their liberty."

BOOK III

Chapter 15

The struggles of the Great Depression and the horrors of World War II left a trail of scars across the American landscape. The country was faced with numerous post-war labor strikes, as millions of workers walked out on their companies, big companies. They struck General Motors, United States Steel, and General Electric, among others.

At the same time, the international scene was dramatically changing. Europe began the slow process of rebuilding, new territorial lines were drawn, and Italy became a republic.

In January 1946, the United Nations held their first General Assembly in London. A month later, in protest of British control, blood flowed in the streets of Bombay, India. In Calcutta, religious ideologies continued to spew hate as the vicious warfare rolled on between Hindus and Moslems. On August 15, 1947, Britain granted India its independence.

Tony, as always, first considered the welfare of his family and to that end, worked long hours, building a solid business at Ferrara's Grocery and Bakery.

Vincenza, still the worrier and ultimate caregiver, helped Tony in the store when she was needed and, with Catherine's assistance, watched over Angelo while Carmela continued to teach at PS 41. With the support of her *famigha*, Carmela was adjusting to life as a single parent.

After receiving a complete tour of Theresa Fortunato's Italian neighborhood in Corona, which included Spaghetti Park and the Lemon Ice King, Mario, in a lighthearted tone, said, "John, I understand why you want to marry Theresa, but to move out of the neighborhood and live in Queens with your mother-in-law and father-in-law . . . I don't know." He wiped lemon ice from his fingers and continued, "And as far as *Mamma* is concerned . . . well, you know the reaction." He hesitated, grinned, and said, "If I were you, I would call the old lady in black from Messina."

Tony took the decision with mixed emotions, but he supported his youngest son with all his heart.

Without any encouragement from John, Vincenza actually did contact the old lady from Messina to perform *malocchiu* . . . and prayed to the Virgin Mary.

Five months after they were married, John and Theresa purchased a home of their own in Corona and were excitedly expecting their first child.

Mario was still reading Dante and writing about injustice. On occasion, he would lend a hand to John and Joe Borelli in their start-up construction and landscape business.

Catherine and Mario, ever in love, remained childless. She worked in the store and took over the bookkeeping task from Tony. And much to Mario's delight, Angelo loved to be with him and his aunt Catherine.

Through it all, the family was inseparable.

JANUARY 31, 1948

A headline in the *Daily Mirror*
MAHATMA GANDHI ASSASSINATED

Mario rushed into the store with a crumpled newspaper. "*Papà*, remember when I told you about a wonderful man called Gandhi?" Taking off his snow-covered coat, he continued, "Yesterday, after a prayer session, some Hindu fanatic shot and killed him. This is not good. He was the spiritual leader for Indian independence. Gandhi led with a torch of civil disobedience in the defiance of British rule. He was nonviolent and espoused love. Again, I say, this is not good."

"I know of this Gandhi; he did no harm. Except, maybe to the British, who, at times have overstepped their power."

"Sometimes, I wonder what people are thinking," said Mario, shaking his head in disgust, "and you're right about the British and power."

After work, Mario walked over to Caffé Roma and recorded his thoughts in a journal. He compared Gandhi's pursuit of liberty to that of Garibaldi. Later that evening, another violent nightmare woke him.

The following week, while visiting at Catherine's parents' home, as Mario was finishing his last piece of apple pie, his curiosity overtook him. He made a request, "Mr. McGuire, please tell me about Michael Collins and the 1916 Easter uprising. I believe that's when Ireland proclaimed its independence from the British."

Owen leaned back in his kitchen chair, lit up his pipe, and responded with a lilt in his voice. "Like your hero, Garibaldi, Collins was a revolutionary. During the Easter uprising, he was lucky enough to escape arrest and, in spite of British power, he was fearless." Raising his voice excitedly, he said, "Michael was one hell of a lad. He led us Irish volunteers with toughness, passion, and courage . . ."

Their conversation continued late into the night.

On the way back to Little Italy, Mario squeezed Catherine's hand and said with a smile, "After what your father said about the British Black and Tans, I wonder where they reside in Dante's inferno."

On July 13, 1950, Maria Ferrara was born in Flushing Hospital to John and Theresa, the only two people ever to have had such a wonderful child—at least that's what they thought. Three weeks later, Father Tim Gallagher baptized the baby at Saint Leo's Church in Corona. The Ferraras celebrated. Vincenza temporarily moved in to help, and Corona was never the same after that.

The following Sunday, sitting at Bethesda Fountain in Central Park, Catherine sighed deeply. "Doesn't it ever end? I'm worried. In time, Korea could possibly turn into World War III." She paused, her eyes saddened, and she asked, "What about Angelo?"

Mario gave her a questioning look and said, "Angelo? Angelo is only eight."

"I'm still worried."

"Don't worry about Angelo yet. Worry about all the men and women—soldiers and civilians—who are dodging bullets today."

"I not only worry about them; I *pray* for them."

While walking to the boathouse, Mario's mind was racing. "I'm doubly troubled. I'm sick about Korea and nervous about Senator Joseph McCarthy. This off-the-wall nut has started a *boo campaign*, claiming that the Reds have infiltrated the government and that they're revealing secrets to the Soviet Union. Another Red Scare may make for another Sacco and Vanzetti."

She slowly ran her fingers through her hair, took hold of his hand, and softly said, "Let's talk about something happy."

He forced a smile and in a conciliatory tone said, "I'm sorry . . . how about if we take Angelo, Carmela, and *Papà* over to Corona?"

Her eyes lit up, and she light-heartedly said, "That sounds wonderful. I spoke with Theresa the other night; she told me that *Mamma* has coexisted with her mother beautifully and has been a tremendous help."

MONDAY, JUNE 11, 1951 . . . 6 PM

As Tony was closing the store, an unshaven man with a swollen half-shut right eye wearing a wool longshoreman's cap appeared from behind a tree. "Hey, Antonio, long time no see." Smiling broadly, he showed his rotting teeth, and said, "The *paesani* want me to give you this." Reaching out, he shoved a summons into Tony's hand.

"Thank you for nothing," Tony said angrily, crumpling the legal document in his rough hands. "Now, get the hell off my property before I stick this paper right up your ass."

He watched the scraggly process server slither down the block until he turned the corner at Houston Street.

Quietly reopening the store, he went straight downstairs to his eight-by-ten, stuffy office that was filled with a potpourri of paper. With his heart rapidly beating and stomach churning, he knew he had to calm down. Tony popped open a bottle of Chianti, cranked up Caruso on his record player, then opened and slowly read the summons.

The words "Defrauded Gateway Bank" jumped off the page, instantly infuriating him.

Besides loaning Nick Castellano substantial funds in the past, Tony co-signed a bank note to assist him in purchasing an adjoining piece of property for expansion. Instead, Nick used the funds from a shell corporation to bail himself out of financial troubles related to his sinking restaurant business that for some unexplained reason was riddled with oddball debt.

They had known one another for years. Trust was implied. Consequently, Tony never monitored the monies being drawn down from the bank. He deferred to Nick and assumed the funds were being used for the proper purpose.

The President of Gateway Bank was none other than Richard Barrett who supposedly was a close friend of the Castellanos and was well aware of the idiosyncrasies involved in the transaction. But somewhere along the way, Barrett became afflicted with a curse known as *Memory of Convenience.*

Because Tony personally guaranteed the bank loan, the summons pointed to him as the sole guilty party. He needed to vent his anguish. The first name that popped into his head was Mike Borelli, but embarrassed by his situation, he called Frank Nunzi instead.

In 1949 Frank had relocated from Little Italy to Cicero, a southern suburb of Chicago. F. A. Nunzi and Company had expanded its check cashing and small loan business into Illinois.

Ready to explode, Tony dialed the long distance operator for the connection and impatiently listened to the irritating series of rings. The phone rang six times before a gravelly voice answered, "Hello."

"Frank, it's me, Tony; how the hell are you?"

"Great!" he roared.

Without any further greeting or casual conversation, Tony launched into a tirade. "I cannot believe it! It's absolutely crazy! How can anyone be so stupid to think that they can get away with this crap?"

"Whoa, what are you talking about?"

"Those rotten sons of bitches," he replied, and he then proceeded to explain the summons in detail.

Frank, noted for his undying loyalty and not his patience, paused for a moment to get a grip on his emotions. His jaw tensed up and he declared, "They think they can place the blame on you? How many times have we seen this? When a deal goes south, those who screwed it up stick their head up their ass."

Pacing the floor while listening, Frank inadvertently pulled on the phone, sending it crashing to the floor.

Then there was a moment of silence.

"What was that? Are you there?"

"Sorry, I was picturing Barrett's head being the telephone. It just hit the floor."

"His head is mush anyway. There's no competence among the lot of them."

"Tell me again; who was involved?"

"Richard Barrett of Gateway Bank, Nick Castellano, and God knows who else." Tony was staring at the ceiling. He said, "I heard that Barrett might be dirty."

"Tony, it's a double-cross. Barrett had to know that Nick's land corporation was a dummy. Nick signs the note corporately and you sign personally. Bam! You wear the target on your back."

"I know Barrett screwed over Gramolini when he tried to get a loan for his butcher shop. But to think Nick would target me as the fall guy really hurts, and it pisses me off. He was supposed to be my friend."

"Anybody with a brain would know you got taken."

Not really listening, Tony said, "Frank, people panic to a point beyond my understanding. I just don't get it. This is out and out fraud. Those bums. To risk so much for so little."

"Say the word! If you want me to whack'em, just say the word. With one phone call it's done." His voice was cold as ice as he wrapped the cord around the receiver and pulled on it.

"What? Are you crazy?" Tony cried out. He was concerned Frank was getting carried away. "Nobody's worth that. But I tell you what, let's break their backs in court."

"Hey, I could break their backs with a baseball bat before they ever get to court," Frank said, slamming his fist down on the table.

"Give me a break, please!" Tony insisted, laughing nervously. He picked up his bottle of Chianti to suck out the last drop.

"I hope they look good in stripes, but then again, they might look better dressed in a tux and laid to rest in a nice pine box," Frank said, his voice trembling with anger.

"You don't give up. Please simmer down; I don't want to regret calling you."

"OK, tell me what I can do and I go do it. Tony, I love you, Vincenza, and the kids, so I'm yours."

"The feeling is mutual. Frank, I'm so frustrated and . . . embarrassed. I can't believe I was so stupid that I didn't think to question Nick. I would like to take this summons and—"

"Now *you* stay calm," Frank cautioned, hearing the rising anger in Tony's voice.

"If Vincenza finds out, it will kill her . . . or drive her nuts. I'm also worried about Mario; he has busted his ass making the business profitable. And John, Carmela, and the rest of the family . . . everybody . . . what will they think?"

"Take it easy. Mario is rock solid and tough as nails, thanks to you. So, forget about it!"

"I'm sick!"

"Let me think. A lawsuit like this is going to be costly. If Nick Castellano is broke, how in the world can he defend himself?" Frank paused. "Wait a second, isn't that sleazebag Hennessy, Mario's old friend, a lawyer?"

"Yes, but so what?" Tony asked.

"I'll tell you *what*. This may be a stretch, but several times when you, Mike, and me went to eat at Castellano's we saw Nick kissing Hennessy's ass. Maybe Hennessy's involved somehow, and if he is it would be easy for them to conspire against you. It's costing them next to nothing and, as far as the bank is concerned, they have all the money needed to protect their flank."

"When I read this friggin' summons, I can't help but question my sanity and my judgment."

Frank said, "You're not listening, and you're beginning to sound like a broken record. I might not be a genius, but you got these scumbags beat every which way to Sunday. I still think I should make the call to take 'em out."

There was a few seconds of silence and then Tony said, "I'm going to Gateway Bank tomorrow and stick this summons up Barrett's ass."

"Why don't you first talk to Rose Gramoli. She's a good lawyer and Carmela's best friend."

"You might be right. Thanks again for being there, Frank."

"Anytime . . . anytime. Call me and let me know what happens. *Sta bona!*"

Looking again at the mangled summons, Tony telephoned Mario. "Please come down to my office. Right away."

Mario stopped eating and rushed to the basement.

Tony exploded.

After listening intently, Mario hugged him and anxiously said, "Call Mike Borelli. If he says the same thing as Mr. Nunzi . . . do it! I'll call Sam Castellano and see if he knows anything."

After talking at length with Mike, Tony took a deep breath and although the hour was late, decided to call Rose. He reached her at home in Greenwich Village and read the entire summons, elaborating on certain key provisions.

She listened calmly while sipping on a cup of steaming hot tea.

Tony, in a state of bewilderment, glumly said, "I don't understand; a friend that I've known for twenty years deserting me like this. Of all people, I thought Nick Castellano was a stand-up guy." Opening another bottle of Chianti, he continued in a scornful tone, "And where do they get off saying I threatened Barrett to make the loan? They did that just to unnerve me because I'm Sicilian. I'd like to break their heads."

"Mr. Ferrara, please don't get upset," she said, as she felt the muscles in her shoulders and neck tightening. "Bring the summons to my office tomorrow and we'll answer the complaint."

Regaining his composure, he softly said, "Rose, I try not to worry. Worry is the worst disease. I tell Vincenza not to worry, but I'm very upset. Thanks for taking the time to listen to my tirade."

In a sincere voice, she said, "Please, you're my second family. I would do anything for you."

Closing the conversation, he muttered, "Thank you so much." Then he hung up the phone, took a deep breath, and closed his eyes.

Chapter 16

Beginning his career as a stockbroker, Sam Castellano had used to the best advantage his the Midas touch. He had parlayed his success into creating his own company, Castellano Enterprises, an emerging investment banking firm on Wall Street.

Early in the morning, Mario telephoned Sam, gave him a quick summary, and in a terse tone, said, "My father is being screwed over by your Uncle Nick and Gateway Bank. Frank Nunzi has a gut vibe that Hennessy may be involved. Have you heard anything?"

Sam replied earnestly, "Sorry, I can't help." He paused, then said, "On the other hand, I sometimes use Hennessy as my lawyer. Let me nose around."

Mario, not able to control his anger, threatened, "I'm not happy. I might have to pay the weasel and Hennessy, that two-faced bastard, a visit."

"The best thing you can do right now is nothing. Let it play out. It sounds as though your father is in a good place."

"Do me a favor. Tell James Hennessy I'm pissed."

"I heard you the first time. I'll be in touch."

Soon thereafter, Mario reluctantly left the store and took the subway to Brooklyn. He had previously agreed to assist his brother and Joe on a massive landscape job in Great Neck, Long Island.

Midmorning, Tony left Vincenza and Catherine in the store, took a deep breath, and, despite his usual desire to avoid Midtown Manhattan like the plague, decided to drive into the tumult.

Rose had become a partner in the prestigious firm of Goldman and Weiss. The firm occupied the entire twenty-eight floor of the upscale TMX building at Forty-eighth Street and Madison Avenue.

Prior to his arrival, she met with Marvin Goldman to apprise him of Tony's situation. "This is the first time since I have known the family that he has asked for help. Usually it's the other way around. Mr. Ferrara has extended himself to many in need."

Looking for a parking space added to Tony's jitteriness. As he drove, he glanced at his watch again and again until he finally spotted a vacant space on the Forty-eighth Street side of the building. In his haste, he never saw the "No Parking/Tow Away" sign.

He knew this was the high-rent district and felt out of place in his worn corduroy pants, plaid shirt, and weathered fedora. Entering the building, he hesitated for a minute looking for a directory. A spaghetti-thin security guard with drawn cheeks questioned him, picked up a house phone, and called the twenty-eighth-floor law firm. Satisfied that he was expected, the guard directed him to a waiting elevator in the stark white marble lobby. With his back against the elevator wall, as the doors were closing, Tony tipped his hat to the guard.

Moments later the elevator doors opened to the reception area of Goldman and Weiss. His heart racing, he removed his hat and pondered why he was there. The receptionist buzzed Rose Gramoli, and he stood anxiously waiting for her to come and get him.

Drinking a cup of black coffee in Rose's small corner office, which she laughingly called "a converted broom closet," eased the tension.

He shook his head sadly and said, "I would appreciate you not saying anything to Carmela."

Taking his hand, she responded softly, "Don't worry; this conversation will be held in utmost confidence. Try to stay calm and tell me why you signed the note for Nick Castellano. Give me all the details."

After hearing his story, she sat back in her dark brown leather chair and with a concerned look said, "Mr. Ferrara, you and Nick Castellano have been friends for many years, and I have a feeling there's more to this than you know. Why not call him, get together, and talk?"

She carefully coached him, explaining her need for certain information before she could proceed.

"If you're not successful, I agree with Mr. Borelli and Frank Nunzi's assessment. I'll take the issue up with the DA. But my hope is that you can preserve your friendship with Mr. Castellano and resolve this amiably."

Tony agreed.

Using her phone, he arranged a meeting with Nick to take place before the lunch crowd ascended on Castellano's Ristorante.

Leaving the building, he courteously nodded to the security guard.

Turning the corner, Tony, seeing that his 1948 blue Plymouth sedan was parked under a tow-away sign, sighed a breath of relief. Then he spotted the two tickets that were plastered to the windshield. He cursed out loud all the way to Castellano's Ristorante.

The restaurant was less than half full when he arrived. Nick was not alone. He was sitting with James Hennessy and Richard Barrett.

Nick motioned him over to join them.

Not in the mood to exchange pleasantries, Tony stood with his hands on the back of the empty chair and looked directly at the man he had called a friend. He quietly said, "What the hell is going on? Since when do we speak to each other through a summons?"

Nick glanced down at his clasped hands and didn't respond.

Becoming more agitated, Tony raised his voice, "I want answers. You know this is criminal. This is fraud. If the bank does not withdraw their demand, I'll have no other recourse but to go to the DA."

Nick slumped down in his chair. Without making eye contact, he said meekly, "I never wanted it to turn out this way."

"Then tell me what the hell happened. What did you do with the money?"

"It's not that easy," Nick exclaimed. He was wiping the perspiration from his forehead. "I made a horrible mistake. I'm just trying to stay alive."

Tony's head pounded. While trying to keep his composure, he pulled his chair away from the table, glared at Barrett, and said in an infuriated tone, "You are an antagonistic piece of shit."

"Do what you have to do. That's life," Barrett venomously whispered.

"I'm going to crush you in your own spit," Tony fired back.

Hennessy jumped up and stood between them.

Tony turned on his heels and avoiding the eyes of curious restaurant patrons, hastily made his way to the hostess station. Many had heard the rising voices of the men sitting at the corner table. His face glistening with perspiration, he politely asked to use the phone.

Hearing Rose's voice calmed him a bit.

"I'm on my way back. I think Frank Nunzi was right. Hennessy is involved with Nick and maybe Barrett as well. We have to talk."

Hearing the anxiety in his voice, she said, "Don't worry, I'll be here."

She hung up and called her lunch date, Sam Castellano, whom she had been dating intermittently since Carmela's wedding. "Sorry, Tony Ferrara just left your uncle's restaurant and is on the way over. It's important that I meet with him."

"No problem. Take good care of Mr. Ferrara. He's a good man. My uncle worries me at times," said Sam, matter-of-factly.

After fighting traffic for nearly an hour, Tony finally arrived back at Rose's building. This time he found a parking space in an unloading zone. Not worrying about getting another parking ticket, he rushed inside, waved to the security guard, and quickly entered the elevator. He held the door open for a hustling deliveryman who pushed the button for the twenty-sixth floor.

When the elevator button for number twenty-eight lit up, the doors opened. The receptionist, seeing Tony sprawled out unconscious on the floor, ran to hold the doors open and screamed, "Call an ambulance!"

Hearing the commotion in the hallway, Rose hurriedly left her office and made her way to the reception area.

"Oh my God!" she cried out. Pushing past those assembled, Rose knelt down and cradled his head in her lap. Whispering, she kept repeating, "Please, Mr. Ferrara, stay with us! Please!"

When the paramedics arrived, she was visibly distressed, fearing the worst. As they worked to revive him, she called Catherine at the store and gave her a quick assessment of the situation. Breathing hard, Rose said, "I'm going in the ambulance with him. I'll meet you at Bellevue Hospital." Tears were running down her face.

Catherine ran upstairs and quickly gave Vincenza the bad news. She tried to comfort Vincenza as she called and left a message for Carmela at her school. She called Tim Gallagher and told him about the situation. She then asked if he would take Vincenza to the hospital.

Catherine stayed in the store with Angelo while Vincenza rushed to the hospital with Tim.

Rose, her eyes beet red, met Vincenza and Tim in the emergency room.

Mario and John were unreachable in Great Neck.

Putting his shirt back on, Mario leaned on his shovel, pausing to admire the results of an exhausting day of planting trees and shrubs on a palatial Great Neck estate.

"Thanks for helping out. Without you, we would be back here one more time," said Joe with his arm around Mario's shoulder. "If you could do me another favor—"

"Shoot," answered Mario, always quick to lend a hand.

"My father needs help at the warehouse. Drop me off there, take the dump truck home, and I'll pick it up tomorrow."

"No problem."

Mario watched as John pulled away in the Borelli and Ferrara pick-up truck—neither of them aware of their father's hospitalization. Twenty-five minutes later, Mario dropped Joe off at Borelli's Sicilian Import and Export in Queens. He arrived home a little while later, tired and dirty, with the B&F dump truck.

The color quickly drained from Mario's face the moment he saw a somber group of people assembled at his parents' home. He broke out in a cold sweat—beads of perspiration formed on every inch of his body from his forehead to the soles of his feet. He cried out, "What's wrong? What's happened?"

But he knew before anyone spoke. There was no music, no laughter. This was a death gathering.

Vincenza was crying.

Carmela and Catherine took him downstairs to Tony's office. The day had been exhausting and they were surrendering to their anguish as they gravely described the circumstances of his father's heart attack.

"What are we doing here and not at the hospital? Call John. Let's go!" he said anxiously, halfway out the door.

"It's no use. The doctor sent us home. John's on his way. All we can do now is pray until morning," Carmela said somberly while hugging her brother. "They will call if things turn for the worse."

"Call . . . if things get worse? That's crap," Mario said. He began pacing the small room. "*Papà* was the picture of health. Twelve-hour workdays were nothing for him. What made his heart suddenly give out?"

"I told you he was under a lot of stress today," answered Catherine, wiping away tears. "He was on his way back to Rose's office when it happened."

Carmela, trembling, added, "She encouraged *Papà* to meet with Nick Castellano at his restaurant. She doesn't know all the details of the meeting except that it was a failure."

Catherine wrapped her arms around Mario and in a fretful tone said, "You know how quickly word spreads in the neighborhood. We heard that the conversation between *Papà*, Nick, Barrett, and Hennessy was heated. *Papà* stormed out of the restaurant. That's all we know."

Holding back tears, Mario pulled away from her and in a menacing tone said, "Barrett and Hennessy! Did you call Mike Borelli and Frank Nunzi?"

Catherine replied, "*Mamma* called them."

"What did they say?"

Sobbing, Carmela said, "*Mamma* was so distraught I didn't ask her anything."

Picking up the phone, he called Mike. No answer. Shoving papers off his father's desk, he dialed Frank.

Nunzi was still in shock from Vincenza's earlier phone call. After recapping to Mario his last conversation with Tony, he said, "Something bugs me. Something just bugs the shit out of me." Nunzi smacked the wall with his fist.

Mario abruptly hung up without a word.

John was rushing up the steps as Mario was leaving. Seeing his brother, Mario grabbed his arm, and hurriedly said, "I think you should call Theresa and tell her you're going to stay the night. I have to leave for a little while."

"Where are you going?"

Mario didn't answer.

He climbed into the dump truck, his eyes filled with rage. He floored the gas pedal and headed to Brooklyn. After blazing through two red lights, he recklessly drove the truck onto the sidewalk blocking Castellano's Ristorante's entrance. He jumped out of the truck, not bothering to close the door, and rushed inside.

He was midway through the restaurant when James Hennessy extended his hand and said, "I'm sorry to hear about your father."

Without a word, Mario picked up a chair and slammed it across Hennessy's chest, knocking him to the ground. He pressed his knee against his chest and proceeded to pummel him. James, who struggled to free himself, had the help of some patrons. But Mario had that extra bit of adrenaline pumping through him, and nothing was going to stop him from beating the crap out of Hennessy.

A number of patrons shouted, "Call the cops!"

He bounced off Hennessy and started to move toward the back office. Diners tried unsuccessfully to calm him down, but he was a man with a purpose. He kicked open the door to confront Nick Castellano.

Nick was cowered behind his desk with a baseball bat firmly gripped in his hands.

Mario, sweat dripping down his face, furiously said, "You rotten, contemptible bastard. My father helped you when you needed him, and in return, you betrayed him. You can rot in hell, but first I have to kill you."

Castellano's cronies came to his aid, slamming Mario to the floor just as the police arrived. As they were trying to sort things out, Mario, now standing, was cursing up a storm in Italian. Suddenly, he lunged at James.

The police were preparing to arrest him, but James pleaded, "Please hold it a second. We're not going to press charges."

"The reason they won't press charges is because they're all crooks . . . and made of shit," shouted Mario, in a tone of disgust as he stomped out of the restaurant. Unable to control his anger, he left his mark by kicking every table and chair within his reach.

Mario's temper was still boiling over as he jumped back into the truck, shifted it into reverse, and floored it, slamming into Hennessy's rose-red Cadillac. He then drove straight to Gateway Bank and dumped the remaining load of manure at Barrett's private back door entrance. He sat, eyes closed for a moment, before speedily driving back to Little Italy.

Back at the house, Mario found the family praying in the living room.

Catherine rushed to greet him, hugged him, and in a tone that echoed her frustration, asked, "Where did you go? I have been worried sick."

Kissing her on the forehead, he softly said, "It's OK. No need to worry."

John and Mario encouraged Vincenza, Carmela, and Catherine to go to sleep. The men would hold an all-night vigil, hoping that the phone would *not* ring.

The following morning, Mario called Joe and filled him in on the previous day, a day from hell.

Slamming his fist down on the table, Mario said, "Barrett, Hennessy, and that double-crossing Nick will pay someway, somehow."

"With those three, you need to watch your back. Let me know what I can do."

"Right now, nothing. I need to think."

Ignoring him, Joe said, "I'll be right over."

THREE WEEKS LATER AT CAFFÉ ROMA

Mario, sitting with his back to the wall, said sadly, "It's been rough in the store. My mother is tough, but it's been hard. Thank God for Catherine's strength. Even Angelo has helped out."

"No matter what, when it comes to family, we're both lucky," said Joe, raising his eyebrows.

"Even though you two are heathens, God shines down on you with favor," said Tim, who couldn't help but smile.

Mario flippantly said, "Please spare me. You have brainwashed me with your ever-loving God. I have prayed my brains out."

"One of these days, I'll try it," said Joe, grinning.

Chapter 17

August 1951

One month later Tony was at home recuperating when Rose called and said happily, "Mr. Ferrara, you won't believe this, but I just heard from James Hennessy. Gateway Bank is dropping the lawsuit."

Vincenza wiped away tears of joy and kissed his cheek.

Excited, he called Frank Nunzi.

"Tony, I knew the bastards would cave."

"*Grazie. Sta bene!*" Tony said happily.

Mike Borelli and Mario were standing at the door with huge grins.

"How are you?" asked Mike.

"*Buono!*" Tony replied.

Mario said, "I'll leave you two to talk. I'm going to give Angelo his first lesson in baking bread. He's nine years old now. He's ready!"

LATER IN THE DAY

"What the hell did you do to Angelo? The kid looks like a ghost," said Joe, laughing at Angelo's flour-covered face.

"Forget about it."

Getting serious, Joe firmly said, "Mario, here's the deal. Sam told me that Hennessy settled with Gateway Bank and paid off Nick's remaining gambling debts and a substantial private loan. Hennessy earned himself a bigger piece of Castellano's Ristorante."

"Too neat for me," said Mario, sounding annoyed.

Joe bluntly said, "Let it rest."

"Listen to him," said Catherine, her patience running thin.

OCTOBER 6, 1955

A headline in the *Daily Mirror*
DEM BUMS BEAT YANKS

> *It was Brooklyn's finest hour. The Dodgers finally beat the Yankees in a hard fought World Series, winning the final seventh game.*

Joe left a note at Ferrara's Grocery and Bakery.

> *What happened to your Yankees?*
> *Hold it. I can answer that. They lost!*

Mario once again celebrated the miracle of life with the family at Flushing Hospital. John and Theresa had three glorious children: Maria, Robert, who was born on May 8, 1952, and the new arrival, Anthony.

1956

APRIL 27, 1956

Mario's concentration was interrupted by a ringing telephone. He was deep in thought, writing a chapter that paralleled Italians and Negroes.

"Mario, it's me, Joe. I just heard Marciano retired. The Rock was undefeated in forty-nine fights and had forty-three KO's."

"So now you're a sportscaster," said Mario, chuckling.

OCTOBER 11, 1956

A headline in the *Daily Mirror*
YANKS WIN

Yogi smacks 2 homers, Kucks shut out Dodgers

Mario called Joe. "What? No note? Or did the big goose egg choke you? Hold it. I can answer that. They suck eggs."

It was late in the day on Friday, November 16, 1956, when Tim Gallagher joined Catherine and Mario at Caffe Reggio in Greenwich Village.

Tim, on his third cup of coffee and second cheese-filled pastry, lamented, "Thank God, Ike has kept us out of the Suez War. It was bad enough with Israel, Britain, and France pitted against Egypt."

"I agree," said Catherine, adding sadly, "Korea still haunts me. We lost over thirty thousand Americans, both men and women."

Mario, holding Catherine's hand, nodded in concurrence and said, "If you think about it, the last three years have been explosive. Besides the thousands upon thousands killed and wounded in Korea, we also had lives destroyed by *that* Senator Joseph McCarthy. The bastard's homophobia and paranoia went right down the sewer when he pushed one too many times and attacked Eisenhower." Taking a bite of *biscotti*, he rubbed his forehead and said, "Thank God no one was murdered behind a cloak of justice, like Sacco and Vanzetti. And now we have a long overdue fight for civil rights."

Tim passionately said, "Father Carelli and I have encouraged our parishioners at Our Lady of Loreto to take special interest and pray for those who are abused in the South. Rosa Parks is a brave lady. She was tired, held her ground, and would not move."

Mario, rubbing his neck, said, "When you think Rosa Parks was arrested for not moving to the back of a bus; if that's not bullshit I don't know what is." Leaning toward Tim, his eyes getting wider, he continued, "This guy, King, has guts. He led a boycott in Montgomery, Alabama, and talked about meeting violence with nonviolence. I like that. I have had enough nightmares about violence to last a lifetime."

"That's because you insist on eating *biscottis* just before you go to bed," said Catherine, grinning.

Ignoring her sarcastic humor, he declared, "The Civil Rights plight somewhat mirrors the American injustice to Italians. Just the color is different." Mario hesitated a moment, collected his thoughts and said, "I'll take that back. Liberty has been trampled. All this crap has to stop." He anxiously shifted in his chair and in a determined voice said, "I think it's time for me to talk to *Papà*, shift gears, track the movement, and write full time. I need to be active in this turmoil."

Catherine, flustered, asked, "And you don't have enough turmoil in your dreams? She looked down at the table in front of her, avoiding Mario's eyes, and pleaded, "Turmoil will wait for you. It's not time yet."

Intuitively suspecting a full-blown argument was about to begin, Tim immediately changed the subject. "Speaking of turmoil, I heard Sam Castellano brokered a deal between Hennessy and Barrett."

Mario, frowning, asked, "What deal?"

"Don't know exactly, except it had something to do with an acquisition for Gateway Bank."

"What's with Sam? I haven't seen much of him lately."

"His focus is a little different than yours. It's called *money*," Tim replied.

"You're right. I told John to go see him. He and Joe are going to need more money in order to expand their business. But I guess they're not ready yet."

Chapter 18

1957 . . . springtime in Little Italy

From the time Tony and Vincenza opened Ferrara's Grocery and Bakery, the demand for Mario's thick-crusted Italian bread, which some called the best in Little Italy and beyond, continued to grow daily, particularly on the Lower East Side. Despite the fact Mario sought to pursue a writing career to expose and fight against injustice, he abided by his father's request to expand the business. As a result, the family put out the word of their impending need—a delivery truck.

Mario didn't have to wait long for the telephone to ring.

"Hello, my name's Brian Maloney, president of Tri-County Trucking." Father Gallagher told me that you're in the market for a small delivery van. You're in luck, I have the perfect vehicle and at the right price."

On blind faith, Mario excitedly said, "Consider it bought."

"It's yours," he responded, chuckling.

That afternoon Mario took a taxi over to the Williamsburg section of Brooklyn. Tri-County, an old-line trucking company, had encountered financial problems and was left with no alternative but to sell off their fleet of vehicles as soon as possible. After surveying the parking lots,

Mario frowned, tugged down on his brand new brown fedora, and impatiently asked, "Where is it?"

"It's in the back lot," replied Maloney, a six-foot-three, redheaded, second-generation Irishman.

"You mean the white van with a hood that looks like it went through a meat grinder?"

Maloney smirked, scratched his blotched face and answered, "That's the one. I'll make you one hell of a deal."

Trying to maintain his composure, Mario slowly returned to the back lot to take another look. Opening the cargo door, he found—much to his surprise—a Sicilian peddler's cart tilted on its side. Barely visible were the faded but still colorful hand-painted panels of Sicilian kings and knights in combat for independence.

Besides the cart, the inside of the paneled van was filled with traditional peddler paraphernalia of trinkets of sorts and case after case of aspirin-sized bottles of tonic. The red, white, and green labels on the bottles were printed with a wizard's staff and the following inscription: "*Count Alessandro's Healing Tonic of Love.*"

Not making the connection with his *papà's* tale of the Count, Mario wasted no time expressing his frustration to Brian. Raising his voice to be heard over the traffic noise, he angrily said, "Now that I'm here, what am I going to do with that piece of dog shit and all the crap that's inside?"

Maloney stepped toward him to within inches of his nose and in an irritated tone spit out, "Look, it runs; and for what you're willing to spend, it's worth twice the price. Loosen up your wallet; you're not in the old country. Besides, I'm giving your priest pal half the proceeds."

Thinking of Tim, Mario bit his tongue and reluctantly agreed to buy the van; though he mumbled some obscenity in Italian. He brushed past Maloney and walked back to the buy-a-wreck van to justify his purchase. He was so preoccupied with his anger that he never heard the soft footsteps of a frail, four-foot-eleven-inch woman dressed all in black. She had a mole on her cheek, and her hair-bun was held in place with a silver darning needle almost as long as Zorro's sword. Standing at the entrance of the storage lot, she startled him by calling out in broken English "Is anybody home?"

"Only me," Mario answered curtly.

"*Buon giorno*, my name is Mrs. Roselli. I have come here again to look for Giuseppe, a peddler from Sicily who brought healing tonic to America."

"Sorry, no peddler. Just this beat up truck and cart," said Mario in an agitated tone.

Her black eyes shone brightly as she said, "*Count Alessandro's Healing Tonic of Love* cured my ailments."

"Mrs. Roselli, I don't know whether or not I understand what you're trying to tell me, but—"

Placing her weathered hands on his shoulders, she interrupted him and said, "Love is a state of being for healing."

"So?" he asked incredulously.

Not wishing to give rise to his impatience, she said, "When you combine the tonic and love, magic happens."

"It sounds like voodoo to me. My *mamma* uses garlic or *malocchiu!*"

Adjusting her bun, she raised her gray eyebrows and indignantly replied, "It's not voodoo! Can't you imagine a tonic healing any ache outside or inside of you? A tonic of purpose?"

In an impatient tone, he asked, "What purpose?"

"A simple purpose of caring and helping each other with love—love that knows no bounds."

"Mrs. Roselli, with all due respect, what you're saying makes no sense whatsoever."

"*Sense?* Let me tell you about *sense.*" She leaned against the truck and continued with determination in her fragile voice, "A simple purpose through love makes sense. And it doesn't stop there."

Mario, not wishing to be rude, but finding his patience running beyond thin, mustered a smile and said, "I'm an Italian, better yet, a Sicilian; I know about love."

She smiled at his sarcastic comment and gently took hold of his arm. "A purpose of respecting and caring for the earth and all living things in it."

"Mrs. Roselli, please—"

"Yes, living things, including flowers, plants, and animals. What can't you understand about that?" she asked in a calm voice, still holding on to him.

He pondered the question, shrugged, and gently pulled away. "I think I've heard enough; I have to go."

Taking hold of his arm again, she looked directly into his eyes and smiled. "Ever wonder why in some religions they call God's vision a kingdom of the living God?

In response, he exhaled in frustration.

"It's not a riddle. The paradise of God is now. No one is excluded. A God of love who accepts all."

Mario, still absorbed in his anger, said, "Tell that to *His Holy Pompous Ass*, Archbishop Stanley. He excludes those who disagree with him or the Roman Catholic Church. What a joke."

"Who is this Archbishop Stanley?" Mrs. Roselli asked. She let go of his arm and patted his hand.

"Excuse me for saying *ass*. But he's just a man who treats my friend Father Tim Gallagher like a peasant servant; who denied my sister a beautiful wedding in Battery Park; and who upset my family over nothing," Mario said in an agitated tone. He plopped onto the crushed hood of the delivery van.

She looked at him in bewilderment and said, "That was over fifteen years ago."

"How did you know that?" he asked anxiously.

"Never mind. What's important is that paradise is more than all religions put together."

"More? You mean paradise is even more than, say, Joe DiMaggio being inducted into the Baseball Hall of Fame?"

Once again ignoring his snotty remark, she continued. "Giuseppe told me, 'Paradise is throughout the earth.' Actually, paradise is throughout all the heavens . . . today . . . this very second."

"It sounds pretty simple, yet it seems somehow complicated. Frankly, I have to go." Mario yanked on his hat, tilting it sideways as he slid down off the hood.

Mrs. Roselli, with a smile so wide it showed the gap between her front teeth, said, "Giuseppe also told me that *Conte Alessandro's* words were simple—that words of spirit and truth are not complicated. But, sometimes his words didn't fall on fertile soil." She was gesturing with her hands as she spoke, "Still, he never lost sight of his vision-quest."

"I don't know; this whole thing sounds strange to me," said Mario, opening the door of the truck, preparing to leave.

Her face muscles tightened. "Please, sir, *Conte Alessandro* was not always appreciated and sometimes he was even hated."

"For what? And please don't call me *sir*," Mario said brusquely as he closed the door.

"People fear the unknown. In Sicily, some thought the *Conte* lived in the slums of Palermo. Others said he lived inside a grotto in *Monte Etna*."

He laughed heartily and said, "*Monte Etna!*" Of course you're talking about my father's favorite fable, *Conte Alessandro di Cagliostro*."

Paying Mario no mind, she beamed and said, "You see, inside this wonderful mountain is a living spring that erupts whenever she's disturbed. With each eruption, the goddess within releases many mysteries she holds inside her womb."

"That's even more farfetched than *Papà's* tale." For some unexplained reason, he couldn't pull away.

Mrs. Roselli again took hold of Mario's hand and said, "Some thought the only reason he could live inside the mountain was because he was the devil himself."

In a smart-ass tone he said, "Crazy. But hey, Mrs. Roselli, I really have to go meet this guy." He tried to pull his hand out of her firm grip. For a little woman, she had the nerve and strength of Hercules.

"Giuseppe loves Sicily! He calls it paradise. His eyes twinkled whenever he spoke of its beautiful coastal waters, orange groves, and vineyards. Oh yes, and let's not forget the *pistacchio* trees."

"I get it; you're working for the chamber of commerce," Mario said grinning.

She returned his smile and rolled on. "There's a story that tells of Giuseppe when he traveled to Rome. A short time after his appearance at the Vatican he vanished—some say in fear for his life. But, I know he was without fear even though he did leave Italy and came to America." She shrugged, rubbed her furrowed brow, and continued, "Giuseppe came first to Brooklyn, and now nobody knows where he's living."

"What was he doing at the Vatican? And what did he do when he came to America?"

"Of course he became a New York peddler," she said, rolling her eyes in astonishment at Mario's questions.

"Of course! Yet, you didn't answer my question about the Vatican." He shrugged his shoulders, sighed a sigh of exasperation, and said, "Forget about it. What can I do for you? I really have to go."

"I wish you to sell me a bottle of tonic." She offered him ten cents.

"If *Giuseppe* gave you a free bottle that's good enough for me. I don't know what to do with this stuff anyway. Take as many bottles as you want and please keep your money," Mario said, smiling.

"Thank you, sir."

In frustration he threw up his arms and said, "My name is Mario . . . Mario Ferrara and please don't call me *sir*. I have to go. Take care of yourself, Mrs. Roselli."

Unfazed by his attitude, she nodded, reached up, squeezed his cheeks, and very softly whispered, "Maybe you can become a peddler."

Mario watched her slowly walk out of the back lot, turn the corner, and disappear from sight.

He rushed back to the front office, borrowed a phone, and called John. You're not going to believe this . . ." After describing what took place in Tri-County's back lot, he asked, "Do you remember *Papà's* story about *Il Conte* and *Monte Etna,* and that with each encounter there's an opportunity?"

"So?" John asked impatiently.

"So, . . . *Papà* said, 'Observe, listen and understand what's taking place, then choose with your intuition.'"

"What's that got to do with the truck?"

"Don't you get it? It's the peddler's cart. I could sell trinkets of sorts and bottles of *Conte Alessandro's* snake oil."

John hesitated a moment; then, half-joking, said, "You haven't been drinking any of that crap, have you?"

"Give me a break, please! Think about it. This could be an absolute godsend to my writing. It could make an intriguing book and maybe even jumpstart my writing career. Angelo could bake bread."

John, mocking him, said, "Why not. I could send Maria, Robert, and Anthony to help." He paused, slapped the side of his head, and blurted, "Are you going crazy or what? All this Dante crap and Italian injustice, civil rights, and whatever else is driving you *stunato*." Stopping to catch his breath, he concluded in a forceful tone, "Why don't you go home? Maybe Catherine can pound some sense into you."

Mario drove the old van back to Little Italy, John's outburst ringing in his ears. Over dinner, paying no heed to his brother's words and without noticing the new chrome kitchen table and chairs that Catherine had purchased, he excitedly began to share with her the day's event.

"This woman . . . I don't know . . . there was something captivating about her."

"I'm glad you told me she was elderly," said Catherine, smiling. Slowly rising from her chair, she leaned over the kitchen table, hugged Mario, and whispered, "Maybe someday you can write about the peddler. Not just yet; in due time. Stay with *Papà*. He needs you. Put the cart in the storage room." She was carrying a handful of dirty dishes to the sink. "Maybe the peddler will take your mind off all the chaos that you choose to surround yourself with. Besides, we still have to pay for this new kitchen set that you never noticed."

Mario, leaping up, lifted Catherine in the air and twirled her around.

Chapter 19

The following morning Mario removed the cart from the van, along with the trinkets of sorts and bottles of healing tonic, and stored them in the back room of the store.

Watching him, Tony shook his head in disbelief and, with his arms extended, said, "What in the hell are you going to do what that thing?"

Mario grinned and replied, "I don't know what I'm going to do with it." He hesitated for a moment, cleared his throat, and said, "*Papà*, besides what you told us as children, is there anything else you know about *Conte Alessandro di Cagliostro?*"

Turning slowly, he gave Mario a questioning look and shrugged his shoulders.

"It's crazy. Yesterday at Tri-County Trucking I met this old lady who went on and on about this guy Giuseppe who she called a peddler. I don't know who owned the cart before, but supposedly that's the *Conte's* healing tonic I unloaded"

Tony tapped his forehead and said, "Wait. I remember last year *Il Sole* had a story about *Conte Alessandro.*" Reaching under the counter, Tony rummaged through a box of old newspapers and found the monthly magazine. He handed it to Mario. Inside, on page 3, Mario read . . .

Fact or Fiction . . . 1785, Palermo, Sicily

Is it fact or fiction that those who supported and believed in the adventurer and mystic, Giuseppe Balsamo, known as Conte Alessandro di Cagliostro of Palermo, were tormented by vengeful reprisals?

This intriguing man peddled bottles of a healing potion of love to cure all diseases and problems that troubled many people in the eighteenth century. He also claimed the discovery and secret of the Philosopher's Stone that allowed him to turn metals into gold. Some would think that would be enough extraordinary assertions and actions for any man, but not for the Conte. He predicted the future, communicated with the dead by holding séances, and sold elixirs. Further, adding to the Conte's tribulations was his belief in Egyptian Freemasonry and the Illuminati, which even today is considered by many as a clandestine order to manipulate the world.

Therefore, as far as self-proclaimed inquisitors were concerned, most of whom were powerful Parisian and Roman aristocrats, Conte Alessandro di Cagliostro had gone far out on a limb. Frightened by this so-called wizard, they made the decision to retaliate. As a result they burned the homes of supporters, wrecked their shops, and even beat many of them to death. Unfortunately, many of those caught in the cataclysm were the poorest of the poor, to whom the Conte had given bottles of his healing potion.

He traveled Europe, Egypt, Greece, Arabia, Persia, and Russia. He was welcomed in the royal courts, and through his antics became the inspiration for Mozart's "The Magic Flute" and Goethe's "Faust." And wherever possible he established healing clinics for the poor. Nevertheless, Catherine the Great ordered the Conte out of Russia.

In a prelude to the French Revolution, he was accused of fraud in the Affair of the Diamond Necklace, which included an innocent Queen Marie Antoinette and a wicked Countess de La Motte who deceived a proud Cardinal Rohan. By the order of a furious King Louis XVI, the Conte was sent to the Bastille along with the Cardinal and Countess. Ultimately, the Conte was found innocent but still was banished from France.

Soon after his release, he returned to the Holy City of Rome, where he and his beautiful wife Lorenza Feliciani, known as Seraphina, attempted to start an Egyptian Freemasonry. The act proved to be blatantly audacious and caused his eventual downfall— or did it? To protect herself against the torturous wrath of the Holy Inquisition, Seraphina betrayed her husband to an inquisitor. He was arrested, tried and convicted of heresy and sorcery, and sentenced to death by burning at the stake. Pope Pius VI excommunicated him and changed the judgment to life imprisonment in solitary confinement within the fortress of San Leo Prison.

Three years later, the people went on a general strike shutting Italy down for a day, thereby pressuring the power elite to acquiesce and grant him an unrestricted pardon. However, the Conte, according to Napoleon, had already died in the filthy dungeon at San Leo, although there is no evidence of a tomb.

There are still people around the world who think of Conte Alessandro di Cagliostro as the King of Charlatans, while there are others who mourn because of the unknown fate of this man. Is it possible that, as some Siciliani assert, he hangs among the mummies in Catacombe dei Cappuccini and at midnight visits those entombed, looking for a way out? Or does he still roam the streets of Rome, Paris, Palermo, or somewhere else?

To this day it remains a mystery.

Mario finished reading the article and looked at his *papà* in amazement.

Tony sat down on a vegetable crate, sighed, and said, "When I was a young boy, the story told to me by your *nannu*, was of this mysterious man Giuseppe Balsamo, known as *Conte Alessandro di Cagliostro*. It was whispered by many *paesani* that a wizard had escaped from the Papal States Prison of San Leo and returned to Sicily. They believed the wizard was none other than Giuseppe, *Il Conte Alessandro*, and that he lived somewhere deep inside *Monte Etna* on an island surrounded by crystal spring waterways. There inside a grotto, the banks of the passage were said to be gilded with gold dust, and it was said that scattered everywhere were sparkling gems of many colors and ornate jeweled chalices." Tony paused and then exclaimed, "And there was light! They said it was as though the sun had penetrated the grotto's walls. Growing out of the granite walls were white roses."

Taken back by his *papà*'s excited tone, he quickly asked, "Who are *they*? And did you say *light*?"

"Yes . . . Yes . . . "

"Please continue."

Tony stood, leaned across the counter, and whispered, "The real secret behind *Conte Alessandro* and his magical powers rests inside *Monte Etna*. It began after Jesus died. A repentant Roman centurion stood at the foot of the Cross and watched in disgust as his comrades played a game of chance for the Robe of Christ. Late in the evening, while everyone was asleep, the centurion took the Robe from the filth that won it and passed the Robe on to Peter the Apostle. In Rome, before he was crucified upside down, Peter passed it on to Paul." Restlessly wiping his brow, Tony continued, "Then, just prior to Paul's martyrdom, he passed the Robe on to several soldiers who watched over him with kindness and understanding while he was chained in a Roman prison. These nine strong men of conviction were overwhelmed to be entrusted with this sacred cloth and thought it best to leave Rome and transport the Robe to an invincible location."

Tony stopped and stood silent for several seconds.

"The Robe of Christ was in the cave and the spring inside the cave was an eternal spring of healing?" asked Mario, questioning the believability of the statement.

Tony was pacing the floor. "Before leaving Rome the soldiers raided the high governor's vault, and off they went with the Robe and a treasure-filled caravan of gold and jewels."

"Why Sicily?"

"The soldiers, familiar with Sicily from past Roman occupations, knew *Monte Etna* and the fire that burned within her soul, the soul of a goddess. After much exploration, they came upon a perfect place to hide their cargo. It was a grotto within the mountain that captured their hearts and imagination. The soldiers never left the grotto." Tony, sipping coffee, paused and smiled. "It was said that a young man wandering around this mountain was lured into the cave by spirits."

Mario rolled his eyes. "Sounds pretty farfetched."

"Let your *papà* finish," said Vincenza, while waiting on a customer. "I myself wonder."

Tony put on his apron, tied it tight, and said, "In the nineteenth century, this myth tempted numerous groups to search for wealth and fame; yet, no one ever found the Robe within the soul of *Monte Etna*."

"What happened to the Robe?"

Ignoring the question, Tony said, "Those bastards wanted to first torture the *Conte* to find the Robe, then kill him. They wanted the jewels and the Robe for their own selfishness purposes."

"Who are *those bastards*?"

Never mind."

"I'll be right back." Mario rushed up the steps to his fourth-floor home. Out of breath he said, "Catherine, please read this."

His eyes locked on her as she slowly read the article in *Il Sole*.

"Interesting," she said, not looking up.

"That's it . . . interesting?"

"OK. Fascinating."

"Forget about it."

Chapter 20

·····································

September 25, 1957

A headline in the *World Telegram*
101st AIRBORNE IN LITTLE ROCK

> *Ike sends 1000 troops to Arkansas to keep the peace and escort Negro students into school. President Eisenhower stated, "The Federal Constitution will be upheld by me, by every means at my command."*

After returning from Ferrara's expanding bread delivery route into Queens, Mario leaned against the counter with a cup of coffee and read the newspaper headline to Tony. Folding the newspaper, he said earnestly, "I tell you, *Papà*, Truman had nothing on Ike. He's also one tough son of a bitch."

Tony nodded.

"For years, I had been writing about exploitation and oppression of Italian immigrants, beginning with the vigilante lynching in New Orleans and the unjust executions of Sacco and Vanzetti. Then came the windbag McCarthy who tried to paint everybody *Red*. And now civil rights and the Negro. Things are bad and getting worse." Mario stood, pushed his hair back, and added, "It's been difficult to stay focused. I don't know much about solutions, but I do have a lot of questions."

"What you need is answers, not questions. So don't be frustrated: spend that energy seeking solutions," said Tony, going back to stocking shelves.

The country was simmering, and it was just a matter of time before things would come to a boil.

JANUARY 1959

Frank Nunzi had arrived in New York just before Christmas and was staying with Tony and Vincenza through the holidays.

It was a typical Friday night dinner. They had enjoyed Vincenza's special *linguine all' aglio e vongole*. The men of the Borelli and Ferrara families, including seventeen-year-old Angelo, settled into the living room, but not before they all had cheerfully joined in singing along with Julius LaRosa's recording of "Eh Cumpari."

Angelo said, "Uncle Frank, thanks again for the great seats at Yankee Stadium. Sitting behind the dugout was great!"

"Love to do it," Frank said, giving Angelo a bear hug.

"Mr. Nunzi, what are your thoughts about the press?" asked Joe. "Last week, they tried to interview Pop about his import business. They also implied something about illegal immigration."

Frank raised his forefinger to his lips. "I have always said, be careful of the press. They enjoy sensationalism. Look at the coverage when Albert Anastasia was whacked, shot dead in his chair. That was in 1957 and they still haven't let up."

Mike Borelli chimed in, "Albert found out the hard way that barbershops are God's waiting room."

"Clever. But seriously, soon after his murder, I was back in the city when someone from the *Mirror* questioned me about a meeting that took place in Appalachian, New York. They thought it was some kind of Mafia summit or something." Frank's mood shifted as he shook his head and said in disgust, "Anyway, they drilled me because I'm successful in business and my name ends with an *i*."

"Didn't you play *bocce* with some of the guys the press are trying to finger?" asked Joe.

Raising his voice, Frank replied, "So what? I might have been on the same airplane with them as well. The press could all go to hell."

"They are already in hell. Don't let them get under your skin," Tony said while filling Frank's glass with Chianti. "To change the subject, did you see where the chicken Batista flew the coop when Fidel Castro pushed toward Havana?"

"Castro is a rebel with guts to spare," added Mario.

"Listening to you for the last week . . . you're the rebel," said Frank gently smacking him on the side of his head. "Be careful what you say in public. Don't put yourself out on *that* limb."

Tony nodded in agreement and said, "Each year the fire of liberty and justice that burns in his heart gets hotter."

"I agree with Mr. Nunzi. Why get branded *stunato*? Express your thoughts to the family and not in the streets," John chimed in.

"You, my brother, are a worrier."

Angelo sat and listened. He had grown accustomed to hearing his Uncle Mario speak of Garibaldi, liberty, and America when riding shotgun on Ferrara's bread deliveries. He especially enjoyed going to Corona and visiting with his cousins—then the treat of the day, lemon ice at the Lemon Ice King.

Carmela was most grateful that Mario had become the father figure in Angelo's life. She was hoping beyond hope that his influence on her son would convince him to go to college.

APRIL 1959

Sam called John. "Giovanni, Sam here; it's been too long. Last night over dinner, Tim Gallagher informed me that you and Joe Borelli are expanding your construction and landscape business and are going to focus on development. Let's get together: maybe I can be of assistance and provide funds for your venture. I have always been interested in real estate development."

John, pleasantly surprised, said, "It's a deal. Where and when?"

"Come down to my office at 40 Wall Street. It's the pyramid-topped building. We'll talk over lunch."

Castellano's successful track record had earned him the reputation as a high-stakes player and powerful investment banker on Wall Street.

When John arrived Sam had a catered lunch waiting for them in the conference room. As they ate, John summarized the business plan for a development he and Joe wanted to build. With the street smarts Joe and John both possessed, John's formal education in business, and Joe Borelli's expertise in construction, a development company seemed a natural course of action to follow.

By the time they had finished lunch, John had completed his briefing on the project's business plan. His responses to Sam's questions conveyed confidence that B&F would be successful in their new venture.

The arrival of coffee signaled the end of lunch. Sam rose from the conference table, walked over to the window, and stood looking out on the Brooklyn Bridge. "Opportunity, it's out there."

"You sound like Joe's pop."

"Whatever you need, call me; I'll be there."

"Thanks."

The telephone rang as John was leaving Sam's office. James Hennessy was calling from a pay phone. "Sam, I thought you might want to hear the latest. Genovese went up the river, and Carlo Gambino is taking over." James hung up and went back to his table to join Barrett for a late lunch at Castellano's Ristorante.

Chapter 21

And so the turbulent '60s begin.

On Sunday, February 7, 1960, during dinner with the family, Mario made a declaration: "I will not spend one more nickel in Woolworth's Department Store."

"What happened, Uncle Mario?"

"In Greensboro, North Carolina, some Negro students decided to sit-in at Woolworth's lunch counter until they were served." His jaw tensed up. "Negroes have been harassed since day-one and that was bad enough, but now it's turning violent. Southerners must have their heads up—"

Catherine gave him "the look."

Tony nodded approvingly.

"That's a thousand miles away; things will get better," said John, not looking directly at Mario.

It didn't take long for the passive resistance of sit-ins to take hold and spread through seven southern states, affecting thirty cities. Things got ugly in Chattanooga, Tennessee, and turned into a raging race riot in Biloxi, Mississippi. In October, Martin Luther King was arrested in Atlanta during a sit-in while waiting to be served at a lunch counter.

JUNE 1960

The phone rang. Joe was on the other end of the line.

"Hey, Mario, I heard Hitchcock's movie *Psycho* is scary as hell."

"Sounds like it's about Nikita Khrushchev, but if you want to go, I'll ask Catherine and call you back."

"I'm not staying at home right now, if you know what I mean."

"Joe, with you, nothing surprises me: you undoubtedly are the horniest guy I know."

NOVEMBER 2, 1960

Mario couldn't wait to give Tony the news. "*Papà*, look at this, the post office just issued a postage stamp in honor of Giuseppe Garibaldi, 'Champion of Liberty.'"

"Wonderful, wonderful."

"Too bad for the Negro that *liberty* in the South is determined by color."

Even though his uncle and mother tried their best, Angelo decided to skip college and work for his grandfather in the family store. He would help Mario bake bread and take over the bread delivery route. Carmela was not happy.

DECEMBER 1960

John and Joe spent countless hours building their development company through a series of checkered endeavors. Much had been learned by enduring failures as well as enjoying successes. All those efforts made B&F stronger.

Although, Mario had major responsibilities in the family-run store, he always made himself available to his brother and friend whenever he was needed. In addition, he and Catherine invested whatever little "extra" money they acquired in B&F development. In spite of their financial efforts and those of Mike Borelli, Mario intuitively knew that

Joe and John were in dire need of additional money. They had set their sights on a major development project that would require substantial equity funds and major lending sources. He convinced his brother that if B&F were to continue to pursue this opportunity, it was time to take Sam Castellano's offer of financial assistance.

Between Christmas and New Year, John and Sam met at the site. Sam was impressed with John's due diligence for B&F to acquire a 200-acre parcel of land on the south shore of Long Island. The site was large enough to accomplish a new development consisting of a variety of housing, a major shopping center, and a business and industrial park. The West Islip town project would be named after a Sicilian seaside village near Palermo called Mondello. Sam agreed to invest and ultimately became a major shareholder.

Castellano Enterprises also secured additional shareholders and arranged financing through Thames, a European bank headquartered in Covent Square, London. Much to the chagrin of the Ferraras, Thames' US affiliate was Gateway Bank. Barrett, in spite of his questionable character and business practices, continued to rise in New York City's financial circle.

To further muddle matters, James Hennessy made partner in Cook and Baker, a prominent Manhattan law firm that represented Gateway.

1961

JANUARY

It was a beautiful, crisp Sunday morning in New York City. After attending Mass at Our Lady of Loreto Church, Mario and Catherine decided to have breakfast at the Sunflower Deli in Greenwich Village. Afterward, they strolled to Washington Square Park to sit on a bench and people watch.

They talked about Kennedy's inaugural speech. Mario said, "What I like about the guy is that he promised nothing: instead he put pressure on the people to help the country."

She snuggled up to him and said, "President Kennedy is right: success or failure is in our hands, not his."

"Maybe people will get off their asses and at least think."

Catherine stood, took Mario's hand, and playfully pulled him up off the bench. "That reminds me, we better get up and walk or the French toast we ate will add to my heavenly hips."

APRIL

Joe came by the store often to pick up a few groceries, and as usual, the conversation turned to the latest newspaper headlines.

"Somebody screwed up royally. The Bay of Pigs invasion was a total failure."

"Fidel Castro is no dummy. He sniffed it out," Mario said, walking Joe out of the store. Each carried a full bag of groceries. "Thank God it was Cuban exiles and not American troops. Korea was bad enough." Standing under Ferrara's awning, he continued, "History will tell you that a little country can always kick the ass of a big country—that is, if the little country is determined. All you have to do is ask the British."

Joe added, "Kennedy is a stand-up guy. Even though Eisenhower planned the invasion, he took full responsibility for the fiasco."

"That's refreshing and courageous, isn't it?"

MAY

It was late in the evening when Mario telephoned Joe. "I don't know if you heard, but a short time ago, Alan Shepard *defined* courage by becoming the first American in space."

"Too bad he's not Italian."

Mario jokingly replied, "You could have volunteered; but how would you like to sit on a rocket that was twenty feet from your ass?"

"Maybe next time I will," Joe countered.

"Forget about it."

"How's your writing coming?"

"I can't keep up. Southern Freedom Riders met head-on in Montgomery, Alabama, with a mob of white bigots that included the Ku Klux Klan. Those guys have no guts. That's why they wear sheets." Rising off the couch, he said irritably, "They beat the hell out of Negroes, whites, news reporters, cameramen; it didn't matter. It's good that King is staying out front. This guy will not cave in, in the struggle for freedom. In fact, I put him alongside of Shepard in the courage category."

"There's not a lot we can do from here," Joe said.

"That's what keeps bugging me."

"Mario, there is always crap going on somewhere."

"That's what keeps bugging me."

"Call Tim," Joe suggested.

"I did. *The Imperial* Archbishop Stanley is sending him to Rome for a while to head up a fundraising program for Vatican Art and Treasure. Apparently, Stanley agreed to help the Holy See in raising money to support a worldwide traveling exhibit of precious art."

"You have to be kidding."

"That's what I said. Then it dawned on me, Stanley is jockeying for position at the Vatican and Tim has a gift in raising money."

1962

FEBRUARY

"Uncle Mario, the White House said we're staying in Vietnam until the Vietcong are beaten. Someday, I could become draft bait."

OCTOBER 23

A headline in the *World Telegram*
KENNEDY SHOWDOWN WITH SOVIETS

> *During his radio and television address, President Kennedy, in a somber tone but with a firm voice, assured the Soviets that the nation was prepared for any course of action.*

>> *The path we have chosen for the present is full of hazards, as all paths are—but it is the one most consistent with our character and courage as a nation and our commitments around the world. The cost of freedom is always high—and Americans have always paid it. And one path we shall never choose and that is the path of surrender or submission.*
>> *Our goal is not the victory of might, but the vindication of right—not peace at the expense of freedom, but both peace and freedom, here in this hemisphere and, we hope, around the world. God willing, that goal will be achieved.*

Mario and Catherine sat at a kitchen table that was covered with half-eaten dishes of *fusilli filetto di pomodoro*. Mario said, "The president chose the right course in deciding to blockade Cuba. You can't have intermediate-range ballistic missiles sitting on your doorstep."

"Mario, what do you think is going to happen?" she asked fearfully.

"I don't know. But watching the president's face last night and listening to the tone in his voice, I have no doubt in my mind that we'll fire on any Soviet ship trying to run the blockade. Liberty is at risk."

Catherine began crying. "That could mean nuclear war."

"Khrushchev is not an idiot. He knows damn well the Soviet Union would become a postage stamp."

"What about us?" she asked and rested her head on his shoulder.

The evening of October 24, Mario, closing the store, said, "*Papà*, if those ships had not stopped and turned course, the Navy would have sunk them."

"I agree. Do you remember when Khrushchev pounded his shoe on the table at the UN? Well, Kennedy just stuck it up his ass."

Thirteen days of high tension finally ended when an agreement was reached between the White House and Moscow.

1963

APRIL

At Caffé Roma, John said, "Joe and I are busting our asses, yet I still worry about Gateway Bank. Barrett drives me nuts with all his innuendos and threats to stop funding Mondello's development."

Joe chimed in. "We're lucky that Sam has kept the weasel in line. There's a lot of money at stake and most of it is Sam's."

Mario blurted, "I can tell both you guys that if sales don't pick up and if development costs continue to go out of sight, Barrett's going to smell blood in the water." He finished his *biscotti* and blurted, "Sam or no Sam, Barrett's still a shark."

"I'm afraid you're right," said Joe.

John stared straight ahead and said nothing more.

JUNE

"Tony, Pope John XXIII is dead. He was a saint," said Vincenza holding a string of rosary beads.

"Too bad; even I liked him. He was not afraid of the cardinals."

"This Sunday, Archbishop Stanley is going to say something at Our Lady of Loreto's Church."

"You can tell Mario and Catherine. Me, I'm not going."

"You never change."

"So, you're telling me I still look young?"

"You're making me crazy."

Tony smiled and walked away.

JULY

Angelo was helping Mario at the store. "Uncle Mario, Martin Luther King has called for a civil rights march and demonstration on August 28th in Washington, DC. It sounds wonderful; I'm going to go down and join the protest."

"What did your mother say?" Mario asked, knowing the answer.

"What else? She yelled, 'You're making me crazy.'"

"Carmela's turning into your *nonna*," said Mario laughing.

One month later, Joe and Mario sat at Caffe Reggio and listened intently to Angelo describe the momentous event that took place on the Washington Mall.

He could hardly contain himself as he repeated the inspiration-filled words "Free at last!" He reminded them, "Those were Dr. King's words from his 'I have a dream' speech. They inspired the hell out of me. That speech will live forever. Uncle Mario, he will take those words to his grave."

Mario's facial expression reflected his enthusiasm. "How can you not love that man? He's amazing."

"Too bad he's not Italian," said Joe, rolling his eyes.

Mario smiled, shook his head, and said, "Please don't go there again."

SEPTEMBER 9

A headline in the *New York Journal American*
VALACHI SINGS BEFORE MCCLELLAN COMMITTEE

> *Joseph Valachi, under federal protection, breaks the code of silence and fingers what he calls "La Cosa Nostra."*

Hennessy called Sam. "Did you see the morning paper?"

"So what? He will sleep with the fishes or hang from a pipe in his jail cell."

SEPTEMBER 15

In an early morning telephone call, Mario muttered dejectedly, "Tim, this time it's Birmingham, Alabama, that spilled blood.

"What?"

"A terrorist bomb killed four Negro girls at a Sunday church service. Things are getting more and more out of control."

That evening Catherine and Mario were watching the late night news when she reached for his hand and said, "I marvel at how Dr. King confronts violence using nonviolent mass demonstrations and civil disobedience to obtain peace."

He let out a heavy sigh. "Tell it to the cops. They're not averse to using dogs and fire hoses, smashing people to the ground, and beating the hell out of them. Look at those kids: they're terrified."

NOVEMBER 23

A headline in the *World Telegram*
JFK ASSASSINATED

> *While visiting Dallas, Texas, President Kennedy was assassinated by a sniper as he rode in a motorcade. Lee Harvey Oswald, the suspected shooter, was arrested soon after.*

Angelo was having breakfast with Mario and Catherine. Mario threw the newspaper down on the table and through clenched teeth said, "Could you believe it? The sneaky son of a bitch fired from a building and shot him in the back of the head."

"This is bad, very bad; something doesn't smell right."

"Angelo, you are absolutely right."

Later in the day, Frank Nunzi arrived from Chicago for a business meeting and was spending the night with the Ferraras.

Sunday afternoon, all eyes were focused on the television set as the police were moving Oswald from the city jail to the county jail.

Frank cried out, "Did you see that?"

The family was horror-stricken as one bullet found the perfect spot and took out the accused.

"How the hell did that guy get in there?" asked Tony as he leaped out of his chair.

Mario looked at Angelo, smirked, and shook his head.

The following day Jack Ruby's name was plastered all over the papers.

DECEMBER

Walking Mario out of Castellano Enterprises, Sam casually asked, "What's your thoughts concerning Vietnam?"

"I think we're sinking deeper into quicksand. Do you realize we're using a chemical to destroy foliage and not giving a damn about anything in its path," said Mario, throwing his arms up in disgust.

"I'm concerned that the war is going to affect the stock market." Sam hesitated a moment, shrugged, and said, "But, you never know. It could be for the better."

"I know you care. I don't," Mario said.

"If you like eating, you better care!"

"When will I get you to understand there's more to life than money?" he asked, looking confounded.

"Maybe never." Sam paused and curtly added, "Speaking of money, I hope your brother and Joe pull out all the stops to make sure Mondello doesn't have a hiccup. The development is being a bit worrisome to me."

Mario nodded his head in acknowledgment.

Chapter 22

1964

March

Sam called for a limousine and picked up James Hennessy at 11:30 a.m. for the short drive to Castellano's Ristorante. As usual, Nick reserved the power table located in the back corner of the main dining room.

Their conversation covered a myriad of things before Sam summarized Mondello's three-year plight and concluded in a confident tone, "James, that's my understanding of the situation as it currently exists. Bottom line—Joe and John are in trouble, courtesy of your client Gateway Bank refusing to continue funding!" Methodically slicing his veal cutlet, he continued, "Barrett is still Barrett. The bastard has also screwed me over in a number of transactions; and in each instance, he benefited none other than himself."

"I understand," said James, breaking apart a loaf of Italian bread.

Sam said, "If Mario wasn't up to his eyeballs at the store, he would be all over Barrett's ass. Right now he's assuming John and Joe can handle the dicey situation. And you and I know Barrett's the same as when we were kids. That weasel, as Joe Borelli calls him, is still a weasel.

Except, now he's a weasel in control of an unbelievable situation—one that we can take advantage of."

"How close did you check things out?" asked Hennessy.

"Close enough. Thames, as lead bank, could be bought out with minimal funds. But, Barrett would have to close his eyes. As his lawyer, that's where you come in."

"Any room for outsiders? This might be a good investment for my family," said James stroking his thick black hair.

"Leave it to me. If you want your family in, consider it done. I'm bellying up to the bar with more of my own money."

"What more can I ask?" asked James, pausing for a moment, and then added with his mouth full of spaghetti, "Sam, you're a lucky son of a bitch."

"What are you talking about?"

Hennessy answered, "Last week I had dinner with Archbishop Stanley. The archdiocese is in desperate need of a retreat center and housing for retired clergy. Long Island could be an ideal location."

"That's no small order," Sam said with a smirk on his face. "And it's extremely ambitious."

"Stanley's got scarlet fever. He wants that red hat so bad he can taste it, and Tim Gallagher is becoming his express train to the world of scarlet."

"That's because Tim's a master at providing anything the archbishop needs, especially funds. He's a rainmaker priest."

Sam stood with his handkerchief in hand, cleaning his glasses. "I don't know how you have the stomach to deal with Stanley and his holier-than-thou attitude."

"He's power, my friend, and where I'm heading, I need power. Always remember, the Vatican, with all its glory, is power," said James. He took a sip of his Chardonnay.

"I can't disagree with you. A run for political office with his endorsement gives you a leg up."

James continued, "Anyway, I volunteered the resources of my office to conduct a feasibility study on Long Island."

"Where on Long Island?"

"With my blessings, anywhere."

"What will it take to point the compass in my direction?" Sam asked.

"Well, after listening to your plan, I have a greater incentive to become a navigator. That incentive is money." Hennessy was edgily glancing at his watch. He went on, "First, I need Stanley to understand that I did him a colossal favor. In turn, I pick up a major coupon for a downstream perk."

Sam neatly folded his napkin and sat back in his chair. "And if I heard you correctly, the door is open for my family to get a piece of the action."

"Anything for the cause," said Sam, raising his glass of Merlot in a toasting gesture.

Nick Castellano came over to chitchat. "You two look like you struck gold."

"Not yet," said Hennessy, rising to hug him.

Sam, placing his arm around his uncle, said, "Thanks for taking care of us: everything was great. We have to run; I'll call later."

The men said very little to each other on the way back to Hennessy's office. They both were deep in thought regarding the conversation they just had.

Leaving the limousine, Hennessy turned, leaned back in, and in a low voice, said, "The only concern I have is whether or not Barrett can keep a commitment. He's a master when it comes to twisting the truth. Actually, the guy's a pathological liar." He paused, tightened his tie and continued, "We both know that Leonard Knight is the money power behind Gateway Bank and he calls the shots. I would feel much better if he told us Barrett will go blind if we're able to take out Thames at a bargain basement price and replace them with a financial entity controlled by Castellano Enterprises."

"I handle Knight's securities: do you want me to call?" Sam asked.

"I'll do it," James responded. "He owes me big time. Just last week, I saved his ass on an ugly situation that could have gone public and created major havoc for him."

James Hennessy was a master strategist when it came to networking the power structure for future favors. Money ranked high in the list of favors and became a lifeline in running for political office, where discretionary funds bought influence whenever and wherever needed.

Before calling Knight, he decided to check out Barrett's interpretation of the situation and paid him a visit.

At the end of a long-winded conversation, Barrett, scratching his head, said in loathing tone, "We may have a bigger problem to deal with."

"What problem?" asked Hennessy, taking off his suit jacket.

"Mario Ferrara. He may not be hands-on right now because of his freakin' book but he's a nutcracker."

"I know all about it. Sam clued me in; don't worry."

"I *am* worried! What if—"

"I said to not worry. What about Leonard and the restructure?"

"I'll handle him," said Barrett, his face flushed.

"Uncle Nick, it's me, Sam. I didn't know Hennessy had any family still alive."

"He doesn't. Why?"

"Forget about it."

"Mario, it's me, Sam. How's John holding up?"

"For a first class worrier, just great. Still, it's not looking good."

"Any thoughts?" Sam asked.

Mario replied, "I haven't been able to figure a way out."

Sam sounded hopeful. "I think I have a plan to solve this mess."

"I hope it doesn't involve Barrett or Hennessy," said Mario with more than a hint of sarcasm in his voice.

"Let me handle that."

"Whatever you can do to help out will be greatly appreciated," Mario replied.

"Forget about it."

Five minutes later Sam called John.

The next day at Caffé Roma, Mario sat facing Tim Gallagher and Joe, whose big arms lay across the table, barely leaving room for the three cups of coffee they were nursing. "Mario, you should be happy; King got the Nobel Peace Prize."

"I'm doubly happy: the Verrazano-Narrows Bridge opened."

"Nothing ever will beat the Brooklyn Bridge," said Joe, tapping his heart.

Mario took a soggy bite of the *biscotti* he had soaked in his coffee. "That's not the point. You can now get to Staten Island from Brooklyn," he said.

"So what?

"Forget about it."

Tim Gallagher shook his head and smiled.

After James talked to Barrett and Knight and thought about the matter, he concluded that everything could work out for him and the archbishop.

"Sam, James here. As I was thinking through the process, it came to mind that we're missing the trump card we need to convince Stanley."

"I'm listening," said Sam.

"A donation of the land to the archdiocese. If that happens I can deliver the archbishop."

"Consider it done." He paused and sharply added, "Only if he promises to open up the doors to Vatican Bank for financial help."

Castellano's financial network, which he tapped many times to facilitate a plethora of transactions, was spread throughout Europe. A missing financial link was Vatican Bank. However, with the archdiocese's involvement in Mondello that void might possibly be filled. But he would need Barrett to broker the deal.

In addition, the power of information, especially when obtained from the right people in the right places, was an effective tool to control any situation. Sam was not averse to using the underworld to track the vulnerability and credibility of certain people. The adage of "one hand washes the other" prevailed in spades. It was the power elite's benchmark, at least until one side needed more than the other.

Later in the day, Hennessy invited himself to dinner at the archbishop's residence. After the two men had a glass of wine in the sitting room, the conversation shifted to Stanley as he espoused his own accomplishments. James interrupted. He rose off the couch and, in his aristocratic way, said, "Your Excellency, wait until you hear about the good, the bad, and the ugly. The cast is as follows: the good is Sam Castellano; the bad, Mario Ferrara; and the ugly, Richard Barrett."

"Go on," Stanley said, sneering.

"Over dinner," Hennessy said arrogantly as he strutted toward the dining room.

The following afternoon Tim Gallagher, at the suggestion of Archbishop Stanley, contacted John and Joe and requested that Mondello donate a 15-acre tract of land to the archdiocese. It took very little to convince them that the development would give Mondello a much-needed transfusion for positive press.

Before the announcement became public, John implored Mario to stay calm. "I know you think I'm crazy, but having Archbishop Stanley involved can't hurt. Besides, it benefits the elderly and makes Tim look good."

"That doesn't change my opinion of *His Holy Ruthlessness*," said Mario, flipping his hand up in disgust.

Joe Borelli laughed, put his arm around Mario, and said, "Wouldn't it be ironic if the Vatican saves our ass?"

Chapter 23

1965

"Uncle Mario, Malcolm X was shot dead in Harlem: they think it was three Black Muslims from the Nation of Islam that whacked him."

"Uncle Mario, I just heard LBJ sent ground troops to Vietnam. Things are not looking good."

Mario was walking with Catherine back to Little Italy from Battery Park when he irately asked, "What the hell is wrong with Alabama? All they know is state troopers, attack dogs, nightsticks, and tear gas."

"That didn't deter thousands from joining Dr. King and Reverend Abernathy on a four-day civil rights walk from Selma to Montgomery."

Not really listening to her, he uttered, "It has to be something in the water. The South is going nuts."

"This may be just the beginning," she said, experiencing a sense of dread she just couldn't shake.

"I hope not."

AUGUST

A headline in the *Daily Mirror*
RACE RIOTS EXPLODE IN WATTS

> *An arrest for drunken driving and alleged police brutality lit the fuse to rioting, looting, and arson that became commonplace in the Watts section of Los Angeles.*

A week later, on a walk through Central Park, Mario stopped abruptly, spun around, and said, "Catherine, when compared to racial unrest, business stress is nothing. We need to put things in perspective."

"Are you talking about Watts?"

"Absolutely. It's a leapfrog of hate from the Southern part of the United States to Los Angeles. The blood-bath ended with thirty-four people dead and thousands arrested."

"This is what I have been worried about," she said, squeezing his hand.

"Bigotry has hit the fan," he said somberly.

SEPTEMBER 28

A headline in the *Daily Mirror*
MONDELLO'S ILL-FATED PROJECT FACES THE WRATH OF GOD

> *Archbishop Stanley of New York, who announced plans nine months ago for a mammoth retirement home and retreat center at Mondello on Long Island, is very concerned that his project may now be in deep trouble.*
>
> *If the dark pall of financial rumors circulating in West Islip proves to be true, Mondello is on the verge of being shut down.*

For John Ferrara and Joe Borelli, a dream of a lifetime had turned into an absolute nightmare. Construction delays and cost overruns ripped their financial forecast to pieces. A substantial infusion of equity money was needed to keep the project from going into foreclosure.

Following a lengthy talk with his brother, Mario recommended a strategy session with key participants to resolve the chaotic state of affairs.

John was sitting in Mondello's construction trailer. He was sipping coffee from the lid of his thermos. "Mario's right; if they'll leave their titles and egos behind, we can unite and solve the problems."

Joe shook the dirt off a set of blueprints. He raised his eyebrows and said, "You're a dreamer! But, just in case, I'll call your mother: she'll pray the rosary for you."

"I think *Mamma* should call the old lady in black above Gramolini's butcher store and do *malocchiu*!" said Mario laughing.

"Don't laugh; that's a good idea," said Joe. His mouth was full of doughnut, and he was unconsciously grasping his *corno* necklace, rubbing the smooth red coral between his fingers.

They followed Mario to the parking lot. John squinted and, in a tone of disgust, said, "The real problem is Barrett and Hennessy. We can't get rid of those two bastards no matter how hard we try."

"Suck it up! We need their help in turning this situation around," said Joe as he massaged his neck to release tension. "I'll arrange a dinner conference."

Mario shook his head in revulsion. "I know it's my suggestion to get together, but I have a hard time sitting in the same room with those two."

"Too bad Pop's in a financial crunch and can't go to the usual sources to solve our money problems." The veins in Joe's neck were bulging as he continued in an exasperating voice, "But no matter what, we need to raise the shortfall of money in order to tell Barrett and Hennessy to screw off. That's the only way we won't have to deal with the two scumbags."

"Don't count on it," said John with his head down.

OCTOBER 4

A week prior to the dinner conference, Sam called a meeting at his office with Joe, Mario, and John to create an agenda and establish guidelines and objectives.

Standing to leave, Mario said, "It's important we keep everyone focused, including *His Excellency, the Braggart* Stanley. Once dinner is over, I don't care what they do."

"You have a long memory," said Sam, peering above his glasses. "I don't disagree, but remember, patience rules."

"*Patience?* Patience, my ass!" Mario bellowed. "Dealing with Stanley, Barrett, and Hennessy—that's not patience; that's a chore! No, . . . I think that's a miracle." He was silent for a moment and then smiled. "Hell, Catherine is always saying I am on earth to learn patience."

Sam, laughing, walked the three men to the door.

"I can't tell you how happy I am that *Papà's* not involved," said John, looking to the heavens. "He would go nuts."

Outside 40 Wall Street, Mario, with his arms around the two men, said in an upbeat tone, "Angelo's having everything down pat at the store gives me more time to be involved."

Joe asked, "What about Frank Nunzi as an investor?"

Before Mario could answer, John jumped in and said abruptly, "That would not be a good idea. You know Frank—"

Mario interrupted, "Let's go,"

OCTOBER 11

The cynical guests entered The Oak Barrel's rustic-style dining room and jockeyed for position around the table. Besides the Ferraras, Joe Borelli, Sam Castellano, and Sam's selected investors, the other key participants were Archbishop Stanley and Robert J. (R.J.) Johnson, an entrepreneur whose professional career spanned thirty years. Johnson was president and founder of JCB Pharmaceutical Company, located in

Charlotte, North Carolina. At the moment he was knee-deep working with accountants and lawyers attempting to keep his initial public offering alive. JCB's IPO and its relocation to Mondello were slip sliding away due to Mondello's inability to complete construction. It was catch twenty-two. Both sides needed each other desperately.

Also, among the invitees were Hennessy, Barrett, and Dr. Susan Chou, PhD, a state senator representing the district in which Mondello was located.

The atmosphere was dismal. As soon as everyone was seated, John wasted no time dropping a pile of files down on the table and cutting to the chase. "The accusations facing Mondello are many, including improper procedures for rezoning the land we donated to the archdiocese. This is in spite of the fact that all opposition was met head-on with public hearings."

"I'm very concerned over this mess," said Archbishop Stanley, his face muscles twitching.

"With all due respect, archbishop, if you would please wait until we discuss all subject-matter before commenting."

Stanley, frowning, grunted.

It was Joe's turn. He began circling the table, telling guests what they feared most. "Let's begin with the ugly truth. The problem is money." He hesitated and slowly began to zero in on Barrett. "Our problems have been compounded by a lack of money and an almost impossible timeline dictated by Gateway to meet sales projections." He paused, leaning his muscular body against the table. "We are desperately in need of financial help to resolve this problem."

Hennessy passed Barrett a note.

Castellano, who was seated at the head of the table, stood as all eyes turned toward him. His manner was calm, firm, and direct. "Due to sizable cost overruns and failure to meet sales projections, Mondello is unable to complete construction for JCB's new pharmaceutical plant and distribution center." Pushing a stack of files toward Barrett, he explained, "Thames and Gateway, though contractually committed to provide financing, stopped funding."

Barrett, never looking up, kept doodling.

Slamming his fist down on the table, rattling plates, James Hennessy cut everyone off. "The situation is not good. Each of you has a lot to lose one way or another." After quickly looking over loan documents, he raised his voice, and continued, "Mondello received an ultimatum: provide one million dollars in additional equity to make up the deficit or the bank will commence foreclosure. If the company performs in a timely fashion, Thames and Gateway will proceed with its previous commitment."

John glared at Barrett. "If Mondello comes to a grinding halt, many people will be affected, including contractors, tenants, and future home-owners. We—"

"*I'm* already affected. I'm devastated by this shameful circumstance," said Stanley, tapping his fingers on the table.

John ignored him, rolled up his sleeves, and continued, "We need to be objective and focus our efforts on solving this impending crisis. If we don't, it will magnify and multiply itself like a rabbit on drugs." Then, forcing a smile, he added, "I think in that case, the archbishop will be affected."

"I told you; I am already affected," Stanley said, grumbling.

John continued, "In a nutshell, because of negative press, sales have dropped sharply. Families purchasing new homes and companies preparing to locate in Mondello are caught in limbo."

The archbishop rubbed his cheeks and said, "Mr. Hennessy, I'm upset over the negative press."

"Pay no mind to the press," James snapped and closed his briefcase.

"How can I ignore it? The article not only addressed improper zoning procedures; it also implied that a representative from the archdiocese is pressuring the town manager of West Islip to approve a bond issue. That allegation has kept me awake nights. It just stinks."

Mario, who learned from Frank Nunzi to listen with his eyes, cried out, "Please!" His patience had run out. He continued in an abrasive tone, "What stinks is your whining, Barrett's deafening silence, and Hennessy's gum flapping. The whole situation smells like a disaster."

Looking pleadingly at Mario, Sam motioned for him to sit down.

Richard Barrett's right leg shook spasmodically under the table as he finally spoke. "The archbishop is right. It's the negative press; and under the circumstances we had no choice but to pull the plug." Avoiding eye contact with Mario he stumbled on, "I tried, but, I had no choice: there was no alternative. Thames looks to me to keep their money secure. And I did try. But, I couldn't do anything out of the ordinary, especially with the Fed closely watching over the banking industry. But I did try."

"Your *but this* and *but that* is driving me crazy," Mario snapped.

With a surprised look, Joe interjected, "Why is Gateway spooked about the feds?"

A red-faced Barrett sat down, shuffled paper, and discreetly flipped Mario off with a motion that only Hennessy could see.

R. J. Johnson couldn't restrain himself any longer; almost leaving his chair, he said furiously, "I hope everyone has finished their bullshit rhetoric. Our company is in the closing stages of an initial public offering. JCB's offering is contingent on construction of a 300,000 square foot structure right here in Mondello. If that stalls, I don't know whether my underwriter and principal investor will sit still." Gritting his teeth while staring at Barrett he threatened, "If they're going to swallow a delay pill, someone better come up with solutions fast—and I mean fast! And please, no more *buts.*"

Everyone smiled except Stanley and Barrett, who slammed his briefcase shut.

Susan Chou calmly said, "I still believe in the project. I'll contact the State's Economic Development Division and inquire about financial assistance."

"As previously agreed, we'll meet back here on the 19th. Let's eat," said Joe Borelli, impatiently pointing to an overflowing buffet.

They spent hours eating, drinking, wrangling, and covering the same ground a couple of times over. Sam, removing his glasses and pressing his eyelids with his fingers and thumb, said finally, "We know the task at hand. If I can be of any assistance before next week's meeting, please call. I'll contact my investment partners first thing in the morning."

Everyone was mentally beaten up. They knew the fuse was burning. Mondello had twenty-three days before the bank note would be called and foreclosure commenced. As the participants were leaving, John stood at the door and reinforced the crucial timeline.

Johnson arranged to meet Joe the following morning at the construction site.

Taking Mario aside, Joe whispered, "I got to go. I have a hot date."

"You never change. You're the only guy I know who could fall in love with Venus di Milo."

With a straight face he asked, "Where does she live?"

"Forget about it," Mario said, laughing.

Joe bolted out of the restaurant like a rocket.

John and Sam were standing in a deserted parking lot. John said, "Did you see Barrett's reaction to your comments? The guy didn't have the guts to look at you or anyone else. And as for Hennessy, he's a chameleon."

Sam pulled off his suit jacket and loosened his tie. "You're letting Mario's emotions take control of you."

"Maybe."

Sam closed the door to his new 1966 silver Jaguar and drove off.

Barrett called the chief financial officer at *Banco Ambrosiano* in Milan, Italy. "Hello, Mr. Russo, my name is Richard Barrett, president of Gateway Bank. Father Tim Gallagher said he spoke with you concerning the possibility of a mutual financing arrangement with the participation of Vatican Bank."

Chapter 24

October 12

Early the next morning, walking through the job site, Johnson raised his voice to be heard over the construction noise. "Joe, I need help." He put out his cigarette and with a pained expression continued, "Due to the delay, it's going to cost JCB a substantial amount of time and money to modify the SEC prospectus and extend our bank loan, which is past due."

Joe slipped a wide rubber band over a set of prints clutched in his hand and said, "I don't know what to say, other than go over the same turf we covered last night."

Although the sun was still rising, Johnson dusted the cover off a Hershey bar, removed its cover, and started to munch. "Do you think Gateway or Castellano would be interested in providing interim financing? I need to keep my company afloat."

"Your guess is as good as mine. However, if I were you, I certainly would call Sam."

Johnson kicked the dirt in frustration and walked away with his head down.

Joe called Sam and clued him in on Johnson's dilemma, then joined Mario for lunch at Lombardi's in Little Italy.

Joe threw his menu down and said in a concerned voice, "Mondello is just a splinter in my ass compared to Pop's stress. He's getting worn out. An immigration inquiry has him not sleeping nights. It's affecting his business. I'm worried for him and *Mamma*."

"I'll meet with Tim and see what he can do to help your family out. The church has its ways," offered Mario.

JCB was now on Castellano's radar screen, particularly after Sam read JCB's prospectus. However, he knew the first priority was Mondello. Without a successful development, a financial play on JCB was worthless. And Sam had long determined that the primary ingredient to any financing alternative was Barrett's cooperation in providing funding. That afternoon Johnson met with Barrett at Gateway Bank.

"Sorry, he's not answering."

"Tell Mr. Barrett, it's Sam Castellano and if he wants to retain my accounts, meeting or no meeting, to pick up the phone and pick it up now," he said irritably to the bank's receptionist.

Excusing himself from the meeting with Johnson, Barrett swiftly walked through Gateway's sterile bank lobby to his office. "What's the matter with you?" he said, his voice quivering. Then true to form, he lied through his teeth to Sam, saying he was meeting with two of his directors.

Sam said curtly, "Buy them a cup of coffee."

"But—"

He interrupted him. "I don't give a damn about your directors. Mondello has consumed my thoughts. After carefully considering my options, I thought it best to buy out my investors. If they agree to my terms, I'll need a substantial increase in my line of credit."

"That's probably a prudent thing to do," Barrett said softly trying to appease him.

"*Prudent*, my ass! Eliminate the bullshit! What about the line of credit?" he shouted into the speakerphone.

In a defensive tone, Barrett said, "Don't lose any sleep over it."

"I take that as a *yes*," Sam said clenching his jaw. "If the answer is *no*, be prepared to close my accounts." He hung up the phone without giving Barrett a chance to respond.

Sam began to prepare for an upcoming meeting with Leonard Knight regarding the bank holding company's investments in stocks and bonds.

Barrett was slumped down in his chair with his face between his hands when the intercom blared. "Mr. Johnson is getting impatient."

"I'll be right there."

After he carefully processed the terms of a commitment letter from JCB's investment banker in regard to their initial public offering, Richard Barrett's greed button was pushed.

"What's up?" asked Sam, answering his private line.

Barrett excitedly proceeded to summarize his review of JCB and concluded, "A takeover should be rather easy."

Sam took him off speaker. "I'll tell you this much, if what you say is true, it's—"

"That's what I'm trying to tell you—multiple opportunities. The dollar-volume generated would be off the charts."

"What about my line of credit?"

"Whatever we work out, it will not affect your line," said Barrett in a conciliatory tone.

"What about contingency plans if JCB's public offering is successful?" Glancing over a dossier on Johnson, he demanded, "I'll need all the pertinent data. Right down to a gnat's ass."

Barrett started to fume. "Hold it—"

"*You hold it*! Remember how you screwed me over in the last deal?"

Getting up the nerve, in a shaky tone, Barrett responded: "Don't break my back. I did you a favor. You heard what happened to the last investor: he went tapioca. Count the money you didn't lose. Besides, this venture will more than compensate you for any brain damage."

"Dealing with you is brain damage enough."

"Pick a time and place, and I'll be there with a backup business plan."

"Let's do it over lunch. I'll meet you at my uncle's restaurant on Tuesday."

"That's great. See you then." Barrett flipped off the phone as he gently laid the receiver in its cradle.

At the construction site, Joe was studying a set of blueprints when Mario called. "I am positive that, given the opportunity, Hennessy and Barrett would stick it to us. Further, I haven't been able to pull anything out of Sam. He's playing his cards close to the vest."

"What's new?"

OCTOBER 13

Barrett phoned James Hennessy at his Fifth Avenue office. From the forty-fourth floor, Hennessy had a fabulous view of Central Park. He stood looking out his window as he spoke.

"Yes?"

"It's about time. I have been on hold for eight minutes," Barrett grumbled while rolling a Cuban cigar between his fingers.

"I was knee-deep in an important negotiating session," said James cheerfully. His desk and floor were covered with files.

"More important than taking my friggin' call?"

"I'll let you know after I have dinner with Anita." James viewed himself as a conqueror of women.

"Anita?"

"She's that insurance broker I introduced you to last week."

"I don't blame you for keeping me on hold. She's a great looking broad," Barrett said chuckling.

"What's up?"

"I'm pissed! *That's* what's up. Where does Sam Castellano get off putting me on the spot like that?"

"Like what?"

"What he said the other night."

James loosened his tie and said, "Believe me, he has a reason for everything he does."

Barrett grimaced. "I don't like it."

"Don't worry," James insisted. "Gateway's in great shape. Ferrara's back is up against the wall, and Borelli is scrambling to nowhere just like a *nigger* in the South." He paused, snickered, and blurted, "You could end up with the entire project."

"That wouldn't be too bad now, would it?" asked Barrett, lifting his feet up on his desk and lighting the cigar.

"If that happens, I want in," James said.

"You *are* in."

James hung up.

Barrett's telephone rang moments later. "Mr. Barrett, it's Mr. Solari from Vatican Bank."

"R.J., this is Sam Castellano: Joe Borelli suggested I call you. Maybe I can help you out."

Mario blurted, "Catherine, I haven't had a nightmare for a long time. But the one I had last night, it was a bitch."

"What was it about?"

"War. I'm concerned about Angelo."

"It will be OK."

"I love you."

"Love you too."

Worried about being late, Joe swerved in and out of New York City traffic, running red lights and stop signs, yet miraculously arriving at Castellano Enterprises without a moving violation.

"The problem is that everything takes more time than what you figure. We can't come up with a quick fix," said Joe, fingering his *corno* necklace. "Mario is a great help. But when he's wrapped up in his book, it's hard to get him to focus on anything else."

Sam glared at him and said nothing.

Joe, trying to appear calm, rested his arms on the conference table and calmly said, "Actually I was hoping you might consider taking down a larger piece of the deal."

Sam wiped his glasses. Shrugging his shoulders, he said, "Right now, I'm leveraged to the hilt."

Five minutes into a mostly one-way conversation, Joe, gazing out the conference room window and sounding exasperated, said, "You're right, we need to go outside the circle and find a new money source to bail us out." Mesmerized by the orderly confusion below, he mumbled, "Let's skip lunch. I'll take another stab at Gateway for a loan extension."

"Why waste your energy? Barrett's not going to budge," Sam said resolutely, putting his glasses back on.

"Maybe he'll take an interest payment as good faith."

"Dream on."

"See you Tuesday." Joe suddenly walked out.

Mario informed Tim Gallagher about Mike Borelli's financial and legal troubles. Tim called the archbishop in an effort to get him to assist with the mangled mess at Immigration. As soon as Stanley got off the phone with Tim, he contacted James Hennessy.

Though the hour was late, James, armed with sensitive information about the Borellis, promptly phoned Joe at home.

At the end of a short, verbal sparring session, James said, "Don't be stupid and pass up this opportunity. Come on board, get the Ferraras to bail out of Mondello and in turn you help a lot of people, including yourself."

There was silence on the other end of the line.

Pressing, he continued in a calmer voice. "Your relationship with Mario is a direct route to salvation. I know you can do it. If anything, think about your old man: he needs money like he needs blood and he's still being investigated by Immigration." He paused for a moment, lowered his voice, and said, "Joe, you have heard of deportation, haven't you?"

Irritated by the relentless pounding, Joe angrily spat back, "My father's having a hard time, but to take advantage of Mario or John . . . no way."

Staying calm, Hennessy persisted, "Don't lose the opportunity to stay in the deal. Of course you would be in a diluted position, but at least you stay in the deal. Then when the takeover of Mondello is complete, I push some money Mario's way to jump-start his writing project. In addition to helping him follow his dream, we'll give him a small piece of the ups. As far as John is concerned, he'll survive," James said.

"I have to go," Joe snapped as sweat started to form on his forehead.

"I'm telling you again . . . listen. It's good for you, your father, and me. Do this one thing. Get Mario to convince John to sell me his partnership interest in Mondello for peanuts. Call me next week," James said. Then he hung up and rolled over in bed to grope his lady friend.

Joe pushed the receiver button, and then called another number. "It's me. I just got off a phone call with Hennessy. We have to talk."

Mario and Catherine had dinner with John, Theresa, and their children in Corona. Afterward, the men took a walk to Spaghetti Park. "John, years ago Papà told me that Gateway and Barrett might be dirty and with Hennessy at his side we're doubly screwed. But beyond us, a lot of people could get hurt."

"I don't know about that: with Sam on our side of the table, the problem will be solved," said John. A moment later with a contorted expression, he slapped the side of his head and mumbled, "Don't you think?"

Unbeknown to Mario and John, Sam was in Rome meeting with Solari at Vatican Bank.

After hours of discussion Sam said, "Mr. Solari, then we have an agreement. You negotiate only with me concerning Mondello. Mr. Barrett and Gateway Bank are totally out of the picture."

"Mr. Castellano, we appreciate your representations to us concerning future opportunities. We at Vatican Bank always keep our commitments. And I might add, they are always confidential."

OCTOBER 14

The Long Island newspapers kept up their doom and gloom attack.

A headline in the *Island Press*
SOMEONE BESIDES MONDELLO IS STUCK IN THE QUAGMIRE ...
COULD IT BE ARCHBISHOP STANLEY?

The news article ended with a quote:

"I pray Mondello will survive the plunge into its deep financial abyss,"
said a befuddled archbishop.

Archbishop Stanley, becoming fearful that negative news might reach the Vatican, didn't take Hennessy's advice and sit tight. Instead, he contacted the reporter responsible for the article.

With a sour expression plastered over his face he said, "If you continue to persist writing sheer gossip, I will have no alternative but to contact our lawyers and commence legal action against you and your rotten newspaper. I demand you immediately retract your malicious allegations."

The archbishop, pleased with his blistering admonishment, summoned his aid and left for a luncheon meeting at the Waldorf Astoria.

The next day the reporter published Stanley's comments in the newspaper.

Upon reading the article, James threw the newspaper down in disgust and telephoned the archbishop to confront him.

Stanley vehemently denied threatening the press.

Standing in the lobby's central Palm Court at the magnificent Plaza Hotel on Fifth Avenue and Central Park South, James concluded a luncheon meeting with his most powerful client, Maggie Bloom.

Hennessy, tongue in cheek, chose Palm Court with its mirrored walls and Italian carvings as a perfect spot to negotiate a deal full of mirrors. Leaving scruples behind, James was running a number of tracks to someway secure himself a solid position in Mondello. It didn't matter whether it was through Sam, Borelli, Barrett, or Maggie Bloom. All James was concerned about was James.

Not wanting to waste any time after the meeting to put things in motion, he phoned Barrett from the bustling hotel lobby.

In a firm and confident manner, James declared, "The money will be deposited in our law firm's escrow account and become available conditioned upon Thames substantially discounting the Mondello loan and selling the note to Bloom's investment company. This is a perfect opportunity for Gateway to divest itself and save face."

"What happened to all your other ideas? Remember you and me and all that crap?" Barrett said reaching for a lit cigar. "There's no way I'm going to call Knight and tell him what you said. I like my job too much."

"If you don't, I will," James said, keeping his voice and temper in control.

"I think you're losing your mind," Barrett said angrily. He crushed his cigar against the side of the coffee cup he held in his trembling hand.

"I'm calling Knight," said James in a menacing tone as he slammed the receiver down. He went to his office.

Dr. Susan Chou met with the State's economic development director to request financial assistance in the form of a bond offering. The director, unable to assure Susan the agency could respond to anything meaningful before Mondello's next meeting, inquired, "Do you think there's some other way out of their quandary?"

Susan grimaced. "Without the State of New York's help, not in their wildest dreams."

Sam, back from an exhausting trip to Rome, read the *Island Press* article that quoted Stanley and went ballistic. "That's exactly what we don't need: the world knowing the development's financial problems. Do you think Tim Gallagher could keep him quiet?" he asked in a late night phone call to Hennessy. Sam didn't want anything to interfere with his tactics in negotiating with Vatican Bank.

"Only when they bury him, will he be quiet. Albeit, I'll contact Tim and see what he can do," said James who was at home entertaining a young woman.

"How's Tim doing?" asked Sam.

"He's busy with his Together Foundation. Too bad he became a priest: he would be deadly in the private sector."

"I'll send him a check."

"Tim will be appreciative," said Hennessy pouring more wine for Anita.

OCTOBER 15

On reading the relentless attacks in the newspapers, Barrett decided to visit Castellano Enterprises. After pacing the lobby, flipping through magazines, and flirting with the receptionist, he was finally summoned to Sam's office.

Barrett, fiddling with his portfolio, removed the unlit cigar from his mouth and said nervously: "The press is killing me and you're getting caught in the bad-news draft. Consequently, I couldn't generate any immediate interest from my banking affiliates pertaining to your line of credit. However, they have taken it under consideration."

Sam, with a scornful expression, growled, "That sounds like a lot of bullshit double-talk. We had a verbal understanding that I would be covered. You have once again reneged on your commitment."

"Things change," Barrett mumbled, shuffling sheets of paper on his lap.

"Tell Knight to call me. Today!" Sam said crustily. Getting angrier by the second, he began to rise from his chair.

Barrett's face turned pale. He accidentally knocked a huge packet of his files to the floor. He said pleadingly, "I prefer not to get Knight involved. Besides, I think we still have the opportunity to take over JCB. Don't we?"

"Forget about JCB, and I *prefer* not to have your ass in my office until you call Knight and take care of this."

Sam stormed out of his office and left Barrett picking up the scattered papers at his feet. Afterward, Barrett rushed to the men's room and threw up.

As soon as Barrett had left, Sam returned to his office and called Solari at Vatican Bank. It was time to lay out a definite proposal to protect his flank.

The following morning Barrett called Sam at home and begged for a luncheon meeting on Monday concerning JCB.

Mario spent most of the weekend in Central Park writing down his thoughts on the circuitous ways and means of business. He and Tony went for a walk after Sunday's dinner. "So, what do you think is going to happen next week at the big meeting?"

"I really don't know. John and Joe are putting a lot of faith in Sam to bail them out."

"What's wrong with that?" asked Tony.

"You told me many times to trust my intuition. I would if I could."

"You're not making any sense."

"That's the trouble. I know I'm not."

Chapter 25

October 18

During a protracted lunch at Castellano's Ristorante consisting of fine Italian Chianti, homemade ravioli, and more Chianti, Sam listened carefully to Barrett's assessment of JCB.

Nick Castellano stopped by their table a couple of times hoping to pick up some of their conversation, but was mostly ignored by the two men.

Barrett, savoring the last of his wine, lit up a cigar and confidently said, "The takeover works with or without Mondello. In summary, we'll convince JCB's investment banker that we'll commit a substantial amount of money and pick up a major piece of the IPO although we have no intention to do so. However, that move will lull Johnson to sleep right up to the midnight bell when his time expires for the public offering to have secured all of its capital requirements."

Sam said, "Talk faster."

Barrett ignored the snide remark and continued, "That's when we pull the plug and renege on our financial commitment. Unless, of course, we get a major piece of the pie." Grinning, he leaned toward Sam. "In the meantime Gateway buys JCB's note from its lender in

Charlotte and prepares to foreclose to get JCB out. Castellano Enterprises then buys Gateway's note. Tell me if that's not a neat package."

"Words. Just words. Where do all the funds come from?" Sam demanded.

"Leonard will pledge ample funds from Gateway's holding company to Castellano Enterprises until your foreign investors are in place. Of course, he and I will personally commit to a sizeable piece of the deal."

"Then what?" he asked stone-faced.

"You and me go to London and we negotiate to purchase Thames' loan—of course, at a substantial discount. Afterward, we foreclose on the Ferraras and Borelli to get them out of Mondello. Gateway Bank loans funds to continue operations." He paused to flick ashes off his yellow tie, smiled, and added, "End result, we control Mondello and JCB. Everybody wins. A win-win without anybody getting screwed . . . except Johnson, the Ferraras, and Borelli."

"You're without conscience," Sam retorted, neatly folding his napkin.

"So?" Barrett said scornfully.

"What about Hennessy?"

"Legal fees. That's all he's worth," Barrett growled.

"I don't know. I'll get back to you." Sam scurried out and left him sitting there with a sixty-dollar restaurant tab. Barrett didn't flinch. He was certain he had come up with the perfect plan to secure himself and Gateway a place in Mondello and JCB.

Returning from lunch, Barrett, back in his office, contacted Leonard Knight. He explained, with pinpoint detail, how the takeover of JCB and Mondello could greatly further their mutual business endeavors.

From his early beginnings as a street loan shark and bookie, Barrett knew the financial game backward and forward, and he manipulated it to the hilt. In the early years he was not opposed to using strong-arm enforcers to collect on delinquent debts. As president of Gateway Bank and its holding company, he was the perfect pawn for Leonard Knight.

Slowly rubbing his hands together he said to Knight, "This is an incredible situation. We take Thames out of Mondello, then the Ferraras and the Borellis. He chuckled while looking around for a match. "In the process we complete the takeover of JCB's pharmaceutical company. Furthermore, it's a perfect front for our money laundering business." He relit his Cuban cigar. "It can be a springboard to supply limitless amounts of money for payoffs, especially in facilitating our drug trafficking business."

Leonard Knight, always careful not to arouse suspicion toward him or his many shady operations, conducted his business with absolute precision and discretion. Knight's thick eyebrows and beady eyes illustrated perfectly his character—his motto: always go after money and power without burdensome ethical reservations or conditions.

Barrett continued. "Lenny, the cherry in the deal is that everything is already in place. It may be a drill, but if we pull it off, we won't be able to count the money fast enough. I'm telling you, it's a perfect scenario."

Knight, stroking his pocked face, was silent the whole time Barrett rambled.

"First, we complete our due diligence on JCB: if it's what I think it is, we make our move. If Johnson resists, we break his head and stuff his tub of Jell-O body in a trunk," he said, snuffing out his cigar.

"Cut the hype. How do we posture ourselves?" Knight responded curtly.

"I have convinced Sam Castellano to bring his foreign money sources to the table. His status as a power player can't hurt." He nervously loosened his tie. "Sam thinks it's the best thing since sliced bread and we don't have to give him one clean, laundered nickel from our side of the deal."

"You make the decision. Don't screw up!" Knight said sternly, hanging up.

Knowing he had stretched the truth, Barrett wiped away beads of perspiration and quickly dialed Sam.

No answer.

Richard Barrett and Leonard Knight were long-time business associates even though Knight struck fear in Barrett's heart. Gateway's holding company owned and operated a lucrative money-laundering business fed by their illegal drug trade. They also controlled numerous automobile dealerships. Nevertheless, their cash cow was wholesale jewelry and diamonds. Still and all, they were constantly searching for a perfect front to conceal their operations.

Barrett had assembled a team of loyal employees who were compensated with above average salaries and excellent benefits.

The team of money facilitators knew the game well. They were well schooled in processing large amounts of money and filing false governmental reports. When it came to securities, Castellano Enterprises was Knight's broker in buying and selling stocks and bonds.

Concerned with the way his conversation ended with Knight, Barrett phoned him back. "The idea of using a real estate development company has limitless spin-offs such as business and merchandise loans." He paused for emphasis and then continued, "Obviously with the right caveats and exorbitant rates. You get the point?"

There was only silence on the other end of the line.

"And when you add JCB's pharmaceutical operation that includes a mammoth retail and wholesale distribution center you have an unbelievable situation."

Again, there was a few seconds of silence.

Barrett began again. "This could be the ultimate mechanism, for the ultimate wash of money. And our drug cartel will flow freely down the highways—courtesy of JCB."

Knight was standing, looking out the window of his penthouse suite in an elegant Manhattan high-rise on Seventy-second and Fifth Avenue. He spoke curtly, "Mention drug cartel one more time and I'll . . . Never mind, go ahead, tell me your plan. But, keep it short. Your running off at the mouth is driving me nuts." He was running late for a dinner engagement in upstate New York, and his limousine driver had already buzzed him twice.

Barrett, while searching for a cigar, said, "Up to this point, hiding the paper trail has been a perennial problem; so we have to move funds through surreptitious routes. When we control Mondello it can serve as a base of operations to launder money."

"I told you to keep it short," roared Knight. He reached for his tuxedo jacket.

"I know . . . but, this is important. There's only so much Gateway Bank can do to move money. The Feds are always breathing down our necks, sometimes with one audit following another."

"That's why you're getting paid the big bucks."

Ignoring the sarcasm, Barrett continued, "Mondello can provide us a home where *problematic* money can rest until it's integrated with *good* money, thereby creating the ideal money mix."

"Alright, already; tell me more. Tell me quick!" said Knight in his haughty style.

Barrett always stretched his thinking to max out the use of money—whether it was good or bad.

Sitting back in his plush chair, he lit up another cigar. "Further, JCB can provide enormous opportunities for placing funds anywhere in the world. Mondello and JCB enable us to purchase lucrative companies at will. At some point, we will be able to discontinue our drug trafficking business and become totally legit."

"You're an absolute idiot!" Knight yelled.

With a pained expression on his face, he tried to respond, but the phone went dead.

Leonard, although in a foul mood, didn't say no; so Barrett assumed he had a green light to proceed. He was well aware that if his proposals were successful, he could satisfy his wildest dreams. If it went south. Well, he chose not to think about that.

After five failed attempts, Barrett finally reached Sam at home. "What's your answer?" he asked, wiping his sweaty palms on his royal-blue suit pants.

"I'm in . . . on the condition that my participation is silent, yet I pull the strings."

"No problem."

"What about the increase in my line of credit?"

"Uh . . . I'm still working on it. By the way, with the Vietnam War heating up, Knight thought you might have an inside track on how we can maximize our holding company's money in the stock market."

After they concluded the phone call, Barrett instantly dialed Leonard Knight. There was no answer, so he left a message with the maid.

"Tell him it's done."

Sam placed a call to Vatican Bank.

Chapter 26

October 19 . . . the morning of the conference

James sat in the conference room of his Fifth Avenue office. He was in a decisive strategy session with Barrett concerning acquisition of an automobile dealership in Elmhurst, Queens, when Sam showed up unannounced. Breaking off the conversation with Barrett, Hennessy greeted Castellano in the reception area and hurriedly left the building with him.

Minutes later, Barrett left fuming at being left sitting.

They sat at a small corner table at Parkview Deli. James put the menu aside and said, "I hope you don't mind meeting here; I'm always concerned that the walls have ears. So what's up?"

"It's almost time to pull the trigger."

James never disclosed to Castellano his meeting with Maggie Bloom. Taking advantage of the current situation, he said enthusiastically, "I'm ready. I spoke to Leonard: he wasn't exactly euphoric, but he's in and his word is good. Barrett's feigned sincerity makes me sick. He knows nothing."

Sam nodded affirmatively and said, "I called some of my overseas associates to see what funds may be available."

"So?"

"Thus far, nothing." Sam chose not to tell Hennessy about his ongoing negotiations with Vatican Bank.

"Using Mike Borelli as bait, I tried to recruit Joe." Hennessy, slowly sipping his coffee, continued, "No word yet."

In an apprehensive tone Sam said, "Take my advice and be careful with Joe. There's a lot riding on this: coupons for your political future, mad money for me, and a monetary lift for your family."

"I'm in all the way," James said. He put his herringbone sport coat on and headed for the door.

"Great!"

Sam, back at his office, immediately called Lenny.

"Lenny, it's me, Sam. If we have to go to plan A, Hennessy's in."

"What about the archdiocese?"

"James will keep Stanley in check."

"Good. After it's all done Hennessy's out," Lenny insisted.

"Whatever," Sam agreed.

Barrett, without informing Castellano, purchased JCB's delinquent note from Charlotte First in North Carolina through an affiliate bank.

Sam soon found out about the transaction from a friendly lending source in Chicago but decided to keep silent. All the while he kept formulating a key maneuver to benefit Castellano Enterprises.

During the week everyone, except Johnson, agreed dinner wasn't necessary. Therefore, instead of the restaurant, the meeting took place at Castellano Enterprises' imposing conference room, a handsome meeting area adorned with hand carved oak panel walls and Italian Renaissance art.

John took a quick glance in Sam's direction and began the meeting with a flare of optimism. "Our updated financial reports are encouraging. If Gateway agrees to an extension, I'm confident we can solve Mondello's financial problems internally."

Joe echoed his statement.

Dr. Susan Chou, prim and proper, spoke next. "The State is unable to do anything on a timely basis. Yet, they remain open for future discussions and have expressed a desire to be cooperative in Mondello's aggressive endeavor."

Castellano, visibly upset by the airy comment, stood and curtly excused her from the meeting.

Barrett kept shifting in his seat. Without looking up he reached into his briefcase.

Joe passed a note to Mario: *"He weasels in his chair after he shits his pants. That's what a weasel does."*

Mario passed the note to John. He nodded, straight-faced, in acknowledgment. His body shook slightly as he struggled to stifle a laugh. No one noticed.

Johnson scowled. "The crap has hit the fan. Inter-Continental Bank commenced foreclosure. In addition, numerous lawsuits have been filed against JCB. I'm at wit's end."

"I thought your lender was Charlotte First," said John.

"Out of fear they sold our bank note to Inter-Continental out of Chicago: they are merciless."

"Maybe I can help," said Barrett with his head down.

"Only if you go to hell," snapped Johnson.

Hennessy and Stanley sat quiet during the heated discussion that followed.

Sam previously had identified a number of alternatives and considered them all: in the end he chose what was best for Sam. Moments later, with Vatican Bank in his back pocket, he made his move.

Looking directly at Barrett, raising his voice he said, "Now is the appropriate time for me to tell Barrett to stick the loan up his ass."

All eyes turned to Castellano.

Then choosing his words carefully he said, "In the best interest of my investors, I have made arrangements to personally provide capital to satisfy Mondello's financial obligations. However, the company will have to be reorganized."

Mystified by Sam's cavalier attitude, John sarcastically asked, "What does that mean?"

"I don't know just yet," Sam said as he stood abruptly, closed his file folder, and walked out of the conference room.

THE FOLLOWING DAY

Sam tendered a take-it-or-lose-it-all offer. Investors, including the Ferraras and Borelli, left with a stinging choice, took it.

OCTOBER 27

Without the need for Gateway's line of credit, courtesy of Vatican Bank, Castellano Enterprises purchased all shares in Mondello at twelve cents on the dollar—all shares, including John's and Joe's.

Barrett was shocked.

Hennessy knew he had been had.

Knight called Barrett.

Barrett called Hennessy.

Barrett, Knight, and Hennessy all called Sam who didn't return any of their calls.

Under pressure by his board of directors, Johnson resigned as president of JCB.

Working the system of manipulation in textbook style, Sam not only preserved, but also increased his ownership in Mondello.

OCTOBER 29

Back in Castellano's conference room, Mario, exasperated, stood in silence with his fedora firmly on his head while Joe and John paced.

Sam entered, holding a steaming cup of espresso and said offhandedly, "In order to preserve Mondello, I had no choice but to verify to the new money that I was cleaning house. That includes staff, contractors, real estate companies, and, unfortunately, your future participation."

They showed no emotion during his solemn epitaph.

Afterward, even though he tried to stay unruffled, Mario couldn't resist the obvious question, "Where's the money coming from?"

Ignoring the question, Sam set his espresso on the copper conference table and coolly said, "That's it."

The three men left in shock.

John saw years of hard work and money disintegrate before his eyes.

Mario's mind was ripped apart with conflicting emotions.

Joe Borelli, dodging a stream of people racing for the elevator, called his father from the lobby, "I'm out!" he said heatedly.

"No problem, you'll be back."

"Why don't I begin on Halloween night and go trick or treating."

"It's a start."

"Thanks, Pop." Joe knew his father had no patience for wallowing in misery.

At the grocery store Tony met with the boys. After hearing what took place in Castellano's conference room, with his hand resting on Mario's shoulder he said, "Sometimes, you need to watch the shadows."

"Mr. Castellano, our board is most pleased with our financial arrangement."

"Mr. Solari, I cannot imagine anything else."

Solari sat back in his red handcrafted leather chair and softly said. "I agree owning fifty percent of Mondello is quite nice. And may I add two other points? First, the loan we made to Mondello must be paid back to Vatican Bank as agreed. If not, our ownership percentage goes up.

Second, if you are able to acquire JCB pharmaceutical, your promise to involve us on the same terms and conditions as Mondello must prevail."

"Mr. Solari, we have a deal," Sam said smugly.

"That's good." Solari was content. With Mondello's financing behind him, he had honored his confidentiality commitment to Sam and could get back with Barrett and conclude his proposed partnership in Gateway's holding company. Vatican Bank was prepared to move substantial dollars into the United States using Gateway as a stepping-stone.

Sam was able to use the funds from the Vatican Bank to purchase the Thames loan to Mondello at a substantial discount.

Chapter 27

November 3

A headline in the *Island Press*
MONDELLO SURVIVES
NO THANKS TO THE FERRARAS AND BORELLIS

> *Men from Little Italy tried to move into legitimate business without guns, but, they were no match for Corporate America. Mr. James Hennessy, attorney for Gateway Bank said, "They reaped what they sowed. Nothing. Gateway and Thames are satisfied to have their debt repaid."*

Tony, reacting to Mario slamming the newspaper down on the counter, said, "If your name was Smith you would not be in the papers. Remember, the world does not know what happened. You do. Don't let your pride get in the way of your common sense. Leave it be; it will go away." Tony, crumpling the newspaper in his rough hands, finished; "And remember what Frank Nunzi told you. Don't trust the press. They exploit."

NOVEMBER 9

Mario and Catherine were sitting in their darkened home. Mario sighed and said, "I'm glad Carmela got home before the blackout. Yet, sometimes I think we're always in the dark."

"Yes. But sometimes the solitude of darkness is helpful," said Catherine.

"You're missing the point."

"No, *you're* missing the point."

NOVEMBER 27

"Uncle Mario, there were thousands of anti-war protesters marching from the White House to the Washington Monument for a rally."

"If you ask me what the hell the march accomplished, I can tell you *nothing*. LBJ is deaf, dumb, and blind."

"Watch what you say," snapped Tony.

Anti-war demonstrations started to build in size and frequency in all major cities throughout the United States. Bob Dylan and Joan Baez, among others, brought their protest songs to the street; and Mario and Catherine never forgot the night they attended Peter, Paul, and Mary's performance at the Bitter End Coffee House at 147 Bleeker Street, Greenwich Village.

In the wake of Castellano's Mondello buyout, John sunk deep into depression and moped for a couple of days, regurgitating the chain of events that wiped him out. One evening after a frustrating dinner with Theresa, he received a call from Mario. "Sam sold us down the river."

"What do you mean?" John asked.

"The more I think about what happened, the more disturbed I get. I'm pissed and depressed," he said in a loud whisper.

"Calm down. Mario, you know that since the beginning it's been an undercapitalized rollercoaster ride. Above and beyond that, Joe and I are not exactly new to being screwed over. But in this case, I don't think Sam had any other choice since he was already heavily invested in Mondello."

"I don't know about that. For sure, he was either oblivious to the turmoil his reorganization caused or he just didn't care. Forget us. What about the others who got caught in the domino effect?"

"Like who?" John asked.

"There's gotta be a list a mile long."

"You sound like you're about to explode. I'll meet you half way. Let's talk about this thing over a bottle a wine at Two-Ton Tony's."

"I'm in!" Mario grabbed his fedora, kissed Catherine on the forehead, and hurried out.

When John arrived, Mario was already seated at Two-Ton Tony's, a hidden-away Italian restaurant near Grand Central Station.

"Mario . . . big hug."

As they embraced, Mario cracked a smile. In the beginning, the conversation revolved around the family. During the second bottle of Chianti and a plate of *gnocchi* and *bruschetta,* Mario switched the subject to Mondello and the ongoing saga of what's next in their upside-down world. "I agonize for all the innocent people who got run over."

"Mario, tell me what the hell you're talking about," John pleaded.

"The game. The game being played by assholes! How to win big by crushing others in the process." Leaning forward, his voice straining, he explained, "I'm talking about the aftermath, the tidal wave of chaos, seen and unseen, that hits people."

"I think I've been too focused on my own problems to give it much thought," John said, finishing off the last piece of *bruschetta.*

"Then let me help you change your focus. Let's begin with the office staff, those who lost their jobs when Sam's company took over and replaced everybody. They all have fixed expenses. Some were single, some married, some with and some without kids. There is a domino effect on their immediate and extended family, friends, neighbors, associates, and merchants . . . you know what I mean," Mario said, not sipping, but chugging his wine.

"You've really been thinking about this, haven't you?"

"You bet your sweet ass I have. The same scenario is true with contractors, real estate companies, landscapers, homebuyers, commercial tenants . . . the list is endless. I'm not only talking money, I'm talking stress, sickness, despair, frustration, and of course, dissension."

"OK! You got your point across. You're making me suicidal. There's nothing we can do about it now; so why give yourself an ulcer?" John uttered, throwing down his fork.

"Think about it. Every time we've got screwed, it was by a network of greed and convenient loss of memory. People get sloppy; friends disappear, and loyalty goes clear the hell out the window and—"

"Quick, bring me a razor blade so I can slash my wrists!"

Mario, ignoring his brother's feigned anguish, raised his voice, and said, "It's survival of the powerful, no matter who gets stomped. Look at Barrett and Hennessy: two leeches motivated by greed set up the dominos, then pushed them over."

It was late and the restaurant began clearing out. John waved off the manager, who started to approach their table.

"Mario, sometimes things are beyond our control."

"I don't know about that. Maybe yes . . . maybe no."

John paused. "I got it. I know you hate rules." Chuckling, he continued, "But this one you'll love."

"Fire away."

"Let's call it . . . the no asshole rule! Absolutely no more assholes in our deals."

"I'll drink to that." Mario tipped his glass and sucked out the last drop of Chianti.

The wine and bitch session was over.

The conversation did wonders to get both brothers out of their respective funks. At least it seemed that way.

Chapter 28

1966

"I'm worried sick," said Barrett, chewing a cigar.

Sam sat back in his oversized black leather chair and tersely said. "Let me make it easy for you. It's simple: you sell Castellano Enterprises JCB's bank note that you bought behind my back. You provide the operating capital, and poof . . . we become partners in a drug company."

Without making eye contact, Barrett was able to squeak out a demand in a high-pitched voice, "Only if you cut me and Knight into Mondello." He wanted Mondello so badly that he was willing to compromise himself and sell JCB's note to Sam.

Sam shook his head and nodded affirmatively. "Tell James to prepare the legal documents."

Sam called Vatican Bank. "Mr. Solari, it's done. We now own a pharmaceutical company."

"Mr. Castellano, we at Vatican Bank are most grateful."

"I'm sure you will honor your pledge of secrecy as it relates to our financial arrangement."

"Absolutely," Solari said smiling. He was preparing to inform his board of directors that he had positioned Vatican Bank to have a piece of the deal on both sides of the table. Barrett and Castellano would never know what took place based on their mutual pledge of silence with Solari.

In the business section of the *Financial Herald:*

> *Castellano Enterprises announced the acquisition of JCB Pharmaceutical of North Carolina. The company will be relocated to Mondello in West Islip, Long Island. R. J. Johnson, former president of JCB, has entered politics in his home state and will run for a congressional seat in the Fourth District. Mr. Johnson stated: "It's time we rid this state and country of white-collar crime. I pledge every ounce of my energy to that endeavor."*

James Hennessy left the law firm of Cook and Baker and accepted an offer to join the New York District Attorney's Office as a prosecutor. His transition to the DA's office was purely politically motivated, as it created a strategic base for his future aspirations.

Hennessy's first call in his new capacity was to Castellano Enterprises. "Just thinking about the short end of the stick you stuck up my ass in the JCB and Mondello deals makes me furious. Listen good. I'm making myself perfectly clear: Don't *ever* cross me again!"

"That's business," Sam said callously. He slammed down the phone and went back to reviewing his memo to the new board of directors of JCB.

Barrett called James. "Whenever you're ready to make your move for public office . . . I'm your man. Money will flow like Niagara Falls. We need each other."

"And don't you forget it," James replied.

MARCH

"Hello, Catherine, it's your father. Tell Mario the Irish Republican Army blew up Lord Nelson's column in Dublin."

"Thank you anyway, but he doesn't need any ideas."

LATER IN THE WEEK

"I told you fear is the thing that keeps people from doing anything that goes against the grain," said Mario.

"What are you talking about?" Catherine asked.

"James Meredith's march through Mississippi is being called the 'March Against Fear.'"

APRIL 1

A headline in the *New York Journal American*
VIETNAM PROTEST DOWN FIFTH AVENUE

> *More than 20,000 people took part in the not so peaceful march down Fifth Avenue, as eggs and obscenities were tossed from the sidewalks. On Eighty-sixth Street several fights broke out among the demonstrators and counter-demonstrators. The police made a number of arrests.*

"This is not Italy before Garibaldi. Right here in America, this war is dividing our country."

"I agree, Uncle Mario; yet when I think of World War II and you and my father . . . I can tell you that if I ever get drafted, I'm going."

"This is not World War II: this is an unjust war. The country is divided."

"You tell me who's right and who's wrong," Angelo said earnestly.

MAY

Hennessy telephoned Castellano. "James, here. Just heard that Joseph Bonanno walked into the courthouse at Foley Square and gave himself up. I wonder what hole he was hiding in for two years."

JULY

A headline in the *Daily Mirror*
NEGROES AND COPS AT WAR

> *New York, Cleveland, and Chicago turn into battlegrounds. Bayonets are poised in defense against rocks and eggs.*

Mario said, "Martin Luther King's call for nonviolence must have fallen on deaf ears."

"I'll tell you this, if I ever figure out who fingered my father to be investigated by Immigration, I won't need rocks or bayonets—just my hands."

"Joe, the world is going down the crapper."

Since the beginning of the year, Mario had tried a schedule consisting of one part hibernation, one part work, and one part writing—a schedule which had tallied to total frustration.

By the day, he had become more distraught. Baking bread and working in the store was robotic, and he didn't communicate much on the home front.

One evening after a quiet dinner, Catherine, in desperation, finally lashed out. "I'm not a mind reader. You're upset and depressed at something. Get it out or get over it."

Mario slumped down in his favorite chair and did not respond. Instead, he internalized her statement and held on to his thoughts.

Catherine, trying to regain her composure, was not ready to give up. "It's about time you stop feeling sorry for yourself, for Angelo, your father, mother, brother, sister, and everybody else. You have become a victim's victim." She kept washing dishes. "We don't talk anymore, and all your interest is somewhere between your ears. If we're going to make it through whatever you're going through, you have to change."

Mario sat, stared into space, and said nothing.

Catherine turned to him, looked him straight in the eyes, and glumly said, "Maybe you need to seek some professional help."

"You got it!" Mario said. Absorbed in his anger, he flung open the door, and walked out.

She buried her head in her hands.

Their marriage was strained and two hearts began to shatter.

He took a slow walk to Our Lady of Loreto's rectory and woke up Tim Gallagher. The two of them were sitting at the kitchen table, beers in hand. After a lengthy conversation, Tim said, "We have known each other too long to bullshit each other. I'm not going to hold your hand. You need outside guidance or you'll lose it all. I have the perfect—"

"So, now you're a shrink besides being a priest," said Mario heatedly, starting to rise off his chair.

"Sit down. I'm not kidding," Tim said firmly placing his hands on Mario's shoulder.

"You're like my mother and brother . . . a worrier."

Tim quickly retorted, "Give me a break: Carmela also called. She's worried about your mood swings. Even Angelo is concerned. Everyone can't be wrong. Please get some help. You're caught up in every cause for justice instead of being concerned with your family and your health."

Drastically changing the subject, Mario said flatly, "I want to know what really happened between Sam, that low-life Hennessy, and Barrett when we got the shaft at Mondello."

Losing his patience, Tim replied, "Where the hell did that come from? That's over: let it rest."

"Nice talking to you. See you around, *Padre!*" Mario stomped out of the room and slammed the door.

Joe Borelli, taking a leisurely stroll with his father through Bensonhurst Park, said: "Mario isn't the same. He's lost his sense of humor. All he does is bitch."

"I haven't seen much of him lately," said Mike.

In a frustrated tone, Joe continued. "Mario's all screwed up. He's caught in a whirlpool. Besides being disgusted with business, civil rights, and Vietnam, he goes off the deep end and thinks there was a conspiracy among Sam, Hennessy, and Barrett regarding Mondello. No one is going to convince him otherwise." He hesitated, placed his arm around his father's shoulders, and dismally said, "To make it worse, I'm afraid Catherine is ready to walk out. I don't know what to do."

Mike, leaning on a rail looking across the bay at the Verrazano-Narrows Bridge and Staten Island, said, "Give him the keys to the Port Washington bungalow. He always loved the place. Maybe that's the thing he needs, alone time."

Mario took advantage of Borelli's offer to get away and do nothing for a couple of weeks. One morning while walking along the beach, he stopped, sat, and watched a glorious sunrise. As he watched the rays of light bounce off the water, his mind churned and his pent-up emotions finally broke loose.

Mario sobbed.

A couple of hours later back at the bungalow, he enthusiastically telephoned Joe and left a message: "I'm heading back. Tell Mike I owe him big time."

Mario, arriving home, ran up the steps, fumbled with his keys, unlocked and pushed open the door. He yelled, "OK. So I'm a hardhead-ed Sicilian. What did you expect?"

Catherine, not looking up, kept reading. He jokingly tiptoed over to her, knelt down, and kissed her cheek. A huge smile spread across her face.

Early the next evening, without notice, John and Carmela appeared at Mario's front door with a pepperoni pizza from Lombardi's and a bottle of Chianti. They came ready to talk.

John, taking hold of Mario's arms, fired out, "Time's a healer and your time is up. It's time to refocus your energy."

"We love you!" Carmela chimed in, trying to temper a looming battle. "Many times *Papà* said, 'In our house, it's always the family that settles things and makes peace.'"

Catherine grinned, looked over to Mario, and said, "That's *your* blood."

Mario, sitting at the kitchen table, smirked.

They continued to verbally work on him into the early morning hours. Prepared to raise the flag of surrender, he said in a conciliatory voice, "I'm hungry; let's go for breakfast."

"Why not. Then we can go to lunch, rest awhile, and then go to dinner," John said, hugging his brother.

The four *paesani*, passing through a cluster of neighborhood shops, kidded each other on the way to Sunflower Deli.

"What do you think?" Carmela asked as she dug into a huge plate of pancakes.

"After brainwashing? I guess I need to swallow my pride, raise money, expand our bread delivery market, and incorporate John's idea of catering."

"So, what's kept you from doing it?" asked John with his mouth full of bagel.

Mario threw up his arms and said, "Don't break my chops. I just told you, pride."

"Tell you what; tomorrow I'll start the ball rolling and call Joe, Tim, and Sam," Carmela said in a peace-making tone, volunteering her time in the midst of a killer schedule.

Catherine asked, "What about *Papà*?"

"To think we would go outside the family for help—no! What he doesn't know, doesn't hurt," said John.

"You're all crazy. But it doesn't matter; I'll take you up on your offer to help," Mario said. He laughed, then, turning serious, he added, "But

I don't think you should call Sam. I'm still gun-shy after the Mondello episode."

Although Joe Borelli was stretched to his financial limit, he dug down deep and found some money for his best friend.

Tim Gallagher did his part by calling in some favors.

John ignored Mario and called Sam who was quick to write a check.

Vincenza supplied an unlimited amount of food to celebrate.

Tony knew something was up, but let it be.

Angelo and Catherine prepared for the onslaught of business.

Later in the week, Mario telephoned Sam and apologized for stonewalling him.

"Forget about it. I accept your apology. I can tell you, selling bread is good and catering is good; but it's also time for you to consider following your dream and starting to write. If you ever need me to stake you in that endeavor, call," said Sam looking through a file, while keeping Barrett on hold.

"Thanks."

Equipped with expansion dollars in hand, Ferrara's Best Baked Bread and Catering was ready to go.

Joe Borelli, genuinely overjoyed for his friend, teasingly said, "Anytime you need outside help, you know what I mean, call me."

They both laughed.

Chapter 29

1967

FEBRUARY

Mario said, "Have you heard that Jack Ruby died of cancer?"

"I didn't know you could inject cancer," Joe said sarcastically. "By the way, I finally convinced Pop to open an additional distribution facility in Chicago. Working together has been a challenge, but so far we haven't killed each other."

"To put up with you, your father's a saint."

MARCH

A headline in the *Daily Mirror*
EASTER SUNDAY "BE-IN" AT CENTRAL PARK

> *Central Park filled with thousands upon thousands of young people who came to celebrate. Nobody really knows for sure what they were celebrating, but they joined beat poet Alan Ginsberg in a statement for love.*

"Angelo, your mother told me you went to hear Ginsberg instead of being with the family on Easter Sunday."

"Uncle Mario, too bad you weren't there. I can't describe it."

APRIL

Mario and Catherine joined an anti-war protest led by the Reverend Dr. Martin Luther King. Beginning in Central Park, they, along with approximately 100,000 protesters, marched to the United Nations.

That evening, sitting on the fire escape, Mario in a contemplative mood said, "I knew it was just a matter of time before King combined his nonviolence-stand and civil rights advocacy with the anti-war movement."

"I'm so happy we took part."

"I agree." He closed his eyes for a moment and shook his head sadly. "But I don't know about burning draft cards: my heart wrenches for our troops in Vietnam. Each day could be their last; we can't turn our backs on those kids." His voice getting stronger, he said, "No matter how much the country is against the war, dissent has to play hell with their minds."

She snuggled up close to him and sympathetically said, "I know."

"The politicians have to stop doing what they are doing and get their heads out of their asses."

The next morning, Angelo and Mario had breakfast together.

"Uncle Mario, Muhammad Ali refused to go into the military. The champ stood by his convictions, and as a reward, the World Boxing Association stripped him of his title."

"No worry . . . just like the Borellis, he'll be back."

JUNE 12

A headline in the *World Telegram*
SIX-DAY WAR ENDS

> *Israeli forces prevailed over Egypt, Jordan, and Syria and gained control of the Gaza Strip, the Sinai Peninsula, the West Bank, and the Golan Heights.*

"What does that tell you, *Nannu*?" asked Angelo.

Tony, slicing provolone cheese, cried out, "Don't screw with the Jews."

Vincenza frowned, lifted her hands, palms facing forward, and waved them, turning them in a motion indicating both frustration and resignation.

Tony and Angelo smiled.

NOVEMBER

Catherine, sipping tea, said, "Mario, I read where Joan Baez was arrested for disturbing the peace at an anti-war protest in Oakland, California. People are really upset with Westmoreland's request for one hundred thousand troops for Vietnam."

"What did she do?"

"The group she was with blocked the doors to an induction center."

Mario shrugged in disbelief and said irately, "Please tell me that we're not turning into a police state?"

DECEMBER

Mario locking the front door to the store turned to John and said, "Angelo told me this morning that over five hundred people were arrested, including Allen Ginsberg and Dr. Benjamin Spock, for trying to shut down an induction center here in the city."

Mario paused and reached for Catherine's hand. "Why don't we take a walk to The Village and see what's going on at Caffe Reggio?"

Ginsberg, along with poet Jack Kerouac, was known to frequent Caffe Reggio in Greenwich Village.

John, taking Mario aside, whispered uneasily, "Be careful—if not for you, for Catherine. Caffe Reggio is a greenhouse for young anarchists. And you never know who's watching to see who shows up."

Mario responded: "The color of blood is red . . . not green, black, brown, yellow, white, anarchist, loyalist, poor, or rich." His voice filled with frustration as he rolled on. "You get the point, don't you? Those kids act from their heart and don't give a crap about what other people think of them. They don't strategize to protest; instead they band together . . . and do it."

"I tried," John said throwing his arms up in despair, "I have to go; Theresa is waiting for me."

Mario shot back, "Hey, John, just like Bob Dylan sings, 'The Times They Are A Changin.'"

Chapter 30

1968

JANUARY

The year began on the dark-side, as the Vietcong launched a surprisingly strong military effort in the Tet Offensive, taking key southern provinces and cities, including Saigon. Although American forces ultimately prevailed, the strength and determination of the North Vietnamese brought a stark realization to the American people that this war was not close to being over.

Whenever Mario considered the impact of the Civil Rights Movement and the Vietnam War on society and his personal quest to right Italian injustice . . . there was no peace. His mind was reaching overload.

He was writing, thinking, baking bread, and rewriting, and then again, thinking, writing, and baking bread. Although Mondello's demise was several years back and Ferrara's business was flourishing, he couldn't put aside the anguish his family had suffered.

MARCH

Sam Castellano, in Little Italy on business, joined Mario for a quick lunch at Umberto's Clam House.

After ordering, Sam smiled and said, "How's it going?"

"Everyday things keep changing. The country is spinning out of control. As a result, I have been rethinking the overall scope of my book." The day was hot for March and the walk to the restaurant had Mario perspiring and thirsty. He paused to take a drink of water. "By the way, are you aware of what took place at NYU?"

"I heard some news, but I really didn't focus on the situation."

"Remember when I told you about a chemical called Agent Orange? Well anyway, about five hundred students demonstrated against the Dow Chemical recruiters who were visiting campus."

"Dow Chemical?" Sam asked with a hint of surprise in his tone that Mario did not pick up on.

Mario's frustration was apparent as he ranted, "Dow and Monsanto are major suppliers of the poison that is being used extensively in Vietnam to destroy plant life so the VC can't hide." Shoving his salad plate away, he said vehemently, "You tell me if using that crap isn't chemical warfare. Give me a break, please."

Sam was uncomfortable with the direction of the conversation, and seeing the beads of perspiration on Mario's forehead, attempted to calm him and play down his concerns. "You really need to take it easy before you have a stroke. The government knows what they're doing."

Glaring at Sam, Mario said, "You're a comedian." He paused a moment; then asked snidely, "Speaking of clowns, whatever happened to Barrett and Hennessy? They seem to have disappeared down a rat hole."

"They're around. Nothing new."

ONE WEEK LATER

Enjoying a cup of coffee at Caffé Roma with Tim and Joe, Mario, in an uplifted tone, said, "Bobby Kennedy declared his candidacy for president."

Tim leaned back in his chair, smiled, and said, "That's good news. It's no secret that he's been upset with President Johnson and his handling of the war. Besides, his vision is to unite—and not divide—our country; it's to create a society where there is no difference between color and class. Best of all, Bobby will bring the Vietnam War to an end."

"How does he do that?" Not giving Tim a chance to reply, Joe rolled on, "You may be a priest, but you're not psychic. I guess you didn't read the morning papers: General Westmoreland is again asking for more troops."

"What else is new?" Mario mumbled and shook his head in disgust.

The following day, an anti-war rally at Washington Square Park turned violent with protestors being beaten by plainclothes police.

The same day, Angelo, while kneading dough, said matter-of-factly, "Uncle Mario, President Johnson is throwing in the towel and will not run again."

"That's the best news I've heard all week."

APRIL 5

A headline in the *World Telegram*
MARTIN LUTHER KING KILLED

> *While the Reverend Dr. Martin Luther King stood on the balcony of the Lorraine Motel in Memphis, Tennessee, a sniper's bullet ended his life. A huge manhunt has ensued. It's a sorrowful day of mourning for all who crave unity and peace.*

ONE DAY LATER IN THE FERRARA'S KITCHEN

"What a dichotomy. A godly, nonviolent man taken out by a bullet to his face," said Tim, his trembling hands holding open *The World Telegram*.

Mario thought for a moment and glumly replied, "King never faltered from his stance on nonviolence, and he gave his life in the cause for justice. Yet, with his death, instead of peaceful reflection, violence is running rampant across the United States." He hesitated a moment, drummed the table with his fingers, and blurted, "Hell, President Kennedy was killed by a white guy. This is bad stuff."

"I pray that this wave of insanity will recede."

"I don't know about that: Catherine told me there have been riots in 130 cities. Johnson reacted by calling out four thousand federal troops to stop the roving bands of idiots that were burning and looting."

"Uncle Mario, France is crippled and almost paralyzed by student protesters inciting people to strike. Paris is at a virtual standstill."

"Interesting . . . "

JUNE 6

A headline in the *New York Journal American*
BOBBY KENNEDY SHOT DEAD

> *After winning the Democratic primary in California, Bobby Kennedy was killed by an Arab immigrant, Sirhan Sirhan. He was the lone gunman. Once again the Nation is shocked into sorrow.*

Catherine's eyes were watery as she sadly said, "This can't be happening again. I don't . . ." Her voice started to break and she was unable to finish the sentence.

"Tell me now . . . that I shouldn't do something," he said irritably.

"Stay calm . . . please."

JUNE 13

Rushing into the store, Angelo, holding high a brown envelope, said breathlessly, "Uncle Mario, *Nannu*, it happened: I just received notice. I'm drafted!"

Tony and Mario stood still and appeared stoic. The fear and dread that the news struck in their hearts was indescribable.

Later, hearing the news, Carmela, Vincenza, and Catherine were panic stricken.

August 29

A headline in the *Daily Mirror*
BLOODY WEDNESDAY IN CHICAGO

> *The Democratic Convention is turning the city of Chicago into a mammoth open-air torture chamber as violence abounds . . . Police clashed with anti-war demonstrators as they marched to the Convention Center. Nightsticks, tear gas, and blood flew everywhere along Michigan Avenue. No one was immune from Mayor Daley's riot police, including innocent bystanders and especially members of the press.*

After reading the newspaper article, Mario threw down his manuscript in frustration. The phone rang. "It's me, Joe." His voice was full of panic. "We need to talk. I'm hearing some rumblings about my father."

December 1

"*Papà*, I just read a disturbing article about Sicily in *Buon Giorno*."

"What happened?" Tony asked in a surprised tone as he tugged on his apron.

Mario, shaking the snow off his fedora, anxiously said, "Peasants had blocked the main highway at Avola. The *carabinieri* were ordered to restore order. So, what do they do? They begin shooting at farm workers and families who were running into the fields to hide: two were killed and many wounded." He paused and shook his head in revulsion. "One more time the message is crystal clear: don't challenge or threaten power. I wonder if that's why every time I think of doing something, I freeze up?"

"Mario, go with your heart."

DECEMBER 2, 1968

Uncle Mario,

Not good news, my infantry unit is shipping out to Korea. I guess that puts us in striking distance of Vietnam. The damn war refuses to end. I'm trying to keep my emotions in check, but the mood here is somber. Everyday, I'll be thinking of you and the family.

Love you.

PS - Please ask Father Gallagher to pray for us.

Anticipating what would likely follow, Mario became too choked up to read the short note to Catherine.

After Angelo left for Korea, Mario became more intense in his writing as he reviewed the chaotic past, including the plight of Italians in America; and he read Dante again for the umpteenth time.

TWO WEEKS BEFORE CHRISTMAS

Sitting next to Catherine on the sofa in their living room, Mario began, "Besides being very concerned about Angelo, I figured out what's missing."

"I'm listening," Catherine said, cuddling.

Pointing to the window, he continued, "Everything we read, hear, and see is out there." Holding his hand over his heart, he said, "I must write so people feel the joy and anguish in here." He wrapped his arm around her, sighed, and said, "If I could do that, people would realize that not only what happens at home and at work, but also everything that takes place in society affects them. Maybe we can all come together, united in liberty and justice."

She held his face tenderly and kissed him.

Sam Castellano, James Hennessy, Richard Barrett, and Leonard Knight, individually and collectively, invested heavily in lucrative war-machine companies.

BOOK IV

Chapter 31

1969

By the time 1969 rolled around, the social system was challenged: the nation faced different value choices. Priorities shifted; lifestyles were changing. At the forefront of the nation's burdens were the Vietnam War and racial injustice: close behind was the environment. And as usual, the plight of the Native American Indian lagged far behind in the consciousness of the public.

Mario spent more time in Greenwich Village and was becoming less content with thoughts without action. It was time for change. It was time to challenge authority.

JANUARY

As the last loaf of bread came out of the oven, Joe elatedly asked, "Can you believe it? Joe Namath said he would kick their ass and guess what . . . the Jets beat Baltimore."

In a shaky voice Mario said, "That's one Super Bowl game Angelo would have enjoyed."

Joe hugged him and kissed him on the cheek. "Before you know it, he'll be home."

APRIL

The death toll in Vietnam surpasses Korea . . . 33,641.

MAY

Mario telephoned Tim and in a surprised tone said, "According to a news article I just read, we're apparently bombing Cambodia. What's that all about?"

"I heard the same thing. It appears that President Nixon is pissed and is determined to find out who leaked the news."

It was a long and exhausting day of baking, bread deliveries, and working in the store. Mario flopped down on his worn living-room chair. He turned on the television set and caught the tail end of an interview with second-term Congressman Robert J. Johnson by Elizabeth Downing, an investigative reporter. Based on his previous track record as a successful businessman, albeit he had had a hand in the untimely demise of JCB, Johnson had become a key advisor to the white-collar crime division of the Justice Department. This prestigious position catapulted him into national prominence.

The interview drifted into scandals associated with the import-export industry.

Mario opened a can of soda and watched the newscast with intense interest.

Elizabeth Downing, or Beth as she was called, leaning toward Johnson in her flaming red dress, began, "I heard the Justice Department is looking into illegal activities conducted by firms specifically importing products from Italy.

"Absolutely correct," he answered.

"Would you mind commenting further on the ongoing investigation?"

Johnson, shifting his overweight body in the flimsy director's chair, replied, "Ms. Downing, I really don't know much about the investigation. Actually, you may know more than I do."

Her curiosity piqued, she continued. "Let me ask you about—"

He interrupted her midstream and snapped, "I really don't wish to talk about it. Please don't ask me again."

"Well then, let me ask you about unscrupulous people in business and their deception of the innocent," Downing said, retreating from her line of questioning.

Johnson went on to tell her about his experiences in the world of white-collar crime. He spoke of men and women that the Justice Department had exposed and convicted. Wiping away perspiration from his bloated face, he bluntly said, "Then there are others, like the Borelli family from Brooklyn, who always seem to escape prosecution."

Never hearing the name Borelli before, Beth Downing was curious to know where Johnson was headed with this insult.

"Tell me more."

"I must be going."

"I wish we had more time to talk."

"We'll finish our conversation off camera."

"Thank you, Congressman, for the enlightening session."

The on-air sign clicked off and the studio exploded with activity.

They sat a moment before Beth broke the silence. "So?"

Johnson was munching on a large Hershey chocolate bar he held in one hand and was playing with an unlit cigarette he held in the other. He firmly declared, "The Borelli family is currently under a congressional investigation; therefore, I didn't want to discuss any details on camera. Nonetheless, I purposely dropped the name to unnerve the guilty."

"I would love to have a greater understanding of how the Justice Department investigates these masters of exploitation," Beth said eagerly, ever seeking the scoop of scoops.

Lighting up the cigarette, he said, "If you're interested in understanding more about white-collar crime, I'll give you a name to contact."

"Please."

"Contact a fellow by the name of Sam Castellano. He's a Wall Street investment banker who understands business and is under contract with the Justice Department as a special consultant."

"He sounds very intriguing."

"When it comes to power, any power from the streets to boardrooms—which includes the power of the Borelli family—Castellano's your man. He's an interesting study and dresses nattily. His trademark is his horn-rimmed glasses, which has earned him the nickname *Peep*," Johnson smugly said. He put out his cigarette and started hacking.

When the television interview concluded, Mario clicked off the TV and sat in silence for several minutes while he finished off a large bag of peanut M&M's. Then he dialed Mike Borelli.

With his mouth full of food, Mike mumbled, "Sorry, Mario, I don't know where Joe could be. Is there anything I can do for you?"

"No thanks, Mr. Borelli. I'll track him down . . . On second thought, if you hear from him, I'm home."

The next morning, as Mario was writing in Washington Square Park, he did a double take as he spotted Beth Downing concluding street interviews with NYU students. She was covering unrest at campuses around the country. Her focus was on anti-war protests at Harvard and Columbia, the actions of Students for a Democratic Society at NYU, and a recent Queens College rampage.

Walking toward the Arch, his mind was racing about Johnson's innuendoes concerning the Borellis and what, if anything, to say to her. He decided to take advantage of the quirky opportunity and engage her in conversation.

Speaking rapidly he said, "Hi, my name is Mario Ferrara. I don't want you to think I'm rude or forward, but I'd like to talk to you about the Borellis."

"About what?" She asked, giving him a suspicious look.

He looked her straight in the eyes and coolly said, "I'm writing a book about Italian injustice and other abuses concerning liberties. I heard your interview with Congressman Johnson and would appreciate the opportunity to discuss it with you.

Her eyes widened. "I'm a risk taker. Let's sit and talk about it over a cup of coffee."

Mario bought a couple of containers of coffee and invited her to a park bench near the Garibaldi statue. Not wanting her to think his motives were anything they weren't, he cut to the chase.

"I know Joe Borelli and have no problem putting you in touch with him on condition you give me the straight scoop."

"I'm game," she replied, brushing back her hair, fighting the breeze that continued to blow chestnut brown curls in her eyes, "I'm preparing a documentary centered on organized crime and how it benefits from the spin of legitimate business," Beth said, looking as stunning in an NYU sweatshirt as she did on television.

In a concerned voice, he said, "To me it sounded as though Johnson was using you for exposure. I think he's on an Italian witch-hunt."

She smiled. "He is a little weird. Apparently the congressman has had some involvement with Borelli in the past. He firmly believes that the family has associated with known mobsters."

"The first part is true: Borelli and Johnson were involved in a real estate development project on Long Island before he became a congressman. The second part is a figment of the congressman's imagination."

"Let me buy the coffee the next time," said Beth, smiling. They decided to meet the following day at Caffe Reggio in Greenwich Village.

Seeking shelter from the midmorning sun, Beth and Mario sat inside at a corner table with Mario facing the street.

Over a steaming cup of latte, Beth said straight forwardly, "I'll trade you. You get me an interview with Borelli, and I'll give you my dossier on Johnson."

"Sounds fair."

"By the way, what's the name of your book?"

"Don't know."

"Interesting title."

"Funny."

Mario took a leisurely walk back to Ferrara's Grocery and Bakery, soaking up rays of sun along the way. After six futile attempts, he finally made contact with Joe at a small airfield in Fort Lauderdale, Florida.

"I don't know what Johnson is thinking, but he's flapping his gums about your family. The bastard is stirring up trouble for anyone whose name ends in a vowel." Mario wiped his forehead, and continued, "Joe, you need to nip his criminal allegations in the bud. Mondello and the past keep coming back like a friggin' nightmare. Beth Downing is a way for you to quell this crap."

"I appreciate the heads up," said Joe, pacing.

"There's nothing to appreciate. Let's stop this rumor maker cold in his fat-ass tracks. Catch a flight out."

"I wonder if that slimeball Barrett is also spreading rumors again. Since Mondello, he has stuck a stick in my spokes at every turn. If he is, I'll bust his head," Joe roared, checking his calendar.

"You don't know if he is. But if it's him, we can turn the table."

"Let's hang the weasel and Johnson by their left nut."

"I'll supply the rope."

"Barbed wire would be better."

"Let me know your arrival time and I'll pick you up at La Guardia. Meanwhile, I'll set up a meeting with Downing for next week."

"Go ahead and arrange it," he paused and then said, "Mario, whatever you do, don't tell my pop."

"What, are you crazy?"

"I know. I'm just antsy. It would kill him. I'll be there Saturday, but don't worry about picking me up; I'll grab a cab."

"Are you sure?" asked Mario, struggling to hear over the sound of blaring horns.

"I have a couple of things going with some heavy hitters in Corona. I'll see them on the way into the city."

"Whatever works." Mario hung up the phone, walked out onto the fire escape, and looked down on a double-parked car blocking traffic on Elizabeth Street. The horns were still blaring and drivers were screaming.

Joe ripped the phone off the wall and threw it across the room.

Mario hastily called Beth. "Joe will be back next week and has carved out time to talk with you."

She bluntly said, "I hope he doesn't have thin skin."

"You'll have to make that judgment. Don't forget to ask him about Richard Barrett."

"Who's Richard Barrett?"

"Ask Joe."

Although preoccupied with business, Joe Borelli had become increasingly anxious to meet Beth Downing and pull the plug on the malicious rumor circulating about the Borellis. He cancelled his meetings in Corona and took a taxi directly to Taormina's Ristorante in Little Italy.

After an awkward introduction, Mario said, "If you two need privacy, I'll bolt."

"Let's have dinner first; then you can disappear," said Beth, not giving Joe a chance to speak.

"You see, Joe, that's what I like about her: it's her tact," Mario said, laughing off her directness.

Beth's appearance was, to Joe, stunning. Her oval-shaped face had fine features and was framed by blunt-cut, thick, wavy chestnut brown hair that fell just below her ears. She looked directly at him, her long dark eyelashes accentuating her eyes, beautiful and intensely green. He came to the meeting in a confrontive state of mind but that look totally disarmed him. Yet he knew he needed to stay focused on the impending discussion.

An hour later, Beth, taking her last bite of *fettuccine Alfredo*, looked at Mario and whispered, "It's time."

"What about dessert?"

"It's time!"

"Don't worry, Joe; she doesn't bite."

Mario left a somewhat nervous Joe Borelli.

Beth was coy enough not to mention the interview with Congressman Johnson, being certain Mario gave him all the pertinent details.

"Mario told me a lot about you, your family, and friendship. However, I'd love to hear it from you and, of course, your assessment of organized crime."

Joe, raising his voice slightly, said, "You're pretty gutsy implying I would have any assessment of *organized* crime or *any* crime for that matter."

Beth, getting out of her chair, said, "Your friend is concerned for your well-being, and I guess he thought that I might be of assistance. He guessed wrong, so forget it."

"Calm down," said Joe in a loud whisper. His dark eyes glared at her.

She stiffened, tilted her head, and pointing a finger in his face, fired back, "No. You calm down!" He had never experienced such fury directed at him from such a beautiful source. It was, to say the least, disconcerting.

He took a deep breath and said, "Look, when it comes to family, I have a very short fuse. I'll stay calm, if you will watch your tongue."

"Now I'm on notice," she said calmly and sat back down.

Joe pushed away his half-eaten plate of shrimp scampi and threw his napkin down. "I can tell you that my father is not involved with any mob of any kind, anywhere. And that's true for members of his family in Sicily, as well."

He went on to make it perfectly clear that Mike was an honest, hardworking person. Then, he said angrily, "Frankly, I'd like to get in touch with Johnson and set his ass straight. Yet, I don't want to give credence to the fat bastard's witch-hunt or possibly breach your confidentiality."

Beth said, "I understand. Please, before I forget, tell me about Richard Barrett." She was cutting her huge slice of strawberry cheesecake into tiny pieces.

Taking advantage of the opportunity, he gave her a detailed synopsis on Barrett and his method of operation.

"Thanks for your candor. I'll make sure the information gets into the right hands." Putting down her pencil, she said, "Tell your father, as far as I'm concerned, the Borellis are a dead issue."

In an exasperated but gentle tone, he said, "Beth, my father knows nothing of this; and he never will!"

"Just for the record, I never said your father was involved in organized crime."

Joe stared and said nothing in return.

They continued to talk a little longer; then they left the restaurant together. Beth gave him a flirtatious glance as she climbed into the cab.

The normal fifteen-minute drive to his home in Brooklyn took Joe over an hour. The delay was attributed to gawkers who were gaping at a disabled car that had already been towed to the side of the highway after having been pulled most of the way across the Brooklyn Bridge.

The moment he walked through the front door, he immediately called Mario. "She's a strange woman."

"Like I don't know? Give me a break . . . please! How did it go?"

"First of all, you didn't tell me she was a looker. Anyway, I convinced her that Pop's a saint and then nailed Barrett's ass to the wall. Johnson will have a field day." Joe sat on the sofa with the receiver in one hand, removing his shoes with the other. Still left with plenty of pent-up emotion, he threw a shoe against the wall.

Mario said, "I'll follow through with Beth and add a little heat."

"Speaking of heat, I've got a date with an angel. I have to go."

"Joe, it's midnight!"

"Alright, maybe it's a date with a devil," Joe said, laughing, as he ended the phone call and jumped in the shower.

The following day, Beth left a message for Mario: "The dinner with your *paesano* was touch and go for awhile. Then again, I must admit he told it as he saw it." She also gave Mario the name of the ACLU lawyer who was conducting an investigation into Congressman Johnson's activities as they related to the abuse of civil liberties."

Catherine, perplexed, asked Mario, "What's this all about?"

"Johnson is trying to rip the Borelli family apart. I'll be back later and tell you all about it."

The ACLU lawyer agreed to meet with Mario at the New York Hilton Hotel at Fiftieth and Sixth in Manhattan.

At the end of the two-hour meeting, Mario expressed his gratitude for the inside look at politics and its contribution to manipulation of the people for the advantage of government.

Before leaving the Hilton, he called Beth who was in the process of making arrangements to meet with Sam Castellano at his office on Wall Street.

"Thanks for the contact: she was very informative, and her thoughts will be most useful in my book concerning injustice."

Chapter 32

June 1969

Mario was deep in thought, after completing a chapter on the 1891 vigilante hangings in New Orleans. The criminal proceedings were dubbed the "Mafia Trial." Nineteen Sicilian immigrants were indicted for the murder of police chief David C. Hennessey. None were convicted; nevertheless, thousands stormed the prison and lynched eleven innocent men.

The ringing phone shattered his thought process.

Carmela said excitedly, "The heat's on!"

"Heat's on what?" asked Mario eating peanut M&M's.

"The FBI arrested seventy-eight people across the United States on securities fraud. Wall Street is reeling. Guess who was one of the seventy-eight?"

"Not Sam?"

"No. Your good pal, Barrett."

"No kidding! Justice prevails! I hope the son of a bitch rots in jail. What happened?"

"The charges varied, but the SEC has focused on an insider scam. Evidently, the accused brokers artificially ran up prices of mediocre or worthless stocks and then dumped them at the higher price. When they pulled out the prices fell like a rock and left those who couldn't afford losing their hard-earned savings in financial trouble. In contrast, the power players made big money."

"That really stinks."

"It's really sad. I thought you would want to know about the weasel."

"Thanks, Carmela . . . I love you."

"I love you too."

Mario hung up the phone with mixed emotions, feeling sorry for those who had gotten hit with monetary losses, yet elated that Barrett had gotten slammed. Just as he jumped in the shower, the phone rang again.

Annoyed and dripping wet, he answered. It was Carmela. "You're not going to believe it."

"Believe what?"

"When we hung up, I turned the TV back on to watch the evening news. In the middle of the broadcast, there was a bulletin out of the DA's office about the bust and they retracted part of the earlier story. Hennessy said that Barrett was only considered a suspect and was not arrested by the FBI. He said Gateway was bilked for five million dollars and was not part of the scam."

"What pure unadulterated bullshit. Barrett had gambled and lost. I bet you most of the funds that went down the drain were generated from his money-laundering machine."

"I don't understand how that works."

"It's not complicated: it's just convoluted. Barrett is a lucky bastard. He has an angel looking over his shoulder and his name is Hennessy."

"You mean the devil. Sorry for the bad news."

"I'm going to call Peep. Take care; . . . love."

Mario called Sam and was informed by his live-in housekeeper that he had gone to Rome but would return by week's end.

Congressman R. J. Johnson stayed focused on the Borelli family.

Chapter 33

July 20, 1969

"We landed on the Moon," Mario said proudly.
"I know. Neil Armstrong, what a guy! Too bad he's not Italian."
"You're kidding, right?"
Joe turned his head as his body shook with muffled laughter.

JULY 26

A headline in the Italian daily *Buon Giorno*
THEY'RE HERE

> *Congressman Robert J. Johnson and his team of investigators have descended on New York City—specifically, Little Italy.*

A month after Beth's meeting with Joe, she invited Mario to an award ceremony of top media moguls at the luxurious Waldorf Astoria Hotel. He accepted.

They met in the elegant lobby, as a steady stream of arriving distinguished guests filed passed them. Beth was dressed in a tailored taupe business suit.

"It's good to see you, Mario," she said.

"Likewise."

Beth's upbringing had molded her into an aggressive woman. She had learned how to use the system to her advantage. In a freakish way, she was ruthless in her passion for success and had no problem in moral interpretation. Before anything else, came Elizabeth Downing.

Moving toward the elevators, she anxiously said, "Let's go up to the Grand Ballroom, find our table, and I'll tell you what I found out about Richard Barrett who no doubt is a tenacious bastard."

As they entered the opulent ballroom, Mario felt a little out of place as he instantly noticed many men dressed in tuxedos. A sufficient number of women were attired in gowns and adorned lavishly with jewelry. Most everyone was milling about or circulating in the dazzling room, moving from table to table.

They had a well-paced dinner and about the time dessert was served, Congressman Johnson, out of the corner of his eye, caught sight of Beth and decided to visit. He moved quickly to her table and, from behind, his cigarette-stained fingers tapped her on the shoulder. Startled, she spilled her coffee as he smiled and sat down next to her, unaware of Mario seated on her other side.

Mario, stiffening up, took Johnson by surprise as he snapped, "It's been a long time. How are you enjoying the battles of Washington?"

Taking a bite of chocolate tart, Johnson smugly said, "You know me, I always love a challenge. It stimulates the mind."

"Oh yes, the mind. Too bad your mind doesn't know the difference between justice and a vendetta."

Johnson ignored him, looked away, struck a match, and lit up a Camel cigarette.

"OK, so much for vendettas; how about Mondello to stimulate you—"

"Mario—," Beth attempted to interrupt.

Miffed at Beth's demeanor, he persisted, "Too touchy? Then let me ask you about your views on police brutality at the Democratic Convention in Chicago."

"What does that have to do with anything?" Johnson asked with a perplexed look, still munching on his tart. Swallowing, he said tersely, "Don't be an ass."

Mario, getting more upset by the second, shot back, "Speaking about asses, what's up your ass about Borelli; or is it Italians in general?"

Johnson scoffed at the assertion and kept eating.

Leaning toward him, Mario whispered, "Be smart. Leave it alone and go back to your cage. The media will find some other manufactured issues to play on."

Blood rushed to the congressman's head.

Beth, irritated over the verbal assault, couldn't maintain her silence anymore. "We give the public whatever information is necessary to shed light on any story." Shoving her empty plate away, she said to Mario, "I can't believe your attitude!"

"Ferrara, don't you get tired of hearing yourself talk?" Johnson added with disgust as he began eating another chocolate tart.

A minute or two later, Johnson spotted Hennessy talking with a smartly dressed elderly couple seated directly across the room. Excusing himself, he waddled over to James who had signaled him.

Seeing the Congressman approach, Hennessy's date tactfully left the table and headed to the restroom to powder her nose.

"It's so good to see you again, James."

"Good to see you too, Congressman. I noticed you were talking with Ferrara," said Hennessy, stroking his hair. "Has the *wop* mellowed out?"

"Are you serious? Ferrara's not changed. He's the same, always up in arms about something."

"What about this time?" James asked deadpanned.

"He's still pissed over Mondello. He forgets that I lost JCB in the bankruptcy. He also accused me of attacking the Borelli family because they're Italian."

Even though Hennessy knew full well that Johnson was anti-Italian, he asked, "Why?"

"I don't know why. He's writing a book about something. What I do know is that Ferrara's a royal pain in the ass. He may have guts but no brains." The congressman finished another tart and wiped his mouth with the napkin he carried with him. Lighting up another cigarette he continued, "Actually, I think the *ghini* bastard just threatened me." He paused and bluntly said, "Joe McCarthy chose commies, and I figure commies or greaseballs, they're all the same."

"What about Joe Borelli?" asked Hennessy.

"I can't answer that in a sentence or two. But, I can tell you I'm trying to tie certain pieces of information together so the government can deport his father. Then we can indict Joe."

"What charge?" asked James.

Johnson snickered and said quietly, "Don't know yet, but we'll create one."

"Congressman, you're aware that Ferrara and I have had some personal problems in the past, even before Mondello. Someday, his feisty attitude will take him down. As far as Joe Borelli is concerned, I'll feed you what I have."

"Thanks. I agree Ferrara is nothing but a troublemaker. Yet, Borelli makes him look like a saint."

Hennessy grimaced and said, "Borelli is a ball-breaker. I would appreciate a favor regarding Ferrara, however."

"I owe you from the past. What do you need?" asked Johnson, accepting Hennessy's chocolate tart.

"Let me know when something hits your desk concerning Borelli. Maybe I can use the information to rattle Ferrara."

Hennessy's five-feet-seven-inch, big-busted, overly made-up redhead returned.

"That's easy!" Johnson chuckled. Then he waddled back over to Beth.

James excused himself and located the phone bank. Making sure he was alone, he called Sam at home.

"Sorry to bother you, but I am at a media bash today and I just ran into Congressman Johnson."

James filled him in on his conversation.

Sam responded in a concerned voice. "I don't care about the Borellis. Mario is possessed in slamming Johnson in his friggin' book about Italian injustice. You didn't mention anything about our investments in CHEMOR, did you?"

CHEMOR manufactured Agent Orange and had secured a lucrative contract with the Pentagon. Sam kept a small empty shipping drum marked with an orange stripe in his study at home for his efforts in raising money for the company's ambitious endeavor.

James said, "Peep, you know you're playing with the first team." He paused and said, "By the way, I have been meaning to ask you—do you think Agent Orange has any other effects? What about long-term health consequences on humans?"

"Don't be ridiculous: there's no way."

By the time Johnson returned to Beth's table, Mario had left. She pumped Johnson for information on Borelli, although she never mentioned anything about a meeting with Joe. However, it was a perfect time to tell Johnson what she knew about Richard Barrett.

Breathing hard, he said, "Years ago, I had an altercation with him which involved the Mondello fiasco. Looking back, you might be making sense. I especially recall—"

Mario returned just then, and Johnson went quiet.

Sorry for the interruption, but I have to leave," Mario said.

Johnson calmly uttered, "James Hennessy said to say hello."

"Who's James Hennessy?" Beth asked.

"Why don't you tell her?" Mario asked curtly. He turned and headed for the door.

The congressman followed him to the elevator bank. He scowled, lit a cigarette, and said, "I'm sifting through every grain of sand to expose your *paesano* Borelli."

"Is that it?" Mario spat back. He was trying hard to restrain himself.

Johnson took a deep drag from his cigarette and blew smoke in Mario's face. Without a word, Mario quickly raised his arm; Johnson flinched. Mario turned and calmly walked into the waiting elevator.

The next day Catherine, bothered by Mario's explanation of his meeting with Johnson, suggested he call Beth concerning Hennessy.

"Beth, I didn't want to tell you in front of Johnson: James Hennessy is a prima donna prosecutor that would run over his mother if she got in the way of his success. Hennessy is your basic scumbag," Mario said, taking a slug of soda.

"Mario, everything is getting complicated and starting to sound convoluted, even for me. I don't like it. Maybe you should cool it. You could be treading on dangerous ground."

"*Dangerous ground*? Trying to clear Joe Borelli is dangerous ground? How much wine did you have after I left?" asked Mario sarcastically.

"I'm close to hanging up."

"I'm there," said Mario banging down the telephone.

Catherine ignored his outburst with Beth and changed the subject. "Rose is in love. But you know Peep: he's in love with his company."

Mario was surprised they were still dating, let alone who was in love with whom.

"Peep is Peep. What else can I say? Sam is self-absorbed: tell Rose to be patient."

Mario was oblivious to Sam's romantic leanings and never knew how very much in love with Rose he was. She was taller than most Italian girls Sam had met, and he had always been attracted to her—even in childhood.

He liked the way she wore her dark hair pulled back, sometimes braided in one long braid running down the back of her head with ribbons intertwined. But Sam liked best when she allowed it to fall onto her shoulders.

She was not the flirtatious type and had no tolerance for small talk. She could hold her own in any repartee. Sam was always impressed with her self-confidence, and, to him, her beauty was something almost mysterious and always strangely attractive.

However, Mario was right about one thing. Sam was focused on his work and would prove slower than most at committing himself to a relationship that might compromise his ability to expand his business at a rapid pace.

Barrett, in an anguished phone call with Sam, said, "I heard James met with Johnson. I also heard Ferrara was there. What in the hell is going on? It doesn't concern CHEMCOR does it? I need to know. My money's at risk. I need to be informed."

"You're a misfit," Sam said. He loosened his tie and continued. "If you want out, the door's open; so go right ahead. But before you do, tell Leonard Knight; otherwise, stay put and stay quiet. That's the only way you won't screw anything up. The next sound you'll hear is a click."

His mind muddled, Mario couldn't take it any longer, and so he again called Beth. She was sitting at her desk reviewing an article draft when the phone rang.

"Hi . . . don't hang up. I promise a civilized conversation."

"That, I could take," she said.

"Did Johnson say anything further about the Borellis?"

"Not a thing. The congressman did say he relished the idea of investigating Gateway Bank and Richard Barrett."

"You made my day. I'll stay in touch."

Two days later, Beth was on Wall Street. She was prepared to meet with Sam Castellano concerning Johnson, Borelli, Barrett, and white-collar crime.

Mike Borelli was served a subpoena to testify before Johnson's committee—*The Threat of International Organized Crime on Foreign Affairs.*

Pacing frantically, Mike called Tony and Frank Nunzi. The three men met a week later at Caffé Roma. After a lengthy and sometimes heated conversation, Frank glared into space and slowly moved his hand across his throat.

Hennessy's business luncheon at Castellano's Ristorante had just ended when Nick motioned him over waving a newspaper. "I hope the son of a bitch shows up in my restaurant; I'll stuff the overstuffed windbag in my pizza oven," said Nick. His eyes darted about the room as he searched for Johnson.

Hennessy grabbed him by the shoulders and shook him. "Don't be talking stupid. On the contrary, you will treat Congressman Johnson with respect and buy him dinner."

"But—"

"No *buts*; just do it," said James as he calmly walked out.

As Joe and Mario were walking into Caffe Reggio, Mario said angrily, "Congressman Johnson is a demagogue, following in the footsteps of his hero, Joe-the-scumbag-McCarthy. He overpowers anyone with a last name ending with a vowel and aimlessly and recklessly destroys lives. In the process he leaves tears in the eyes of mothers, wives, and children."

"Mario, he's scumbag number one. What he's doing to my father is unconscionable." With his fists clenched, he said furiously, "Johnson better have eyes in the back of his head."

"Be careful. Years ago *Papà* told me that vendettas could come back and bite you in the ass."

Joe nodded solemnly and said nothing in return.

AUGUST

Mr. McGuire called to say: "Catherine, tell Mario that British troops arrived in Belfast to stop the rioting and reestablish law and order. Of course Catholics were involved in the turmoil. Eight were killed and hundreds wounded."

"Dad, I don't think so. He doesn't need to be stirred up even more."

Chapter 34

August 29

Sweat poured down his face as Mario sat at the kitchen table writing feverishly about last evening's turn of events.

> Stalking through the labyrinth of Central Park, a lone alley cat, hunting stealthily for prey, flipped when lightning struck within inches of her sleek body. Feigning the actions of a cheetah, she headed for parts unknown.
>
> It was a hot August night, just about midnight, when reality hit me. I, Mario Ferrara, was alone and lost in a heavily wooded section of Central Park near Bethesda Fountain. There I stood, with tired eyes, dull ears, and overburdened mind, not understanding my deep thoughts of fighting through a maze of everyday struggles, which in general make life so stressful.
>
> I had become frustrated with business. I was writing, listening, and trying to connect with those in the government, business, and religious segments of society to create a better world.

You would think at age fifty-four I would know better, but like many others before me, I had wandered off the straight path and lost my sense of direction.

It was just a moment later when explosive bursts of thunder and crackling lightning ushered in a storm traveling rapidly through the city, unraveling nerves and sending late night revelers scrambling for cover. Pounding raindrops and swirling winds showed no partiality, whipping everything in its path, littering the pavement with fallen branches, sending garbage cans rolling, spilling their trash onto the slick, wet streets.

When the torrential rainstorm ended, an ominous silence descended upon the city. Unable to find shelter, I became one sopping-wet human being. Yet, I was happily looking at a clearing sky filling with twinkling stars. That in itself was OK: it was what followed that still, today, makes my heart pound and fills my senses with fear.

Despite that, I know the good that it revealed. No matter how difficult, I must strain my mind to escape its terror and tell the consequences that come from thoughts, choices, decisions, and actions.

I'm not one hundred percent certain how it all came about, for I was truly discombobulated at the time. I do remember running helter-skelter through the labyrinth looking for an exit out of the wretched woods, when I finally spotted a faint light in the distance. The closer I got, the more joy poured into my heart, filling it to overflowing, for I recognized it was a stairway lit up by reflecting rays of a rising sun guiding all peoples onto the straight roadway of life.

Ready to climb the stone steps on the extreme right, I stopped to catch my breath and glanced back at the dark woods that were threatening to dash my hope; yet all the time I was giving thanks to the Divine Love for my approaching freedom.

As I reached for the top step, a sullen, pasty-faced woman dressed neatly in a pinstriped suit carrying a shiny, worn briefcase blocked my way. My nose immediately was sent into shock by the overwhelming fragrance of her sickly sweet-smelling perfume permeating the air and being propelled outward and upward to the heavens. However, it was her empty eye sockets that pushed my heart near to exploding.

Not able to go around her, though I tried three times, I leaped, ran back down the steps, and headed in another direction. A moment later, I ran up the steps to the extreme left only to be startled by a man dressed in silk robes carrying both a television set and a huge leather bound book. The pages were singed and smoldering with an aroma of incense. He smiled. His lips bled. I started to panic. It was apparent that he had a severe overbite. He had no ears and his decaying fangs added to his shortcomings.

I smiled back, then let my feet do the talking. After running back down these steps, I raced through a darkened underpass and slowly climbed the thirty-eight steps of the center stairway to a striking cast-iron bridge. Just as I approached the top step, a bony, stooped-over, meticulously attired gentleman with furrowed brow was in my face. His top hat wasn't quite large enough to cover the peeling scabs on his balding head. This stately man pulled a little red wagon overflowing with scrolls and reams of white paper. Raising his arms high, he kept shrugging his shoulders, while letting out drum-roll garlic farts.

I was so close to reaching the top step and almost feeling the thrill of victory, yet foiled by the three spooky roadblocks, I faced the agony of defeat. Racked with anguish, I turned to go back down the stairway, tripped on the next step, and stumbled the rest of the way down, finally reaching the bottom step on my bottom. I stood, ran, and finally found my way past the Bethesda Fountain and back into the dark woods from which I had come.

Traveling at what felt like the speed of a cheetah, I fell over what I thought was a toppled tree limb. Caked in mud, I stood, looking directly at a ruddy-cheeked robust man outfitted in a shiny blue and white baseball jacket and ragged red hat resembling a WWII aviator's cap. There he was, slumped against a gnarled tree, complete with sunglasses bound with duct tape and cigarette in hand, hacking his lungs out.

Smiling, he said, "Hi, I'm Jack."

Terrified, mumbling, I barely spit out, "I'm lost." Looking closer at him, I whispered, "Hey, aren't you—"

"Never mind that. But, as for being lost, why didn't you try the rising-sun-soaked-stairway?"

"Are you kidding? Didn't you see me retreat from those three weirdoes that preyed on me on those very steps?"

"I thought that might have been your concern and that you are very afraid to try again."

"One doesn't have to be psychic to see my trembling hands!"

Gesturing with uplifted arms, Jack howled, "Not to worry. I'm familiar with those imposters you encountered. They would wish you to believe they can take away your liberty. They are each cunning in their own way—always starved for more humans to mirror their wickedness; and there they will remain until— "

"I don't know whether you know it or not, but all this is scaring the hell out of me. Have pity man!"

"Today's your lucky day. I'm here to escort you on a journey that will shed light and lead you onto your straight path. You will hear, see, and understand the good; but also experience the bad and the ugly," Jack said between wheezings.

"I must be losing it; what in the hell is going on?" I cried out.

"Exactly, my amico! That's it: you just entered the vestibule of hell."

"What! But how? Do you know the way out?" I yelped.

"Follow me," he whispered.

Jack turned to move backward, and I, left with no choice, followed.

"Hey, really, aren't you . . .?"

He ignored me.

As I ran into the darkness to catch up with Jack, all I could think was . . . why me? My heart, mind, and soul were not prepared for this encounter. But ready or not, there I was, shouting, "Jack, slow up; . . . for the love of God, stop for a second, I'm getting exhausted."

"Don't bug me. Just stay close."

I shrieked, "Why this?"

"Because, I, Dante, say you need to suck it up, stop fighting shadows and cowardice, and follow me."

"Dante! I knew it! You're Dante!"

"OK, so you're a genius. I'm Dante. Now will you listen to me?"

"You're not being reasonable," I blurted. My heart was near to exploding from running.

"Me, *reasonable?* Mario, your eyes are full of fright. You have lost your boldness and passion and have become a prisoner of the mind!"

"Your words are irritating the hell out of me!"

"That's the goal: to remove the living hell you have embraced. Look, by giving you this tour, I'm risking my state of being in Limbo. Limbo is where my friends and I reside. Don't screw it up."

Still in shock, I said nothing, just smiled.

"Mario, you have responded correctly."

Needing time to think and trying to stall the impending trip, I meekly inquired, "Who are your friends in Limbo?"

"I know you don't give a rat's ass about my friends, but I'll answer your question anyway. Limbo is a peculiar place: actually, it's extraordinary. There are many writers, scientists, philosophers, and poets that sit and ponder in Limbo. Among them . . . never mind; I will say no more."

A split second later, hearing sighs and wailing that curdled my blood, I turned to my right and spotted a huge contingent of pockmarked, naked people jumping and skipping around, bumping into one another as they chased blank sheets of paper that were flying about.

The area was infested with a multitude of worms and maggots swirling at their feet, not to mention the swarms of mosquitoes and wasps biting and stinging them over and over again.

I didn't know which way to run; shaking, not looking where I was going, I bumped into Dante.

"You'll thank me for this later," he whispered, grinning, as he took hold of my arm.

Before I could ask a question, Dante bellowed, "The vestibule, an area for the Uncommitted, is set aside for those who lived life with no blame or praise. These wanderers were inflicted with "the fear of the unknown" and for that reason they were not willing to choose. They were only concerned with self."

Still shaking, I uttered, "Their screams are freaking me out." I was getting sick. Looking beyond the haze I barely made out a flaming sign hanging over a covered wooden bridge . . .

YOUR CHOICE . . . ENTER HERE . . . ABANDON HOPE

Dante, while nonchalantly swatting at the airborne attack, said, "These miserable wanderers weren't even worthy enough to be accepted into hell itself . . . let alone paradise. They were just plain cowards; they made no choices. Therefore, they never committed to anything."

I asked, "Why the army of mosquitoes, wasps, worms, and maggots?"

"Oh, that's to get their sorry asses moving in some direction . . . any direction. Giving up hope to get out . . . believe it or not . . . some crazies would rather relocate to a lower floor of the inferno. But it's too late. The good news is the worms and maggots are always fed by the Uncommitted's trickling stream of blood and tears," Dante said, doubling over in laughter.

Again taking me by the arm and looking me straight in the eyes, he asked, "Can you handle the truth?"

After losing my dinner, I meekly nodded.

Dante said, "This pit is my constant reminder of how and why at times I compromised my thoughts, choices, decisions, and actions. Yet, your visit kindled and aroused my desire to find a way out. Let's make a deal!"

The next thing I knew, a ringing noise jolted me to the floor. Catherine leaned over and wondered what in the world I was doing in a fetal position with a smashed alarm clock in my sweaty hand. She helped me to the kitchen table and put on a pot of coffee.

Mario called out, "Catherine, I just finished writing this; please read it."

MINUTES LATER

"You just had to eat that last piece of cold pizza before going to bed."
"Is that it?"
"Well, it is interesting," she said with a slight smile.
"I'll take a page from *Mamma's* repertoire. You're making me crazy!"
She leaped up and hugged him.
He was shaking with laughter.

That afternoon at Central Park, at Mario's insistence Catherine climbed with him the steps near Bethesda Fountain, which coincidentally numbered thirty-eight. Back at the bottom they sat at the fountain and held hands.

In a reflective mood he said, "Angelo would have loved Woodstock—music, love, and peace."

"Didn't it turn out to be somewhat of a disaster?"

"Well . . . it depends on what your definition of *disaster* is. As an example, the facilities were overcrowded, but, no problem. Lack of food and water, no worry. Torrential rains, so what? Alcohol and drugs . . .

could be a problem, but, no problem. Naked people—leave it to Joe to be sorry that he didn't go for that reason alone. To sum it up . . . no trouble."

"That was a good synopsis," she said smiling. "I would have loved to have seen The Who."

"My rock-and-roll wife."

Chapter 35

November

"Mario, it's me, Tim. I just heard the FBI arrested Sam Melville."

"Never heard of him."

"He's the radical who was involved in the recent terrorist bombings against what he called 'the Establishment.'"

"So that's the guy who hit the RCA building in Rockefeller Center and Chase Manhattan Plaza."

Tim added, "He also bombed the Criminal Courts Building as well as a number of others. Someway, somehow, miraculously no one was killed."

"Why don't we get together? How about next Friday?" Mario asked.

"OK."

Even before Tim was ordained, he gave his time all the time and then gave some more, assisting the poor and disheartened. Involved in many endeavors, he relied heavily on his old friends, as well as his new ones, for assistance.

For Tim, the best place for peace and quiet was Calvary Cemetery in Queens with its intricate maze—not of hedges, but concrete. He and

Mario often had their talks as they walked through rows of tombstones. These tombstones were shadowed by a forest of aging trees that filtered the sunlight. It shaded the green lawns in some places but allowed the sunlight to break through in other places, highlighting patches of green and featuring nature at its best.

Actually, it didn't matter whether it was Calvary, Saint Paul's, or Trinity Cemetery, Tim just loved to get lost in nature, especially if it was accented with tombstones. "If obituaries are the Irish sports pages, does that make cemeteries the ballfield?" asked Mario who mercilessly teased him about his obsession with death.

This time, Tim picked Trinity Church with its small, inviting cemetery. They walked awhile, bantering back and forth. Then, shifting gears and turning serious, Mario said dejectedly, "Without Angelo, it's been rough at the store. John is going to pick up more of the slack." Looking skyward, he threw up his hands in frustration and said: "The war sucks. My heart goes out to those who are getting their limbs torn off or bodies blown apart. I don't understand why in the hell we don't get out."

Tim listened.

"The kids at Columbia and campuses around the country are right on. The longer I sit back and do nothing, the more frustrated I get by the minute. Dante's inferno, that's the hell we're living. We're all slaves to the system."

Tim listened.

"Are you still breathing?"

"You haven't lost me yet," assured Tim, studying a tombstone dating back to 1796. "Did you read about *My Lai*?"

"I did," answered Mario. "It was so bad I couldn't talk with Catherine about it. It's hard to believe that over five hundred Vietnamese civilians, mostly women and children, were massacred."

"The army charged Lt. Calley with murder," Tim said.

Mario, shaking his head in disgust, said, "They had no choice. There was too much explicit photographic evidence to do anything but that."

"Too bad you couldn't come to Washington for the Moratorium March. There had to be close to three hundred thousand people participating in the anti-war protest." Tim paused to button up his overcoat as a stiff wind blew through the cemetery. "It turned out to be a peaceful walk, especially since Senator George McGovern and Charles Goodell were participating. And God bless Corretta King: she was there, right up front. It was a wonderful experience."

"That's what I want to talk about . . . an experience. Any experience is difficult to describe, whether good or bad. But, a nightmare in the inferno, that's way beyond difficult," said Mario. He was watching a family of squirrels enjoying life, racing each other up a tree. "Dante's poem came alive. I probably have spent too much time analyzing his prose on thoughts, choices, decisions, and actions."

"For some unexplained reason, I never read the *Divine Comedy*. Tell me, how did Dante describe God?" Tim asked, leaning on a tombstone resembling a movie marquee.

"He described God within the context of paradise, the way you described God to my family before you went to the seminary."

"Refresh my memory."

"Tim, you basically said that God is in all, and there are no boundaries on earth, or for that matter in the universe, that separate us. Unfortunately the more you read, the more you studied, the more structured and tight-assed you became."

Tim smirked.

Mario, taking hold of Tim's arm, smiled and said, "What you said to me then was in your heart, not in your theological training. You also said that everyone sees life differently and that's what makes us unique and special individuals. We are separate in our vision, but we are one in our hearts."

Mario waited to catch a reaction.

"I said that? That's pretty good stuff." He picked up a discarded coffee container off the grass. "Tell me more about your trip with Dante into the inferno?"

"What's unnerving is that I understand hell and the trauma associated with turmoil. It's much harder to understand paradise."

"That's a distinct possibility since we all get caught up in everyday trappings," Tim commented.

"To me, it seems that we're trapped in structure, a subtle bondage." Mario paused, taking in the serene surroundings. "Yet, doesn't bondage go deeper than the secular world? To take it a step further, isn't bondage caused by organized religion's fear of other belief systems? Look at

Ireland—Catholics against Protestants—or the Middle East—Jews versus Muslims; and so it goes, on and on."

"If you're talking about liberty again, think about this: the Indians have taken Alcatraz Island."

Mario stared at him and said, "What the hell is going on? Unrest is turning into a tar baby."

They left the cemetery and began the walk-and-talk back to Little Italy as the chilling wind picked up.

LATER THAT EVENING, THE TELEPHONE RANG ONCE.

"Tim, do you know it's midnight?" asked Mario in a whisper so as to not wake Catherine.

"Doesn't Tim ever sleep?" murmured Catherine as she rolled over.

"I didn't feel like we finished our conversation. For one, please let go of your deep-felt resentment of Barrett, Hennessy, Stanley, and Johnson. Let it be."

"Sounds good to me," Mario said. He had put a pillow over his head to muffle the sound of his whispers.

"You also talked of liberty. Yet, I sensed fear in your voice and thought pattern. No one can be free if they fear. Let go and freefall into your destiny."

"Hold on a minute." Mario walked into the kitchen, stuck his head under the faucet, took a drink of water, and picked up the extension phone. "Look, I do what I do for one reason: because I know things are not as they seem or as they should be."

"Mario, my best advice, no matter what you write, is to be clear in what you ask people to do. That's a grave responsibility. However, in all my endeavors, God has responded in time and shown *me* the way."

"What's your secret? Do you have a special pipeline?" Mario asked chuckling.

"There's no secret. It's about my will. I abandon my will to God and pray; that's my saving grace. Prayer carries me through my rejections, misunderstandings, and anxieties. I try to do whatever God asks of me and serve every day as though it were my last."

"My father is right. You're a saint! Or, you're taking a huge dose of spiritual placebos."

Smiling, Tim blurted, "Screw you!"

"Such language! And coming from a saint," Mario teased. And then he continued, in a more serious tone, to share his thoughts, "Still, the way I feel right now, I'd have to hibernate for months just to clear my head before I could even begin to pray. I don't know how many times I've not done what I should have done."

"You can't beat yourself up. Forgive yourself and go on. If you screw up, so what?"

"You stole that line from *Papà*," Mario accused.

"Sue me," Tim said. He chuckled.

"I guess I am a person who needs to be always in control."

"It's worse than that: you're Sicilian. Indifference and detachment—refusing to let anything push you one way or another—will keep you in a peaceful state of mind. Stand for what you are, for what you believe, and don't worry about the consequences."

"Only if you send me to the Caribbean," said Mario, amused by his own wisecrack. "I appreciate your words of wisdom. I just hope they don't get me in trouble like they did on our infamous trip to Coney Island."

"Great memory. If you need me, call . . . I'll be there. Remember, God searches for and calls all people to himself, including a hardheaded Mario Ferrara. Goodnight *paesano*."

THE NEXT DAY

Sam, even though he was in a meeting, took Tim's phone call.

"Peep, I had a long talk with Mario and I'm a little concerned. I love the guy and his family and know you feel the same way."

"What's up?"

"I'm not 100 percent sure, except, I know he's searching."

"Let me know what I can do."

"When I figure it out, you'll be the first to know. Besides that, the other reason I called was to see if you received an invitation to the Together Award Ceremony."

"Sure did, why?"

"Are you going?"

"Don't know. I'm buried in work."

"That's what I was afraid you would say. Here goes the surprise. You're the recipient of this year's Saint Francis Medal. I'd love you to be there to receive it."

"I'm honored and flattered. Thanks, Tim. I'll be there."

Sam was leaning on his antique table from Palermo, "Sorry for the interruption, Lenny. Now tell me again exactly what Johnson did."

"Mario, what's the matter?"

"*Papà*, I don't know; but I can't sit still."

DECEMBER 22

Uncle Mario,

It finally happened. Our infantry unit has been ordered to Nam. Not a very good Christmas present. But, at least, maybe I'll get to see Bob Hope. A little bit of humor. Not too funny, but whatever it takes to keep a positive outlook. I would rather laugh than cry. The guys in my squad keep talking about going out there to kick some ass. Nothing more than talk. Inside we are all nervous. I miss the famigha. Love to Aunt Catherine, and yes, I have written Mamma, Nanna, and Nannu.

Love,
Angelo

Chapter 36

....

1970

<small>FEBRUARY</small>

Unconditional love for humankind, along with his outgoing personality, was Tim Gallagher's major asset—and curse. He could charm the socks off anyone and knew most everyone in the neighborhood, from the poor to the super-elite, including members of the Mafia. That out-of-the-ordinary combination allowed him to provide money and a variety of other favors when needed and for whomever needed them.

On more than one occasion, Tim provided Gateway Bank opportunities to loan money for church and nonprofit development projects. In turn, Leonard Knight made sure Barrett introduced Tim to contractors and benefactors who could be of assistance to the archdiocese and other nonprofits; a simple example of *one hand washing the other.*

The neighborhood knew Tim. The neighborhood loved Tim.

Nevertheless, the downward slide of Tim Gallagher, Catholic priest, began with "old man Levine," as the kids called him. Mr. Levine's frail, bent-over body never dampened his cheerful attitude. He owned a candy store, complete with soda fountain, at the corner of Mott and

Houston Street. It was barely surviving financially. Further, it was in need of serious work to keep the health department from shutting it down. However, a bank loan was a major problem for Mr. Levine who, at the age of eighty-one, was viewed as a bad financial risk.

Tim had a soft spot in his heart for the corner store, having fond memories of it as the boys' old hangout; so, he came to the rescue and approached Barrett for a loan. Within days, a business loan of thirty thousand dollars was approved on the condition that Father Tim Gallagher personally guarantee the loan, a condition that was an absolute joke. Tim's financial statement was all zeros. Nonetheless, he agreed and Gateway Bank funded the loan.

Four months later, Mr. Levine suddenly died and the loan went bad. Tim met Barrett at the bank as he had requested. And Richard Barrett, with a heart colder than dry ice and a slimy handshake, snarled, "Tim, I can't believe the son of a bitch dropped dead. I'm screwed big time if you don't come to my rescue right now." Picking at his pudgy face he continued his tirade in a state of panic. "My ass is in a sling. In order to make the loan you requested—and I mean you—I told my loan committee that I relied on your ability to pay me back. I'm calling the loan due and looking to you for repayment." He sat back and lit up a Cuban cigar.

Tim was mystified by Barrett's callousness. "Wait a second, you said my signature was just eyewash and had nothing to do with the loan whatsoever."

"That's not my recollection. Besides, don't give me that crap. You know better. You signed the note; you owe the money. Period. I cannot afford scrutiny, especially at this time," Barrett said, waving the loan documents in Tim's face.

"Right now I'm in shock and disbelief at your attitude."

"I'm sorry, *Padre*. Call your friends; you got a million of them. Let them bail you out."

The normally jovial priest went ballistic. "I'm not going to impose on my friends for some pure unadulterated bullshit."

"You have a problem, Gallagher: fix it or I sue and notify the archdiocese."

"I'm in the middle of Our Lady of Loreto's food drive."

"That's tough. I'm sick to my stomach right now, so food drive to me means shit!"

"The reason you're sick to your stomach is because you're a rotten bastard," Tim said, rising to his feet.

"Screw you, penguin," Barrett said loudly enough to cause bank customers to turn their heads.

Joe Borelli was deep in conversation with Mario when Tim called. "Joe, I'm glad you're back from Sicily. I hope things went well."

"How are you doing?"

Ignoring the small talk, Tim anxiously said, "I need a favor. Please check out why Barrett's so nervous about old man Levine's loan. Maybe it's Lenny Knight."

"Barrett again. He's a money-sucking maggot. Weasel and Knight would stop at nothing to protect their financial empire. They need their heads broken."

"Don't be going crazy. All I ask is for you to check thinks out," said Tim letting out a heavy sigh.

"OK."

Mario, without saying a word, walked off the loading dock of Borelli's warehouse building.

BACK AT THE STORE

"*Papà*, if Joe is right, Gateway will collapse when the Fed can prove—"

Tony pointed to a customer milling about and whispered to Mario, "Say no more."

A COUPLE OF DAYS LATER

With a tone of contempt, Joe said, "Tim, apparently Gateway's money-laundering business has been shaken by Barrett's loan policies. There have been countless times he made unsecured loans to his buddies without Knight's knowledge. The pay-off for Barrett was sexual favors."

"Keep going," said Tim.

He lowered his voice and continued, "He's way over-extended on his financial commitments. A number of loans are in default, including a multi-million dollar loan to an investment banker for a corporate takeover that went south. Although small by comparison, Levine's loan going bust can be the final straw that the Feds need to launch a full investigation into Gateway. The egg-sucking weasel got caught up in his manipulative game and is scared shitless of Knight."

"Go on."

"Barrett's an idiot. He's in a state of panic because of your tweaked financial statement, the one that he prepared. And now he is accusing you of fraud. Anything to save his ass."

"You're right, Barrett's balls need to be broken."

"Keep cool, *Padre*. I'll get the bastard in the end."

"Go in peace," Tim softly said, sliding the panel separating the two closed.

Joe opened the curtains, made the sign of the cross, and left the confessional with his head down.

The peering eyes of the little old Italian ladies of Little Italy were on him until he disappeared out of Our Lady of Loreto's Church.

After having heard confessions the rest of the afternoon, Tim placed calls to Sam and James expressing his concern of an approaching tidal wave that could ultimately cripple his street ministry. He waited for their response.

One week passed and, not hearing from either one, out of desperation he made another call to Joe. "Hi, Mr. Borelli: it's me, Tim. Is Joe there?"

"Joey is out of town," Mike answered. "Timmy, how are you doing?"

"I'm doing OK! Do me a favor: when you hear from Joe, tell him I have had enough. I'm ready to trump Barrett with his money-laundering scheme."

Mike's intuition told him this was the wrong card to play.

He called Mario, who quickly contacted Tim. "Tim, back off. Leave it to Joe and me. We'll set things straight."

According to Barrett, bank examiners checked the loan package and requested Gateway go after Gallagher. The same directive applied to all the bank's unsecured loans. As for Tim's financial state, getting blood out of Christopher Columbus would have been easier, and he had been dead for centuries.

Tim was rightfully concerned that a lawsuit could damage the credibility of Together, a nonprofit foundation that benefited youth in the inner cities. That was problem number one. Right on the heels of that predicament, through an anonymous tip, the feds had discovered that certain funds supporting Vatican Art and Treasure and his Together Foundation were coming from illegal sources. That was a bigger problem. The end result: Tim was being investigated for racketeering.

A new federal statute known as RICO (Racketeering Influenced and Corrupt Organizations), gave law enforcement a way to control money obtained from illegal operations. Therefore, RICO became the vehicle the federal government used to confiscate properties owned by Together, all the mortgages of which were held by Gateway Bank.

Tim was mentally and spiritually crushed.

Word spread quickly in Little Italy.

Archbishop Stanley's ego was rocked, as the archdiocese faced a potentially damaging blow. In the course of a telephone conversation, he squealed, "James, it's very bad. The scrutiny is killing me. Besides, everything's at stake, including our relationship with Gateway Bank. We must not forget they made the loans for my buildings in Mondello."

"The best thing you can do is stay the hell out of it. I'll worry about Gateway Bank," James said harshly.

Stanley whined, "Well, I guess one priest for the sake of the Vatican is no major loss. Tell Tim I'm sorry I can't help, but I'll pray for him."

"Sure thing," he said in a tone of indifference.

James delivered the message of Stanley's offer of prayer.

Mario arrived at Our Lady of Loreto's Church right after the phone call.

"I really didn't expect anything different," Tim said, visibly shaken. He gave Mario further details of the archbishop's stance.

"Stanley is a ruthless bastard," Mario growled, putting down his bottle of soda.

Vatican City was oblivious to all that was taking place in Little Italy. The powers that be were more concerned with the Pope's announcement of his newly appointed cardinals. To no one's surprise, Archbishop Stanley finally got his red hat and became a cardinal.

When Mario heard the news, he called Tim, "Hey, now I know God's got a great sense of humor."
"What are you talking about?"
"The Pope, in his infinite wisdom, named Stanley a cardinal."
"Mario, the Pope is the Pope."
"Tim, Stan Musial is a Cardinal. Stanley is no cardinal."
"Give me a break."
They both laughed.

Cardinal Arthur Stanley revered the title as well as the pomp and circumstance that accompanied it. His motto was never buck the Vatican or any of its authority; consequently, when he was deposed in a lawsuit between Gateway and Tim, Stanley played ignorant.

Nonetheless, he did admit that Tim forwarded funds to Rome for the benefit of the Holy See. Under direct questioning, he answered, "Father Gallagher acted alone; therefore, I cannot confirm the source or the amount of money contributed."

FEBRUARY 18

A headline in the Italian daily *Buon Giorno*
FATHER TIM GALLAGHER HAS BEEN ARRESTED ON RICO CHARGE
OUR LADY OF LORETO'S PARISHIONERS ARE IN SHOCK

Mario appeared at the offices of the archdiocese at different times, hoping to catch up with Cardinal Stanley, all to no avail.

Silence, woven in a memory of convenience, validated Tim's former statement that he didn't expect anything from the Church. Through it all, the cardinal never lifted a finger to assist him.

Adding to the trauma, was the sound of silence from Tim's friends at the archdiocese.

"The Church is out of control. Tim needs a way out of this bullshit," Mario said as he reached Joe at a construction site.

"So what's the answer?" asked Joe, raising his voice to be heard above the noise of a bulldozer backing up.

"There's no answer, not just yet. But, we need to think hard on what can be done. Stanley manipulated Tim into being a pimp for the Vatican and now sends him down a rat-infested alley without a bat."

"Your metaphor is really bad."

"I know; that's what pisses me off."

"You know you can count on me. Let me make some calls."

"Thanks, Joe," said Mario. He pounded on the phone booth with the receiver, shattering the glass.

Not reacting to the mishap, he stood on the glass fragments, dialed Barrett, and shouted, "Weasel, let go or I'm going to rip your head off."

Barrett responded with a shaky voice, "Stick it up your ass," and hung up.

Mario phoned right back, but Barrett refused to take the call.

Pounding again on what was left of the phone booth, he dialed Sam.

"Sorry, Mr. Castellano is in a meeting."

"Tell him it's me and it's super important."

"I'm sorry, Mr. Ferrara; I buzzed him again, but he ignored me," said the receptionist.

He insisted, "Please go and interrupt him; I'll take the blame."

Sensing the urgency in Mario's voice, she left her desk and rushed back to Sam's corner office.

"Mario, what the hell is so important that you can't wait for a return call?" Sam asked. He was fingering the starched white collar that was irritating his neck.

He proceeded in bringing Sam up to date.

"I can't help. I'm sorry: you know I love Tim, but this is a very sticky situation. It could screw me up big time. I can't afford to have my reputation tarnished. If something went astray, I would be dead on Wall Street." Sam was anxious to return to his meeting with Beth Downing discussing the nuances of white-collar crime.

Mario, frustrated, said, "Thanks anyway." He again pounded the phone booth.

Mario swallowed his pride and most reluctantly called James Hennessy who had been elevated to the number two spot in the DA's office.

James, in conference, refused to take the call.

Mario recalled Tim counseling R. J. Johnson after the Mondello debacle and frantically called Washington. The congressman was out of town and couldn't be reached.

He tried contacting the cardinal again and again, with the same result: he was always unavailable.

MARCH

Three are dead in an explosion of a townhouse in Greenwich Village. That, plus several other bombing threats, have been attributed to The Weatherman, a radical terrorist organization.

A month had past since Tim's arrest; Mario became frustrated. His bitterness and resentment over the chain of events were getting the best of him.

The story of Sacco and Vanzetti that would jump-start his writing career never materialized; his book on Italian injustice was fragmented at best. One of his best friends was in deep trouble with the law and couldn't find a way out.

Sam's underground network produced the right kind of information—but not enough of it—concerning Gateway's operation. Sam was out of the picture, at least publicly, as it related to Tim. However he had posted bail for Tim through a discrete third party.

Joe had exhausted his contacts.

Mario felt totally helpless and concluded that maybe true justice was an illusory quest and it was time for a change.

Mario and Catherine were ready to take a much-needed vacation. They left for the Rocky Mountains of Colorado on the first of April.

Chapter 37

April 4, 1970

A headline in the *World Telegram*
SUICIDE TAKES THE LIFE OF REVEREND TIM GALLAGHER

An intense investigation that began on February 9 ended in death. A generous, yet humiliated priest apparently was unable to cope with an indictment that came down from the Justice Department on April 1.

He was found dead in Our Lady of Loreto's Church in Little Italy.

Here are comments from some of Father Tim's friends and associates. Richard Barrett was quoted: "What a shame. I warned him many times to stay away from those who leeched on him for personal gain. He will be missed."

Cardinal Stanley stated, "The Lord forgives. I'll pray for his soul."

Sam Castellano, contacted in Palermo, Italy, on a business trip, said, "He was a wonderful human being. A lover of mankind." Mr. Castellano further stated that upon his return he would set up a trust fund to enable Father Gallagher's work to continue in support of his Together Foundation.

Long time friends, Mario Ferrara, Joe Borelli, and James Hennessy could not be reached.

"Mario, Tim committed suicide," cried out Joe Borelli in a static-filled telephone call from his import/export office.

"Tim! Suicide! What happened?" Mario cried out in shock. He slowly sat down on the bed beside Catherine whose eyes immediately welled up with tears.

"Tim apparently lost it. He called and asked for you," Joe said, his voice breaking. "Tim said, 'Tell Mario, I'm sorry for letting him down and not to wait any longer. He will know what I mean. I love you guys.'" The minute I got off the phone, I raced over to Our Lady of Loreto's and was met by a whole bunch of cops who told me that Tim had taken his life."

"How did it happen?" Mario asked, pounding his forehead with his hand.

"Looks like he grabbed a kneeler from the confessional, jumped on it, and hung himself from the cross behind the altar."

There was a fairly long pause before Mario swallowed hard and said, "Did he leave a note?"

Joe's tone reflected his anguish and his anxiety. He was apprehensive. He felt there was more to this than was apparent. "No, but they found a copy of a letter in his back pocket addressed to the Pope."

"Did you—?"

"I couldn't convince the cops to turn it over, but I was able to get a copy," Joe said.

"How? Who the hell would take a chance to give you a copy?"

Joe was silent.

"Do me a favor and read the letter to me," Mario said, sliding off the bed and onto the floor of his hotel room. Catherine, in tears, sat by his side.

"Sure, here goes."

April 2, 1970

Holy Father,

I have attempted to write this letter numerous times, but for one rea-son or another, always vacillated. However, enough time has passed; the time of reflection and contemplation is over. The season of recon-ciliation and spiritual freedom is upon us—a time for peace.

From the beginning, with openness I have spoken from my heart. I personally delivered to Cardinal Stanley and copied you a detailed explanation on past and present events that took place with Gateway Bank, Banco Ambrosiano in Milan, and Vatican Bank. Until now, I waited and hoped that one day, you, Holy Father, or the Cardinal would respond. Subsequently, what is now distorted and kept in secret would be made clear and brought out into the open.

However, I did not perceive that my attempt to communicate with the hierarchical Church would be met with a conspiracy of silence. Further, I compounded a sad state of affairs, reacting by creat-ing my self-imposed bondage that in turn impeded my actions.

What I neglected to consider was that a challenge for truth would be dragged down deep into Rome's silent maze of catacombs by institutionalized intellect. Apparently, there is a fear associated with things being brought into the light.

Since the investigation and now the indictment, I choose to break my own silent bondage. I will resign my priesthood. With absence of malice, I will reenter the community at large and move forward with the same excitement and enthusiasm as in the past. I do so without seeking any opinion, encouragement, or approval from the Holy See.

In concert with the decision to end my silence, I have decided to copy this letter to the FBI along with the appropriate enclosures that speak to the issue of criminal behavior.

I had wished to be obedient to the Holy See, but I must first be true and obedient to my call. Therefore, I have renewed my heart with unconditional love.

With thanks, I am
Sincerely yours in Christ,

Reverend Tim Gallagher

"He must have been talking about money laundering. And, if you remember, the rumor mill always spoke about Barrett's involvement with drugs," said Joe, his voice rising in anguish.

Mario, having a difficult time controlling his emotions, said, "Tim's dreams may have been shattered, but that letter doesn't sound like suicide to me. I don't like it. He would never do this."

"That's what I think," Joe roared.

"Did you get hold of the documents he was sending to the FBI?"

"No, there were no enclosures to be found."

"We have to trust our gut," Mario said as he began to pace.

"I know; this is serious shit."

"Do you think someone whacked him?"

"I don't know what to think," Joe said taking out his bible of names. "I'll start making calls the minute we hang up."

Mario, becoming furious, said, "Something's not right. If I find out he didn't commit suicide, I'll find the bastard that killed him and—"

"I'll call Peep and see what he knows."

"I need to think this whole thing through before I call *Papà*."

There's something else I better tell you." Joe motioned his warehouse foreman to leave.

"It can't be any worse . . . can it?"

"I don't know. James Hennessy was the last person to see him alive. Tim apparently was invited to the DA's office for a so-called interview. If he committed suicide, then whatever took place with Hennessy must have broke his back."

"How did you find out?"

"One of Pop's spies at the DA's office told me."

"Hennessy—that back-stabbing son of a bitch. I'd like to get my hands around his neck," Mario said. He kicked a wastepaper basket across the room.

Joe said, "Let's stay calm. At least right now." The veins in his neck were nearly bursting.

Mario shouted angrily, "*Calm,* my ass!"

As he hung up the phone, Catherine, crying, said, "Please, Mario, sit. Let's pray."

Drained, he sat, buried his head in her chest, and sobbed.

That same day, James Hennessy decided to run for District Attorney of New York County. He called Barrett and said, "Open up your checkbook. It's time to take you up on your financial commitment. I'll call the cardinal and Sam. Oh, and believe it or not, I have a new political advisor! He wants me to be seen in The Village and appeal to the crazies. Let's meet at Caffe Reggio."

Chapter 38

....

April 5, 1970

The next morning, Mario still in shock, wandered downstairs to pick up a New York newspaper. He tucked it under his arm and headed to the hotel coffee shop to meet Catherine. Leaping off the front-page bottom-right of the World Tribune was an article outlined in black titled "Priest Gives Up," followed by an interview with Cardinal Arthur Stanley and the Honorable William Phillips, "a respected jurist" who was to have presided over Gallagher's trial.

Next to Stanley and Phillip's commentary, ran a story of the GOLDEN CARE AWARDS:

Once again this glorious affair is upon us. The organizers promise this year's gala will be bigger and better. For the first time, the celebration will be covered nationwide on television.

The GOLDEN CARE AWARDS honors leaders and achievers who have given unselfishly of themselves in the interest of our global community. Their contribution to humankind cannot be adequately expressed in words.

This year's recipients of the prestigious award are the following:

GLOBAL COUNCIL FOR A BETTER WORLD	DR. SUSAN CHOU
BUSINESS AND LABOR	GEORGE LAWSON
MEDIA	MS. ROBIN WHITEHALL
EDUCATION	MS. JANET TURLEY
GOVERNMENT	CONGRESSMAN ROBERT J. JOHNSON
MEDICINE	DR. MARGARET HERNANDEZ
RELIGION	CARDINAL ARTHUR STANLEY
ENTERTAINMENT	DONALD PARKER
INTERNATIONAL	NITKA SOLZWOLK

By the time Catherine arrived, Mario was extremely upset and was ready to leave the restaurant. She pleaded, "Mario, please calm down; people are staring."

His face contorted in anger, he said in a loud whisper, "What pisses me off, more than Stanley, who is nothing more than a rotten, self-serving bastard anyway, is Johnson who is blind to justice." He slapped his forehead. "Even Sam folded his arms for fear of repercussions. As far as Hennessy and Barrett are concerned, they're consistent—low life scum."

At the urging of Catherine, John and Carmela called to calm Mario down.

He didn't return either call; instead, he chose to contact Cardinal Stanley. He yelled into the phone, "I'm coming back to sit outside your building and wait for—"

The cardinal gently laid the receiver down on its cradle and left his office.

Carmela tried again: this time he returned her call and in frustration barked, "Something is terribly wrong."

The suicide death of his childhood friend Tim Gallagher haunted him mercilessly.

At the end of a midday hike down a snowy trail, Mario and Catherine watched the sun give way to darkness. Growing weary, Catherine found a sunny spot where the snow had melted and the ground was dry. She spread a blanket, and she and Mario sat for hours on a crest of a hill in Rocky Mountain National Park, high in the Rockies. They embraced, turned, and gazed at a magnificent display of stars dancing to the beat of the universe. Eventually, the thin, cold air encouraged them to return to Grand Lake Lodge.

Catherine tried to convince him that Tim's death was indeed a suicide and to give up his obsession with justice. "It's time to let go of what you consider the unjust ways of structured religion and society in general and settle down." She reached for his arm and said, "Please, be happy, bake bread, and be available to the family. If you want to write, write about the Yankees."

In turn, he tried to convince her that he couldn't let it go. "I can't do it, at least not now. If anything, it's time for me to push harder. Someone has to end this charade: please join me."

"I love you, . . . but, I can't; it's your thing to do. So, go do it. Please try to understand me."

The next morning, Mario, while sipping his orange juice and admiring the majestic snow-peaked mountains, hugged Catherine and softly whispered, "I do understand you . . . please understand me. I have to do what I have to do."

Her eyes filled with tears as her heart filled with dread.

The flight back to New York's La Guardia Airport was long and quiet. Catherine slept most of the way back. After picking up their luggage, they hurried toward the taxi stands. On the way, as luck would have it, Mario ran into James Hennessy. They exchanged some nasty words about Tim Gallagher's untimely death and Cardinal Stanley's indifference.

James said, "To tell you the truth—"

He was interrupted by Mario who growled, "Do you mean in lieu of lying to me?"

"Don't give me any of your crap. Stanley told Tim on a number of occasions that he needed to temper his enthusiasm for his so-called neighborhood ministry. I personally tried to help, but was unsuccessful." A big-busted blonde, towering over him, held on tight.

Inches away from Hennessy's nose, Mario roared, "Bullshit!"

Catherine pulled him away to a waiting cab. Thirty minutes later they were back home in Little Italy. He was still wound up like a coiled spring.

"Mario, for once listen to me. This is not going to be a hard decision."

"Go!" he snapped.

"That's what I think we should do ... go. Let's go to Lido's and enjoy a good glass of wine and food. I'm hungry."

"Actually that does sound good."

Lido's in Greenwich Village was their "date place": it was a small Italian restaurant, with red-checkered tablecloths and fine homemade cooking.

They talked non-stop from the minute they sat down, slowing up every now and then to drink some fine Chianti and enjoy their macaroni with *fra diavolo* sauce. Three hours later, arm in arm, they left Lido's and chatted all the way back home where they talked some more.

It was a wonderful evening as Mario and Catherine behaved like newlyweds again.

They fell asleep in each other's arms from pure exhaustion.

Barrett, over a lunch meeting with Sam at Steve's Kosher Deli, yammered, "If you had stopped contributing money to Together, I could have foreclosed Gallagher out and benefited by owning a number of profitable properties."

"Why didn't you ask me to stop?" Sam responded sarcastically.

"Knight's also pissed that we missed out on the opportunity."

"Please tell Lenny for me, just as I'm telling you, to go get screwed!" Sam pushed his unfinished pastrami sandwich aside and leaned in close to Barrett.

Barrett, ready to light his Cuban cigar, stopped, held his lighter in mid-air, the flame flickering in the small space between the faces of the two men. He cried out as if in astonishment at Sam's belligerence, "Sam!"

"Don't *Sam* me! You amaze me: at times you show just how stupid you really are."

Barrett sat still and lit his Cuban.

Sam turned and shouted, "Stupid!" Then he bolted out of the restaurant.

BOOK V

Chapter 39

April 21, 1970

A headline in the *Daily Mirror*
IT'S HERE . . . THE GOLDEN CARE AWARDS

> *Lincoln Center is amply prepared for the onslaught of media. Dr. Susan Chou, chosen as Person of the Year, stated in an interview: "The United Nations continues to provide our global community multi-faceted programs that benefit humanity. And I am proud to be part of this wonderful international organization. As director of human rights for the UN, I have on occasion worked closely with Cardinal Stanley and Congressman Johnson. Both have been most supportive in our endeavors."*

At Caffé Roma between sips of espresso, Mario expounded on his theory. "Joe, with organizations and programs you have to deal with structure and ego." He hesitated, smiled, and in a lighthearted tone, said: "Tim talked about love. I figure with love, you don't need organizations or programs."

"That sounds oversimplified. Mario, please don't be going off the deep end."

Mario popped two peanut M&M's into his mouth. "I'm *already* in the deep end."

Later in the day, Mario purchased a ticket to the Golden Care Awards and waited patiently for nightfall. At Lincoln Center, he maneuvered his way through a horde of humanity until he located his reserved seat.

As the evening wore on, he found that he actually enjoyed the intermittent entertainment, and he listened intently to a litany of orators as well as to the accolades that accompanied each award.

Cardinal Stanley was the last to receive his award and speak. In a condescending tone he said, "The Vatican is the conscience of Christ. In that context, I pledge to lead the laity in their service for the Church." He continued with self-praise, speaking of how he supported young priests who labored for the betterment of society, in particular the poor and oppressed, and concluded, "I was deeply saddened at the recent loss of Father Tim Gallagher, a fine, uplifting, energetic priest." He paused, shook his head and continued, "Up to the very end, I was there supporting and defending him as well as working endlessly with his Together Foundation. I share this award with him," said the beaming cardinal.

His statement was not earth shattering, but it was enough to tip the scale of reason inside Mario's head. He had had it. The anguish of the past exploded and began a defining moment in his life.

While all the award winners were standing on stage acknowledging thunderous applause, Mario decided to leave his seat and head down the main aisle. Walking ever so slowly, he took security by surprise by suddenly attempting to climb on the stage shouting "Hypocrite! Hypocrite!" Within moments, he was in the grasp of the private bodyguard of Congressman R. J. Johnson.

Dr. Susan Chou came rushing forward. Part of the standing-room-only crowd was booing and part was cheering. She leaned down and said in a disturbed manner, "Mr. Ferrara, why are you making such a spectacle of yourself? If you want to voice your opinion, come to our roundtable discussion tomorrow at the Waldorf Astoria. I assure you, you will have a chance to speak."

Forcing a smile, Mario said, "Thank you. I accept your invitation."

By then the Lincoln Center security squad had Mario physically restrained. They quickly escorted him from the building.

The following day in the Empire Room at the Waldorf, the roundtable discussion was in full gear when Dr. Chou introduced Mario as a man in search of justice and liberty.

"I'm sure many of you have read Elizabeth Downing's enlightening new column—published where else, but in the *World Tribune*—concerning this revolutionary individual. Mr. Ferrara overlooks no sector of our society or culture, including religion, in his quest for liberty and justice."

The audience greeted him with silence.

Mario, dressed in a black turtleneck and black pants, stepped to the podium and removed his fedora. Picking up the microphone, he turned and scanned the audience through a barrage of camera flashes.

In a strong and confident voice, he began, "To express oneself by just using words is not sufficient, especially when demonstrating justice, liberty, and love. Having said that, I'm still going to give it a try."

In anticipation of what was to follow, Stanley squirmed uncomfortably in his chair, as did Johnson.

With heightened intensity in his voice Mario said, "But there comes a time when enough is enough. For me, that time is now. It's no secret that all human beings are born free. There's no distinction in dignity and equal rights. We are all entangled in a web of life. So, our choice to claim liberty is based on our understanding of togetherness.

"In the words of Father Tim Gallagher, 'Let us, together, synthesize our total being with love to create a world more human and more divine.'" Hesitating a moment to choose his words carefully, Mario continued, "I have given his statement much thought and have come to the conclusion that Christ, Buddha, Mohammed, Gandhi, and King all can't be wrong. Or, have we shut our eyes, closed our ears, and lost our understanding of love?"

Barrett was in the audience with Hennessy; leaning toward him, he said defiantly, "Maybe Ferrara can join Gallagher in everlasting peace."

James waved him off.

Stanley, taking a tight grip of Congressman Johnson's arm, grimaced and whispered, "What's this bastard up too?"

"Leave him be and watch him bury himself," said Johnson sharply.

Ignoring a heckler, Mario declared, "It doesn't matter whether it's government, business, religion, or any segment of society: it's time to take away the keys from the jailers of our minds . . . our wills . . . and our souls."

Mario kept talking. "Each person's relationship with their deity is at the very heart and soul of spiritual liberty. Now it's time to dismantle the concrete bunkers of religious segregation and plant seeds of infinite love . . . unity . . . and liberty."

Cardinal Stanley was appalled and could not believe what was taking place at the podium. Turning to Johnson, he said: "This clearly shows his unruly attitude. How dare he disparage my church! Though I'm not a vengeful man, we must remove him from the public eye."

The congressman was fuming and nodded affirmatively.

LATER THAT EVENING OUTSIDE THE WALDORF ASTORIA

"As Christians, we live in harmony with our congregation," said a southern preacher's wife. She was wearing a pale lavender, ruffled blouse, a style that would have seemed more appropriate for a much younger, much slimmer woman.

Mario responded calmly, "That you may do. Tim told me, 'We all form one community because we're all together in the bosom of God.' So that begs the question, do you live in harmony only with *your congregation* or with all religions and ideologies?"

"What gives you the right to speak out in such a manner?" asked the woman, adjusting her wide brim hat. The hat reminded Mario of Bella Abzug for it had become a trademark for this icon of 1960s radicalism, a civil rights activist and anti-war protest leader. The lady who stood before him in the wide brim hat was, however, it seemed to Mario, the very antithesis of Bella Abzug.

Mario gave the preacher's wife an incredulous look and replied, "It's not what, but who. In the beginning, I kept myself in check: now my tongue is raw from silent abrasions. From those who do not believe as you, I hear a cry for shelter from the storm of isolation."

"We adhere to the law of the Gospel. We know the way, the only true way," insisted the woman.

"But don't we need to recognize the common path, rather than ignore it? It's pure folly to condemn other belief systems."

"You're making too many presumptions. We are concerned with the poor, the lonely, and the helpless."

"That's good. But, don't we need to be concerned for the rich and the worldly as well? We must give up pretenses and be sincere in our efforts for everyone."

She huffed, and placing her hat back on her head, she countered, "In urban and outlying areas, we have built shelters for the homeless, schools for our children, and churches to reach out to society."

"Build and build and then build some more. Are they projects for all or for a select few?"

She answered smugly, "We are self-sufficient and that allows us to do more for each other."

"Yes, that may be true. But, haven't you just grown more powerful and vain? You now have a well-oiled machine. True. But how much good does it accomplish?"

"This is useless. I'll pray for you," said the woman tugging at her tightly fitted, white knit skirt.

Mario smiled and gently said, "And I'll pray for you."

A young man wiped cheese from a hot slice of pizza off his face. He was listening to the ongoing dialogue. "You've got to admit the guy has quite a tongue."

His friend raised her eyebrows and said, "Yes, he does. But if he keeps taking whacks at the establishment, he could get it cut out."

A neatly attired man in a three-piece suit was leaning on his cane. He called out to Mario, "There was a report in Richmond, Virginia, detailing Christianity's extreme right and their plan of action. They are preparing to use everything in their power to reverse an approaching tidal wave of spiritual freedom. In addition, I know of someone with influence who was visiting New York and read Ms. Downing's column and your quote on the subject of Christianity and religion. I can tell you, Mr. Ferrara, these things do not bode well for you. Some feel you are the devil himself."

Mario shrugged and calmly said, "People can think and say what they want. That's their liberty. My liberty is to say, 'Love one another.'"

"You're possessed," someone yelled.

Another person, not looking at him, uttered, "But there is only one way."

With a look of bewilderment Mario responded, "Do you not know? Have you not heard? Christ himself would be crucified today for the same reasons he was crucified then."

"How dare you be so bold," an Evangelical minister cried out.

"Because . . . I *do* dare. Is it because I'm telling you the truth that has made me your enemy?" Leaning on a mailbox, unfazed by the minister's statement, he continued, "Bondage siphons away the very breath out of life. It will always be counterproductive. Consider for the moment that bondage includes the mental as well as the physical state of a human being."

APRIL 23, 1970

A headline in the *New York Daily Mirror*
THE GOLDEN CARE AWARDS . . . OR A . . . PREVIEW TO HELL

> *Ferrara's given a few folks a headache without the booze. Where does it all go from here? No one knows for sure.*

One of the morning newscasts featured the Golden Care Awards with a blistering commentary on how an upstart the likes of a baker by the name of Mario Ferrara could have recklessly maligned a cardinal of the Roman Catholic Church.

The famed news anchor continued with a fiery closing statement, "Ferrara, though he might be Cardinal Stanley's worst nightmare, is not fit to tie the shoes of His Eminence.

Beth Downing called Joe Borelli.

Mike answered, "I'm afraid not; Joe went back to Sicily to take care of some unfinished business."

"It's important that he call me when he returns."

"All I can do is tell him."

"Thank you, Mr. Borelli."

Chapter 40

Mario exited Grand Central Station. The pouring rain, hitting off the blacktop and pelting his fedora, continued to soak his already sopping-wet jacket. The station crowds that usually could be seen hustling from place to place found themselves shrouded under umbrellas and were carefully making their way though puddle-filled streets.

While standing on the corner of First Avenue and Forty-fourth Street, Mario was about to enter the United Nations building when he noticed a figure shuffling across the avenue in a red cap and a blue and white baseball jacket.

Drawn to the figure Mario followed him. He tried to avoid becoming a hood ornament by dodging horn-blaring traffic as he crossed First Avenue. Blocks later he was out of breath and disoriented. The man in the red cap apparently had gotten swallowed up in a swarm of people, causing Mario to give up his futile search and return to Little Italy.

He arrived back at a deserted Spring Street Subway Station—deserted except for the man in the red aviator's cap, moving around a concrete pillar. Mario quickly moved to the exit, right on the heels of the mysterious stranger.

The blaring alarm startled Mario. He knocked the taped-up alarm clock to the floor, waking Catherine.

She turned over and asked, "What's going on with you? How many times have I told you not to eat before going to bed? It's just like eating a meatball sandwich before swimming."

Mario, sitting up, smiled, and said, "You're turning into *Mamma*."

APRIL 27, 1970

A letter from Angelo

Uncle Mario,

It's getting worse. Trying to stay alive is a bitch. The Vietcong survive by ambush, hit, run, and hide. It doesn't matter how much we pound them with bombs; these bastards have built a tunnel system that rivals the subway. Too many guys are being blown apart. I hate to admit it, but at times I'm scared shitless and can't wait to get the hell out of here and go to a Yankee game with you; and I never want to see a jungle again. Give my love to Aunt Catherine. And don't worry; I wrote Mom a long letter as well as Nanna and Nannu.

Love you.

MAY 1

A headline in the *Daily Mirror*
NIXON ORDERS TROOPS INTO CAMBODIA

President Nixon, hoping to bring the war to an end, went on national television and announced to the American people that he was sending combat troops into Cambodia to destroy North Vietnamese and Vietcong sanctuaries and supplies.

MAY 3

A headline in the *New York Journal American*
OHIO GOVERNOR JAMES RHODES SUMMONS NATIONAL GUARD

> *On the heels of President Nixon's announcement that US troops have invaded Cambodia, campuses across the United States erupted in angry protests. At Kent State, students on a rampage attempted to burn an ROTC building. National Guardsmen bayoneted two men.*

Two days later National Guardsmen opened fire on unarmed onlookers and students demonstrating against the war. Thirteen wounded, four dead . . . two of the students that were killed had been on their way to class. Why the sudden and violent response? No one seemed to know.

MAY 12

Mario fell to his knees in anguish and let out a loud mournful cry when he saw two army officers standing at the front door of 231 Elizabeth Street. Minutes passed before the army chaplain somberly announced, "Specialist Angelo Ferrara was killed in action on a search and destroy mission a day after his unit crossed the border into Cambodia."

Carmela was at work.

Catherine knelt down beside Mario, held him tightly, and rocked him back and forth in grief.

Tony rushed outside the store and wailed loudly.

Vincenza collapsed slowly, her back against the counter behind her as she slid down the cabinet and sat on the floor. She lifted her head, resting it against the cabinet, and sat in silence with her eyes closed: her profound grief was written on her face.

A short time later, Mario and Catherine, along with Father Carelli, began the sorrowful walk to PS 41 to tell Carmela that her dear son had given his life, as his father before him in World War II had given his life for a land of liberty—America.

Chapter 41

IT WAS A MOMENT IN TIME NEVER TO BE FORGOTTEN.

The faded, red, green, and white striped canvas awning soaked up the rays of a rising sun. The hanging flap read *Established in 1929 . . . Ferrara's Grocery and Bakery*.

Long after the morning rush, the tantalizing aroma of Mario's thick-crusted bread was still permeating the air throughout the store.

Tony Ferrara, tugging on his stained white apron, shook his head in disbelief at the lingering, arm-thrusting women blocking the doorway. Vincenza had joined the two who were talking nonstop in Sicilian dialect about their respective ailments, the Vietnam War, and *la famigha*.

Hurrying out of the store, Mario, wearing a new dark brown fedora and carrying a leather bag strapped over his shoulder, smiled, gave a goodbye hug to Tony, kissed Vincenza's cheek, and barely squeezed his still strapping body past the black-clad ladies.

Mario smiled. Long gone was the Italian struggle of assimilation. A new tapestry woven by the Italian American had unfolded, interlacing the Old Country with the New World. Nonetheless, the spirit of the neighborhood was still embedded in *la famigha*.

Thirty minutes later, his hurried walk took him to the Arch at Washington Square Park. Mario stopped momentarily at the statue of Giuseppe Garibaldi to reflect on his hero's quest for liberty. After a quick stroll around the park to collect his thoughts, he entered a packed Caffe Reggio.

The area had simmered down somewhat from the early sixties when The Village was a hotbed for anarchy, the Beat Generation, and anti-Vietnam War rallies. Nonetheless, the coals of rebellion were still smoldering.

Standing in the middle of the relatively small smoke-filled coffee-house, he glanced about, hoping to see peace activists who had frequently rendezvoused at the well-known gathering spot: but they were not there.

Mario sighed in disappointment, tilted back his fedora, and waited patiently for a table to open up. Minutes later, fumbling to close his bag while maneuvering through a bustling room, he reached a far corner table just as sheets of paper from it spilled across the floor.

Sitting down, his heart pounded in anticipation as he slowly picked up his hand-written notes, chose a few to look at, and stuffed several back into the bag. Nervously smiling at the waitress, he ordered a cappuccino, took off his fedora, and began reviewing his document.

Every so often, he paused to take a look around and to study the faces of the people who gathered: students and professors from New York University and members of the gay, lesbian, and business communities, as well as residents and tourists.

Indeed, Caffe Reggio was a microcosm of society where those of different color, religion, social status, and nationality mingled.

Thirty-nine minutes, one *biscotti*, and two cups of *cappuccino* later, there still was no Alan Ginsberg, Jack Kerouac, or Bob Dylan.

Ginsberg or not, it was time.

Taking a deep breath, Mario climbed onto a wobbly chair, startling the overflowing crowd of patrons.

Unknown to Mario, Richard Barrett, James Hennessy, Congressman R. J. Johnson and Cardinal Stanley were walking along McDougal Street, having just minutes before left a symposium at NYU where Barrett, Hennessy, and Johnson were featured speakers on international banking and Cardinal Stanley spoke of the wonderful outreach programs of Vatican Bank.

As they walked into Caffe Reggio, Hennessy could not believe his eyes. He stopped abruptly and pointed out Mario to Johnson. Filled with curiosity, they pushed their way past the door to observe and listen.

Mario bellowed over the noisy chatter that filled the room.

> *Hello, allow me to introduce myself . . . My name is Mario Ferrara. I'm a revolutionary! Too many years I have waited to speak my heart. So . . . I say why not now? May those who have ears, hear and those who have eyes, see.*
>
> *In my hand I hold a Declaration of Liberty and call for a general strike against any government . . . religion . . . business . . . or . . . structure that perpetuates darkness and chains the spirit.*
>
> *Let a Revolution of Liberty for all humankind begin now and continue until we cannot go another heartbeat.*

Hennessy, Barrett, Johnson, and Stanley blended into the crowd and were not noticed by Mario.

With a steady voice, Mario continued,

> *For all who desire to join this adventure, I will read the Declaration and leave a copy to be signed.*

DECLARATION OF LIBERTY

There comes a time in the course of human events, when it becomes necessary for the one body of Peoples to dissolve with love the powers of darkness within any structure, religious or secular, that bind the mind and suppress the spirit.

Therefore, we declare the causes that impel us to separation . . .

ONE . . . When and where the hierarchy and other leaders in the religious or secular realm seek to be served rather than serve and do not hear, see, or understand the needs of the peoples.

TWO . . . When and where the development of hardness of heart obscures and suffocates the peoples' dignity and endowed abilities.

THREE . . . When and where there exists a conspiracy of silence that originates and perpetuates contempt for basic human rights.

FOUR . . . When and where religious rules and regulations administer guilt, create fear, and distort truth.

FIVE . . . When and where hypocrisy deforms and chokes the spirit of brotherhood and sisterhood toward one another.

SIX . . . When and where humankind is exploited and discriminated against by those who butcher fundamental freedoms.

SEVEN . . . When and where doctrine is enforced by arrogance and power.

EIGHT . . . When and where places of worship are for the sake of structure and materialism only.

NINE . . . When and where discrepancy between word and deed cripples the pursuit of happiness.

TEN . . . When and where there exists any other wickedness against the peoples.

For the support of this Declaration, with a firm reliance on the protection of Divine Providence, we mutually pledge to each other our Lives and our Sacred Honor.

Mario Ferrara

Taking a breath, he shouted to be heard over patrons clanging china, shuffling, and whispering:

So . . . if you care about life . . . and if you care about truth, nothing will stop the revolution.

You have a choice.

You decide if the declarations are true or not. If they are not true, condemn them.

If they are true, meet the challenge, . . . sign the Declaration, . . . join the revolution, and take action in a general strike.

The time is now.

Together . . . without any separation whatsoever we can claim our liberty.

Mario paused to catch his breath.

A woman seated at a nearby table asked her friend, "Can togetherness create a new breed of humanity?"

"Who knows? Maybe?" was his response.

Mario fearlessly exclaimed:

Strike and paralyze any entity that engages in bigotry, thereby, planting want, fear, and slavery in hearts and minds.

Tell the insider of big business with their subtle intimidation to stick it.

And demand basic rights for those who are denied jobs, fair wages, and decent working conditions.

Strike the ego.

Strike the system . . . and shut the injustice down.

Strike them all!

The crowd was anxious and becoming disorderly. A voice from nowhere yelled out, "Hey, get your ass out of here or I'll bust your head."

Mario facetiously said, "That's not nice." Turning serious, he added, "I'm sure you know . . .

We are Spirit.
We are Truth.
We are Billions.
We are Family.
We are Love.

And when love is violated, liberty is raped.

Mario spotted Catherine at the door. She was an hour late in meeting him at the coffeehouse. Smiling at her, he jumped off the chair and without losing a beat continued in a firm voice,

I ask you to withhold your presence, money, and talent from any religious structure, service, or event that immortalizes a charade and breaks the covenant of life.

Strike churches, mosques, and temples whose cornerstones are bonded by a bankrupt religious spirit which is fruitless and worthless and produces nothing; in the process, they blind truth and obstruct unity.

Take action. Exercise your birthright.

Slowly moving toward Catherine, Mario, his eyes wide with excitement, continued:

Strike any business or professional enterprise where manipulation can cause, among a myriad of things, resentment, anger, and paranoia that eat away like gangrene.

Strike and walk out on those employers who have hardness of heart and leave turmoil in their wake.

Walk out today!

Strike the merchant that is in conflict with these declarations; stay away and let cobwebs grow on their merchandise.

Wearing a handwoven shawl, an elderly woman with a shaky voice asked, "What about utility companies?"

Mario shook his head in frustration and replied, "I don't have the slightest clue of what public utilities, energy companies, and refineries are thinking . . . But taking advantage of necessities is simply unfair. Forced to make a decision between food, medicine, or heat is just not right and should no longer be tolerated. So . . . now is the time to buy candles, sweaters, walking shoes, and bicycles."

He wiped his forehead and declared:

> *Stand up against the looters. I'm talking about those who use the system for fraud and abuse, causing frustration and mistrust.*
> *Strike!*

Hearing the ruckus inside Caffe Reggio, MacDougal Street started to fill with the curious, adding to those already assembled in front of the coffeehouse.

Mario, standing in the doorway, motioned the gathering crowd closer.
Catherine, with a finger to her lips, pleaded, "Please, you've said enough; let's go home."
He kissed her on the cheek and whispered. "I love you. But the time has come. Please forgive me."
She stood by his side.

Raising his arms high, he said with determination:

> *Evaluate your situation. I ask you, has your wallet or purse been affected by injustice? Has injustice affected your job, your pension fund, and your buying abilities for necessities? If the answer is yes to anything I just said, then it's time to strike.*

Waving his fedora, he continued:

> *The Strike may be painful in the beginning, but in the end, it will be sweet and simple as we will live in liberty.*

Listening to Mario's verbal assault, Barrett, gasped and said, "Knight will be livid."

Johnson was gagging on his croissant.

James scoffed and said, "This is his waterloo."

Stanley was nervously fiddling with a gold cross hanging around his neck. Outside, people gathered on the sidewalk. Many pressed against the windows to catch a glimpse of the escalating tension inside.

Mario took a drink of water, and then cried out:

How can we sit, watch, and do nothing to help those who cannot afford health insurance? Why not insist the government provide a health-care system that provides quality care for every person without cost . . . rather than forcing many of the ill into bankruptcy?

HealthCare vs. Warfare. Your choice.

Let's not forget the environment. Remember the spectacular show of support for the environment on Earth Day? It was wonderful; however, every day should be Earth Day. It's time for clean air and safe drinking water, everywhere for everyone.

And then there's Peace vs. War, easy choice.

Strike those in media who, rather than respect liberty, exploit it by controlling what's printed in newspapers, magazines, books, or said on radio and television.

In answering a college student wearing an NYU sweater, Mario nodded knowingly and replied, "Too bad, but you are right; too much bad news and not enough good news. And yes, malice and deceit, sensationalism and gossip work their way into the printed word. And so go the television networks. Sad but true."

In a concerned voice she asked, "How can we change it?"

Mario, his eyes focused on the young woman, thought for a moment and gently said, "How to change it? It's your choice. My choice is not read or buy newspapers, magazines, or rag sheets or watch television or listen to radio programs that feed on malice, that's how. And, as for those who manipulate the strings of media, it's their choice to awake out of the abyss and live love. And time is on the side of love. Strike the malice!"

A young actress was adjusting her Ray-Ban sunglasses. She was amused by the verbal exchange. "This is great: someone having the guts to speak out. I want to hear your thoughts on the great white lie."

"*Great white lie?*" Mario asked, scratching the back of his neck.

"The great white lie is . . . 'let's do lunch' and lunch never comes," the actress explained.

He howled, "Aha! Short memories or memories of convenience. Expressing integrity is to integrate words with deeds. Yet, this is a huge weakness in all aspects of our society; it reaches corporate boardrooms, the capital steps, religious institutions—everywhere."

She hugged him and rushed off to catch up with part of her film entourage.

Mario removed his jacket, draped it across his arm, and stood holding it there as he spoke to those who remained determined to confront him. Slightly raising his voice, he said:

Another thing. Who is accountable anyway? When the media chooses the role of lapdog to serve the spin masters or bulldog to harass the meek, or when sensationalism comes before truth, it brings tears to my eyes. Do people only want to hear bad news and not listen to good news?

"I think you're a no-good bastard," a male voice cried out from somewhere in the crowd.

"Is that your best shot?" Mario asked.

A reporter for the *World Telegram* shoved a tape-recorder microphone in Mario's face and defiantly asked, "Who is to determine what's right?"

Mario snapped, "Well it's sure not the spin-doctors. Their position is to hide or expose whatever or whomever they wish and whenever they choose. Their lot in life is to protect the interests of their clients at any cost."

Looking straight at the grimacing woman he said, "So, let me ask you who determines what's right?"

"You're not being fair. You're prejudiced against the media."

Mario, keeping his eyes on the fashionably dressed reporter, said, "Media needs to be renewed with a challenge of personal ethics guided by love. I believe accepting the challenge would lead to a new manner of operating, one embracing what is called integrity. The truth shall set you free!"

"That sounds pious. Don't you believe we do our best?"

Mario cheerfully replied: "There's nothing finer than reporters who engage in unbiased journalism. But creating a story by indicting the innocent is a disgrace. Those who place truth and justice before awards, ratings, or other measurements of success need to be applauded."

"You speak from both sides of your mouth."

"I try to speak the truth, and those who hear, should listen."

He shouted:

> *Strike, . . . every sovereign nation and government . . . local or national . . . where there exists degrading treatment and crimes against humanity resulting in tyranny and injustice.*

Mario paused, scanned the faces of those who were standing, took a deep breath, and earnestly said, "This strike is a call for change. And in order to show solidarity, let us, one week from today, . . . shut the system down in a national strike."

Many taunted him.
Many cheered him.

Pandemonium broke out in the caffe and out in front on the street.

In the midst of the commotion, one word—loud and clear—emanated from the rear of the room. Starting slowly, then gaining momentum, the throng inside and out chanted "liberty . . . liberty . . . liberty."

The crowd followed him outside.

Stanley's face spewed contempt. "He needs to be stopped."

In an agitated tone, Johnson said, "Cardinal Stanley, I agree. This rotten bastard needs to be gagged and jailed tonight."

There was bedlam on the street.

Johnson became vehement. "This man is an anarchist, a rebel with no motive except to undermine the government. In fact, he wants to undermine society in general."

At the direction of the congressman, the police dragged Mario to a waiting patrol car. They loudly admonished Mario for his unruly behavior and then released him with a stern warning.

John and Carmela, having received a panic call from Catherine, rushed to The Village.

When they arrived, a large contingent of media was already in place recording the turmoil.

"What in the hell are you doing; have you lost your mind?" Carmela shouted, trying to be heard over the yelling crowd. "Listen to me. Be quiet! No more of this nonsense. Go home with Catherine."

Mario listened but did not reply.

"What makes you so sure that anyone will join a general strike?" a strong female voice called out.

At first, he didn't respond. But, the Ferrara in him would not rest.

He decided not to take Carmela's advice to be silent and determinedly answered in a confident tone, "Today a revolution has begun. Join the ranks of bravehearts who are bold enough to believe that we can win an ongoing struggle against the powers of darkness—powers that perpetuate injustice. And join the ranks of those who have the courage to remove themselves from the grip of darkness."

John stepped in to end it right there; but Mario, unwavering, continued, "The decision is ours . . . to strike the system and free ourselves from bondage. I ask . . . what will history write about this generation? Will it say we were so fragile and fearful that we sat back on our asses and did nothing?"

Catherine nudged him to stop. Ignoring her, he rolled on, "Or, will it say, we were willing to risk our reputations . . . risk everything—even life—and serve each other in a revolution of liberty, born out of love."

The instant Beth Downing arrived at the scene she began writing as quickly as her hands permitted.

John again stepped in front of Mario in support of Catherine's attempt to stop his incendiary words. No luck.

Mario enthusiastically said, "Let this generation set the pace and give hope for those who follow. I look forward to hearing your voices and seeing your actions as a united people . . . a family . . . in a revolution of liberty. Let's do it."

A male voice within the steadily growing media group fired out a question, "Mr. Ferrara, what do you think you can accomplish?"

"Me—nothing. All of us . . . liberty . . . liberty with love!" he thundered.

Another reporter shouted, "Mario, who is the enemy? It seems as though no one is exempt."

Smiling, Mario replied, "So, you did listen."

His adrenalin still pumping full bore, Mario was unrelenting.

> *Strike in the cause of liberty and with courage . . . march . . . gather . . . protest . . . demonstrate, and if necessary, employ nonviolent civil disobedience.*
>
> *Lie down in roadways and across railroad tracks . . .*
>
> *Spread yourself across runways at airports, form a human chain on the waterfront, block city hall, block the capital, use your imagination . . . act and strike.*

After he simmered down somewhat, Carmela exhaled loudly in frustration and approached him. "How in the hell do you think you're going to pull this whole thing off? I'm worried about you. I don't need any more sadness in my life."

"You know damn well, I believe . . . Catherine believes . . . Tim believed . . . that all we need is love!"

Moving closer, she reached for his hand. "You don't need to stand on a soap box for me. I love you and don't want to see you destroyed."

In a conciliatory tone, he said, "I'm sorry if I sound insensitive. But I believe if what I said is true nothing will stop The Strike and Revolution; . . . truth is the key to liberty."

Carmela, John, and Catherine stood by helplessly.

"Mario Ferrara has taken a different look at humanity. He simply invites people to join in a revolution not with weapons, but with love," said one reporter to another.

The other reporter shook her head in disbelief and said, "You're forgetting how Ferrara in his call for a general strike was meticulous in not leaving any segment of society out of the equation. He has attacked our very foundations."

Some of the press gathered around Cardinal Stanley, who in an aristocratic manner, stated: "Mr. Ferrara is here to impair goodness and create havoc. Not only is he a blatant heretic and sinner, but he's also an enemy of the government. He needs to be incarcerated for the public good."

Hearing this, Mario began to move toward the cardinal but was restrained by the police who were watching the situation closely. Mario bellowed, "Tim Gallagher talked about being more human and more divine. I know I have a long way to go. But, you! Why don't you take the express train to hell?"

This time, Mario was escorted to a waiting police wagon for the short ride to the Sixth Precinct. The patrolman in charge was Enrico Mascotti's son. Pete Mascotti had recently made Sergeant on the New York City Police Department and was a long time family friend. This made the task of placing Mario in handcuffs very difficult for him.

During the walk to the police wagon, Pete pointedly said, "Mr. Ferrara, how many times have I told you to watch what you say and how you act? Please, I can't control the powers that be. Use your head."

"I always try to use my head, Pete. But, I try never to forget my heart. Besides, what did I do?"

"What did you do? How about inciting a riot?"

Catherine pleaded with Mascotti to let him go.

"I'm sorry, Mrs. Ferrara. I have no choice. The congressman will press charges. He insisted that we arrest him; so did Cardinal Stanley. This time, Mr. Ferrara has gone too far."

John, Carmela, and Catherine, at loose ends, rushed back to Little Italy to talk with Tony and Vincenza before anyone else, particularly the media, reached them.

Afterward, John immediately called Sam at his office to apprise him that Mario was being arrested for inciting a riot. Without hesitation, he excused himself from his private luncheon engagement with Leonard Knight and called Rose. "Sorry to bother you, Rose, but I'm rushing down to the Sixth Precinct to bail Mario out."

"I heard the news."

"Can you—?"

"I'm on my way."

Mario, appearing confused, smiled nervously at Sam who was quite somber.

Sam irately said, "Do you realize what the hell you did?"

Mario fired back. "Pete Mascotti gave me his opinion. Give me yours."

"You offended half the friggin' planet—that's what," said Sam, not backing down.

"Peep, I finally had the guts to speak my convictions."

"Hold it. Listen to what I'm trying to tell you."

"You *hold it*!" Mario said, slamming his hand against the wall. "*Papà* told me many times, 'Always be strong: don't compromise your heart for the sake of a favor or being accepted.'"

"You're impossible. Too bad Joe is in Palermo; maybe he could pound some sense into your head. As for now your ass is grass," Sam said throwing his arms up in disgust.

After Sam posted bond, they started down the front steps of the station house when members of the media swarmed around them. A reporter shouted. "Hey, Mario, any last words?"

"Liberty! Now!"

Sam shoved Mario into his new silver Jaguar for the ride back to Elizabeth Street. When they arrived, Catherine greeted him with a chagrined look on her face, "I thought we agreed? That we had an understanding?"

"That's exactly what I thought," Mario shot back.

Carmela and John hugged their brother.

Tony wasn't sure of what to make of the situation.

Vincenza prayed.

Sitting at the kitchen table, John frustratingly said, "You really are hopeless. Understand one thing—you're a one-man target."

With a glint in his eye Mario smiled and said, "No, I'm not. Tim Gallagher said, 'The small voice within is how you make a final decision. It's called faith.'" He paused and continued, "When you don't worry about consequences . . . I call that liberty. So, little brother, the small voice within told me to give out your address: that way they'll get you before they get me." Mario was smiling.

"Smart ass."

Sipping his coffee, Mario said gently: "John, imagine yourself ready to take *the happy trip*. You're lying in bed and the clock is ticking away and you ask yourself this one question: Did I do what I knew—not what I thought—I should have done to fulfill my destiny?"

"You mean, whether or not I should have added more basil to the pasta I made you and Catherine?"

"Talk about being hopeless," said Mario, laughing as he reached into his bag. "Here's a poem from me to you."

NEW WIND

A new wind is blowing,
And we know not
From which direction it comes,
For this wind is swirling.

But, if we listen closely,
We will hear the heartbeats
Of humankind blowing in the wind.

A new wind that caresses all beings
With a warmth of love
And fans the flames of light, energy, and life.

A new wind that blows away
The clouds of confusion
And clears the air,

So, we can recognize one another.

Chapter 42

June 6, 1970

Congressman R. J. Johnson soundly criticized Mario in a special broadcast from his office in Washington, DC. Soon afterward, he returned to New York to hold a two-day conference at the US Court House. In attendance was a select group of bankers, including Richard Barrett and members of the Federal Reserve. Their purpose was to discuss international banking.

Johnson had come armed with information received from Beth Downing, courtesy of Joe Borelli. He knew Barrett had sidestepped a number of questions by alluding to the fact that Knight, and not he, made all the decisions. Also, in an attempt to divert the congressman away from Gateway Bank, he divulged information relating to Castellano's offshore entity. Not falling for his maneuver, Johnson lost his patience and accused Barrett of participating in a money-laundering scheme.

He stoked the flames just enough for Barrett to feel the heat.

Somehow, Leonard Knight unearthed the findings of the conference and was furious.

On the second day when the session concluded, Barrett called Knight from a pay telephone outside the courthouse.

"Leonard, it's me."

Knight thundered: "You're an imbecile! You call yourself a banker. My four-year-old grandson could do better than you. Think! For God's sake, think!"

Barrett swallowed hard and stayed silent.

Knight continued his verbal assault. "How about this for an idea? Maybe the blimp congressman can play the Hindenburg and go down in a ball of flames."

"I have been giving that some thought," said Barrett chewing on his cigar.

"*Some thought*?" he snapped.

Concluding a lengthy discussion, Knight, totally incensed with Barrett, pounded the phone on his kitchen table before he clicked the line dead. He then called James.

"*Mr.* Hennessy, it's time for you and me to have a quiet dinner."

The following day, Barrett discovered someone had wired his office at Gateway Bank. He went berserk. He called Congressman Johnson, and Johnson's aide informed Barrett that the congressman was attending a conference at the United Nations.

An hour later Barrett located the congressman and invited him to lunch at the UN Plaza Hotel. Barrett told the congressman that he would be delivering damaging documents pertaining to Sam Castellano.

In the course of conversation, Johnson vehemently denied any knowledge about the wire. Barrett banged on his plate with his soup-spoon and furiously cried out, "Watch your ass."

Heads turned. Practically foaming at the mouth, Barrett continued in a hushed tone, "Politicians come and politicians go. I know the *wops* would love to see you go. And if the public finds out about some not-too-discreet situations that you know that I know about, you couldn't get elected to the piss-boy's union."

Johnson scoffed, chose not to respond, and calmly walked out of the restaurant. Leaving the hotel, he took a taxi directly to Castellano

Enterprises. Despite the fact that he did not have an appointment, he was able to command a meeting with Sam.

The congressman, wasting no time, stood in front of Sam's Roman antique desk and arrogantly said, "Consultant to the Justice Department or not, I'm here to tell you that you're officially under scrutiny for moving unreported income out of the country. Sam, my friend, you have been exposed. You're finished. Your little bit of heaven in the Caymans is really an offshore haven, not heaven."

"Who the hell told you that?" he asked curtly, losing his composure.

"Why, your pal Barrett," snickered Johnson as he munched on an Almond Joy. "He also told me how you coerced him into selling JCB's note to you for your hostile takeover of my former company. As a reward for your business acumen, I'm sending a team of auditors to review your company records."

"Get the hell out of my office, right now!"

Johnson froze as a cold chill ran down his spine.

"Now!" Sam shouted.

The congressman shuffled out.

Sam slammed his office door closed, removed his glasses, and called Joe Borelli.

Joe listened carefully and finally demanded, "Cut to the chase and tell me what you want; and no bullshit please."

Six months had passed since Sam had been pressuring Joe for repayment on a loan pertaining to a business deal in Palermo, and Joe was still fuming.

"We have known each other a long, long time, so let's not either of us bullshit the other. First off, your loan goes away. With that out of the way, we can continue. You're a smart boy. You know the repercussions that can occur because of the Borelli skeleton in the closet called *immigration*. Ultimately that ugly problem has spokes that can radiate in many directions, even to the Ferrara family and Frank Nunzi—if you get my point."

"You're pussyfooting around: tell me what you want me to do."

"Listen carefully to me: it's a twofold opportunity. We keep Mario and his family out of the debacle, and you get the money you need to help Mike. Deportation is not good, and I would not want Frank Nunzi pissed at me. Just push the right buttons. There's a lot at stake, so make sure it's the right buttons."

"*Right buttons*? Are you not talking about egg-sucking weasel Barrett or James-the-scumbag Hennessy?"

Sam, breathing heavily, said nothing.

The phone went dead.

A federal agent was waiting in the lobby to serve Sam a subpoena to appear before a Congressional hearing on *International Relations and Global Organized Crime.*

Rose Gramoli called Carmela and Catherine and invited them to lunch at The Fig Tree, a quiet eatery in Greenwich Village. They met at the front door and decided to eat inside because the wind was stirring up street dust and dirt out on the patio.

Once seated, Rose, with menu in hand, simply inquired, "What in the world has possessed Mario?"

Catherine, eyes heavy from a lack of sleep, replied, "I don't know. I tried everything to get him to quit. Mario has this restlessness that can be triggered by so many things, beginning with Italian injustice which he calls a mirror image of the civil rights movement: when you add Tim's suicide and Kent State . . ." She ran her hands through her tousled hair. "Then the final blow, Angelo's death—well, he has just gone ballistic. He's impossible!"

Carmela chimed in, "Rose, you know my brother. When he gets focused, he's focused; nothing is going to move him in a different direction." She was wiping away tears. "First and foremost, Mario has never let up on his quest for truth and justice. And when it comes to Tim's death, Mario doesn't believe for a moment Tim committed suicide. I agree with Catherine: with my dear son Angelo's death added to the equation, you have nitroglycerin bouncing around in Mario's head." She paused to take a drink of water. "That's my brother, and I don't think anyone can stop him. You can give it a try, but I think it's futile."

"Sadly enough, I'm afraid both of you are right," said Rose uneasily. "After talking with Sam, I brought us together to determine if there is anything we missed that might help him. I thought if we share our knowledge about his idiosyncrasies and what we know—"

The waiter delivering their drink orders interrupted her. The interlude caused the conversation to drift in a variety of directions as each picked at their salads. Suddenly, Rose, without looking up, asked, "What is there about Mario, Gateway Bank, and Johnson?"

"Why all the interest?" Catherine asked.

Rose finished a bite of lettuce and placed her fork across her plate, tines facing down to indicate she had finished her salad. This action seemed also to indicate some frustration and a desire to get to the core of Mario's problems, to search out skeletons in the closet, to discover hidden agendas and roadblocks that she might encounter in trying to help him.

There was a long pause, but no answer from Rose. Ignoring Catherine's question and the reluctance of Catherine and Carmela to answer hers, Rose continued, "Sam has volunteered to help Mario in any way possible." Straightening her body in her chair, she finished almost defensively, "He's worried about Mario's welfare and health."

In a follow-up column in the *World Tribune*, Beth quoted Mario:

> *The call for a general strike is going to test the patience of structured society. All who join should do so with sincerity and be prepared for sacrifice that may go unnoticed and without reward. The Strike will transform truth into action and open avenues not conceived possible. In this revolution, we must control our emotions, act only out of good, and be prepared to forgive.*

Some supporters of the general strike arranged a forum at a local high school in Glen Cove, Long Island. Mario, making his way through an unsettled auditorium scanned the audience while mentally preparing for an onslaught of questions.

"Some say, you bring liberty to captives. Who and what is a captive and how do you bring them liberty?" asked a neatly attired young man.

Without hesitation Mario replied, "There are captives entrapped in their self-ridden guilt who miss the harmony and enjoyment of life. Then, there are those who see problems but no solutions. They're making life nothing more than a chore held together by their negativity."

Crossing his arms, the young man gave Mario an irritated look and said, "You didn't tell me how you will bring liberty to captives."

He shrugged and gently said, "I never said I will bring liberty to captives. You said it. All I bring is a message that identifies where the crack is in the jailhouse door. With love, each person can liberate themselves."

The next day, after his last bread delivery to Colacci's Groceries in Corona, Mario drove to Bensonhurst to have lunch with an unshaven Joe Borelli at Carmine's Pizzeria.

"You look like hell."

Joe was wrapping spaghetti around his fork. "Hot date; but forget about that. Mario, the more I think about it, why screw with it? People would rather be in chains than set free. If they stay in chains, all they have to do is live within the limits created by their mind."

With a surprised look Mario shot back, "Hey, just when you think you have had enough, that's when you push ahead even harder. If you want to bail, that's OK."

"Oh, screw it. No more strategy, let's go kick ass," said Joe grinning.

"You are a screwball."

Not making eye contact, Joe changed the subject, "By the way, how come you gave up on Castellano? I thought he was your meal ticket to a bestseller."

"What makes you think I've given up? Maybe I should follow up on my investigation of Johnson and his Italian witch-hunt."

"You're going to be up to your eyeballs in The Strike. If there's anything I can do to help, let me know."

"That's probably a good idea. I'll take you up on it."

Joe pumped his fist in acknowledgment.

The next afternoon, Joe called Mario and in an annoyed tone said, "I still have not come to grips with how you're going to make it happen."

Mario enthusiastically replied, "Faith. That's the only thing that works. With faith you *gotta* believe: that's faith, that's Yogi Berra. Free-falling—that's faith.

"Now, Yogi Berra I understand, but that *faith* thing is another issue," Joe said chuckling.

"Did you lose part of your spine?" Mario asked jokingly.

"Mario, I'm going to kick your ass."

"Anytime."

"OK, but first meet me for a bottle of wine."

"You got it: see you down at Two-Ton Tony's."

Frank purposely flew from Chicago to New York to have a face-to-face meeting with Tony Ferrara and Mike Borelli.

On a muggy night over a glass of Chianti, Frank took a long sip and said, "Tony, I called Mike before flying in. We both agree that it's going to get ugly. But no matter the result, we stand behind Mario."

"I never doubted that."

Mike, looking perplexed, asked, "Tony, I'm curious; do you know where he's going with this thing?"

"I wish I knew. I don't, but I do know Vincenza's spending a lot of time in church."

On a nationally syndicated radio talk show, the reporter said, "There have been positive rumblings all week long about your call to join the Revolution and General Strike. How should people prepare to enter the melee?"

Mario collected his thoughts and with strong conviction said:

> *Be prepared to be persecuted.*
> *Be prepared to go to jail.*
> *Be prepared to lose your job.*
> *Be prepared to lose your friends.*

And be prepared to gain your happiness and liberty!

"Do you wish to say anything else to our listening audience?"
"Yes, . . . tomorrow is the seventh day—do it!"

JUNE 12, 1970

A headline in the *New York Journal American*
IT HAPPENED
THE GENERAL STRIKE, A DAY LIKE NO OTHER

Mario Ferrara's call for a general strike has struck the jangled nerves of the people, causing them to reverberate in a response that has surpassed anyone's wildest imagination.

Yesterday, in an air of celebration, cities and towns throughout the country were virtually brought to a standstill. Despite warnings from the police, hundreds of thousands, young and old, turned out, determined to march in protest of hidden bondage. People flooded streets carrying placards and shouting "Liberty."

The wire service reported that demonstrations across the United States were spontaneous and unorganized.

In many instances, no buses, planes, trains, or taxis moved.

Offices, factories, retail stores, schools, courts, and banks were closed.

Broadway was dark as performers took to the streets to entertain.

Hospitals, nursing homes, and emergency services operated on a maintenance-type schedule.

AAA reported that all tollbooths were vacated and service stations closed.

Newspapers, television, and radio organizations struggled to keep lines of communication open.

Movie sets shut down.

The New York and Chicago stock exchanges were vacated at noon.

It's unbelievable.

Chapter 43

June 13

The morning after The Strike began

"Tell him to stay put. I'll be at the bank in fifteen minutes," James Hennessy curtly said to Barrett's secretary.

Entering Gateway Bank, ignoring the receptionist, he went directly to Barrett's office and barged in, growling, "What in the hell are you thinking? Johnson is going to put your ass in jail."

During Hennessy's outburst, Barrett just sat back with a blank expression on his face, striking matches.

"Haven't you learned when to keep your mouth shut? I'm telling you: you're dog shit."

"James, I hope the bastard, Johnson, disappears," said Barrett, his mouth dry from anxiety.

"That, my friend, will not happen. Don't call me; I'll call you."

He turned and stomped out of the bank.

Back at his office, Hennessy was rushing to the main conference room for a meeting with Sam when he was stopped by his secretary. "Mr. Knight is on the phone."

"I'll pick it up in my office."

Taking a deep breath, he spit out, "James here."

"I'm returning your call. What's up?" Knight asked brusquely.

"Your boy Barrett is a wreck: somebody wired his office."

"I know. I wired his office."

"That was not a good move. He thinks Johnson's the culprit and wants him to disappear."

"The pinhead is right about Johnson needing to disappear. But Barrett's weak, so it's up to you, James."

"What's up to me?"

Knight gritted his teeth and said, "It's time for Johnson to take a hike and not come back."

"Lenny, if you're talking about his congressional race, that's not for another five months. If it involves anything else, I want no part of this conversation."

Knight sat at his desk cracking English walnuts and tossing the shells in an otherwise empty trashcan. As a shell plunked into the can, he said in an arrogant tone, "*Mr. Hennessy*, you are part of *this conversation* whether you like it or not. And we can continue *this conversation* when we get together for dinner Friday night. My place."

James hung up. He then called Joe Borelli and insisted, "Meet me at 2:00 p.m. in the lobby of the Plaza."

Following the blistering phone call with James, Knight dialed Barrett and in an icy tone said, "If you like your position in life, start thinking of all available options. Creativity is the name of the game. Tap your contacts and resources—but think. I told you before to think and you better think good if you enjoy breathing. And be careful what you say to Hennessy."

"But—"

"*But* nothing. Screw up and you're dead meat!" roared Knight.

The next sound Barrett heard was a dial tone. He struck a match and watched it burn until it singed his fingers. Standing, he flipped off the phone.

Sam had spent twenty-five years building a successful enterprise and was determined to avoid a collision course with a congressional investigation committee.

To divert Johnson away from Castellano Enterprises, Sam needed outside help and Joe Borelli was his man. After a half-hearted embrace, accompanied by slaps on the back, Sam filled him in on his concerns and said, "I need you to find out which corporate executives use bribery, blackmail, or payoffs to gain favors." He paused and handed him a folder. "Barrett is a perfect example. The thing that's keeping the weasel alive is bribing his auditors."

During Sam's dissertation, Joe decided not to respond.

Sam extended his hand and bluntly said, "Think in terms of dollars." Joe nodded but didn't commit.

Since Mondello, Joe had participated in a variety of business ventures, compliments of his father, and had become a master at fitting pieces together. In pursuit of Sam's goal, Joe knew his father's contacts would be invaluable to him. They would be helpful in identifying corporations fitting the profile Johnson was using in his hunt for white-collar crime. Joe was keenly aware that an inconspicuous method of obtaining information was access to personal dossiers, access that could be leveraged for substantial benefits.

Besides money, which everyone understood, Richard Barrett dumped gifts, trips, and sexual exploits into the mix. These methods of gaining favors and turning heads the other way earned him the title *King of Manipulators.* Barrett's favorite mousetrap, however, was to purchase promissory notes of politicians in financial trouble and broker them to the highest bidder.

Gateway Bank was in Joe Borelli's bull's eye. Explicit data found its way to Johnson via Beth Downing.

Watching harbor traffic from the Battery Park promenade, Joe offhandedly said, "Peep hired me to represent him at a CEO conference concerning the workplace and white-collar crime."

"Sounds interesting. Any news about your father and the Immigration Service?" asked Mario.

"Not yet. Pressure's still on. Sam finally agreed to pull some strings."

"Don't let up. Johnson shows no mercy."

Joe did not disclose the actual purpose behind his financial arrangement with Castellano.

Sam, not at all happy about a confrontational conversation he had just had with Barrett, arrived ten minutes late for a meeting with Hennessy at the DA's office.

He stood after a carefully crafted session with Hennessy. "I'm not going to let some backstabbing dickhead destroy my company," he said, barely opening his mouth.

"That's for you to take care of," said James, escorting Sam down the hall to a rear entrance. "By the way, thanks: CHEMOR's stock is off the charts."

"Don't thank me, thank Vietnam."

Sitting at a small table in the UN cafeteria, Cardinal Stanley, still upset with Susan Chou, whined, "In spite of the fiasco at the Golden Care Awards, you convinced me to let Mario Ferrara voice his opinion at the forum, and it's biting me in places I cannot say."

"With all due respect, Your Eminence, if something disturbs you, first look within and determine whether you are the cause of your own disturbance," said Susan. Her hazel eyes peered at him over her cup of coffee. The cardinal didn't know how to respond, so he simply scowled.

With legal pressure starting to build, Sam arranged a meeting with Mario at Caffè Roma and in a troubled, low voice he said, "Mario, listen to me and listen good. Watch your back."

Mario, with a stunned expression, shot back, "What!"

"I'm worried about Joe. I've heard he's close to participating in a deal with Hennessy and Barrett."

"Hey, we live in America. He can do anything he wants. I wouldn't be afraid to turn my back to him anytime day or night."

"Mario, a word to the wise is sufficient," Sam said, quickly changing the subject. "By the way, how's the book coming?"

"It's on hold. I have been preoccupied tracking The Strike. The writing is spotty; it waxes and wanes."

"Why not travel and get a firsthand look?"

"Sounds good to me, but I'm really financially stretched right now."

"Let me know how much you need, and I'll have a check ready whenever you want."

Mario hesitated a moment, shook his head, and said, "I've lost my pride. Thanks Sam. I'll take you up on your offer." Rubbing his neck, he continued, "I *did* hear what you said about Joe: I'll be careful. But for the life of me, I can't understand why Hennessy and Barrett."

"I sure as hell don't know."

"Didn't you hire Joe to attend some conference or something?"

"Not anymore," Sam said stone-faced.

It was 5:00 p.m. straight up. Mario decided to take the subway to Joe Borelli's house in Bensonhurst rather than fight rush hour traffic.

With Mike at home, Joe thought it best he and Mario walk and talk. As they made their way through the neighborhood, Joe said, "One of the things I wonder most about is how Peep is able to compartmentalize whatever the hell he's doing."

"It's a gift. Hey, I need a favor: Sam's funding a cross-country trip so I can tract The Strike. The problem—and it's a good problem—is that our bread and catering business is picking up and John could use some help."

Joe grimaced and said, "I have a problem, too: no time. I'm still working my way through company profiles."

"You're working on *what*?" he asked, surprised.

"Don't you remember the CEO conference and white-collar crime? Why? Is there anything wrong with that?"

Mario paused. "No, my mind is in ten different places. If it doesn't work, it doesn't work."

"No big deal. I'll ask Peep to give me some slack," Joe said placing his hand on Mario's shoulder.

"Finish your job first: then if you can, I would appreciate you giving John a hand."

"You got it."

On the way back from Bensonhurst, Mario decided to visit Our Lady of Loreto's Church rectory.

"Father Carelli, how's it going?"

Straining to keep his temper under control Father Carelli ignored Mario's question. He said calmly, "Mario, you indicted the churches."

Mario shook his head sadly and said, "I'm sorry you feel that way. But don't you agree there are those who get more protective of their theology the higher up the ladder they climb? They forget simplicity."

Father Carelli, placing a book on the kitchen table, sternly said, "Canon law is the law of the Church."

Mario fired back, "A law that turns people into slaves bound by words and not free in the spirit is a miserable law. I agree with Tim that the spirit is our ticket to liberty."

"But how do you think we can practically use this ticket you're talking about? Or, maybe I should say, why can't we use it if it is as easily available to us as you say?" Father Carelli asked, exasperated.

"That's not the question. The question is, why don't we use it?"

"What's the answer?" asked Father Carelli in a tone that showed that he was dubious.

"Courage! To be a braveheart, you need courage to go deep into the water and cut the cord of the mother slave ship."

Beth accepted an invitation from an overly anxious James Hennessy to lunch at Pierre's, a posh uptown restaurant. James, using all his charm, failed in his attempt to gain additional information concerning the Ferraras and Borellis.

She, in turn, failed at using her charm, working her five-foot-seven-inch, head-turning figure to the max, teasing him to gain further insight on Barrett and Knight.

Ending an afternoon of jousting for favors, they called it quits. Neither caved in to the other's whims.

Barrett placed a frantic phone call to Hennessy. "I was just served a sub-poena. That son of a bitch Johnson has me testifying before his committee on tax evasion, drug trafficking, and money laundering."

Chapter 44

June 30, 1970

T<small>HE</small> S<small>TRIKE IN</small> <small>BLOOM</small>

With Sam's financial assistance and the support of *la famigha*, Mario prepared to intermittently journey across the United States in support of The General Strike.

The first stop in Chicago was at Marcucci's Italian Restaurant on West Taylor Street where Mario had lunch with Frank Nunzi. "I spoke with your pop last night. Even though he said he wasn't worried, he's worried. Your *mamma* is worried and prays all day." Moving the plate of *vitello scaloppine ai funghi* closer, Frank frowned and said, "Catherine is worried. But her love for you gives you the freedom to do this thing."

Mario listened intently while picking away at his *insalada di stagione*.

"John, Theresa, and Carmela are worried; even the children are worried. Now me. I'm worried, but I trust your judgment. So, whatever I could do for you, I do."

His eyes tearing, Mario nodded, and smiled.

Walking along Michigan Avenue, Mario was tugged from behind by wind-blasted, fiery words.

"You seem averse to structure as well as authority of any kind: is that true?" asked a person in a pinstriped suit.

Keeping his composure, Mario turned and replied, "At times, structure is an impediment to liberty. As far as authority is concerned, many times it is entrenched in institutionalized intellect rather than reality."

"That response seems pointed and without a solution. Can you elaborate on what you just said?"

Mario obliged, replying, "At times, those in authority become insensitive to life and are caught in a maze of entanglement. So, instead of a foundation of love, we find one of hypocrisy and hardness of heart."

"What's your suggestion?" asked the person in the pinstriped suit.

"We must shed the ego."

"Bullshit!" snapped the person in the pinstriped suit as she turned her back and strutted off.

"Do you really think people can buck the system?" asked a truck driver whose stomach rolled over his belt.

Mario replied, "Everyone is a dominant force on earth. No one is bigger or better. No one is greater or superior. We're all on an equal playing field."

Scratching his head, he asked, "Don't you ever want to get off your soapbox? People have been trying to change society for thousands of years. Total equity. That's a tall order. Jesus Christ couldn't do it, what makes you think you can?"

Mario smiled and replied, "I didn't say I could. All I can do is what I'm able to do."

At O'Hare Airport, Mario, answering a frustrated advertising representative, said, "Yes, you will be inconvenienced, but don't be intimidated. This is not a popularity contest."

The young African American gave him a skeptical look and asked, "How in the world can you convince hate groups to love?"

Mario nodded and said, "It is beyond my comprehension how anyone can wish to live a life comprised of hate. The Kennedys, King, and Gandhi, just to name a few, were victims of hate. The thought of hate makes me tremble and feel terribly sad. But I know you can't fight them by mirroring their hate, using violence against violence. The only way I know is to bring flowers and love them."

"That seems like an awful waste of good flowers."

"Maybe. But, I don't think so," said Mario smiling. He took a deep breath and in a firm voice rolled on, "So, I implore all men and women to rid themselves of hate, built-up prejudices, pride, greed, and blindness to the injustices that are created on earth. Isn't it about time that all the words and pledges of all institutions and structures have a common goal—that all work diligently toward creating a better world?"

"Count me in the revolution," she said hugging him.

A gentleman, fiddling with the thinning hair he had combed across the top of his head, spat out, "Idealist."

Mario shot back, "No. Realist!"

The gentleman scoffed and said, "Give it a rest." Then he stomped off.

Mario shouted out after him, "Wait, please wait. One more thing: I hope that all the actions I spoke of have no other motives than the love of one another."

A robust man wearing bright blue suspenders said to his wife, "This guy makes Blackbeard look like a saint. He is a rogue and should be dealt with accordingly."

Before boarding his flight to Los Angeles, he called Catherine, "So far so good. Nobody's throwing tomatoes—yet."

"Just be careful; I love you."

"I love you too."

On Wilshire Boulevard in Beverly Hills, Mario was having a conversation with a financial officer from a Fortune 500 firm located in Southern California. "There are many corporations that depend on each other for loyalty. They rely on longtime friends and supporters before undertaking any radical action."

In response the young executive grabbed Mario's arm and asked boldly, "Are you so perfect that you've never screwed up?"

"I have messed up more times than I care to remember. I only hope I have enough humility to own up to my mistakes and swallow my pride." He paused, waiting for the roar of a motorcycle to pass. "I'm not asking anyone to go beyond his or her capabilities. Just do what you feel you're capable of doing. Nothing more. Experience is achieved by experiment." Mario leaned toward the young man and in a low menacing whisper said, "Please be so kind to let go of my arm."

As he turned away a crazed, well-dressed, middle-aged woman ran up and attempted to spray Mario with red paint. She was shouting, "Communist! You red bastard!"

She missed, hitting the young executive instead.

Mario kept talking.

A frustrated businessman holding three folded newspapers under his arm asked, "Why do corporations and companies prostitute themselves for gain?"

With a look of bewilderment Mario replied, "*Why do some corporations and companies prostitute themselves for gain?* You just answered your own question." He shrugged his shoulders and said, "My question is, what reward awaits companies of greater size that use unscrupulous methods to crush smaller competitors or use their power for hostile takeovers and leveraged buyouts?"

Leaning against the wall, he rolled his eyes and continued, "In the world of business, you have the worst of the worst. Price gouging and unsafe or shoddy merchandise paves the roadway to bottom-line profits." He grinned, and added, "And then you have the best of the best, those that not only fulfill their obligation in the workplace but also financially support countless sectors of society, including religious communities, homeless shelters, food banks, safe-houses: the list is endless."

The businessman asked, "So what is the end result?"

Mario hesitated, slowly shook his head, and softly said, "The end result of all that may be accomplished will not last unless love, and only love, is the driving force behind the acts."

Barrett called Hennessy and invited him to lunch.

"Can't do: I'm jammed. What's up?"

Spewing contempt, Barrett said, "I cannot believe people are flocking to Ferrara's cause. He's promised nothing but rejection, hard work, and maybe jail."

"Don't worry about it. The *wop* is marching right toward a propeller blade."

"I hope your crystal ball is right."

"Two crystal balls. Sam called and said he heard from Joe that Mario is out of control. Now go make some loans and let me get back to work."

Barrett was not convinced. "We should accelerate his march to the propeller blade."

"Please. Go back to work," a rankled Hennessy bellowed.

While shaking cigar ashes off his dark brown suit Barrett nervously said, "Wait a second, what about our deal? Is Borelli's old man going to export our drugs to Italy, or not? What the hell is going on? Knight is all over my ass."

Mario took a short respite at home, then took a train to Washington, DC. Somewhere along Constitution Avenue, a gray-haired woman leaning on her cane asked Mario, "Do you feel more secure in your comments after last night's enthusiastic crowd at the Washington Hilton."

"Strength in numbers doesn't mean anything, except to the weak-minded," Mario said smiling. "This is not about winning or losing: it's about doing."

In front of the Lincoln Memorial, a man standing over six feet tall with Stetson hat in hand, said with malice, "I recognize you from television coverage of last night's conference. I'm from Texas and you have just found trouble."

Unnerved by the man, Mario appeared to be studying the marvelous statue of Lincoln. He said, "There is no place to hide from truth. Living truth may bring trouble, but I say, *So!*"

"You're lucky that gun laws in Washington are strict."

"Mr. Texas-man, Sir, guns should be under strict control every-where."

"I could live with that," said one of the women with the Texan.

"Let me ask you, war or preparation for war, which one is the greater calamity?" asked the young Texan.

"If you'd ever experienced war, you would be able to answer that yourself," answered Mario glaring at him.

With a sour expression on his face he fired back, "If I were you, I'd watch my back."

"If you were me, you would be free of fear. Then you wouldn't worry about watching your back."

"Before this is all over, you're going to beg for mercy."

"From you?"

The man moved toward him, grabbed his arm, and proudly said, "From those who care about righteousness."

"Do they understand justice?"

Standing nose to nose, the Texan said through tight jaws, "They will get you. You are a dead man."

Mario shrugged. "Tell them, or *they*, whoever you think *they* are, that *they* can kiss *my* ass in Macy's window," he said and yanked his arm away from the man's tightening grip.

Walking down the memorial's steps, a young woman who identified herself as a reporter for *Viewpoint*, a monthly magazine, asked, "Mr. Ferrara, what's your opinion as it relates to cruelty to animals?"

He tipped his fedora and said, "Please don't call me *Mr. Ferrara*: call me Mario. Now in answer to your question, manufacturers notorious for exploitation of animals need to be treated with rigor mortis of the wallet. You know who they are; boycott their products. Strike and shut them down."

On the way back to New York, Mario stopped off in Philadelphia. Outside the Cathedral Basilica of Saint Peter and Saint Paul on Race Street, a priest pointing his finger sternly at Mario said, "You're not being fair in your assessment of good hearts."

"*Good hearts* you say. *Good hearts* would reach out to all people of all religious traditions," Mario said and walked away shaking his head in disbelief.

A man struggling with pocket folders holding numerous manila files stood in front of him. He was staring at Mario with a scowl on his face. The man growled, "Religion is the moral fiber of our country."

Rubbing his forehead, Mario sympathetically asked, "Are you so preoccupied with sterile sermons and the word *religion?*" Raising his voice, he continued, "I think the word *religion* should be struck from the dictionary. All anyone would have to do is look up the word *confusion* and get the same definition. Why not break the fetters of religious institutions? If each person listens to the small voice within, they will know what to do—even if they have to stand alone for what they believe."

Mario turned around to acknowledge a middle-aged woman wearing bright purple high heels who was tapping her feet impatiently. He asked, "Did I hear you correctly? You ask, who is my God? I did not know God belonged to anyone, but instead to everyone." He tilted back his fedora, wiped his brow, and said, "It's time to dismantle the concrete bunkers of religious segregation and captivity and rebuild with infinite love, unity, and liberty."

"You have broken every rule under the sun. Don't you think you have gone far enough?" asked a woman with expressionless eyes who had just finished taking a photo.

"Let me answer your question with a question. Am I breaking the rules of tradition, or am I just not accepting these rules?" Mario said. And after hesitating a moment, he blurted, "Another thing: is it more important to keep rules or be kind and thoughtful to others?"

The woman bristled.

Overhearing a heated conversation that was taking place to his far right, Mario decided to approach the small group that had gathered.

Mario joined in the discussion and declared, "With certainty I can tell you that excessive pride, conceit, and arrogance permeate fundamentalism. Too bad fundamentalists have no respect for human dignity and continue to grow fat with money by exploiting innocent people."

Chapter 45

July 1970

ON THE NEWSWIRES

In an answer to a question by a newspaper reporter from *The New York Journal American*, Mario said:

> *In government, it's possible that staff can literally stonewall anyone from getting anything accomplished. In many instances, they become the vessels of power. Consequently, protection of civil service status can turn nice people into not-so-nice people. In that event, why not eliminate their cloak of security and give those who care the opportunity to work and fire those nasty bastards who don't? And let's not forget those who have an insatiable appetite for power, commonly called the power brokers.*

An article in the magazine *Grow* discussed a farmer's approach to making things right:

It appears there actually is a farmer who collected weapons of war and turned them into tools for farming. In an interview with our Tom Girard, the farmer stated: "I figured, what the hell? We sure tried everything else. My grandkids are my concern and where we're heading doesn't look good. I love'em and want'em to grow old. I'm asking my neighbors to turn their swords into plowshares. I can tell you something real simple. If all military everywhere rid themselves of weapons, then there will be no more war."

He continued, "And by the way, while we're at it, help me put pressure on the city folks for clean air. I sure as hell like looking up at the stars at night and quenching my thirst with good water. Oh, I might add a little bourbon . . . but of course, only for medicinal purposes."

A story in the *Omaha Daily* featured a move among a number of farmers to rid themselves of surplus crops by distributing them among the poor. Their pledge, "No child will go hungry," spread throughout the farming community. The story quoted a longtime farmer, Noel Bartlett, as saying, "The farmer doesn't need a law to understand the dignity and sacredness of the land."

A female reporter for *Round The Clock*, a twenty-four hour all news radio station located in Boston, reported the following:

There doesn't appear to be any systematic approach to Ferrara's Strike in a cause of liberty. It seems driven by grass roots and may I add . . . wild grass.

News bulletin

At Berkley, protestors were out of control and the National Guard was called out.

Ferrara blasted participants on both sides. "Their participation in this event was inexcusable. Both sides shed blood in a flagrant disregard for the process of liberty, love, and nonviolence."

A freelance journalist reported the following:

Mario Ferrara was arrested for disturbing the peace in Newark, New Jersey. The judge, before sentencing, rebuked him. "You, sir, are a glutton for punishment."

Ferrara replied, "Your Honor, I am what I am. I don't hide behind any law. And I don't give a damn about rules and regulations if they break the law of life."

The judge countered, "My dear man, you are impossible and arrogant. The judicial system rules."

And Mario responded, "That's your opinion, Your Honor."

To the surprise of all those in the courtroom, the judge decided to give him a suspended sentence.

Outside the courthouse, a taxicab driver yelled, "Hey, Mario, aren't you worried someone may put a bullet in your head?"

"That's a perfect spot; I got a hard head," Ferrara roared back.

The taxicab driver laughed.

In an editorial, it was reported in the *Madison Ledger:*

> *Young and old alike have acted on Ferrara's assertions and are picket-*
> *ing insurance companies that sweep their responsibilities under the rug*
> *and ignore legitimate claims while continuing to raise premiums indis-*
> *criminately.*
>
> *The police have been present in each instance to keep order.*
>
> *Ferrara smirked and said, "Whatever you do . . . do not make a*
> *claim, or your policy will be cancelled."*

The *Denver Times* exposed an oil and gas company price-fixing scheme that had Wyoming reeling. The reality of that ugly situation sparked public outrage. Truckers joined in forming a chain of trucks around a number of refineries creating a blockade.

Chapter 46

July 27, 1970

In the early morning hours, a rock was thrown through the front window of Ferrara's Grocery and Bakery, barely missing a customer. The word spread quickly through the neighborhood and somehow reached a reporter from Channel Seven.

"Mr. Ferrara, did you hear your sister's comment last evening?"

"No," said John, standing in the door.

Holding a handheld recorder the reporter said, "Let me play it for you."

He heard Carmela say earnestly, "It doesn't matter what you say or what you do to my brother. He will love you. It's true that he's been arrested numerous times, but Mario doesn't wear down. If anything, it fires him up to prove that the message of love can wear down your bitterest enemy."

John stared at the reporter and in a confident voice said, "Mario's tough. Sometimes he goes against his own words, but I know he's constantly trying to temper his emotions with love. Me, on the other hand, I'm a major step behind him." He paused. With his voice rising a bit he said, "So, if you threaten my brother, sister, or my family, my first thought is going to be to beat the hell out of you; then I think of Mario and cry."

The reporter looked into the television camera, bewildered and said, "I don't know if I really understand what John Ferrara just said."

Mario was ambling up Broadway toward Saint Paul's Church when a minister blocking his way growled, "You talk about unity for a common cause. Yet, there are so many religions and so many factions within religions that it's impossible to achieve your perception of the world as a Utopia."

Mario couldn't help but smile and in a conciliatory tone said: "I agree with the first part of your statement. And what you say about factions is true of governments, as well: each is protective of their respective domains." He hesitated to collect his thoughts before continuing, "So, we either cut our wrists or we believe our ability to reach unity is in the diversity that exists. And if we believe, we then can create a society inspired by God, through love."

"It will never happen because there's too much sin in the heart of man," said the minister bluntly as he stepped aside.

A visiting cardinal from the Midwest stood by silently with his arms folded. He finally questioned Mario. "By what authority do you speak?" he asked firmly.

In a surprised tone, Mario answered, "I speak from the same authority that you speak."

Frowning, the cardinal said, "My good fellow, are not all men accountable before God? Should they not fear God in repentance and faith to receive salvation?"

"Doesn't that mean men and woman alike are responsible and accountable to one another?"

"You tell me how that can be accomplished."

"With love in the human and divine of who we are."

"How do you know whether it's the human or the divine responding to the task at hand?" inquired the cardinal.

Leaning against a light pole, Mario answered calmly, "If it's the will of God, you will know because the will of God is reflected in liberty which is devoid of fear."

"But, fear is subjective and sin can be conducted in liberty," the cardinal said, tapping his foot impatiently.

"In liberty there is no fear, only unconditional love. So how can sin be conducted in liberty?"

"Sin cannot be dismissed so lightly."

"We no longer are slaves to your definition of sin."

Agitated by the statement, the cardinal said, "You need to be concerned about sin. God speaks of sin, and you don't want to be dammed, do you?"

Reaching out to him, Mario softly said, "Christ lives in the light of liberty, and liberty is without the shackles of guilt. And if you put on Christ, you will know what you're allowed not to do."

The cardinal glared at Mario and gravely said, "To trust judgment without guilt doesn't work."

"Guilt is bondage. In liberty, if one falls, forgiveness saves."

"Then you agree when sin enters the soul, one should seek confession for forgiveness?" asked the cardinal, as he gave Mario an irritated look.

"Before I respond, I wish to ask you a few questions." Keeping his composure he respectfully asked: "Isn't it true when talk turns to sin, we immediately wonder whether we're good or bad? Didn't Christ say, 'Let the one among you who is sinless be the first to throw a stone?' Who is sinless anyway?" Moving closer to the cardinal, he continued. "So I say, the simple act of repenting, seeking forgiveness, and forgiving others frees the soul not only of the harmed, but of all people."

The cardinal ignored Mario's questions and impatiently asked, "What do you mean when you say all are free?"

Mario sighed and said in a positive tone, "Thoughts, choices, decisions, and actions not only affect the individual, but the community at large, indeed the entire earth. Therefore, if we don't forgive and accept forgiveness, we are all held together in bondage. Then again, if we forgive and accept forgiveness, we are free."

"Is that reality?" asked the cardinal stroking his salt-and-pepper beard.

"You can answer that for yourself. But, why not create a state of mind that speaks to forgiveness and not sin? Forgive self first; then see other people in yourself and forgive them. Because when you forgive yourself, you become blind to sin."

The cardinal took umbrage at Mario's comments and said indignantly, "Religion is reality! A measuring rod of right and wrong."

"Religion has been made a profession; otherwise, there would be no need for the word *laity*." Mario paused and said matter-of-factly, "We just need to live in the light of love."

Becoming even more annoyed the cardinal asked, "How do you know the light you speak of is the right light?"

With a wide smile Mario radiated enthusiasm and said, "The light of love is the light of God."

"I will pray for you," said the cardinal, turning to walk away.

Mario tipped his fedora and kindly said, "Thank you, Your Eminence, and *I* will pray for *you*."

Standing close by was a woman who identified herself as a parochial school teacher from Florida. "Why do you persist in condemning the institutionalized church?"

"I speak my mind. Church or no church. What can they do to me? Take away my heart?"

"Shouldn't you have respect for those in authority?"

"Do they have authority over my heart? I don't think so. As long as I try to live love, I'll be indifferent to human opinion and not let anything or anybody push me. Therefore, a person's stature or human approval means nothing to me."

"I'll pray for you."

"Thank you and I'll pray for you as well."

"I have heard enough. I demand you stop preaching the ways of God," said an impeccably dressed man gritting his teeth.

"You judge for yourself whether it is right for me to obey you or my heart. Oops, another question. Do the laws of religion hypnotize you?"

"You will be condemned to hell."

"I've been there: I thought I recognized you. Didn't I see you there?"

An elderly gentleman raising his hand-carved cane spoke in a tone that indicated his skepticism at Mario's attempt to change things. "People are people. They have heard these words before and still don't know what the hell to do."

Looking directly at him, Mario responded with confidence, "Yes, that's the challenge. To let them know that they already know all they will ever need to know. You can strategize, have philosophical discussions, establish doctrines, and take notice of myths. But, I wonder, if in the process we miss the simple understanding and result of loving one another." Mario took a deep breath, "You see, there's a natural impulse and mutual advantage to helping one another. So, whether or not we interact with one another, we affect one another. If one person gains, everyone gains; on the other hand, if one person loses, everyone loses. That's a plain and simple fact. So bear one another's burdens and joys."

"Yeah, yeah. Give us some more of your bullshit. I need to fertilize my lawn," said a woman in a dark gray three-piece suit.

"*Scusi*," said Mario amused, "no bullshit to fertilize lawns. Just seeds of love. But, if that's what you think, that's your choice."

"You don't know what the hell you're talking about," cried out a man holding on to his hairpiece as a gust of wind buffeted the area. He hesitated and then, pointing at Mario, angrily fired off another salvo, "You are going to get a lightning bolt up your ass."

Mario looked bewildered by the man's outburst and peacefully replied, "Eh? You say I should worry about the wrath of God? I don't think so: God is love. Love brings joy and frees the soul. So you see? There is no wrath—only love."

An investigative reporter from the *Washington Herald* caught up with Congressman R. J. Johnson at the Capital and said, "Ferrara, playing off the word *liberty*, has launched a major assault against our nation's strongest institutions. What's your personal take on his campaign?"

Stuffing the wrapping of a Clark candy bar in his pocket, he said in frustration, "He's a cruel human being who preys on the unsuspecting.

The poor folks who don't have the slightest clue on how to protect themselves are in much need of assistance."

"What about the Borellis?"

"No comment."

"What about Gateway Bank and Richard Barrett?"

"No comment."

Two older gentlemen waiting for a bus at Lexington Avenue and Fifty-fourth Street were casually talking with each other.

The taller one, rubbing his chin, said: "Awhile back, Mario said, 'Companies that abuse, threaten, or discriminate against employees should face a sit-in or sick-out.' His words especially affected the good-old-boy network. In my company memos flew everywhere to head off any possible disruption."

The other man, with wrinkled brow, added, "Interesting. In my company, within the circle of power, intimidation became the word of the day. Speaking of group action, a vice president in a heated exchange with an employee barked, 'Try it and we'll starve you and those other slimeballs into submission.' The immigrant worker, not backing off spat back, 'When it comes to liberty . . . you're not the boss over me.'"

At the Arch in Washington Square Park, Mario, making eye contact with a woman who was prancing about, said in a lighthearted tone, "You seem anxious to speak."

The petite young woman quickly responded, "At a coffee shop in Albuquerque, a waitress made a simple mistake on a meal ticket. The proprietor humiliated her by shouting at the top of his lungs, and she responded with red-faced silence and tears.

"Noticing the incident, a young construction worker put on his jacket and walked out; others soon followed. Within minutes most patrons left the restaurant, accompanied by wait staff, hostess, and cooks. A defiant owner stood outside and flipped the group off.

"The tension was relieved when an elderly woman dropped her cane, then her drawers, and mooned him."

Mario smiled. "Very interesting story. Were you there?"

"My mother was the waitress."

A young man wearing tattered jeans with a guitar flung over his shoulder said, "Mario's just like a little kid, full of enthusiasm. As many times as I have heard him, I have never heard him compromise his viewpoint when it comes to unity. Defiance, courage, and love—that's Mario."

His girlfriend, who had long blonde hair and a gentle smile, responded, "He may be a minority; you and me may be a minority: but majorities always follow the actions of minorities."

AUGUST 5

A business editorial in *FINANCE* magazine

> *At a Rotary luncheon in Boston, Massachusetts, Mario Ferrara was asked his opinion regarding the banking industry. After a blistering attack on Gateway Bank, he continued his response, "I ask, what good is a bank if it uses insider information for undue gain, charges exorbitant fees, and takes advantage without conscience? Why not eliminate these vacuum cleaners?" Staying at the podium he fired out a final salvo, "Another question: why don't we demand that those in banking who are driven by self-importance attend the school of Mr. and Ms. Manners?" Some attendees laughed; others swiftly left the luncheon.*

Congressman Johnson, during an interview at LaGuardia Airport, commented on Ferrara's statement. Putting out his cigarette, he nodded in assent and said, "I somewhat agree with him in regard to banks. However, in my opinion, he's carrying this liberty-thing too far. His approach to problem solving is based on naiveté. He's a disgrace to America. I'm embarrassed to know him."

The reporter, pressing, said, "How do you answer Mario's accusation that Gateway Bank in New York is king manipulator of the financial world and baits the piranha that feed on people?"

He cleared his throat, lit up another cigarette, and said: "I can't speak to his statement; but I can speak to specific issues, such as fraud, money laundering, and tax evasion. I pledge to the American people that any financial institution caught engaging in criminal activity of any kind will be punished to the full extent of the law. Trust me. Indictments will be issued."

During a deposition James Hennessy was interrupted by a telephone call from Richard Barrett. It was his fifth attempt to reach him.

Barrett was stabbing at a loan portfolio with a letter opener.

"Ferrara is a son of a bitch. Did you hear what he said about the bank?" he snarled.

"You dragged me out of a deposition for that?"

"It's important."

"Only in your mind. He's still just a gnat on an elephant's ass. You need to worry about Johnson and his investigative committee, not Ferrara," James said. He was looking at his watch.

"Lenny would like to send both of them on a trip up the river of no return."

Losing his patience, Hennessy barked, "What the hell do you want me to do about it?"

"You know Lenny and his nasty personality," Barrett said as he grimaced. He had inadvertently stabbed his finger with the letter opener.

"Have Sam Castellano call him. He thinks Peep walks on water."

"Good idea. Sorry for the interruption, James; I'm having a hard time sleeping lately." Barrett hung up, closed his eyes, and sucked on his wounded finger.

AUGUST 7

A reporter from Radio Station WKNY interviewed Mario outside the New York Stock Exchange. Deep into the interview the reporter challenged Mario.

Reporter: *Mr. Ferrara, I disagree with your assessment of the press. The press is most objective when it reports on the financial marketplace.*

Mario: *Don't give me that crap! There are a number of newspapers that are notorious for manipulation and fabrication of half-truths and untruths. They are the slime that should lose half if not all their circulation. I challenge those who work in the industry to walk off the job where untruth is present.*

Reporter: *Alright, let's change direction. Do you think business can really change?*

Mario: *If the business community changes, the world changes. Business supports all of society: politics, media, religion, government, education. The list is endless.*

Reporter: *You're placing a great deal of credence on business.*

Mario: *The business community tears down and builds, it destroys and creates. It is ruthless and it is full of heart.*

Reporter: *That's a most confusing statement.*

Mario: *Not really. It's all about choices. So, will the heart of business slip into the inferno, or will it understand with its heart and accept its inherent and trusted responsibility?*

Reporter: *That's a lot of—*

Mario: *Please let me finish! On the other hand, if we can look beyond the concrete pyramids that harbor self-proclaimed pharaohs, we might be able to catch a glimpse of our heart.*

Reporter: *That might be a push.*

Mario: *Maybe. Still, I can't help but wonder if just a single individual changed, then, wouldn't the world change?*

Later that same afternoon the reporter interviewed Sam Castellano.

Reporter: *What is your opinion of Mario Ferrara's statements regarding the investment community?*

Sam: *To some degree, he's correct. It's a mixed bag. There are some investment bankers who are expert market makers and then there are the manipulators, the bulldogs. They juggle and create a market by inflating stock prices for their own monetary advantage, not caring about anything or anyone. They are engaged in get-rich-quick schemes, fueled by insider trading and conspiracy. I guess that's what Mario was talking about.*

Sam had no sooner returned from a meeting with Leonard Knight when his phone rang. It was Mario calling from Tony's office. "I heard the radio interview. Thanks for your support."

"No thanks needed. I only spoke the truth," Sam said. He was reading his messages.

"Say hello to Rose for me."

"Sure will. On second thought, I would accept a thank you in the form of a favor, Mario."

"Fire away!"

"You're creating a lot of heat on Wall Street. Out of fear of scrutiny, takeovers and mergers have been stifled." Sam took Mario off the speakerphone and continued, "Unfortunately, one transaction that was shut down cold was a multi-million dollar merger our company was brokering. I need your help. I would appreciate you letting up on Wall Street and going after something else for a while."

"That's a hard call."

"If I could conclude that transaction, I could make it worth your while. You would be able to write forever."

Rubbing his forehead, he uttered, "Sorry, I can't do it."

"Just thought I'd ask," said Sam shifting papers from one part of his desk to another. "No problem."

Tilting his chair backwards, Mario said, "Let me ask you a question. What's happening with Johnson's investigation into Castellano Enterprises and the Caymans?"

"Right now all is quiet."

"I don't know, Peep: Joe has told me enough horror stories about Hennessy and Johnson becoming strange bed-fellows. If I were you, I'd watch my flank."

Sam took off his glasses, rubbed his eyes and mumbled, "Thanks."

Knight, still smarting from Mario's scathing assaults on Gateway, phoned Barrett at 10:00 a.m. "Meet me for lunch at Pierre's. Right now."

Forty minutes later Knight was sitting across from Barrett, his face red with anger. He said, "You better do something about Ferrara. He's a piece of shit."

Barrett chewed on an unlit cigar. "What do you want me to do?" he asked.

"Get a Quija Board and figure it out!" growled Knight. He grabbed the cigar out of Barrett's mouth, violently crushing it on the table in front of them. "Call James Hennessy. Call Sam Castellano. I want this son of a bitch shut up!"

"But—"

"Don't be *butting* me again," Knight said. He shoved his tobacco-riddled salad aside. "Castellano makes a ton of money off our stock and bond transactions. He's got Ferrara's confidence. Tell him to use his brain to stop this troublemaking bastard or I . . . never mind."

Both men fell silent.

Knight's face was still flushed. In a loud whisper, he said, "Why in the hell can't you think of a way to entice Sam to help us? Give him a bigger piece of our offshore banking deal with Hennessy. Give him your piece."

Again both men went quiet.

"What?—no *buts*?" Knight snarled.

Barrett, perspiring profusely, sat in a comatose state.

"And of all people, Sam should be able to pull out all stops to turn this bastard into a wanted criminal. He owes me big time and I'm getting tired of negative results."

Out of Cuban cigars, Barrett began chewing on a pen.

"Say something, you dumb shit," Knight shouted, slamming his fist down. Heads turned.

"But—"

"I'll tell you a *but*. *But*—if Ferrara is not stopped, you're more than finished. I expect a call by tomorrow evening."

Back at Gateway Bank, his lips blue from a leaking pen, Barrett called Sam and James and left identical messages on their home phones. "I hate to tell you this, but you have a colossal problem with Lenny. Call me."

Upon arriving back at his uptown office, Knight called Hennessy and left a message, "James, it's Knight; I've had it!"

AUGUST 10

An editorial comment from the *San Francisco Gazette*

> *Through sacrifice and inconvenience comes light. People have begun to recognize one another in the interconnectedness of human life. Family has resurrected. Over dinner, parents and children are actually talking with one another.*
>
> *Yet, an interesting dynamic is taking place. Although the average person is making a difference, in a number of instances friend has turned against friend and family member against family member. Lifestyles are affected and inconvenience is commonplace.*

Congressman R. J. Johnson granted an interview to the magazine *Art Today*. It took place at his recently acquired historic brownstone in Greenwich Village. The trade publication was preparing a feature article about this high-powered politician who had an extraordinary talent for painting.

In his home studio, among the clutter of artists' brushes, canvases, easels, and paints stood Johnson's beautiful streetscapes. Midway though the interview for this human-interest article, the topic changed from paint to Mario Ferrara and the General Strike.

The congressman, breathing heavily, said, "I feel sorry for Mr. Ferrara. In the beginning, I thought him a kind man, albeit a man frustrated about the state of society. Now I see him as an anarchist, an irrational and desperate human being who has gone to the extreme in his zeal for liberty. I was there at Caffe Reggio and heard him speak. The man has lost his mind."

The reporter accepted a piece of chocolate from the congressman. "Can you tell us about your disagreement with Richard Barrett?" he asked.

"If you're referring to last week's meeting of the *Congressional Committee on Banking and Money Laundering*, it wasn't anything substantial," he said with his mouth full of cherry pie.

"You don't think his statement 'Washington's impaired brain and snooping eyes are gravely deficient' could be considered substantial?"

"No comment," said Johnson opening a storage closet stuffed to the brim with art supplies.

Chapter 47

Interwoven in the Revolution of Liberty were turncoats, those who acted and took part in the General Strike except when threatened monetarily or intimidated socially. Then, they simply bailed out.

As usual with any high profile protest, it provides an excuse for the hoodlum element to emerge. The General Strike had shifted into a bedlam-riddled debacle with bands of thugs roaming the streets, turning over automobiles, attacking people indiscriminately, torching churches and businesses, and looting stores—all recorded for everyone to witness.

AUGUST 18, 1970

Mario commented on the criminal element in a telephone interview. "It is disheartening to see the smiling faces of thieves running through the darkness of night. Although, in the midst of madness, you can always count on the fire department and a strong cadre of police to quell civil insurrection." Mario lowered his head and gave a deep sigh. "It's a sad commentary: time and again, it's mostly the innocent who are injured, be it monetarily, physically, or spirituality."

During the last couple of months, the pandemonium took a mental and physical toll on Mario.

A major television network requested that Mario participate in an exclusive interview to be conducted by a distinguished moderator.

Mario agreed.

It just so happened the program aired the Sunday following a volatile DC protest. The Revolution's General Strike was deteriorating by the minute.

The program had barely begun when Mario calmly said, "I want to thank everyone who joined the Revolution and supported the General Strike. You are true bravehearts. Now in retrospect, I think I may have made a mistake."

Shifting in his chair, he took a deep breath. "The great experiment is over! I'm sick to my stomach over the riots and general unrest. Hooligans have pushed the patience of law enforcement to the brink." Holding his forehead he said dejectedly, "Abuse of liberty has made us all losers. I'm weary of the struggle: the powerful still wanting to maintain control at any cost. I'm weary of encouraging people to stop creating structures that ultimately lead to egotistical pyramids." His voice became raspy. Looking weak, he reached for a glass of water.

"Do you wish to continue?" asked the moderator, who stopped glancing at his prepared questions.

"Yes I would, thank you." Setting the glass of water down, he continued, "The thought process behind forming an organization is usually grounded in goodness. Then enters ego and self-righteousness and all good thoughts go clear to hell. From the beginning of time we have organized and reorganized."

"What do you consider the major problem?"

"Separation! Separation of entities by name creates separation of entities in reality. We need to let go of all titles and not replace the entities in existence today with other entities that someday will turn to power seeking."

"Where do you begin?"

"Nowhere. Everywhere. So this morning I made the decision to do nothing."

"Excuse me? It seems as though you have forgotten all the good that people have accomplished. Every day at the news desk we hear good things," said the interviewer.

"If you hear good things, why do you focus on bad things? Besides, I have not forgotten the good that people achieve. Though, I don't believe there's a need to reward a natural act other than with a simple thank-you."

His voice breaking a bit, Mario explained his new view of change: "Catherine, my beautiful wife, is right. The experiment proved you cannot change society quickly. It takes time; it takes one person at a time living every act in the Divine. Liberty or slavery. It's a choice of the individual, a choice with or without love."

"That's a major shift in your position."

"It is what it is."

The reporter, raising his eyebrows, said, "You do realize there's been much rhetoric about love. And now the word *love* is opened to much interpretation. You could go insane trying to accomplish the impossible?"

"Not really. Originally, I questioned my sanity and began to doubt everything. I still believe that if you shed the past and live in the moment, time is on the side of love. Pure, unconditional love will lead to a spiritual journey of inner peace and ultimate liberty.

"The Strike is not even three months old. You spoke of persistence, never giving up: what you're saying now is inconsistent with your challenge."

"The only thing that's consistent is love and truth. I'm not afraid to say I was wrong on a number of counts. The one assertion that I was not wrong in making was that the fire of love carries enormous energy."

"I'm sure you're aware of the protest in Washington, DC that turned vile when fire hoses were used against demonstrators. I'd like to get your reaction to a chant echoed that unfortunate day. Let me play it for you and our audience."

Mario sat listening to voices blaring from the studio's speakers. "Ain't no power, like people power . . . Ain't no power, like people power."

The moment the tape stopped, Mario, wincing, said in disgust, "I reject the word *power* because power begets power. New power exists or is created to control those who had power. Even the lowest of the low in character has power today."

"What's the solution?"

Excitedly he shouted, "Love! The answer is love. Love transcends reason and is both the subtlest and the strongest force in the world. If each person listens to the small voice within, they will know what to do, even if they have to stand alone for what they believe."

Mario, leaning on the interviewer's table, insisted, "My faith is as strong as ever. Yes, I do have haunting memories of the past three months that I'll take with me. I also have very sweet memories from this experience to carry with me into the future."

"Where will you be going?"

Mario smiled and said, "Little Italy. Where else?"

After the newscast, Sam reached Mario at home. "You did the right thing. I was proud of you. Now that it's over, I can tell you firsthand your buddies Hennessy and Barrett were intent on burying you like they buried Tim. They were the ones who tipped off Congressman Johnson about Tim's Together Foundation and spread rumors about the Borellis. Further, through my grapevine, I found out Johnson was ready to label you a subversive of the United States Government. The only good news I have is that Cardinal Stanley has a case of laryngitis."

"Peep, those three miserable bastards should do all society a favor and off themselves," said Mario. He was stretched out on the floor of his apartment listening to Frank Sinatra's "That's Life."

"Let's grab a bite next week," Sam said sounding upbeat.

"Sounds good. But if we're going to talk about those scumbags again, I better bring a barf bag."

Minutes after the newscast ended, Barrett called James. "I knew the *wop* would wear down. He and his great ideals have crumbled."

"I agree. Now we continue to feed the media poison and sway public opinion. Then we cut him at the knees and crush him into the earth," Hennessy said.

"I like that. I'll call Sam Castellano," Barrett quickly offered.

He didn't quite get James's final comment "Don't! Let me do it." It was muffled because Hennessy's face was buried in his young lady's breast.

Barrett hung up and dialed Sam.

"Right now is the time to bash Ferrara's skull in," Barrett cried out in a threatening tone.

"What in the hell are you talking about?" demanded Sam.

"You know. You should want to lead the pack. Ferrara hasn't done jack-shit in helping you. Remember? He screwed up one of your vital mergers, costing you millions." Lighting his Cuban cigar, Barrett continued, "Besides, I just spoke to James; he agrees that it's time we stop screwing around and bury the bastard."

Sam, in an intimidating voice, said, "Tell you what. Go play in the street with broken glass and let me talk to Hennessy. In the meantime, keep your mouth shut."

"You can't talk to me like that," Barrett said biting down on his cigar.

"I just did. Now be a good little boy and take your hostility to the street."

"What the hell? Knight wants Mario crushed and Johnson off my back. We have a deal."

"Let me tell you something," said Sam, grinding his teeth, "and you had better listen if we're going to stay partners: the next time I hear Johnson's name mentioned, I pull all my accounts, spread the word to my associates, and they pull all their accounts—and guess what: Lenny will forget all about Mario."

"It was that friggin' Borelli who tipped Johnson."

"I'm taking care of Joe. Leave him to me and please shut up. Please!" Sam hung up and called Joe.

"Tell me again about Johnson and Barrett," Sam said anxiously.

After giving a short rundown on his assessment of the situation, Joe blew up. "Barrett screwed me over in Mondello, so I returned the favor by leading Johnson to Gateway's watering hole. Johnson's witch-hunt put a strain on my family which caused my mother's stroke," said Joe, hitting the wall with his fist. "I hate the son of a bitch."

Rubbing his sweaty hands on his pants, Sam calmly said, "I am getting no benefit from your tirade. My problem is that Johnson's knocking harder on my door. I need you to keep him away, permanently. Let's grab lunch: it's time to arrive at a new approach and financial agreement. You have the right stuff to assist in both cases."

"I'll see you tomorrow," Joe said, chugging a beer.

Sam called Knight, then James, and left the same directive for both: "We have a major problem on our hands. Call me."

Barrett began destroying documents.

Leonard Knight left a message. "James, the shit is going to hit the fan and I'm the blades. Call me."

"Sam, James here, things are going straight down the shitter. Call me."

"Sam, it's Lenny. We need to put our heads together and fix what's broke and what's not broke. Call me."

"Leonard, it's me, Barrett. We're going to need a good law firm."

Unable to change his situation, Joe fought to control his anger, which was increasing by the minute. "Mario, the motherless bitch, Johnson, served me to appear before his committee, *The Potential Effects of Organized Crime . . . Infiltration in the Import/Export Industry.* Since I became partners with Pop, Johnson's been on my ass. My bet is that they're trying to divide and conquer the Borelli family."

SEPTEMBER

Mike Borelli offered Mario the use of his Port Washington bungalow as a means of escape and a place to refocus his life. Catherine thought it best if Mario had alone time to think things out and stayed home.

He no sooner unpacked his luggage than the telephone rang. It was Catherine. "I'm taking the next train out."

"I'll be waiting at the station," he said excitedly.

Two weeks later, after much conversation and reflection, Mario and Catherine agreed it was time to return to Little Italy and resume a nor-mal life—time to go back to baking bread and writing. At least that was Catherine's understanding of their agreement.

Months passed, Mario's mind drifted, and his mood shifted.

Chapter 48

1971

APRIL 24

Snuggled together on their couch, Mario and Catherine were watching the late-night news. Reaching for his coffee cup Mario said, "It's not surprising that over five hundred thousand people, including lots of Vietnam veterans, demonstrated against the war. What's sad is that fourteen hundred were arrested on the steps of Congress."

Catherine asked, "Did you know about John Kerry?" She opened the paper to the article and handed it to Mario. "He's the navy captain who earned a Silver Star—the one who took part in the demonstration and testified before the Senate Foreign Relations Committee."

"That I could understand: what I don't understand is what possessed Lieutenant Calley," Mario said, slapping his forehead.

JUNE 6

As she stood in front of Most Precious Blood Church in Little Italy, Sister Francesca's lined face and furrowed brow reflected her concern for humanity. She first met Mario and Catherine at Our Lady of Loreto's Church after Tim Gallagher's death.

"I recall how upset you were some months ago with Cardinal Stanley and the hierarchical church. It is apparent now, as it was at the time, that your stance against the Vatican will lead nowhere. Why persist?"

Before he could answer, a priest who was with her spoke in a firm voice, "During The Strike, I heard your words. I wondered at the time if you knew what you were saying. Your position against structured entities and buildings makes no sense. They are the very elements churches use to deliver their message."

"I understand, but isn't it true that Jesus told the woman at the well that you will worship God neither on this mountain or in Jerusalem but true worshippers will worship God in spirit and in truth?"

"The church needs to guide us there. We have a society that needs structure," said the priest looking for approval from Sister Francesca.

"I say to you, structure as an institution is an impediment." Tilting back his fedora he smiled and said with much conviction, "The Holy Spirit looks at the heart, not at the structure."

"I'm afraid you need a doctor."

"Thank you for the advice," said Mario bowing at the waist.

Sister Francesca shook her head as a slight smile broke from her thin lips.

JUNE 28

"Sam, it's me, James. Joe Colombo was shot in the head at an Italian American civil rights rally in Columbus Circle. The guy who whacked him was killed instantly by Joe's bodyguards, right in front of the cops."

"So?"

Soon after the Pentagon Papers were published, they triggered a different thought-process in Mario's mind.

"Please, not again," Catherine begged.

328 THE POET, THE COUNT, AND THE PEDDLER

He excitedly said, "I knew it! Vietnam was a total screw-up! Don't you see? It's all government gobbledygook; it's arrogance; it's power. Religion, military, government, business; it's all power. I have reflected back on the chain of events during The Strike and have come up with an interesting idea."

"I hope it's only on paper," Catherine said apprehensively.

"That's exactly what I'm thinking. Paper, with a sharp edge."

Sitting at Tony's kitchen table, Frank Nunzi was cutting himself a huge piece of provolone cheese. "I had a long conversation with Mike. This deportation issue with Mike is dead serious. My contacts in Washington carefully checked out Johnson and his mode of operation. They confirmed Mario's suspicion that the man is a rotten bastard."

Tony said, "That's an understatement. He's also harassing Joe."

Holding a piece of cheese with his knife, Frank said through clenched teeth, "Johnson's hatred of Italians is really getting on my nerves. It needs to end. Maybe he could do us all a favor and drop dead."

"We're not that lucky."

"Maybe no, maybe yes."

At Umberto's Clam House, Mike and Joe Borelli were having lunch with Mario. Ripping apart a loaf of Italian bread, Mario said, "Johnson is just plain no good."

"Tell me about it. Pop and me have been under the microscope for too long."

Pushing away his plate of half-eaten *zuppa di pesce,* Mike wiped his mouth and said, "I spoke with Frank last week. He's also concerned about the congressman."

Mario took hold of Mike's arm and said, "That's understandable; the bastard has been bit by the power bug. We both know Frank Nunzi. If it's at all possible, he'll reach the right people and get him off your back."

"I hope so."

Joe blurted, "Hey, Mario, what do you think about the riot at Attica? At last count thirty-two prisoners and ten hostages have been killed."

"Unbelievable. Remember Sam Melville? He was one of them," Mario added.

"Who's Melville?"

"He's the guy who blew up a number of buildings in the city."

LATER IN THE WEEK, AT DINNER WITH THE MCGUIRES

Owen McGuire opened the conversation. "The situation in Ireland is still volatile. The IRA continues to strike out against British troops; Irishmen are being killed and injured. Hundreds arrested. The British will not let go."

"Mr. McGuire, it's all about control and power. Be it Ireland, The Strike, or Italian injustice, it's all one big nightmare in the inferno," said Mario.

"Dad, Mario has read Dante one too many times," Catherine said, giggling.

"Laugh all you want; Dante's words are ingrained in my thought process. He is right on as far as religion is concerned. Religion is a state of dictatorship. All you have to do is ask that backstabbing Cardinal Stanley." Putting aside his knife, he asked, "How about this for a book title: *Me and Dante Down by the Inferno*?"

"I would rather you spend more time listening to Simon and Garfunkel sing "Me and Julio down by the schoolyard" and let it rest there."

Mrs. McGuire placed her arm on Mario's shoulder. Circumventing a potential argument, she gently said, "How about a nice big piece of apple pie?"

The following day Elizabeth McGuire's life was turned upside down. Her beloved husband of sixty-three years died of a massive heart attack. The moment Catherine got off the phone with her mother, she and Mario rushed to her side. The entire Ferrara family shared Elizabeth's grief. Owen McGuire was buried in a serene ceremony in Calvary Cemetery.

JULY

A young reporter from *Human Rights Today* was shopping at Ferrara's.

"Hello, Mario. You probably don't remember me. We met briefly during The Strike. A friend of mine has been telling me about your meeting with Senator Claude Pepper. I'd love hearing it directly from you."

Leaning against the counter, Mario answered, "Sure. During our conversation, he told me a story about when as a young congressman from Florida, he and his wife were invited to Germany.

"The night of their arrival, pounding steps of storm troopers on the cobblestone streets of Munich abruptly awakened them.

"After a frightening, sleepless night, the senator's host informed him of the Fuhrer's impending visit to the city for a luncheon engagement. They arrived at the same restaurant before Hitler and his entourage. Sitting at opposite tables, their eyes met a number of times, although neither acknowledged the other. When it came time for Senator Pepper to leave, the only way out was to pass directly in front of Adolph Hitler.

"The senator maneuvering through the quiet, yet filled dining room, stopped momentarily at Hitler's table, and as he glanced down, their eyes locked for the last time; yet neither said anything.

"Thirty years later, Senator Pepper, regretting his silence, told me, 'Sometimes a simple act of saying something, even the word hello, may change the day, the month, the year, a lifetime, or perhaps history itself.'"

"That is a wonderful story," said the female reporter. "In a strange way, it dovetails with what a friend of mine who works at the UN said. He said there exists a conspiracy of silence that originates and maintains a contempt for basic human rights. And he said the Native American is no stranger to this contempt. Nations fall prey to the same misery they inflict upon one another. Fear! Fear of retaliation, of skeletons that may be exposed in their own closet."

Shrugging his shoulders, Mario added, "The weak and the poor are always getting screwed by the rich and the powerful. It makes me wonder about people. Are they afraid to speak? Is speech more threatening and frightening than physical violence?"

Outside the store, Mario stood pondering for a full minute the question asked by a middle-aged man. Then Mario said, "You ask, aren't we tired of marches and protests? I can add to your question." He continued with his arms wide apart, "Aren't we tired of the ongoing rhetoric and insanity running rampant in society, or have we accepted insanity as sanity?"

"You're pathetic," the man answered defensively.

Mario stepped toward him and said, "That's your opinion and that's your choice." Then unable to contain himself, he added, "So let me ask: are *you* contributing to the insanity that exists in the streets?"

Someone yelled, "You're the one that needs a loony bin."

"Sure, you can think me insane. That's your opinion."

1972

APRIL 8

"Sam, it's me, James. Crazy Joe Gallo's forty-third birthday gift was a couple of bullets in the chest. He was shot in Umberto's Clam House, staggered outside where he fell, and was picked up by an ambulance. He was dead by time he reached the hospital. The rumor is that he was whacked in retaliation for the hit on Joe Colombo."

"What else is new?" Sam hung up and called Solari at Vatican Bank.

Once again laughter returned to the Ferrara household. Mario, between the times he spent trying to recoup precious lost time with Catherine, spent the year baking and conducting research for his book.

NOVEMBER

Popular North Carolina Congressman R. J. Johnson won reelection for the fourth time.

1973

MARCH 30

A headline in the *New York Daily Mirror*
LAST US TROOPS WITHDRAW FROM VIETNAM

America's longest war finally comes to a halt.

With tears welling up in her eyes, Catherine cried out, "Thank God!"
Mario mumbled, "A little too late for Angelo."

APRIL 11

Over lunch Joe said, "Mario, they subpoenaed Pop to appear in front of another Johnson committee."

"The guy is vicious. It's about time I call him. Enough is enough."

"Instead, why not call Mr. Nunzi—the man has guts to spare—and see if he has come up with any ideas?" Joe asked.

Mario said, "I'll do it. The reason he's without fear is that he really doesn't give a damn about anything . . . except loyalty."

"Maybe Johnson should worry about his backyard. Since Carl Bernstein and Bob Woodward from the *Washington Post* blew Watergate wide open everybody is running for cover," said Joe nervously grinning, trying to temper his own anxiety about his father.

Mario clenched his fist. "You're right. Power crumbled. Yesterday, Nixon's top aids quit. Halderman, Ehrlichman, Dean, and Kleindienst are no more. And now Dean is fingering Nixon."

MAY 4

"James, R.J. here. I have decided to retire."
      "I was depending on you to—"
      "I said I'm retiring. There's nothing further to discuss."

BOOK VI

Chapter 49

July 4, 1973 – Independence Day

A rising sun had created brilliant prisms of light, reflecting off towering glass edifices. New York City residents were just beginning to stir.

In an exclusive section of uptown Manhattan, an everyday ritual was in progress. A slightly bent-over man wearing a black and scarlet warm-up suit was crossing Sixty-second Street toward Central Park to begin his morning walk when out of the blinding light came a speeding truck. A moment later the white delivery van quickly disappeared into the sunglow leaving the fragile creature to die on city pavement.

JULY 5

A headline in the *New York Journal American*
CARDINAL STANLEY CRITICALLY INJURED
HIT AND RUN DRIVER NOT FOUND

> *The cardinal, in an intensive care unit, is teetering between life and death. An investigation is underway.*

AUGUST 3

At approximately 1:00 a.m. on a hot night, a wide area of the East Coast was buffeted by an angry thunderstorm. Although the rainstorm lasted only an hour, substantial damage occurred. Numerous sections of the city, including Greenwich Village, lost its electrical power, leaving darkened streets deserted except for a lone male figure walking briskly toward the Washington Square Subway Station.

Nearby, a heartbeat later there was a flash of light, an earth-shattering explosion, and then, fire riddled with debris engulfed the sky. In a matter of minutes wrenching sounds of wailing sirens and flashing lights of emergency vehicles sped along West Third Street. It wasn't dark or still anymore.

AUGUST 4

A headline in the *World Tribune*
CONGRESSMAN R. J. JOHNSON DEAD
PERISHES IN BLAZING INFERNO

> *The former congressman's charred body was found in the vestibule of his brownstone. Johnson, former Chairman of the Justice Department's White Collar Crime Unit, was in the middle of a deposition at a hearing on organized crime in the New York City area.*
> *An arson investigation has begun.*

The first police officers arriving at Congressman Johnson's home secured a large area, enabling firefighters to do their job in safety while keeping the curious at bay. Based on the details uncovered about the explosion and ensuing blaze, the fire captain's quick assessment pointed to arson. By the time homicide detectives arrived, the inferno was under control.

In a syndicated column, a well-known reporter wrote:

> *I wish to remind my readers that last month Mario Ferrara was arrested and later released for the near fatal hit and run of Cardinal Arthur Stanley. The vehicle crushed the cardinal's fragile body, leaving him to die on the filthy streets of Manhattan. Only by the grace of God does he live. Witnesses said the white delivery van was traveling at such a high rate of speed that they were unable to identify the driver or license plate.*
>
> *Ferrara was again arrested in late July for a gangland-style assault on Dr. Susan Chou, director of Human Rights at the United Nations. Dr. Chou was severely beaten on her way to a television interview that was to cover Ferrara and his past antics. Ferrara was released later the same day.*
>
> *Mario Ferrara had plenty of motives in both cases. Could it be that the charred body of retired Congressman R. J. Johnson marks the third in a series of assaults—including a murder—by someone seeking revenge? Congressman Johnson gained notoriety for his unrelenting pressure on the financial community as well as on organized crime, which included the Borelli family who are long time friends of the Ferraras. The congressman's brownstone was located near New York University where he frequently lectured.*

"Hey, Ferrara, it's me, Barrett. I apologize for not calling sooner to congratulate you for whacking Johnson. You did me a huge favor. But, trying to take the cardinal out, now that was stupid. Once a *wop* always a *wop*."

"Stay put! I'm coming down to the bank to throw your ass out the window."

AUGUST 16

A headline in the *New York Journal American*
MARIO FERRARA ARRESTED

> *A wild incident occurred at Gateway Bank. Mario Ferrara was arrested for aggravated assault on Richard Barrett, president of the bank. In a bizarre twist, hours later, when questioned by police Mr. Barrett refused to press charges.*

Hennessy knew he could effectively use Mario's track record of having a hot and volatile temper against him. Therefore, soon after the fire at Johnson's residence, he cranked up his intense investigation.

The fact that Mario had previously threatened Stanley and Johnson publicly, had more than one motive, and had opportunity and capability to commit the crime of murder made him a number one suspect in the fire and hit and run. The Chou assault was a puzzle.

Hennessy and Barrett were at a luncheon meeting at Castellano's Ristorante.

"We set up Ferrara perfectly." Hennessy paused to sip his Chardonnay. "He beats up a respected banker who becomes fearful of greater retaliation and drops charges. I love the power of this job."

"Good for you. Now go kill the bastard," Barrett said. He stuck two cigars between his swollen lips, laughing wildly.

"I always knew you were a compassionate soul," Hennessy said sarcastically.

An editorial in the *New York Journal American*

> *It's questionable whether Ferrara is a liberty patriot or a tyrant. Did his challenging words create harmony or unrest and fear? It is beyond comprehension how up until now he has escaped prosecution.*

It didn't take Frank Nunzi long to arrive in New York. He, along with the Borellis, was sitting at Tony Ferrara's kitchen table. Frank, leaning toward Mario, took hold of his arm and sternly said, "Why are you letting your emotions control you, rather than the other way around? I told you to let me take care of problems that seem out of control. There are ways."

"Barrett is a scumbag."

Vincenza pulled on her hair.

Catherine shook her head in despair.

"Listen to Frank," Tony blurted, glaring at Mario.

In almost a whisper, Mike said, "Enough. He understands."

Joe looked at Mario through bloodshot eyes and smiled.

With her hands tightly clenched around her water glass, Catherine said unhappily, "No matter what you say, he will do what he wants to do."

"What the hell does that mean?" bellowed Mario.

Her eyes tearing, Vincenza pleaded, "Please, no more."

Chapter 50

September 1973

It was 5:00 p.m. and there were several customers remaining in the store picking up last minute groceries. Upstairs in his apartment, Mario was snacking on a cold piece of pizza when he answered a loud knock on the door. Standing on the other side were two men dressed in dark suits who introduced themselves as homicide detectives. The taller of the two handed Mario a search warrant.

Mario's first thought was Catherine. Blood quickly rushed to his head. He recalled with some relief that she was staying with her sickly mother. With his heart pounding he realized he had no choice. He reluctantly allowed them to enter the apartment.

At the time Mario was preparing a manifesto, a white paper of sorts, and was eager to publish it much like Thomas Paine did with *Common Sense*. He had previously distributed drafts to Joe and Sam for comments.

Spread out on the kitchen table were pages of his manifesto, magazines, and newspaper clippings tracking the death of Congressman Johnson, the hit and run of Cardinal Stanley, and the brutal attack on Dr. Susan Chou.

Certain pages of the Manifesto read . . .

POWER: THE ROOT OF DARKNESS

There is an invisible power of unspoken favors called the network of favors. No one is actually in charge because power rotates to a need, and the need incorporates itself into gain at the expense of anyone who may be in the way of power's progress.

Then, there's the power within the power called the ultimate power. The ultimate power is comprised of Business, Government, Media, and Religion—and when you control those sectors, you control society.

However . . .
Don't be fooled: there are many levels of power beginning with the super rich and ending with thepoorest of the poor and with every other financial and social class in between.

Each level of power succeeds to the determent of others. To eliminate power, the force must come from within and without. Power needs to be taken away and destroyed.

Power is intimidation.
Power is manipulation.
Power is deceit.
Power is misinformation.
Power is arrogant.
Power is control.

In the dictionary the word power should be covered with blood.

No distinctions equals no power.

Hennessy had previously determined that only the most seasoned and skilled officers should handle the investigation. He directed a sergeant and lieutenant, both of whom had twenty-plus years of service on the force, to make certain their scrutiny would be conducted by the book.

If he were to bring charges of murder in the first degree in the death of Congressman Johnson, he would need everything as airtight as possible.

The investigators knew that Hennessy suspected Mario of being behind the wheel of the white van that critically injured Cardinal Stanley and the cold-blooded attack on Susan Chou. Nevertheless, no substantial evidence was found to support an arrest.

Ferrara's delivery van showed no damage except a broken headlight, for which he was ticketed a month prior to the hit and run.

At the time of Susan Chou's brutal assault, Mario was at dinner with Sam Castellano. Sam's statement regarding Mario's presence at his home at that time provided an airtight alibi.

As far as Johnson's death was concerned, much to Hennessy's delight, there was an eyewitness who claimed he saw Mario at the crime scene.

The high-ranking detectives, whose faces showed no emotion, requested Mario accompany them to the Fifth Precinct for further questioning. There he was drilled relentlessly.

They released him after four grueling hours.

Arriving back home, Mario quickly reached for the telephone. "Hi, Mr. Borelli. Have you heard from your delinquent son?"

"He's back in a couple of weeks. Anything important?"

"No problem. Just tell him to give me a call when he gets back."

"OK."

"How are you doing?"

"Just great kid . . . just great."

"Take care."

Mike called Joe in Palermo, Sicily.

Mario took a deep breath, trying to calm himself down before he phoned Sam.

"Something's not right."

"What do you mean?"

"The cops drilled me about Johnson's death."

"Don't tell me you spoke to them without contacting Rose?"

"I've got nothing to hide. They can go get screwed."

"Stay put. I'm calling Rose."

Rose Gramoli had earned the respect of her peers as an esteemed litigator and had become a partner in the prestigious law firm of Goldman and Weiss.

The following day Catherine returned home and Mario filled her in on the previous day's events. That evening Catherine uttered as she was lying awake in bed, "I'm worried."

"They're crazy. This whole thing is going to go away."

Her voice was trembling, "*Papà* is worried. If *he's* worried, there's reason to worry."

Exhausted, he mumbled, "Please go to sleep." Placing Dante's *Divine Comedy* on the floor beside the bed, he turned off the small bedroom lamp and rolled over.

It was a long night as he drifted in and out of sleep trying to recall at each wakening his last horrifying nightmare.

One week to the day later, Mario was picked up on Prince Street and taken back to the Fifth Precinct for further questioning.

The lieutenant, an enormously big man, handed him a piece of paper that was taped to the dashboard of Congressman Johnson's Mercedes.

Mario, stone-faced, read the note slowly.

Before we can secure liberty, we must first derail the power train of hell; leave it there and watch it burn into ashes.

The detectives' initial approach in the interrogation process was to be sympathetic and logical. Eventually their patience turned to frustration. The lieutenant kicked over a metal folding chair and barked, "Who the hell do you think you are?"

Mario shrugged and replied, "A Sicilian immigrant; a simple individual with nothing more than my thoughts."

"OK, wise guy, tell me your thoughts."

"One thought is that we're all bound by love."

The detective clenched his fist and said irately, "Tell you what. Give me a whole bunch of thoughts at once or I'm going to get really pissed."

Mario rubbed his forehead. He complied with the lieutenant's request, speaking calmly, "My thoughts are nonviolent, and I would like to think we can match our words with deeds and try to live the ideal. Some call such thinking Pollyanna. I call it life. I believe all people can change for the better. I think how wonderful life would be if each one didn't wrong another. Do you want me to go on?"

"What's the matter with you?" boomed the detective.

Before answering, he thought about it for several moments; then, in a resolute voice, said, "During the Revolution, my eyes opened, my ears sharpened, and my heart understood. It was an experience that transformed my entire thought process."

The other detective paced the room and said nothing.

Mario continued, "Tim Gallagher said we're all one in God. Tim made me think about how can we be in God and all things? Simple conclusion: that means we are in one another, and still we sit back and do nothing. We are free in the spirit, but for some reason we bind ourselves into things we see rather than things we don't see."

The detective stopped pacing, glared at him with a look of contempt, but said nothing.

Mario, taking a drink from a paper cup, crumpled it, threw it into a wastepaper basket, and raised his hands in recognition of the successful shot. "Then I went into the inferno with Dante and came to the conclusion that we need to destroy the power of darkness."

The lieutenant crossed his arms, looked down at Mario, and said: "The revolution, God, and the inferno. OK, *wop* . . . Keep talking."

Biting down on his lip to restrain himself, Mario continued, "I do think about hate. Then, I remember if we live love, we eliminate hate. I think about kids roaming streets and how they can mold themselves or remake themselves into love."

In a sarcastic tone a detective said, "Then you're telling me that you love Cardinal Stanley, Dr. Chou, and Congressman Johnson. You're just an all around nice guy."

Mario shot back, "First of all, Johnson is dead. Nonetheless, to love your enemies is better than loving your friends because if you're able to love your enemies, you will have manifested the Divine. At least that's what Tim Gallagher told me."

Agitated by the statement, the lieutenant barked, "Tim Gallagher's dead. So stop quoting him. But what I did hear you say is that Cardinal Stanley, Dr. Chou, and Congressman Johnson are your enemies."

Mario was staring straight ahead. "I think it's about time that I talk to my lawyer." The detective turned the table over.

Rose was furious. She went straight to the stationhouse and blew up. "What in the world are you guys doing? He hasn't been read his rights: he's being harassed and detained against his wishes." Pointing her finger, she finished, "I'm going to bring a list of charges against the department that will make you throw up."

Both detectives looked at her with contempt written on their faces.

"Charge him or let him go!" she demanded.

Bottom line—they released Mario.

The sergeant who interviewed Johnson's friends, adversaries, and associates concluded it would be most difficult to prove Ferrara's guilt.

He informed Hennessy, "Sure, he's an obstinate bastard, and he had motive and opportunity, but those we questioned only offered opinion and not fact. And there's the possibility Ferrara could be innocent. After all, the guy who saw someone running from the fire scene is nearsighted."

The quote from Mario's manifesto found taped in Johnson's Mercedes could have been planted by any number of individuals. The result: basic and essential facts were missing. Frustrated, the investigative team completed their search without turning up one piece of hard evidence. In their report, the detectives indicated that they might have the wrong man.

However, Mario, with no established alibi except that he was home writing, was still the prime suspect. Hennessy had long decided that a preponderance of circumstantial evidence would be enough to get a conviction of murder. With a firm grip on the New York City Police Department, he was able to convince them that before it was all over, his office would assemble enough corroborating evidence, present a strong case, and obtain a guilty verdict.

While reviewing his file, Hennessy said to the detectives, "When Congressman Johnson demanded Ferrara's arrest for inciting a riot at the United Nations, his hatred grew and he sought revenge. That's how simple it is; Chou's attack and Stanley's hit and run add fuel to the fire, metaphorically speaking of course."

James Hennessy, elevated to assistant District Attorney of New York County, went for broke and decided to charge Mario Ferrara with murder in the first degree. The street fight that started in childhood continued; except this time, it was a life and death fight.

Three weeks later, detectives arrived back at 231 Elizabeth Street with arrest and search warrants for the murder of Congressman R. J. Johnson.

The moment Mario returned home from his bread deliveries, the detectives made their move. Rummaging through his home, they turned up Mario's research papers, articles on Watergate, the Pentagon Papers, and a briefcase that held his manifesto and a working draft of his manuscript *Me and Dante Down by the Inferno.*

Twelve minutes later, Mario, in handcuffs, was being escorted out of his home—a detective on either side. Joe Borelli pulled up in a taxi. "Hey, what the hell?"

The police said nothing.

"Call Rose. They think I killed Johnson," Mario shouted, as he was being shoved into a patrol car.

Joe hurried into the store, waved to Tony, and reached for the telephone. "Rose, they have arrested Mario for Johnson's murder. They're taking him down to the Fifth Precinct."

Catherine rushed outside the store just in time to see the patrol car pull away from the curb.

Tony steadied himself against the counter.

Vincenza was upstairs, sick in bed with a fever and unaware of what was taking place.

Chapter 51

October 1973

Wasting no time, Rose left some unhappy clients sitting in her office and headed for the police station, arriving in fifteen minutes flat.

In a troubled voice, Mario said, "I know I have been slandered and charged with being an anarchist and a scoundrel. I may be a fool for the sake of liberty, rattling cages every now and then, but I'm not a murderer." Wiping his forehead, he continued, "It's shades of Sacco and Vanzetti."

Rose shook her head in desperation and said, "Please forget Sacco and Vanzetti and start thinking of your survival. You know James Hennessy. You think him a ruthless bastard, and I'm certain he feels the same about you. I need you to be focused because he will exhaust every means possible to get a conviction."

"Tim told me on a number of occasions that if we have faith, whatever we ask, if it's right, it's already been granted," he said in a monotone voice.

"Sounds wonderful . . . Bullshit! Let's get serious. Remember your life is at stake here," Rose cried out.

Mario sat motionless and listened.

"You told the police you were alone in the apartment writing at the time of Johnson's death. Mario, that was 4:00 a.m. You could have been sleeping."

"I was writing."

"Is there anyone who could corroborate your story?"

"Just the pictures on the wall."

"There you go being a smart ass."

"That was a stupid question. Who the hell is going to corroborate me writing at 4:00 a.m.?"

"Where was Catherine?"

"She was at her mother's. My mother-in-law has been seriously ill."

"Place yourself in the shoes of the police. It seems that whenever anybody gets killed, injured, or a building is burning, you're either at home by yourself or writing at a park!"

"Who's the smart ass now? I enjoy being home, I enjoy the parks, and I enjoy writing."

"Mario, don't be such a hardhead. Keep in mind I'm on your side."

"Johnson was a rotten bastard."

"What in the hell does that mean?"

"Actually, it means Johnson was a rotten bastard."

Rose was leaning on her elbows on the table in front of her. "I'm trying to fit the pieces together, and without facts we could be in serious trouble. Please stay focused."

Mario began to pace the room in silence.

"You need to settle down and recall everything you did prior to the congressman's death," cautioned Rose, who was now holding a pencil and legal pad in her hands.

"Nothing. I was just writing."

Peering at him, she clasped her hands and softly asked, "Mario, don't you own a white delivery van?"

Giving her an incredulous look, he said, "So what? There are thousands of white delivery vans."

In frustration she fired back, "You're not on murder's row yet, but Hennessy will do his damnedest to get you there."

He shrugged and said, "That's no surprise."

"Cardinal Stanley was close to death by the time he arrived at Lenox Hill Hospital. Eyewitnesses were not sure about the driver or plates."

"Rose, you're beginning to irritate me. When Johnson went up in flames, I was at home writing. And when Stanley was hit, I was in Battery Park writing. Besides, my van has a big *Ferrara's Fresh Bread and Catering* sign on it."

Taking a deep breath she said, "Alright. I need to ask you one more time. Did you have anything to do in any manner, in any way whatsoever, with arson and the subsequent death of Congressman Johnson, the hit and run of Cardinal Stanley, or the assault on Susan Chou?"

Mario stopped pacing the room, looked directly at Rose and said: "You know better than that. Was I angry? Yes. Did I kill somebody? No. Am I sorry to see Johnson dead? No."

"I don't know how I can make this any clearer. This is going to be one hell of a fight. Hennessy is possessed. His political future rides on this trial."

Mario tapped his forehead and with a gleam in his eye said, "Maybe we have to call the little old lady *Mamma* used for *malocchiu*."

Mario's words broke the tension and they shared a needed laugh.

Rose bluntly asked, "Do you have any concern about Joe Borelli?"

He gave her a quizzical look and said, "What does Joe have to do with anything?"

"I may be stretching, but then, again, I may not. Suppose he sought revenge in your behalf, or possibly, to get even after Johnson's brutal investigation of his family."

"You're stretching. *I'll* give *you* a stretch. Hennessy's pissed because neither Johnson, Chou, nor Stanley endorsed him for DA. Vanity is his Achilles heal, so he tries to whack Stanley and Susan and then torches Johnson."

Angrily gathering her notes, she cried out, "I think we better call it quits."

He paused and reached for Rose's shoulder and in a pacifying tone said, "Thanks for everything. I do appreciate your concern and support."

Tears were welling up in Rose's eyes. She hugged him. "You don't need to thank me . . . not yet. I know how hard you work in your belief of a better world. Sam and I agreed that the patience you have shown and the suffering you have endured is beyond the tolerance of most. Stay strong."

Back at her office, Rose reflected back on the day's events. She felt she needed time to put things in perspective and decided not to return any phone calls, including Catherine's.

Sam called Joe to ask him if they could meet for lunch.

"Peep, I don't have the stomach to eat. But I'll come down to your office anyway."

When Joe arrived at Castellano Enterprises, he was escorted into the main conference room. He stood motionless looking at the spectacular view of New York Harbor and the Statue of Liberty.

Before Sam had a chance to sit, Joe said, "If it's the last thing I do, I will find the person or persons who framed Mario; and when I find them, I will personally see them dead."

Sam took off his glasses and wiped the lenses with his handkerchief. "I understand your feelings. But you need to cool it and let the cops do their jobs. The Feds have become involved and are assisting the DA."

"I'm telling you, Peep, if I find them first, I will personally see them dead," boomed Joe. He was still staring out the window.

"I'm begging you to think seriously about what you're saying."

Looking fiercely at Sam who was still standing near the door, he said, "You want me to *think seriously*? I'm as serious as life itself. I'm going to make sure Mario doesn't suffer for nothing!"

"You're going to get yourself killed in the process."

"Are you in?"

In a concerned tone, Sam answered, "I'm not your guy. After today, I never want to talk to you about it again." Putting his glasses back on, he looked at Joe with an expression that indicated the discussion was over.

Stomping out of the conference room, Joe turned and bellowed, "Forget about it! Braveheart my ass; you're a pussy."

Sam rushed back to his office and called James Hennessy.

"I have never seen Joe Borelli so out of control: tell Barrett and Knight to lay off everything before it bites them in the ass. At least for now."

"Borelli gets on my nerves."

"Don't go there," said Sam.

"OK, I'll call Barrett; why don't you call Knight?"

Chapter 52

October 4

Mario Ferrara was officially charged with murder in the first degree and was refused bond.

Catherine became nauseous and spent the night in tears. Tony, Vincenza, and the rest of the family were in agony, yet hopeful that this injustice would be rectified.

Rose quickly set up a list of people who could visit Mario. She called each of them and explained the rules and procedures for visitation and arranged with her secretary to take calls from people on the list and set up a visitation schedule.

The following morning, Catherine took a depressing taxi ride through Queens, crossing the East River over the Rikers Island Bridge. The forbidding three-lane bridge connected the Borough of Queens to the penal colony, a land of darkness. The island of multiple jails held society's exiles, detainees waiting for or on trial and the convicted.

She approached the prison checkpoint; her heart ached with fear and sadness. The dread of seeing Mario in this place sent an icy chill down her spine.

Following an emotional visit, Catherine painfully said, "Whether we talk or sit in silence, every visiting day I will be here to hold your hand. Together, we will get through this horror. I love you. There's nothing that will separate us."

He held her tightly and closed his eyes. "I love you too."

They lingered a bit too long in the embrace according to the control room deputy who told them to separate. The long embrace resulted in Mario receiving a strip search before being returned to his cell. After Catherine left Rikers Island, she couldn't wait to get home and take a shower. She felt as if she were washing away the grime of sadness.

Later in the day, Catherine, sitting in her kitchen wiping away tears, took a sip of water and said, "Joe, they can't do this. It's so wrong. I don't know how *Papà* and *Mamma* are going to survive this torture."

Holding her hand, he gently said, "Don't lose hope. Between Sam and me, we will find a way. We'll tap into every contact we have and pull every string we can to get him acquitted. When you add my father, Mr. Ferrara, and Frank Nunzi, what you have is dynamite."

She shook her head in despair and said, "This is not a business deal. He's accused of murder: there's no contact to help—"

He interrupted her and in a positive tone said, "Don't be going negative on me. Hennessy has always been a rotten bastard; there's got to be a kink in his armor."

Frank telephoned Mike at midnight and said, "The more I think about it, the more upset I get. We need to watch this mess closely: it could turn into another Sacco and Vanzetti where innocent men were wronged and martyred by those who espouse justice."

"When it comes to treatment of Italians, Hennessy is as bad as Johnson was. And he considers Mario an anarchist. The only good news is that we don't have to deal with the congressman," said Mike.

"This morning, I spoke with Tony. He's livid. Vincenza's been sick in bed, and Catherine is miserable and can't sleep. John and Carmela are worried out of their minds and don't know what to do. The Ferraras are in a bad situation."

"I'll go visit the kid on the next visitation day if Rose doesn't already have someone else scheduled," said Mike.

"Good. I made plane reservations for later this week; I'll go see him then. I'll give Rose a call to set up both visits."

Rose pondered the question for days: How could a jury possibly convict Mario of the willful, deliberate, and premeditated killing of Congressman Johnson without hard evidence or at least plausible circumstantial evidence? She knew Hennessy only had circumstantial evidence. Nevertheless, he was a man on a mission, fueled by a personal vendetta and possessed with one objective, a conviction. It was going to be a trial of wits.

Rose stopped by the jail on her way out of town. She said, "Mario, I'm going into hibernation: Mike Borelli was kind enough to allow me the use of his Port Washington bungalow. I'll be out of reach for a couple of days to evaluate our options. In the meantime Marvin Goldman will be available if you need anything."

"You'll love the place. Have dinner at Paulie's. It's a wonderful Italian restaurant on Shore Road."

"Stay calm and take care of yourself."

Rose left him and walked out of the jail feeling the weight of a pretty heavy burden. The life and death of her best friend's brother was at stake.

Upon her return from Long Island, Rose set forth her preliminary strategy. She went to see Mario and warned him again not to let his feelings cloud his thinking.

"First of all, forget Sacco and Vanzetti. Secondly, Hennessy's melodramatic style will have the jury in tears, chiefly when he describes in excruciating detail Johnson's desperate struggle to escape his artist studio; how his scorched body was found at a doorway with a defective lock."

Though listening carefully, Mario showed no emotion.

Rose, noting Mario's reaction, ploughed ahead emphatically. "It's James Hennessy's game we're playing. Consequently, we need to discredit every assertion and cause him to stumble in his own rhetoric."

Mario nodded in agreement.

On awakening the morning after another restless dreamed-filled night, he quickly reached for pen and paper and began writing furiously. He couldn't stop his hand from shaking.

> I was standing alone in a Boston courtroom. Webster Thayer, of high reputation, sat on the bench scowling at Nicola Sacco and Bartolomeo Vanzetti. His patience was growing short as he waited for the verdict to be delivered.
>
> Throughout the trial, I sat between Nicola and Bartolomeo, closely observing Judge Thayer's actions. The pompous ass would revel during the brutal attacks on the two passionate radicals by the prosecution.
>
> Appealing to the handpicked jurors' patriotism and bias, the State of Massachusetts presented a trumped-up case, taking full advantage of the paranoia caused by the Red Scare.
>
> Everyone, except the prejudiced judge, thought the jury would be out for days. But, when they briskly walked back into the courtroom after six short hours of deliberation, I slapped the side of my head in utter frustration. Much to my distress and the distress of Sacco and Vanzetti and of millions of supporters, the jury returned with a verdict of guilty.
>
> Afterward I suffered with these men, along with millions of others, through six arduous years of appeals for a new trial, appeals that failed. A plea for clemency fell on deaf ears.
>
> I sat in terror, as a calendar dripping with blood floated before my eyes. All dates were blackened out except for August 23, 1927. Handwritten in blood-smeared letters was an invitation.
>
> *Come to the Death House at the Massachusetts State Prison and witness the executions of two innocent Italian anarchists. See firsthand a travesty of the Justice System.*

A militaristic prison guard grabbed my arm and said through clenched teeth, "I cannot believe the demonstrations in support of these two *wops* throughout the United States. And not only that, countless protests have taken place in cities worldwide: in Paris, London, Berlin, Warsaw, Buenos Aires, Mexico City, Rome, Moscow, Barcelona, Milan, Havana, Tokyo . . . all over. His face soured as he asked in revulsion, "Why the outrage?"

My hands became sweaty and my face flushed in fright as I observed Nicola Sacco enter the death chamber.

He shouted, *"Long live anarchy!"* And then he softly murmured, *"Farewell, my wife and child and all my friends."*

They slipped a hood over Nicola's head. He cried out *Mamma* as the executioner, with professional precision, pulled the switch.

My body jerked violently. I felt as though the surge of electricity had passed through *my* limp body.

Minutes later it was Vanzetti's turn. Before Bartolomeo entered the same execution chamber, he solemnly declared:

I wish to say to you that I am innocent. I have never done a crime; some sins, but never any crime. I thank you for everything you have done for me. I am innocent of all crime; not only this one, but of all, all. I am an innocent man.

As the guards were strapping him in the barbaric electric chair, Vanzetti blurted, *"I now wish to forgive some people for what they are doing to me."* With that said, the signal was given to pull the switch.

A day of death began with two Italian immigrants exterminated because their political views were different than that of the establishment. I shuddered . . . and sobbed.

My eyes went dark as death masks were quickly made. Their bodies were taken to the Langone Funeral Home in Boston's North End.

The day of the burial, Hanover Street filled with tens of thousands of mourners dressed in black slowly following the hearses carrying two innocent men. While walking in the funeral procession to Forest Hills Cemetery where Nicola and Bartolomeo were to be cremated, I held a small bouquet of red carnations close to my heart.

At the cemetery a man holding a burlap sack and dressed in black silk robes, a stiff white collar, and a derby hat purposely blocked my way. I gently tapped him on the shoulder. He turned and snarled. It was Judge Thayer. He slowly opened the bag and handed me the plaster death masks of Sacco and Vanzetti.

My heart stopped: the masks reflected my face.

Having learned jailhouse procedures the hard way during her previous visit to Mario, Catherine gave Mario a quick embrace and placed her hand on his shoulder. She asked, "What's the matter? You seem jumpy."

He did not wish to respond to her question. Changing the subject, he blurted, "How's your mother?"

"Mom's not doing well. Even with her new medicine, her high blood pressure is taking a toll. She's sleeping a lot."

"I'm sorry."

"She misses my father terribly. So, tell me, Mario, why are you so edgy?"

Having gotten permission from the on-duty deputy, he reluctantly gave her his notes and said, "Read these."

She read them, kissed him on the cheek, and then softly said, "Mario, it's another nightmare. That's all it is . . . a nightmare."

Due to an unrelenting media blitz, the DA's office was under extreme pressure as the saga concerning Mario Ferrara consumed the public's interest.

Outrage from the street over a ruthless crime kept Hennessy in the spot-light with no letup in sight. The press had hounded him with a nagging question: "Was anyone or any group behind Mario that would or could support a conspiracy theory?"

At Castellano's Ristorante, Rose discussed the case in detail over dinner with Sam. Most disturbing was his dissertation on why and how Mario could have been involved in the death of Johnson and the hit and run of Stanley.

"Lastly. Despite the fact that I was with him the night Susan was ferociously beaten doesn't preclude his involvement. He could have ordered a hit. Although, I can't figure out why?"

"Thanks for depressing me, but in a strange way I owe you," Rose said while massaging her forehead.

"We'll call it square in the morning," said Sam, chuckling. And then turning serious, he said, "And don't forget Joe Borelli; he could be the wild card. I just have a gut vibe about him."

"I hear you."

ONE WEEK LATER

"I have vacillated enough. It's time that I go visit Mario," said Sam who had made an unexpected appearance at Rose's office to ask if she could have lunch with him.

Rose said, "No problem. You pick the restaurant and I'll make arrangements for your visit next Tuesday. Mario respects you, and if you can give him words of encouragement that would be wonderful."

"I'll do just that. Let me know what time and I'll rearrange my appointments. By the way, forget what I said about Joe Borelli: he's clean."

"That's a relief."

"Moreover, Joe assured me that he and his father, as well as Frank Nunzi, could be counted on for financial support in Mario's defense. Mike has made a phenomenal comeback since Johnson's committee decided to call it quits. Mike's one tough son of a bitch. As for me, you have whatever you need."

"You're fantastic: I'll tell Mario," Rose said smiling.

Sam stood, hugged her, and as they started out the door, he blurted, "Please don't say anything to Mario; you know he's hardheaded and would probably refuse the money."

"I guess you're right." Taking hold of his hand she added, "I love you."

"I love you too."

In preparation for his visit to Mario, Sam, back at his office, cleared his calendar.

Tuesday, entering the jail that held Mario for the first time, Sam shuttered at the overall filthiness of the facility. The cold, gray steel bars and mucky, spider-web-cracked concrete floors added to his uneasiness and depressive state of mind.

Sam said uneasily, "Mario . . . you look good."

"I don't know, Peep. This gray suit needs tailoring," Mario replied with a slight grin.

"How are you holding up?"

"What I'm doing is a lot of thinking."

"What about?"

In a tone of restlessness, Mario answered, "Hennessy will stop at nothing to hang me. Rose seems to have everything under control; yet, I don't have the slightest clue how we're going to bury the snake in his own arrogance."

"Leave it to Rose."

"You know why I'm confused? Because my innermost self is telling me I'm screwed and tattooed. I think that's what Tim meant when he said I'll know what's next," said Mario, his eyes glazed over as he looked about the room.

"This is not the time to get deep," Sam said uncomfortably.

Mario, his voice raising a couple of decibels, said, "All I want is to get the hell out of here and beat the crap out of Hennessy. You know he's a piece of shit that needs to be flushed."

"Quiet down!" Sam retorted. The control room deputy motioned for Sam to lower *his* voice.

Ignoring Sam, Mario said firmly, "Up until now, I never worried over consequences or lost my nerve. *Papà* told me, 'In times of turmoil, trust no one, just trust your family or God.' Words. They sounded good at the time, but right now my ass is on red-hot coals."

"We're behind you all the way. Hennessy will screw up before this is over, and I might be able to facilitate that."

"Whatever!" said Mario waving his hand in a helpless gesture.

Sam took off his glasses and laid them on the table in front of him. He looked directly at Mario and said, "Be tough. I've made sure Rose has at her disposal whatever she needs, including the best investigators money can buy."

Mario stood, massaged the back of his neck, and said, "I appreciate everything, but keep your money. Just give me Hennessy's head." Mario walked toward the deputy who would take him back to his cell.

As the heavy metal door opened to let him out, Sam's parting comment—one that seemed so empty and trite considering the circumstances—was "Stay cool: I'll be back next week."

"Sure," Mario said smiling sadly. The door slammed loudly behind him. The noise, reverberating for what seemed an eternity, jarred Mario to the core and left him feeling very alone.

On November 15, during one of his many visits to Rikers, Joe Borelli cried out in annoyance, "Liberty, justice, and peace my ass. Give me five minutes alone with Barrett."

"You and Rose. Both of you think Barrett did it."

"He's disappeared, but I'll find him and beat him with my bare hands until he confesses," growled Joe through clenched teeth.

"Take it easy; you're going to get a heart attack," Mario warned.

"Look who's calling the kettle black. Peep told me you wanted Hennessy's head. Hey, if you really want his head, you tell me. Nobody else. Understand?"

"Joe, give me a break . . . please! I was shooting off at the mouth and you know it. Nothing more," he said wearily. "Maybe I *should* fold my arms and let it be."

"You know something, Mario? You're all screwed up. Last week you told me you had no doubts and were ready to stand tall and kick ass." Joe stared at him and shook his head in despair. "A messenger of liberty and love: . . . you and Dante . . . down by the inferno. Wasn't that what I heard? Right now, Mario, you sound like a pussy that just had a lobotomy."

"Why don't you kiss my ass!" Mario whispered through clenched teeth.

"I give up!" Joe said, shaking his head in frustration.

Rising, Mario leaned on the table and quickly said in a peaceful tone, "Truce. Let's show everybody how love works by example. Love is a healer and forgiveness, a perfect stress reliever."

The deputy motioned for him to sit back down.

Joe slapped his head and cried out, "Nothing but bullshit. If you need me, call me. But don't call to tell me how love is going to save your ass and the world. I'm out of here."

Walking through the visitor's area, Joe threw his hands up in disgust. Hearing that cold, rusted steel door clanging shut, he made the sign of the cross.

Catherine telephoned Rose. Sobbing, she said, "I don't know whether I can make it down today to see Mario. Mom had a stroke and has been rushed to Bellevue Hospital. I'm there now."

"Don't worry about Mario: stay with her. We will let him know what has happened."

An hour later, John and Carmela arrived at the jail for their weekly visit. Before they had a chance to say anything, Mario said, "Rose just got a message to me from Catherine. Nothing is going right. Besides putting up with me, her mother had another stroke." With elbows on the table in front of him, he was holding his head up with both hands. He forced a smile. "So how's it going for you two?"

Carmela's voice was breaking. "We're OK. *Papà* told us about Mrs. McGuire. We'll go visit her later. But how are you doing?"

"I just had a long talk with Joe. He's pissed at me. He said I'm not facing reality. He may be right. Other than that, I'm fine." Standing to stretch his legs, Mario continued in a tender tone, "I don't want you second-guessing or spinning your wheels on what you could have or should have done."

"We love you, Mario," she said, touching his hand.

He wasn't listening to her. "Don't you see? I dared myself to fight a battle against injustice. I'll never have to say *what if?* For me, knowing the agony of defeat is better than living with not having taken my own dare. No regrets," said Mario, his eyes half shut.

"We understand," said John in a low voice.

"I'm not done." Mario stopped eating the peanut M&M's that Carmela had given him. "I'm ready to get on the witness stand and kick James Hennessy's ass."

"You need to listen to Rose. You really need to listen to her," said John, the inflection in his voice indicating he was getting firmer in his stance.

"I'm all screwed up . . . I know it, but I'm writing a poem called 'Trust.' I'm going to give it to Catherine."

Carmela murmured, "That's nice."

"I'm sure she'll love it," John said gently. Then he fired out, "Putting all that crap aside, how are you doing coping with all this?" John made a sweeping gesture indicating he was talking about being in jail.

He shrugged and said, "Tim Gallagher gave me insight about prayer and how it kept him sane. I've taken his advice. Prayer has kept me from going batso. Tim said prayer is silence or action. He said everything is prayer and if you're in tune with the Holy Spirit, it becomes a beautiful melody, and then comes peace."

"Tim committed suicide! So tell me, how are you really doing?" asked John, pressing Mario.

"I'm worried to shit. How's *Papà* and *Mamma*?"

"*Papà* is making phone calls to everyone he thinks could help, and *Mamma* is praying up a storm," said Carmela, squeezing her brother's hand.

John glumly said, "I told *Papà* not to come to see you here. It would kill him."

"I agree," said Mario, looking despondently around the visitor's area.

John and Carmela left Rikers Island and immediately went to visit Vincenza.

"*Mamma,* Mario's OK. He's got God on his side," said John with his arm around her.

She grimaced. "Excuse me. I'm an old lady, but I'm not senile. I'm not only worried. This time I'm worried *for real*! I would like to smack that James-fella right in his face."

Carmela, holding Vincenza's hand, said, "Please take it easy. Rose is working extremely hard preparing a great defense. Everything is going to be all right."

"Your *papà* has been on the phone with Frank Nunzi for hours. I'm worried."

John, trying to comfort her, sympathetically said, "Don't worry: I'll talk to *Papà.*"

Vincenza sat with her arms around Carmela. "I'm sorry," she said. "I'm not feeling too good, so I can't cook food for Rose. Please, make sure she eats good to stay strong. Come back tomorrow and we'll talk more. Right now I need to lie down: tell Mario I love him."

Holding back tears, Carmela and John kissed Vincenza goodbye.

Standing outside the store, John took hold of Carmela's shoulder. "Mario is worrying the hell out of me. All his talk about spirit . . . God . . . love . . . and whatever else . . . is driving me crazy. He's out of control. As Papà would say, what he needs right now is a swift kick in the ass."

"Don't sell him short," Carmela said opening her eyes wide. "And don't tell Catherine: she has enough to worry about."

John opened the door to the store, took one look at Tony, and lied in answer to his request for a report on Mario's attitude and bearing.

The next day, Joe—looking for assurance that Mario's state of mind was what it should be and not wanting to upset Catherine—took Carmela and John to lunch so they could talk.

Walking out of the Sunflower Restaurant, Joe looking frantic said, "Maybe, you didn't pick up the same irrationality that I did. I'm telling you, I think he's one step away from the plunge."

Carmela calmly said, "The best thing we can do right now is to support and love him."

"I agree," added John.

A week later Carmela visited Mario by herself. She was pleasantly surprised by his cheerful attitude. "You seem fine, Mario. But I have to tell you, Joe Borelli's worried about you."

"I told you, the last time I spoke with him I wasn't right. Besides, how can you accomplish anything in life without being off the wall, even if just a little bit? It dawned on me this morning. I remembered what *Papà* said and it made sense."

"What was that?" asked Carmela.

"I'm sure you'll recall it. One day when he was in one of his philosophical moods, he said, 'When I'm feeling helpless . . . weak and sad; that's when I feel like a giant . . . because I am forced to depend on God.' I now understand his feelings because I see that when you exhaust your mental gyrations there's no place to go; so you surrender to God." He paused and said gently, "It doesn't make sense. Why don't we run there first *before* becoming suicidal?"

"Mario, tell me you're not thinking suicide?" Carmela exclaimed.

"No. I was just using a metaphor."

"I think you're full of crap. The next time I come down, I'm bringing Father Carelli with me."

In a light-hearted tone he said, "Carmela, please. I'm fine. Furthermore, I would never think of committing suicide before I beat Hennessy and Barrett to a pulp."

"Now you sound like my brother," Carmela said with a slight grin.

Afterward, she hurriedly called Father Carelli.

DECEMBER 10

Elizabeth McGuire lapsed into a coma and never regained consciousness. She passed away at 11:14 p.m. Three days later, Catherine and the Ferraras took the heartbreaking ride to Calvary Cemetery were she was buried alongside her husband Owen.

Mario, sitting on the end of his bunk, sobbed and prayed for Catherine—and for faith to sustain them both.

Chapter 53

1974

The visitation schedules settled into a routine with family members, usually two at a time, making sure that Mario had someone visiting at every opportunity since they were so limited.

The visitor area deputies came to recognize Mario's regular visitors and greeted them by name when they signed in.

One of the people that Mario included on his visitor's list was Beth Downing. Although Beth had been to the jail many times before to interview inmates, she had never gotten over how repressive it all was.

The latest visit to see Mario was enough to convince her that it was time to have a serious talk with her editor.

"It seems to me that he's been set up. There's no doubt his principles are strong and his uncommon and adventurous mind, as mysterious as it may be, led him to try jumpstarting a revolution, an attempt which backfired." She took a large drink of water and continued in a confident voice. "On the other hand, Barrett appears to have an affinity for wreaking havoc. I wouldn't be surprised if in the end we discover he was behind the murder. I don't trust him. Furthermore, it will be interesting to see if Mario's statement today comes to fruition."

"What statement are you talking about?" asked her editor.

Checking her notes for accuracy, she said, "He told Congressman Johnson that authority is swayed by the power-structure of money. He said, 'Right or wrong, money is key to protect positions of power. But me, I'm on a collision course with structure and its established institutions. Money is not wagging me and I'm not looking back.'"

"What did he mean by 'not looking back'?"

"Mario was hell-bent on tying religion to every social category, including politics. At one point, he said, 'In order to make progress, we cannot repeat history. Look back, bring it forward, turn it sideways or upside down; it's the same. Why not create history? Be bold and cut a new path.'" She was gazing out from the editor's sixty-fifth-floor office, down to Fifth Avenue and Saint Patrick's Cathedral.

The editor asked, "Wasn't he devastated by disappointment after disappointment in his high expectations?"

"Actually, he refuses to deal in negativity. Mario will fight with his very last breath for what he believes."

"I hope you're being objective as a reporter and not being blinded by idealism. Go ahead and write your story."

Back in her office, a harried Beth phoned the jail and was able to talk to the deputy she had noticed watching her with great interest during her last visit with Mario. She was able to charm the deputy enough to get him to bend the rules and get Mario to the phone.

In an uplifted tone, she said, "I just received the green light to write an article on blind justice. This will fit well with public sentiment that is riding with you. Demonstrations are taking place throughout the city protesting the trial."

"That's good for the cause of liberty," Mario said, sounding robotic.

"Don't worry. It's going to work out alright."

"Thanks, Beth."

Mario Ferrara was riding a rollercoaster of bewilderment.

Rose Gramoli and Marvin Goldman, along with experienced investigators, were working non-stop gearing up for trial, as telephone calls and letters were coming in to her office by the thousands; some were calling for death, most for liberty.

In a conversation with Marvin Goldman, she said, "Hennessy is a prosecutor with political desires. He had joined Johnson in his vendetta against Mario and Italians in general. The assertion that Mario is an anarchist fuels the prejudice of those who idolized the extreme right-wing congressman."

"Is that your opinion or is it fact?" Mr. Goldman wanted absolute clarification.

Rose didn't answer.

After months of day and night sessions of reviewing investigative reports, the anxiety level began to diminish at the Goldman and Weiss law firm. Rose's confidence increased dramatically upon completion of the firm's due diligence, a procedure that was meant to uncover all basic facts and beyond—a procedure that, in Mario's case, uncovered nothing incriminating.

She concluded that Johnson's home went up in flames due to an abundance of flammable materials stored in an airtight closet inside his artist studio. Either a cigarette left carelessly burning or a buildup of chemical fumes caused the explosion. Therefore, unless some unexpected evidence turned up, Mario's testimony would only be used as a last resort, a trump card she was hoping never to play.

Rose spent countless hours with Mario constantly reminding him to pay attention to all the testimony of witnesses and all the evidence presented. Throughout her coaching, he never asked what his chances for acquittal were.

Emotions ran high as the trial of trials was about to begin. The law firm of Goldman and Weiss, with a style all its own, was one of the best in the city, and it was prepared to proceed aggressively and resolutely in Mario's defense.

On the other side of the table, in an interview with a reporter from the *World Tribune*, James Hennessy was quoted: "*It's a done deal, he's the bread and I'm the toaster!*"

Both sides agreed that the selection of acceptable jurors in this case would be difficult due to enormous pretrial publicity.

MAY 1

Knowing the fate of their friend was about to hang in the balance in a New York courtroom, Joe and Sam thought it appropriate to crack open a bottle of Chianti in Mario's favorite place, Bethesda Fountain in Central Park. After the second bottle of wine was consumed, their talk changed dramatically.

"Peep, everything seems out of whack. In fact, in my opinion a number of people could have knocked Johnson off, including Catherine. Her love for Mario is beyond understanding. She watched him being swallowed up by the whale. Catherine might look the part of a pussycat, but underneath, she's a crazed tiger. Keep in mind that at Tim Gallagher's funeral she humiliated Hennessy with a roundhouse slap to the face."

"*Slap* you say? Oh my God! That's a sign of a killer all right," he said sarcastically.

"OK, how about Beth Downing? She would do anything for a story," Joe said. He was standing on a park bench chugging his Chianti. He paused and blurted, "Oops, did I just say that?"

Sam snickered and said, "You're making no sense."

"OK, what about Barrett? He is a number-one scumbag-maggot-weasel shit face. As payback for the federal investigation against Gateway Bank, he decided to whack Johnson," Joe said, waving an empty wine bottle. "Stanley was a good diversion, and Susan Chou was just a robbery gone bad," he said, pulling the cork out of another bottle.

"Hold it, my wine is superior to yours." Wiping his chin, he handed his bottle to Joe. "I agree with you about Chou, but it's time you get realistic." Looking to the heavens, Sam said, "I'll do you one better. What about His Eminence the Cardinal? He conspired with Lenny Knight—who despised Johnson—to take him out. *Why*? you ask. I'll tell you why. Johnson was getting dangerously close to uncovering Stanley's illegal funding sources for Vatican Art and Treasure. Above and beyond that, the cardinal became extremely fearful that Tim's death might be tied to him. Now . . . that's two huge motives. But, Knight screwed up by failing to take Stanley out in order to keep everything quiet."

"Sounds good, but too complicated, especially when you bring in Knight. Hey, what about *you*, Sam. You never did forget that Johnson left you at the altar with broken promises in Mondello. Then to add insult to injury, when news of Johnson's investigation leaked out, it tainted your fair-haired boy image on Wall Street and caused you to lose millions. Simple solution . . . you torched him." Joe's eyes were darting from side to side as he unfolded his theory. "And you admired Tim for the good work he did and blamed windbag Stanley for his death. So, you decided, as long as Johnson was going bye-bye, it was a good time to avenge Tim's death by taking the cardinal out. However, I have to tell you, Sam, that was a feeble attempt at making it look like an accident," Joe said. He was admiring another empty wine bottle.

"That's bottle number three and you're quite drunk, my friend. Talk about motive, *you* hated Johnson too. First, for his malicious effort to deport your father to Sicily. Second, for his persistent, nasty investigation and ongoing attacks on you and your family that ultimately caused your mother's death." Holding on to a park bench to steady himself, Sam continued, "In addition, you were pissed at Stanley to the point of insanity over Tim's suicide, murder, or whatever it was. As a result, with Mike's contacts it was a cakewalk for you to orchestrate a hit on both of them," Sam said.

Stupefied, they looked at each other in disbelief.

"Holy shit! Joe, think about this. Mario firmly believed that Stanley someway, somehow, provided the rope in Tim's death. On the flipside of the equation, Johnson torpedoed Mario at every turn in the Revolution and General Strike, twice having him arrested. Worst of all, both Johnson and Stanley caused devastating effects, not only on Mario, but on Catherine and the family. And that was his breaking point." Sam, wiping his mouth after a slug of wine, whispered loudly, "Let's face it: Johnson and Stanley were Mario's waterloo. I think trying to take them out was his only way to see justice fulfilled. He succeeded with Johnson but failed with Stanley."

Joe, smashing an empty bottle against a park bench, shouted, "No way!" Falling backward onto the bench, he blurted, "Could it have been John?"

Sam called Joe the following morning and whispered, "Do you think maybe it was Frank Nunzi?"

"You're still drunk."

The day before trial, Joe visited Mario. "Hey, are you going to be all right?"

"Of course," Mario mumbled.

"You have to get fired up," Joe commanded, taking hold of Mario's arms and looking him straight in the eyes. "Don't be going philosophical . . . not now."

"Take it easy. I'm just learning to control my anger and beginning to understand life better," Mario said calmly.

Trying to restrain himself, Joe said, "I'm telling you, Rose and even Beth Downing think that son of a bitch Barrett could be the killer. I'd like to slit his throat from ear to ear."

"That's a bit harsh," Mario said in a sarcastic tone and took a deep breath. "What I was trying to say is that you need to love your adversary."

Joe rolled his eyes. "There you go again. I'll tell you what. You can love them all you want—after you kick the shit out of them in a courtroom."

Mario, in a voice devoid of emotion, said, "Right. Anyway, you become more peaceful when you love because you eliminate all other agendas except for love. It's unbelievable."

Preparing to leave, Joe hugged Mario. "*You're* unbelievable! Please, Mario, stay focused and we'll win this thing. I guarantee it!"

"Joe, . . . you're the best," Mario said, smiling. He kissed Joe on the cheek.

Frank Nunzi called Mike Borelli and said, "I'm worried about the jury and Mario's enemies. The mob that lynched the *Siciliani* in New Orleans were motivated by fear, fear born out of prejudice. A dying police chief, David Hennessey, supposedly said it was *the dagos* that did it. They believed him and a vendetta against the Italian community began." Slapping his hands together, he continued, "It took six thousand people to brutally massacre the eleven *Siciliani* who were found innocent."

That's about the right ratio," snapped Mike. "They had no comprehension of what real justice is; they only knew vigilante justice. You're right, that's what I worry about too."

Pretrial publicity ran the spectrum. Forever ready to pounce on the smallest leak or rumor, the press resembled crouching tigers.

The *New York Journal American* reported:

> *A reliable source from the District Attorney's office, speaking on the condition of anonymity, confirmed that Mario Ferrara is ready to deal. One option for Rose Gramoli, the defending attorney, is an insanity plea.*

Hennessy had gained a solid reputation from having never lost a case. However, the term *plea bargain* was a major contributing factor to his successful track record. In the case of Mario Ferrara, the trade-off for a plea would be life in prison without parole. But only if he confessed before the gavel sounded. Some legal experts questioned Rose's lack of experience in trials of this magnitude.

An editorial in the *World Tribune* ran as follows:

> *James Hennessy has fought off innuendo after innuendo of unfair practices in preparing for this trial. How can a prosecutor do his work under a microscope?*

The Italian daily *Buon Giorno* reported:

> *Hennessy is a hoodlum with a badge, nothing more than an official leader of a lynch mob.*

The evening before the gavel came down, Vincenza was able to visit Mario to reassure him. "Mario, me and your *papà* are praying for you. Don't worry. I love you."

"*Mamma*, I'm not worried. How can I be worried with you and *Papà* looking after me? I can't lose. Your love made me understand who I am!"

"I'm worried a little bit just the same."

"Please don't worry. If you worry, then I worry, and if I worry . . . I can't concentrate."

"OK . . . OK . . . I won't worry anymore. I love you, my son."

"I love you too; see you soon," he said.

Tony, with his arm around Catherine, was waiting in the holding area for his turn to visit Mario.

The media was poised to report on testimony given, as well as cross, redirect, and recross examinations, all of which were about to unfold. Representatives from newspapers across the country and restless native New Yorkers converged on New York's Criminal Courts Building at 100 Centre Street to catch a glimpse of the hero or the villain, depending on their perspective. Jury selection was arduous and took ten days to complete. The power-hungry Hennessy was basking in the media-spotlight of the carnival-like atmosphere that pervaded the courthouse. The trial began.

Chapter 54

....

May 3, 1974

The *New York Tribune* editorial stated:

> *For months, a drama of deep proportions has been unfolding with a plethora of emotions in the case of the People of the State of New York v. Mario Ferrara.*
>
> *Now, get ready for a down-and-dirty street fight between two high-profile lawyers pitting wit against wit. Both are among the best in criminal law.*

An aging Judge William Phillips, known as a tough, no-nonsense jurist, had earned the nickname *Justice* from several citywide law enforcement officials. However, his colleagues in the legal profession viewed him differently. It became common knowledge that in order to protect his definition of the legal system, Judge Phillips would be amenable to breaking the rules. One defense attorney attributed the diminutive judge's actions to his "Napoleonic complex."

MAY 4

A headline in the *Daily Mirror*
HANG 'EM HIGH "JUSTICE" BEGINS

A newspaper reporter's background search uncovered the fact that Hennessy and Ferrara had known and competed with each other since childhood. She reported:

> *Their lives and career paths have crossed a number of times, creating a dynamic display of personal animosity that most likely will accelerate as the trial progresses.*
>
> *James Hennessy, who graduated near the top of his class at Columbia Law School, is noted for his silk suits, flashy ties, and flamboyant style.*
>
> *Prior to becoming Assistant District Attorney, he worked with the rich and powerful in business and finance, gaining well-deserved kudos. Those efforts earned him a partnership in the prominent New York City law firm of Hannifen, Shultz, and Wilbur that specializes in banking and real estate litigation. The court became his turf and he knows exactly how to maximize it to his advantage.*
>
> *Mario Ferrara is an Italian American whose family immigrated from Palermo, Sicily, in 1923. His family owns and operates Ferrara's Grocery and Bakery in Little Italy. He is known locally for his hard-crusted Italian bread.*
>
> *Ferrara's trouble began when he decided that baking bread was not enough to satisfy his appetite. Instead, he became a staunch advocate for liberty and instigated the General Strike that all will remember well. Some wonder if he might have bitten off more than he could chew.*
>
> *The life and death of Mario Ferrara is now hanging in the balance in this high-stakes showdown. Witnesses include those attesting to the defendant's character and experts that are compensated to testify as to his emotional state of mind.*

When the prosecution was pushed for their assessment of the defendant, they quoted a news article written shortly following the call for a revolution of liberty and general strike:

> *Who is Mario Ferrara? This reporter is not certain that even Ferrara knows. He may be either a scoundrel or a true seeker of liberty. Then again, he may be just a baker-turned-writer with an over-zealous imagination. In any case, he did start a firestorm.*

A sea of media, joined by a curious crowd, jockeyed for space outside one of Manhattan's imposing structures, the Criminal Courts Building. Inside the overcrowded Courtroom Four, with its air conditioner out of service, all was absolutely still—all except for the stormy oratory of James Hennessy.

Hennessy, ever the professional, was concluding a confident opening statement to the jury. Addressing the eight males and four females, he finished, "Ladies and gentlemen, the State will prove beyond a reasonable doubt that Mario Ferrara planned and committed murder by arson of Robert J. Johnson, a distinguished United States congressman from North Carolina. The prosecution has prepared a case supported by meticulous evidence that in every instance points to the defendant." His voice resounded throughout the courtroom and his arms were raised in a gesture of hopelessness. He continued, "I have no theory whatsoever to explain how my esteemed colleague, Rose Gramoli, can presume to offer a reasonable defense for Mr. Ferrara."

Hennessy was very clear as to whom he would call as witnesses and how the jury would be lead through a maze of deceit that resulted in murder.

Rose approached the jury box, smiled, and gently reminded jurors, "Mario Ferrara is presumed innocent until proven guilty." Catching the eyes of individual jurors and holding them for a time, then moving on to another pair of eyes, she continued, "Not a startling statement, but factual. In order to remove reasonable doubt, the prosecution has the unbelievable task of proving evidence that is circumstantial at best to be credible." Turning to Hennessy she said with a confident smile, "The prosecution, in my estimation, has an impossible task. Impossible for one reason: you cannot convert a lie into truth. Truth is at risk!"

She further explained in excruciating detail the improbability of the prosecution's evidence.

The State was ready to call its first witness.

Chapter 55

The trial proceeded with predictions of pretrial hype coming to fruition, much to the delight of the media group. Incendiary statements by both sides kept everyone on edge.

Lawyers went well beyond the scope of legal procedures, notably in direct- and cross-examinations. Speculation and rebuttals were twisted to the point of downright confusion.

Some witnesses testified to hearing Mario talk about Johnson in derogatory terms: others testified to his outstanding character.

Cameras rolled while both seasoned and amateur reporters interviewed those who knew, and those who said they knew, the cast of characters. Unsubstantiated rumors linking Mario to communism or other *ism's* abounded.

The trial took place in two different arenas. One was Courtroom Number Four in the Criminal Courts Building; the other was in the media.

The jury repeatedly heard "that's hearsay," "that's irrelevant," and "that's immaterial."

Judge Phillips had both lawyers approach the bench so often some joked they had worn a path in the tile floor.

There weren't any unexpected developments or announcements—except for Rose's bombshell: "Mario Ferrara, at his request, will take the stand and testify. You will see, hear, and understand for yourself the man who is on trial for a crime he did not commit."

If it had been a prizefight, the scorecard would have been mutilated and both sides even. Two different approaches were put to the test. James, a condescending and sometimes-belligerent prosecutor, pitted against Rose, always controlled and friendly. Newspapers sold out quickly, and people watched the nightly news with obsessive interest.

At the last recess just before closing statements, Rose held Mario's hand. She said in a low tone so as not to be heard by onlookers, "I'm curious. You often speak of reconciliation and say it's important to live the message of love. Now that you have been maligned repeatedly by Hennessy and others you thought were friends, can you forgive?"

"I don't know. At this very moment, I feel like some friggin' beast in the dark is kicking my ass. Yet, somehow, I think I believe Tim. He said that the Holy Spirit is always setting things in place. Besides, nobody knows all endings."

"Can you forgive?"

At first he fell silent; then smiling, he asked, "What do you think?"

Mario fell silent again: then reached into his pocket, pulled out a folded piece of paper, and gave it to Rose. It read:

LIVING SPIRIT

When you feel weak and oppressed,
Turn to the living Spirit in faith and hope
And be consoled, with overwhelming love.

When you hunger and thirst for justice,
Rely on the living Spirit
To grant strength and courage.

When you feel the pain of bondage,
The living Spirit heals and resurrects
And becomes your liberty . . .
Forever.

Mario smiled and said, "Yesterday, out of nowhere, an encouraging letter came from an old *paesanu* and in it was a quote by George Eliot. Let me read it to you."

Who shall put his finger on the work of justice, and say, "It is there?" Justice is like the kingdom of God—it is not without us as a fact, it is within us as a great yearning.

He looked at Rose and exclaimed, "Enough said!"

As the trial neared its end, a brazen reporter thirsty for sensationalism, broke into Tony and Vincenza's home. As luck would have it, the evening he chose for illegal access was the very night Joe and Mike Borelli came to visit, which translated into very bad luck for the intruder.

Soon after the intruder was discovered, the Borellis arrived. Joe was livid and his face flushed bright red as he dragged the startled reporter, who stood over six feet tall and weighed over two hundred pounds, down three flights of steps to the front door. Once outside, with a choke hold around the big man's neck, he escorted him across the street and shook him violently before giving him a boot-in-the-ass send off.

Catching his breath, Joe calmly went back inside to share a meal with Vincenza, Tony, and Mike. Although she had prepared a wonderful meal of *vitello scaloppine ai funghi*, Vincenza, not feeling well, excused herself from dinner and went to bed.

The men sat for hours comforting each other with words of encouragement and hope.

On the way to the subway after dinner, Mike asked his son, "What's the latest on Barrett and Castellano?"

"Pop, you ask hard questions," Joe replied. He placed his arm around his father's shoulder as they kept walking.

AUGUST 10, 1974

A headline in the *New York Journal American*
NIXON RESIGNS

> *Nixon becomes first president to resign. Gerald Ford sworn in. The
> country can once again proceed with integrity.*

While reading the paper, Mario uttered, "Power bites the dust."

SEPTEMBER 9

It was four months and six days since the first gavel sounded. The
much-publicized trial and media spectacle was coming to its long-awaited end. The players had all seen some moments that tried their patience
almost beyond endurance. Even Judge Phillips had experienced some
schizophrenic moments presiding over a twisted and much-maligned
ordeal.

CLOSING ARGUMENTS COMMENCED.

In full stride, Hennessy made his closing arguments. His booming voice
ricocheted off the walls and high ceiling of the old courtroom.
Spectators, standing or sitting shoulder to shoulder, kept fanning themselves to avoid keeling over from the stifling heat.

In an exasperated tone, Hennessy said, "In conclusion, let me review
key elements of how the defendant, Mario Ferrara, cunningly deceived
those who trusted him."

Hennessy, mastering the art of theatrics, snarled, "Simply said, Mr.
Ferrara used image as the line, trust as the bait, and action as the hook."
Stroking his full head of black, wavy hair he said in a sincere, we-all-
know-it's-true tone, "Mario Ferrara is nothing more than a calculating
human being with a depraved and degenerate mind."

Fiery words, together with choreographed arm and hand gestures, caused the courtroom to erupt. Some spectators jumped to their feet with shouts of joy: others jeered and beat on the wooden benches.

Judge Phillip's gavel slipped out of his hand and flew through the air, just missing Hennessy, as he roared, "Quiet! You people are a disgrace to the judicial system!" Rising out of his worn leather chair, he grunted and yelled, "Another disruption, and I can assure you this entire courtroom will be emptied."

Rowdy onlookers finally settled down, while the Judge, fighting hard to retain his composure, instructed Hennessy to continue.

The defendant, who was seated upright in his chair, never took his eyes off the Assistant District Attorney.

Marvin Goldman, leaning toward Mario, whispered, "Stay calm. You know his ego and his method of operation. His ethics get lopsided when it threatens his personal notoriety and success."

Mario, tight-jawed, nodded.

Hennessy never missed a beat. "Furthermore, I can tell you, as sure as hell burns with its eternal fire he is not, as some defense witnesses described him, kind and lovable, a man who loved whatever the circumstance. The only thing Mario Ferrara loves is chaos." Skillfully playing to the jurors' emotions, he lowered his voice and continued, "Let me remind you that the defendant chose as heroes and role models Giuseppe Garibaldi and Sacco and Vanzetti. Believe me when I tell you that these men were rebels espousing poisonous anarchy."

Moving toward the bench, he stopped suddenly, looked directly at Mario, and then, pausing for several seconds, shook his head as if in disbelief and continued: "It's no wonder the defendant is a magnet that attracts and employs evil. With willful and malicious intent, Mr. Ferrara was hell-bent on a destruction that was consummated in an atmosphere of blasphemous assertions and tyranny."

He hesitated a moment, allowing jurors to absorb the impact of his last statement before he continued. "During The Strike, the defendant's rebellious actions were documented by law enforcement agencies, both locally and nationally."

Standing behind the prosecution's table with tape in hand, he said, "Please permit me to replay a short segment of an interview by Elizabeth Downing taken shortly after the Golden Care Awards." Gesturing with his hands, he explained, "Ms. Downing is a noted and well-respected freelance journalist who has been given the coveted Investigative Reporter of the Year award by the National Press Club. She conducted the interview for New York Radio Station KVUC."

Sneering at the defendant, Hennessy turned, smiled at the jury, and said, "But before I play the tape, on a personal note, permit me to reintroduce the speakers on the tape, three outstanding servants of the community that were duly honored in 1970 at the Golden Care Awards.

"Prior to being elected to public office, Congressman Johnson was a successful businessman and philanthropic benefactor. I will miss his friendship."

Standing near the back door of the courtroom, a member of the press commented to an associate, "Johnson made his mark by playing hardball in business and politics. The reason he looked like a whale was because he ate opponents' body parts."

Her associate swallowed his gum as he stifled a laugh.

The confident prosecutor in a tone of compassion said, "My relationship with the cardinal is summed up thusly: Proudly displayed in my office is a photograph taken at the Vatican of the Pope, His Eminence Cardinal Arthur Stanley, and myself. This giant of a man is a staunch, loyal religious figure who gives unselfishly of himself."

Mario leaned toward Rose. "Bull. The only thing *giant* is his ego. Stanley defines ruthlessness. Moreover, kissing the pontiff's ass was the only reason he became cardinal."

She looked away to hide the smile creeping across her face in spite of her best efforts to rein it in.

"Dr. Susan Chou is a champion of human rights," Hennessy said. He straightened his shoulders and lifted his head as if his comments about Chou were somehow a reflection on his character as well. "I had the opportunity to work with Susan at the United Nations on a number of occasions. She gracefully hosted a forum after the Golden Care Awards in which she supported the defendant. In appreciation, Mr. Ferrara ordered a hit on Dr. Chou."

"Objection!" shouted Marvin Goldman.

"Overruled!" roared Judge Phillips.

Moving to where Mario was seated Hennessy glared down at him saying, "The defendant here rounded out the group of those interviewed. Now then, Ms. Downing's voice is the first voice you will hear."

The prosecutor motioned his legal assistant to turn on the recorder. Someone had readjusted the tracking mechanism and volume control, and when the recorder was turned on, this adjustment resulted in the emanation of a horrific screeching sound.

Wincing at the mishap, Judge Phillips cried out, "Mr. Hennessy, I'm quite sure you have everyone's attention *now*." The look on his face clearly showed he was quite pleased with his impromptu humor.

Hennessy, with an expression that indicated he was not amused, continued, "Sorry, Your Honor. Ladies and gentlemen, I apologize. The recorder has been reset. Here goes." The tape began to play.

> Beth: *Will each of you please sum up for our audience your attitude and approach to religion and its effects on society as a whole? Dr. Chou, will you kindly lead off?*
>
> Dr. Chou: *Certainly. Religion has been a key element in shaping our diversified cultures. It has sought justice and, in many instances, led the fight against inequities. Religion established a foundation for human rights in a society governed by the law of righteousness. However, religion needs governmental assistance to protect the birthright of each individual. In my opinion, only an enforceable human rights law can fully preserve human dignity throughout the globe. Only when we have this law can we begin to shape a better world.*
>
> Beth: *Thank you, Dr. Chou.*
>
> Beth: *Congressman Johnson, your viewpoint.*
>
> Congressman: *It will be my pleasure. The United States has*

endured because of the Constitution. The law of the land. That pre-cious document has allowed us to grow as a nation and today our country remains an international leader. We are in a position to defend freedom, justice, and the rights of all human beings. First, this accomplishment has to be attributed to a nation under God, driven by strong Christian grounding. We also have to look at a strong military, a strong economy, a strong judicial system, and of course, a strong government. All these elements, when combined, protect and preserve our freedom.

Beth: *Thank you, Congressman.*

Beth: *Cardinal Stanley, if you will please?*

Cardinal: *Elizabeth, I thank you for this splendid opportunity to share my heart. In order for religion to grow and maintain its stature in society, its people must adhere to the law of the Church, or for that matter, the law of whatever religion to which that individual belongs. The Church with all its wisdom knows the right path for humanity, a path paved by those who gave their lives in observing the doctrine of the Holy See, which leads to eternal glory. We cannot have a bunch of renegades, each espousing their own interpretation of faith, under one roof with those who are seeking the true path. President Lincoln said, "A house divided against itself cannot stand."*

Beth: *Much thanks, Your Holy Eminence.*

Beth: *Mr. Ferrara, please close out our segment.*

Mario: *Sure. At Caffe Reggio I called for a revolution of liberty and general strike. There is no doubt that religion is tied to every segment of society. For that reason, we need to overthrow and rebuild any sector or entity that instills fear or slavery in the hearts and minds of the peoples. Those who use twisted, perverted, or self-indulged thinking, theologies, or laws are the real cancers to our well-being. So, again I say if you care about life . . . and if you care about truth . . . accept the challenge, join the revolution, and strike now! Together, we can bring the dark forces of power to their knees. Liberty is ours!*

Beth: *Thank you, Mr. Ferrara.*

Beth: *I wish to thank my guests for their frank and open com-*
ments. Goodbye and may everyone find happy roads ahead.

As the tape ended, Hennessy stood at the jury box, rolled his eyes, and said: "Mario Ferrara's obstinate viewpoint about life and sacrile-gious attitude is clearly indicated by his words here. The world is his enemy, and anyone who doesn't agree with him is expendable. The State has presented conclusive proof, beyond any doubt, that his I-don't-give-a-damn attitude ultimately got the best of him. His Declaration of Liberty was an excuse for insurrection."

Hennessy, back at the tape recorder, sighed a heavy sigh and requested: "The next segment takes place on July 7, 1970. Please listen carefully to the news coverage of that infamous day at the United Nations. This is Ferrara while he was being held at bay at the UN entrance." Hennessy turned on the tape recorder.

> *Secrecy is the enemy of liberty. Courts my ass, screw the dictators,*
> *march to their general offices and lie down in the doorway. The*
> *worse that can happen is a vacuum cleaner, and not a tank, will roll*
> *over you.*

Hennessy stopped the tape recorder abruptly and commented that the person who was speaking on the next section of the tape was a reporter from the local television station, Channel Nine.

> *Many police vehicles are moving up and down First Avenue, main-*
> *taining control by entrapping activists on the west side of the*
> *avenue. Different law enforcement units, along with the National*
> *Guard, are poised for action in front of the barricades that stretch for*
> *blocks.*
> *At this moment police are attempting to remove protesters who*
> *have formed a human chain blocking the diplomatic entrance to the*
> *United Nations building. Many others are marching, sitting, and*
> *chanting. People old and young, people from various ethnic groups*
> *and social classes, people who are obviously well educated and peo-*

ple who are probably uneducated are forming this chain; and they are creating a strong field of solidarity. Onlookers are cheering activists with peace signs, encouraging them to stand strong. At last count over a hundred had been arrested.

Hennessy, shutting off the recorder, asked the jurors what that tape told them about Mario. Scowling, he pointed to a nervous melon-shaped figure with a bald head. The man was wearing a wrinkled suit. "You have heard good things about the defendant's character. But let me tell you about character. The testimony of Mr. Richard Barrett here brought closure to a mystery surrounding Mario Ferrara and his relationship with Father Timothy Gallagher and the Together Foundation." He turned and focused his eyes on the jury.

"Father Gallagher, the defendant's childhood friend, was a fixture around the Ferrara household, and he understood the Italian definition of loyalty. His parishioners would say of him, 'He could be Ireland's poster boy.' Father Gallagher, with his red hair, freckled face, and broad smile, was well known, respected, and trusted by members of his community. Well, I'll tell you this: in the end, the face of Ireland's poster boy could have been on a poster all right, a wanted poster. His willingness to befriend everyone got him in serious trouble. His actions humiliated Cardinal Stanley and the Vatican."

Cradling an enormous portfolio, Hennessy explained how the documents therein were submitted as evidence and distinctly revealed how Mr. Ferrara's undying loyalty to Father Gallagher led him to repeatedly threaten Mr. Barrett with bodily harm. He explained how Mario's barrage of telephone calls and appearances at Gateway Bank resulted in Richard Barrett and his family suffering extreme mental anguish.

Turning his attention to Mario, he described how the defendant cleared the top of Mr. Barrett's desk with one hand while grabbing him by the throat with the other. And, Hennessy, pausing to wipe his brow, maintained that this altercation caused Mr. Barrett to suffer a heart attack, after which he spent four days in an intensive care unit "barely hanging on to life." Further, he reminded the jurors that Mr. Barrett's testimony indicated this incident had not been the first vicious altercation with the Ferraras.

Hennessy first looked to Barrett, then straight at Mario. With a sneering smirk on his face, he concluded: "To fully understand what Mr. Barrett experienced, one only has to look at the defendant's upbringing. His father, Tony, a Sicilian immigrant like the defendant, is a dichotomy unto himself, quiet and passive, yet volatile and aggressive. And above all, he has an infamous reputation for associating with the wrong people. Well, I don't think I need to say more. I'm sure you get the point."

With the culmination of Hennessy's stinging discourse, Mario jumped out of his seat and started climbing over the table separating him from the Assistant District Attorney. It took the court bailiff and Mario's lawyers to restrain him from attacking a retreating prosecutor. All the while, Mario was calling Hennessy and members of his family, dead and alive, a few choice names in Italian.

The courtroom turned from decorum to disarray. Spectators and jurors were stunned. The media group was recording the escapade for the evening news and morning papers.

"You're out of order! You're all out of order!" the frazzled judge roared, slamming down the gavel sharply.

Mario shouted, "No, you and this lying-piece-of-shit District Attorney are out of order!"

Embarrassed and infuriated by the outbreak, Judge Phillips realized his courtroom was again out of control and demanded the bailiff clear the room. Law enforcement officers dragged a frustrated and incensed defendant from the courtroom.

The judge called for a one-hour recess and instructed attorneys for both sides to immediately go to his chambers.

Ferrara's defense attorneys, disturbed at Hennessy's dirty theatrics, engaged in a fierce argument that ended without any resolution—other than the judge's unlikely decision not to hold Mario in contempt.

When court reconvened, a composed Hennessy sighed heavily and said, "Ladies and gentlemen, you just had a front row seat to what can be the dangerous antics of Mario Ferrara. You saw firsthand evidence of his explosive temper. He is not a loon . . . just an aggressive, rebellious man. Love—you say? A campaign of *love?* I don't think so. The defendant organized and indulged not in a *love* campaign but in a *hate* campaign."

Avoiding eye contact with Mario, he leaned on the lectern and with a touch of sadness in his voice continued, "It's not pure coincidence that in the last year, the three well-known and respected individuals who challenged and debated Mr. Ferrara at the internationally acclaimed Golden Care Awards have been attacked. Two suffered near-fatal injuries. The other wasn't so lucky. The congressman was burned to death."

"Objection!" cried out Rose Gramoli, leaving her chair.

"Overruled!" snapped the judge.

At the courtroom easel, Hennessy talked the jurors through a series of crime scene and victim photos.

He said, "The State has shown you in finite detail how the defendant carefully plotted and methodically committed this heinous act against Congressman Johnson. It's a classic case of deliberate and premeditated murder. Much of the testimony given in this trial and much of the evidence presented here show that Mr. Ferrara often took radical measures as he engaged in acts of rebellion. Could this murder have been one more such act?"

Turning his attention to Beth who was seated with the reporter pool, he said: "You heard a disturbing interview conducted by an independent and unbiased reporter. All those who Ms. Downing interviewed expressed their concern for humanity except for the defendant, who made an insensitive and radical call to *strike*. One merciless assault, one near fatal hit and run, and one brutal death have left our city in fear and in shock. Gone forever is Congressman Johnson's courageous fight for a strong government to protect you. And we don't know how many more people are on the defendant's hit list."

"Objection!" protested Marvin Goldman.

"Overruled!" shouted the judge, banging his gavel.

James paced.

"Mr. Hennessy, we are waiting," barked the judge.

"Yes, Your Honor. The prosecution, through its expert witnesses, provided clear-cut evidence of Mario Ferrara's guilt. You heard the riveting eyewitness testimony that placed the defendant near Congressman

Johnson's home the night of the fire. The words the witness spoke were the final nails in Ferrara's coffin."

Hennessy stopped pacing and stood behind the lectern. He glanced at Mario, and added that when the arresting detective's evaluation of the defendant's state of mind was added to the mix, obvious conclusions were inevitable. He raised his voice in telling the jury that there was nothing left to consider or deliberate over; that Mario Ferrara was guilty of premeditated murder of a United States congressman.

Holding up a large photo to the jurors, Hennessy argued: "Congressman Johnson was a man of integrity who fought for justice every step of the way. But the interview in which the congressman chided Ferarra for being an anarchist planted in his crazed mind a seed of revenge—a seed that grew into a murderous plot. The congressman's life was taken without cause." He hesitated a moment, glared at the jurors, and said, "And now, Mr. Ferrara's life needs to be taken *with* cause."

Rose became furious and frustrated by Hennessy's bizarre, well-crafted eulogy and commentary. Objecting aggressively, she was once again in danger of the judge finding her in contempt of court. The previous two times, he levied heavy fines and threatened jail time. The judge perceived Hennessy's comments differently and overruled the objection, allowing the Assistant DA to continue.

Pleased with the ruling, Hennessy strutted a bit and coolly resumed: "Ladies and gentlemen of the jury, Mario Ferrara had no desire to serve anything or anyone except himself. His aspirations were born out of evil resulting in depravity. Mr. Ferrara stalked his prey one at a time until he finally devoured one of them."

Walking within a few feet of Mario, he insisted, "It was only by the good grace of God that other innocent bystanders of our city were not killed or maimed for life. You, as members of a civilized society and as jurors, have the power and the responsibility to be objective, and that means making a decision here that's devoid of emotion. Mario Ferrara must repent and pay society the ultimate price for his crime—the premeditated murder of Congressman Johnson."

Raising his voice, he continued, "Therefore, it is quite clear you are left with no other choice but to return a guilty verdict—a guilty verdict of murder in the first degree. You owe it to yourself, and you owe it to the people of the great state of New York."

Avoiding Ferrara, Hennessy swaggered back to his table, turned to the jury, and calmly said, "The prosecution rests its case. Thank you." He sat down and stroked his hair.

Chapter 56

Judge Phillips called for a quick recess.

Spectators and reporters headed for exits down the corridor, some in an orderly fashion; others resembling a cattle stampede: pushing, shoving, moaning, and groaning.

The majority of the press congregated in a cold, sterile hallway on the thirteenth floor. Joe and Sam huddled in a corner not far away. The reporters were concluding that, circumstantial evidence or not, the noose was tightening around Mario Ferrara's neck.

The creases in Joe's face had deepened. He said, "You have to remember that Hennessy and Mario have had absolutely no love for each other. Feelings have been the same between them since childhood, except now Hennessy's vendetta is playing out to a jury."

Sam grimaced and, in frustration, said, "If Mario would only have let go . . . about Tim, Johnson, Stanley, and Barrett, it may have never come to this."

Joe threw up his arms and said, "How could he let go? Mario never trusted Johnson and he despises Barrett. Did you take a good look at the weasel? He still wears high-water pants. Bet it doesn't keep him from stepping in his own shit. There are always piles of it wherever he is."

Ignoring his comment, Sam repeated, "Mario still should have let go."

Joe angrily responded, "Johnson tried to destroy me with wild accusations and showed no mercy to my family: he tried to deport my father!

That son of a bitch Barrett stole a bunch of money from me and reneged on commitments. He used it and other illegal gains to acquire the luxuries of life—a trophy wife, a mammoth vacation home on the Hamptons—and you say Mario should have let go?"

"It's not about you," barked Sam.

Joe waved him off. "Forget about it."

"You need to tone it down."

"Why in the hell is everyone trying to hang Mario?"

"This conversation is going nowhere. All we're doing is getting on each other's nerves. It's because of you that my hair keeps falling out," said Sam with a slight smile.

Joe, still tense, said, "Hold it a second: here comes John. Let's not worry the worrier any further. Coming up behind him is Catherine and the rest of the family."

Sam said, "I'll be right back. I need to check in with the office."

John, his lips tight, said, "Joe, I'm worried. I should have taken Frank Nunzi's advice."

Carmela cut in, "What's that going to get us?"

"She's right. We need to be the voice of reason. Rose's closing argument is going to win over the jury," said Joe, struggling to stay upbeat.

"What the hell are you smoking?" John asked irritably.

Tony, glaring at John, snapped, "Calm down!"

"I'm at wit's end," added Joe.

Catherine stood in silence listening intently to these comments that indicated the level of exasperation in the group.

Vincenza, emotionally distraught, was at home resting.

Mike Borelli was at LaGuardia Airport waiting for Frank Nunzi to arrive.

Recess was over and everyone started to scramble back into Courtroom Four.

Joe, making his way through the first set of double doors, came face to face with Hennessy. He had caught him in the eight-foot airlock before the second set of double doors that lead into the courtroom. He leaned toward him and contemptuously whispered in his ear, "If I had known a woman was a sure and easy way to get the judge to turn his head, I would have seized the opportunity in Mario's behalf."

"Screw you!" James growled.

Sam returned just in time to stop Joe from going any further.

Chapter 57

Judge Phillips entered the courtroom visibly upset. In the men's room, he had overheard two reporters.

One of the reporters had said, "That's right, James Hennessy clerked for Phillips during law school. Phillips should have known better than to take this case. How could he be unbiased?"

The other reporter replied, "If the defense loses this trial, it's headed straight to Appeals Court. It sure would make for interesting print."

"This time, the judge will be hard-pressed to declare his allegiance only to the law."

"I wonder what the hell he was thinking," one of the reporters said, raising his voice to be heard over a flushing toilet.

In the courtroom, spectators fidgeted in their seats, anxiously waiting for the trial to reconvene. Yet, they were finally feeling a little relief from the heat. The long-awaited fans had finally been brought into the courtroom.

Once the bailiff called the court back to order, Judge Phillips demanded the fans be shut down to stop their annoying whirling sound. This action caused a loud groan to rise in the courtroom.

Holding herself rigid, Rose gave Judge Phillips a quizzical look as she approached the bench in a slow, deliberate manner. The courtroom was now eerily quiet, except for the sound of her stiletto heels clicking on the tiled floor. Her pacing lasted only a few moments, although it seemed much longer, before she suddenly stopped. Turning, she curled her lips as she glanced at Hennessy and then moved to the jury box.

Walking along the jury box railing, she again made eye contact with every member of the weary jury. With a soft voice she said, "You . . . and you . . . and you, . . . each one of you will have to look deep into your hearts, your minds, and yes, . . . even your souls, to discern the validity of the evidence presented in this case. Remember, the only question you need to answer is, is Mario Ferrara guilty of the crime of murder? Nothing more!" The jurors, sitting tall in their seats, listened intently.

At the table for the defense where Marvin Goldman was seated with Mario, she picked up a thick file folder, flipped through a number of pages, and slammed down the portfolio, sending sheets of paper flying every which way. Judge Phillips bolted out of his seat, spilling a glass of water over his freshly pressed robe.

The courtroom burst into laughter, but before Judge Phillips's ire could strike they quickly resumed their silence.

Rose bit her lip to suppress a smile. Pausing, she lowered her voice and, in a belligerent tone, said, "Ladies and gentlemen, what we have here is a carefully orchestrated frame-up, an almost perfect web of deceit and entrapment. It's so preposterous that if it were not so sick and perverted it would be laughable.

Glaring at Hennessy, she accused, "You have been presented with innuendo after innuendo—a preponderance of imagination woven into circumstantial evidence without a single shred of hard fact."

She turned back to the jurors. "The prosecution's case is devoid of logic. It is inexcusable that the police didn't look elsewhere to unearth the true perpetrator of this crime. It could have been the Weatherman Organization who actually blew up their own building in Greenwich Village, . . . or other terrorists that resented Congressman Johnson's extreme 'patriotism.' Remember Sam Melville and the downtown bombings?"

She paused and moved slowly to the jury-box railing before continuing. Her tone was solemn. "Then there's the other alternative; just suppose a crime was not committed—a theory that still needs to be investigated. Let us remember, the congressman perished in his art studio and it's quite plausible that the tragic fire may have been an accident."

Rose stopped to take a drink of water. She wanted to give the jury time to ponder this possibility and thus reinforce the theory of reasonable doubt in their minds before she proceeded. She changed her tone. It was less solemn, more confident—a tone meant to move the jury to accept her comments as authoritative. "His art materials, many of which were flammable, were stored in a small airtight closet. A buildup of fumes, a smoldering cigarette, the pilot light on a water heater, and who knows what else, could have contributed to igniting that fire. The prosecution, in a rush to judgment, quickly dismissed all accident theories." Her voice began to mellow as she finished. "I can tell you with assurance that Mario Ferrara did not in any manner whatsoever take part in any act that resulted in the fire causing Congressman Johnson's death."

Leaning on the edge of the defense table she continued: "Our investigation cut to shreds the testimony of a so-called eyewitness. The witness stated he observed Mario near the congressman's house moments after the explosion." Pacing in front of the bench, she said, "Let me remind you it was pitch-black that tragic evening. We were a city without power or moonlight. No specific expertise is needed. No expert witnesses on lighting or astronomy. What's needed is common sense!"

Walking toward Hennessy she said loudly so there would be no mistaking her message, "The witness was proven to be not only nearsighted, but also a habitual liar known to conjure up any story to get his name in ink. Thus, to be specific, what you have observed and heard as evidence and supposed collaboration of fact, I prefer to call *cow dung*!" This comment produced giggles.

While waiting for things to settle down, she stood in front of the prosecutor's table. With a wide smile on her face, Rose looked at Hennessy and said softly, "I don't believe the prosecution knows how to define *proof*, let alone present it."

Hennessy scoffed.

Pointing to an easel prepared by her legal team, Rose said earnestly, "Members of the jury, before you is a case of contrived tales, hatred, and vengeance. You were told that Mario had revolutionaries as heroes and role models. That's true. However, they forgot to mention that two of those revolutionary heroes were George Washington and Gandhi. I thank the prosecution for bringing that fact to the forefront." Smiling, she bowed slightly to Hennessy.

"You have heard character witnesses, young and old alike, who knew and collaborated with Mario. One word summed up their portrayal of him, *love*. He fights against bondage and is fearless when confronting authority. If Mario is an agent of *change*, the change is to take away darkness and shed light."

Her assessment of Mario gained the undivided attention of everyone in the courtroom. Again, Rose turned to Hennessy, saying, "Let me tell you what Mr. Hennessy did do in his overzealous approach to get a conviction. He excluded key elements of pertinent and substantial segments of Ms. Downing's interview."

The judge interrupted to warn that her repeated disparaging remarks concerning the prosecution should be tempered.

"I understand, Your Honor," Rose humbly replied.

Satisfied that he had exercised his authority in a convincing manner, the judge told her to continue.

As part of her courtroom strategy, Rose was determined to get under Hennessy's skin, but she hadn't expected Judge Phillips to constantly come to his rescue.

Rose announced that she would play a different portion of that same interview. She started the tape recorder.

> Beth: *Mr. Ferrara, I think our audience would be interested in hearing your thoughts on why you were so inclusive in your Declaration of Liberty.*
>
> Mario: *There's a season and a time for everything, including living and dying. In this revolution, it's time to tear up and knock down, to plant and rebuild. So, we need to challenge all peoples, especially those in a position of influence—the elite and the powerful in all segments of society. We need to challenge them to allow the peoples to live liberty.*
>
> Congressman: *May I comment?*
> Beth: *Yes, Congressman.*
> Congressman: *Religion is our nation's strength. To live the Christian life is what America is all about.*

Beth: *Yes, Cardinal . . .*

Cardinal: *I am a shepherd of the Roman Catholic Church. I carry a full burden of sorrow in my heart for its people. I am obedient to my superior, His Holy Father. I know, without a doubt, that our flock needs to be faithful and obedient to the Church, the Holy See. You must understand, Elizabeth, without leadership and guidance you have chaos. Without leadership and guidance, religion dies.*

Beth: *Thank you, Your Eminence.*

Beth: *Dr. Chou, if you wish, I would love to hear your thoughts.*

Dr. Chou: *I have a different vantage point than the gentlemen here—one that includes the view of a diversity of cultures in the international community. From this vantage point, I see things differently and wonder if what Mario Ferrara says isn't valid. Maybe some of what he says should be heeded. Maybe, in following some of his advice, we could create a better world. How much of what he says is true, I don't know. I need to give that further thought.*

Beth: *I certainly appreciate your insight.*

Mario: *It's interesting to hear the congressman's and the cardinal's response concerning religion, . . . yet, I never mentioned the word religion.*

Beth: *I'm afraid our time is up. I thank you all for your heartfelt commentary. Following a short break we will be right back.*

The jury may or may not have noticed that Beth's words effectively closed out that particular segment of the interview in such a way as to disallow Cardinal Stanley and Congressman Johnson a chance to respond.

Rose turned off the tape recorder, moved back to the lectern, and said, "Ladies and gentleman of the jury, my summation will be short and simple. Mario Ferrara, at great risk to his defense, took the stand and spoke to you. You observed him and listened carefully to his words." She paused for a moment in order to catch the jurors' body language. "Mario answered the most probing questions directed at him by our *esteemed*, pompous, publicity-seeking Assistant District Attorney."

In response to her remark regarding Hennessy, the judge intervened and said sternly, "Ms. Gramoli, once again you are out of order."

"Yes, Your Honor."

Judge Phillips, shifting uneasily in his chair, gave her a look that would have frightened Genghis Khan.

Ignoring him, she turned her attention back to the jury. Smiling, she moved toward Mario and continued her appeal. "You looked into his eyes. Are they the eyes of a murderer? I defend him, not because he is my client, but because I whole-heartedly believe and trust him."

Gesturing with her hand, she said, "Do you remember how, when seated in the witness chair, he was grilled relentlessly by . . . you know who?"

Jurors chuckled.

Hennessy scowled.

Judge Phillips sneered, and when he raised his gavel everyone in the courtroom immediately settled down.

Turning serious, Rose continued, "Do you remember Mario's response when Mr. Hennessy asked the number one question of the trial? 'Mr. Ferrara, you say you speak the truth: please tell the court in your own words, what the word *truth* means.'"

She opened a file and said, "Now, if I may, let me read how Mario responded to this condescending prosecutor."

"Ms. Gramoli, you're testing my patience," said the judge, his eyes twitching.

"Sorry, Your Honor."

James Hennessy was fuming.

She waited a few seconds to add to the tension felt by her listeners and then said, "Now to continue with Mario's response." She read from the transcript:

Truth is defined in the dictionary as "conformity to fact," but to me

Liberty is Truth.
Truth is wisdom.
Wisdom is logic.
Logic is common sense.
Common sense is the inner voice.
The inner voice is energy.

Energy is one peoples, one earth, one universe.
One universe is the Spirit of Life.
The Spirit of Life is Love and Liberty.
Love and Liberty is Truth.
And when you embrace Love and Liberty you cannot deny
Truth because you then deny yourself.

But, Mr. Hennessy, let's face it: you really don't understand
what love or liberty mean. So how in the world can you understand
truth?

"Ladies and gentlemen, I do remember the tight-lipped expression on Mr. Hennessy's red face, as well as your smiles," Rose said, enjoying the reaction of the jurors to this statement. She glanced at the table where the prosecution team sat and she beamed. Then, she continued: "The prosecution, stretching the truth beyond reason, asserted that Mario caused the explosion resulting in the death of Congressman Johnson. Mr. Hennessy would also like you to believe that he was behind the wheel of the van that injured Cardinal Arthur Stanley and that he ordered an assault on Dr. Chou. But, I know and you know that someone or some entity other than Mario Ferrara, committed those outrageous and barbaric acts. Why? For one purpose and one purpose only: to fulfill a vendetta against Mario and society."

She walked over to her display board and pointed to large red handwritten letters that formed the bold words: "Who? Who would commit these heinous acts? Religious zealots? Right-wing extremists? Who?"

Moving back to the jury box, Rose said, "I ask you to think and then, think again. Furthermore, as for the arresting detectives' opinions of Mario Ferrara's mental state; that's exactly what it was; an opinion, not a psychiatric evaluation. Their testimony was inconsistent and incoherent."

Positioning herself behind Mario, she placed her hands on his shoulders. "Mario Ferrara is not an evil man, nor is he guilty of committing murder or creating mayhem in any degree. Although, I certainly can tell you what he *is* guilty of. He is guilty of speaking his heart; nothing more.

His words placed fear in the minds of those who are rattled by truth and liberty. Mario told the truth, and it is the truth that will set him free."

Pushing the edge of the envelope, she pointed at James Hennessy and bellowed, "*I* know it and if you had half a brain *you* would know it." Turning to spectators, she continued, "Each and every person in this courtroom knows it. Mario Ferrara is innocent! As a trial lawyer, I have placed my entire reputation at risk. Mario is a friend I have known for years, and without hesitation I would place my life in his hands. But instead, he placed his life in mine."

Standing in front of the jury, Rose softened her voice. "I ask you, please look deep inside and let your conscience decide. Your conscience is an extension of the community." Clasping her hands in a prayer-like manner, she said, "If you do what I ask, the one and only verdict you can deliver is not guilty!"

In an unusual move, looking away from the jurors, she focused on the standing-room-only crowd.

"Mario Ferrara is not guilty! Let him experience his definition of truth—liberty. Set Mario Ferrara free!" Turning back to the jurors, she smiled. "Let your hearts as well as your heads be your guide. The defense rests its case. Thank you."

Judge Phillips called another quick recess.

Hennessy hastily conferred with his cocounsels in preparation for his final rebuttal argument.

At the jury box, Hennessy calmly said, "Ms. Gramoli's attempt to distort the truth has failed. Her statements were frivolous. Her unruly and childish antics are an embarrassment to the court."

Staring at Rose with contempt, he roared, "This is a case of murder: it's not about Mario Ferrara's eyes. All her rhetoric and all the testimony of defense witnesses have not presented one iota of evidence to prove his right to live. To the contrary, all evidence supports the fact he deserves the death penalty."

Hennessy hesitated momentarily, and then leaned forward. "On second thought, I will not dignify Ms. Gramoli's preposterous remarks with further comment. Everyone in this courtroom knows the negative effect the defendant had on our great country by his incendiary challenge of a revolution of liberty and general strike. Mario Ferrara's actions have shown a total disregard for the law. He has incited people to overthrow the American system."

"Objection!" shouted Rose.

"Overruled!" thundered the judge.

Hennessy said, "The defendant was not satisfied with disruption and turmoil. No! He took revolt to the extreme by taking the life of another human being, namely Congressman Johnson."

Looking at Judge Phillips, Hennessy cried out with vengeance, "Mario Ferrara and his revolutionary participants are anarchists, much like his role models Sacco and Vanzetti. Only this time, he became the murderer! I beg you, do not allow this killer to take another breath of fresh air! I ask you to find the defendant guilty of murder in the first degree!"

Bowing his head, James Hennessy walked to the prosecution's table, turned to the jurors, sat, and softly said, "I beg you; . . . thank you."

Chapter 58

....

The Honorable Judge William "Justice" Phillips sat erect. He wrinkled his brow as he addressed the jury. Wasting no time, he gave instructions in his harshest voice.

He began, "Jurors, you have heard all the evidence. I want you to listen carefully as I give the rulings of law that apply to this case." He paused to take a drink of water and continued: "Remember this: whatever Mr. Hennessy or Ms. Gramoli may have argued is only relevant if supported by evidence. Above all, you must follow the law whether you agree with it or not. I ask of you nothing more than a just verdict."

He then completed jury instructions. The whole process was moving forward at this point like a well-oiled machine.

Throughout the judge's commentary, Mario Ferrara sat straight, his eyes focused on the jury.

"This court is adjourned," the bailiff cried out.

Jurors, displaying mixed facial expressions, slowly filed out of the jury box. The courtroom erupted with activity. Spectators, including members of the media, began discussing the tactics used by the lawyers in the case and the potential outcome of the trial.

Reporters rushed to pay phones to call their news desks while film crews headed to the exits.

Hennessy approached Rose and extended his hand, but before he could open his mouth, she whispered loudly, "Kiss my ass, you rotten bastard!"

Grinning, Hennessy flipped her off.

The bailiff, along with two sheriff's deputies, came forward and handcuffed a seemingly unnerved Mario Ferrara. As he was being escorted out of the courtroom, Rose reached for his hand.

"Don't worry; we got 'em where we want 'em," said Mario with a slight smile.

One reporter was lagging behind the others. She was still inside the courtroom gathering her belongings when she noticed the sheriff's deputies leading Mario into Judge Phillip's chambers. Through her personal experiences with the judge, she was keenly aware his chambers led to a back door in close range of the freight elevator. She alerted her film crew to move quickly and cover the back of the building.

The press lauded James Hennessy for staying his course, for holding on in spite of intimidation from a certain segment of society.

One noted television commentator referred to him as "the pit bull of the judicial system." Others in the media shredded Rose Gramoli for taking a case that might have been beyond her capabilities.

Mario's family, friends, enemies, and a large contingent of curiosity seekers had assembled in front of the Criminal Courts Building. The undecided weather matched their moods, as heavy, dark clouds lingered over the courthouse.

John and Carmela moved through the noisy crowd looking for Rose. Suddenly, there she was, a crumpled form leaning against a huge granite column outside the entrance.

John walked up behind her and startled her by speaking before she saw him. "Rose, where do we stand?" he asked.

Straightening herself, she said in a grave voice, "It's always difficult fighting a shadow of circumstantial evidence." Taking a deep breath she continued, "But I believe the jury heard and understood our case."

They started walking toward Tony.

Tony hugged Rose and thanked her in a tone that revealed he was in better spirits than earlier in the day.

John, with a sour expression on his face, added, "Maybe Hennessy and his overzealous approach alienated the jury. And with any luck, it will come back and bite him in the ass."

"Carmela, what do you think?" asked Rose.

Carmela answered honestly and with tears in her eyes, "I don't know. I guess I'm really worried."

Tony listened and said nothing.

Joe and Sam found their way to the Ferraras and Rose.

Mike was still at the airport waiting patiently for Frank's private plane to arrive.

Sam kissed· Rose and, in an optimistic tone, spoke first. "I know we're going to prevail. In the waning minutes of this . . . this marathon trial . . . you reached the hearts and minds of the jurors. You've done one outstanding job!"

Tony embraced Joe and Sam and said, "Vincenza and I can't thank you enough for your support and undying faith in Mario."

Joe, not really paying attention, slapped his hands together and said irritably, "From the beginning, I was concerned that Mario's obsession with past crusaders would come back to haunt him." Cracking his knuckles he spat out, "I think it's ironic that Mario himself could be the subject of a major chapter in the book he's been writing forever. It's a great title, *Me and Dante Down by the Inferno*; too bad he—"

Sam, perplexed at Joe's words, stared at him and snapped, "Leave it be. You're starting to get on my nerves. It's hopeless to try to change

Mario. You know he is just as determined in his pursuit of liberty as Garibaldi was."

"I still think that's crazy," Joe snapped.

"You two are always the same," said Tony, forcing a smile.

Their conversation was interrupted when Carmela noticed Catherine pushing her way through the crowd and heading toward them.

"Here comes the love of Mario's life," John said with a smile.

Her eyes beet red, her voice cracking, she said, "My heart's broken. I'm angry, I'm bitter, and I'm all cried out."

Catherine's face revealed the strain of the trial.

Carmela, reaching out, hugged her.

Turning to Joe and Sam, Catherine said, "I'm proud of both of you. I know Hennessy tried to entrap you into saying something negative about Mario. Still, you stayed strong in your convictions."

Hennessy had badgered Joe as a hostile witness, accusing him of being an enabler who fanned the flames of his explosive friend. He was a little softer on Castellano.

Joe bluntly said, "That rat-bastard Hennessy is going down like the Titanic."

"I hope the son of a bitch dies of a heart attack and joins Johnson in hell," Catherine said, unaware that she was raising her voice, causing people to turn and stare at her. Her words shocked Joe and Sam. This was not the woman they knew. They did not respond.

Beth Downing approached the group, gave Joe a flirtatious glance, and with notebook in hand turned to Rose. "Ms. Gramoli, I commend you on an excellent job. I especially enjoyed the way you took on Hennessy."

Joe was not the only one who was taken in and inspired by Beth's personal charm. Her charisma was apparent to all. A small crowd gathered to hear the conversation. Beth continued, "His reputation is at stake, not only as prosecuting attorney, but as a man with other future political aspirations."

"Thanks for your kind words," Rose replied.

"How did Judge Phillips' decision to allow certain pieces of evidence that seemed out of context play out to the jurors?"

"That's a hard read," said Rose cautiously, fully aware that Beth might quote her in the morning papers.

Sam, with a smile, said, "John, the more I think of Rose's closing argument, the more confident I become. Mario is going to beat this injustice."

"Peep, I hope you're right."

Joe, placing his arm around Tony, was thinking of the fact that Vincenza wasn't there, that she was bedridden. He tenderly asked, "How are you holding up?"

"I'm worried sick and Vincenza prays the rosary all day."

Joe sighed and shook his head.

Beth Downing, motioning Joe aside, invited him to dinner. "It's my treat," she offered.

He rolled his eyes and grinned.

The line of spectators stretched along the front of the building and across the street. They were craning their necks to catch a glimpse of Mario Ferrara. Cameras were clicking, tapes were rolling, and people were pushing and shoving, as looming clouds opened, letting rain do a free fall.

Those that had assembled outside were arguing about Mario's motives and his prospects for acquittal.

"His manifesto reflected his unstable personality."

"He tried hard to live what he spoke."

"Mario Ferrara is the devil himself incarnate."

"Could be a hung jury!" exclaimed a voice from the media group.

Another reporter, looking puzzled, responded. "I don't know. But whatever the verdict they return, many facets of society have already been impacted."

"If Mario's convicted, Rose Gramoli's tactics will be questioned forever. I wasn't sure whether she was grandstanding or being clever. The
jury had to be confused."

"Mr. Castellano, was Mario Ferrara a success or failure?" asked a
reporter who pushed a microphone in Sam's face.

"Mario doesn't believe in failure or success, only progress. But if
there is a measurement, I have come to the conclusion that if failure was
an end result for Mario, what better vision quest can a person have to fail
at than Mario's?"

Traffic slowed to a crawl, enabling drivers and passengers alike to
gawk at the media show taking place.

In a surreal atmosphere, a few teenagers nestled in the drenched
crowd, started chanting, "liberty . . . liberty." By time the third *liberty*
had sounded, many more voices had joined in, in support of Mario.

The arresting detectives, with shocked expressions frozen on their
faces, were among the unruly throng.

"Look, there's Mario!" Catherine excitedly cried out.

Two sheriff's deputies appeared, escorting a shackled Mario Ferrara
to a waiting transport van. Instead of going out the back door as they
originally planned, the deputies, at Hennessy's insistence, led Mario out
the front door of the Criminal Courts Building in shackles.

In a conversation with Barrett, he said, "Make sure you recruit
enough people to assemble in front of the building when court adjourns.
It will be a perfect opportunity to humiliate and taunt him before he
heads back to Rikers Island and awaits the verdict."

Mario's face brightened the instant he saw Catherine and his *famigha*
and *amici*. Chants of *liberty* continued bellowing out from the crowd as
rain came pouring down.

Catherine, sobbing and holding on to Tony said, "Mario told me, he
doesn't regret his past actions in the cause of liberty and for us to be
strong whatever the outcome of the trial. He wants us to know that he'll
love us forever."

The police transport wagon slowly pulled away from the curb to take Mario back to his jail cell on Rikers Island.

In all the excitement, no one paid any attention to a white delivery van double-parked in the shroud of huge raindrops that were beating down on Centre Street.

Tony, concerned about Vincenza, rushed home.

The time had come to await a verdict.

A headline in the evening edition of the *World Telegram*
FERRARA'S FATE LEFT IN THE HANDS OF TWELVE

Chapter 59

....

Windshield wipers on the police transport wagon were losing the struggle to keep pace with the blinding rainstorm, causing the sheriff's deputy to slow the vehicle to a crawl. Up ahead, flashing red and blue lights from emergency vehicles flickered through the rain.

As the van approached the intersection, the deputy could see that two police officers clad in yellow slickers were diverting traffic around a tragic accident. Apparently a cement truck had broadsided a Volkswagen bus, flipping it on its side. Paramedics were attending to two figures sprawled out on the wet blacktop, one male and one female.

A patrolman signaled the deputy to stop. As the patrolman approached the driver's side of the wagon, the deputy rolled down the window and said, "Looks pretty bad. Do you need help?"

The deputy grimaced as the police officer slowly raised a .45 caliber pistol hidden under his raincoat to the deputy's head. Smiling, the police officer pulled the trigger. Blood splattered across the windshield. In tandem, hooded occupants from a white delivery van smashed the opposite window, sending glass flying everywhere.

With a gun pointed at his face, the other deputy was motioned out of the vehicle, where he was pushed to the ground and shot repeatedly in the back. His body recoiled with the impact of each bullet.

At the same time, the tires of a NY-A1 ambulance slid on the wet pavement as it came to a halt beside the transport wagon. The rogue cop who shot both deputies calmly walked to the rear of the wagon and unlocked the back door.

Mario sat shackled, unable to move, his mind racing, trying to process the trauma he was experiencing. As the door flung open, he stiffened up and cried out angrily, "What the hell is going on?"

Without a word spoken, two hooded men of enormous size blindfolded and dragged him from the van to the ambulance that sat with siren wailing. There they unshackled him. As the ambulance pulled away, another rouge cop jumped behind the wheel of the police transport wagon and then sped off in the direction it was originally headed.

A short ten minutes later the ambulance slowed, the door was pushed open, and Mario was shoved out before the vehicle came to a full stop. The moment Mario's body hit the pavement, he was rolled, pushed, and shoved toward several people anxiously waiting for him to arrive. His body ached: tasting blood with his tongue, he slowly lifted himself up.

A moment later, a man dressed in a navy blue blazer slapped him hard across the face, and squealed, "Don't you wish *you* had the power?" Mario's body cringed with pain. Holding his hands up to his bloody face, Mario felt blood begin to ooze from his nose.

A heavyset figure slammed Mario back to the ground and began kicking him. He yelled, "Here's my liberty: a gift from me to you."

Another man yanked him up and held him in place while a female kneed him in the groin. She said laughing, "That's what we call *tough love.*"

Bleeding and bruised, he could feel his eyes swell under the blindfold. Mario said nothing as he stood in the middle of a circle, hearing moving vehicles under his feet.

One of the hooded men stood at a steel pillar holding a knotted rope. He first ripped Mario's blindfold off; then he removed his hood and snickered. "I hope you're tougher than that Irish bastard Gallagher. He whimpered when I hung him from the cross."

"You rotten son of a bitch: I should have known," Mario mumbled as blood dripped from his chin.

In a rough, sarcastic tone the man spat out, "Why so ungrateful? What better spot than the Brooklyn Bridge to provide the best view of the city skyline. But before you swing, I have a surprise."

Another man laughing wildly grabbed Tony Ferrara by the neck and pushed him out from behind the group. Tony's mouth was still duct taped as a short, stocky man squeezed the looped-end of a rope over Tony's head.

With a clenched jaw, the man yelled, "It's only fair that he goes first." He paused. "Take a good last look at your *papà*," the stocky man cried out as he pushed . . .

Chapter 60

September 10

The morning papers covered the aftermath.

A field reporter's assessment stated:

It's been a vicious affair . . .

Throughout the trial, especially when seated in the witness chair, the 60-year-old Ferrara, although appearing stoic, showed signs of wear and tear.

During The Strike, he survived beatings, mud slinging, and foiled attempts on his life. He was arrested nine times and had ample opportunities to give up and let society function in the status quo.

Still and all, the more adversity he faced, the more determined he became.

Mario Ferrara may not have fully known the letter of the law, but he knew the law of the streets.

On a nightly news program in Kansas City, a news anchor closed out his segment with the following editorial:

Mario Ferrara was consistent. There was nothing new in his rhetoric and he promised no miracles. He just wanted to remind us of our birthright. I myself have wondered what would have been the results if just for a moment we had taken him seriously and had given the message of love a try in embracing the cause of liberty.

But then, I gave it a little more thought and determined Mario meant not a few people should live love, but everyone on earth should live love. Obviously, "everyone" would include all children, men, and women, wherever they were and whatever position they held: they would all have to live love. Thereupon, after further reflection, it dawned on me, Mario Ferrara is not a revolutionary . . . he's a nut. Yet, I must admit he never gave up.

Beth Downing's weekly column read:

He conveyed news of liberty to the poor and oppressed. I was there among people who believed, and I can assure you as an agnostic, I personally sensed their energy and aura of hope.

Mario Ferrara was held up as a sacrificial lamb to satisfy the carnivorous appetite of the members of the power structure that claim righteousness for their own existence and meaning.

If the inquisition has returned, the question is, for how long?

In an interview with a reporter from the *Law Beacon*, Rose Gramoli said:

Once in a while someone fights back. Mario Ferrara had no organization; he became an avenger of truth, an advocate of sorts, a champion of the oppressed. He called for no one to follow him. He invited people to join him.

Mario said, "Each person needs to take responsibility for himself or herself and change into love."

He confronted people when necessary and assisted people in time of need. Those in society whom Mario has unnerved have tried to pin a heinous crime on him in order to get him out of their hair.

Father Carelli wrote an article for the *Catholic Reader.*

Although he may have gone against the wind, my reflection of Mario Ferrara's plea for love is simple. I heard no clichés about loving someone, but not having to like them; I didn't even hear words about distinguishing between the sinner and the sin, or talk about who is your enemy and who is your friend. Nothing!

He didn't advocate that we love with our total being or subscribe to that radical thinking without first putting into practice what he spoke of without subterfuge or deception. He challenged people to be different by thinking only with love.

Mario Ferrara surely did it his way.

BOOK VII

Chapter 61

A husky prison guard was standing over him. "Mario! Mario! Quick, wake up! The jury has reached a verdict!" Jolted out of his nightmare, Mario leapt out of bed and smashed his head against the flaking metal frame of the upper bunk. He shuttered at the thought of his nightmare as he quickly dressed.

The ride back from Rikers Island to the courthouse seemed to take forever.

Mario threw a kiss to Catherine as he took his seat next to Rose and turned to watch the jurors enter the room.

Everyone in Courtroom Four sat motionless as the jury foreman read the verdict:

We of the jury find the defendant, Mario Ferrara . . . Not Guilty!

Word spread swiftly . . .

Inside and outside the courthouse, spectators and reporters reacted with varied emotions.

Mario smiled.

Rose jumped up and hugged Mario.

Judge Phillips grunted and sat in silence.

Hennessy slammed his briefcase shut and stormed out.

Barrett wiped his sweaty hands on his wrinkled silk suit and rushed out of the building.

Catherine, tears of joy running down her cheeks, rushed to Mario with her arms opened wide. He picked her up and held her close.

Tony hurriedly telephoned Vincenza, who was overcome with emotion and unable to talk.

Frank and Mike stood by Tony's side with their arms around one another.

John, Carmela, Joe, and Sam were ecstatic as hugs, kisses, and tears abounded.

Beth Downing stood ready with notebook in hand.

Dr. Susan Chou waved to Mario and slowly walked out of the courtroom.

Cardinal Stanley had already taken an Alitalia flight to Rome and was unaware of the verdict until he landed. As he moved through the airport, he heard two stewardesses talking about the "wonderful news" that Mario Ferrara had been acquitted. He suddenly became quite pale with fright.

Hearing the results of the trial, Leonard Knight threw his radio against the wall.

A reporter tried to corner Mario as he was leaving the courtroom. He shouted, "Mr. Ferrara, what's next?"

With his arms around Catherine and Tony he shouted, "I'm going home to Little Italy and celebrate with *la famigha.*"

SEPTEMBER 11, 1974

A headline in the *World Telegram*
FERRARA'S NIGHTMARE IS OVER

Chapter 62

October 11, 1974

In celebration of a victorious verdict, Catherine and Mario took Tony and Vincenza to La Boheme at the Metropolitan Opera. Tony left with tears in his eyes—tears that had nothing to do with the opera itself; it reminded him of *Teatro Massimo,* the elegant opera house in Palermo.

Vincenza was sobbing—not for Mario this time—but at the emotional heart-wrenching love story.

Somewhere in the theatre were Joe and Beth who had begun dating soon after the trial ended.

The next morning at breakfast, Mario said, "Catherine, I know I should be sitting on top of the world . . . but my stomach turns. Something still bugs me."

Smiling, she said, "Your stomach turns because you ate *Mamma's* cold meatball sandwiches when we got home."

"I'm serious."

She reached for his hand and said, "Sorry. What does your intuition say to you?"

"*Liberty* and *unfinished business.*"

"Listen to what Tim told you. Pray for guidance."

Mario grinned and said, "Suppose the guidance is . . . ah, never mind."

"What?"

"Not now, maybe later."

NOVEMBER 1

A headline in the *New York Journal American*
HALLOWEEN HOLD-UP TURNS DEADLY
GUN FIGHT IN BROAD DAYLIGHT KILLS TWO . . . WOUNDS ONE

> *Mike Borelli, longtime resident of Bensonhurst, was shot dead during a bold robbery attempt at Rossi's Grocery store on Avenue U in Brooklyn. Mr. Rossi fired two shots before being killed by a lone gunman wearing a clown mask. The manhunt continues.*
>
> *Joe Borelli, Mike's son, was taken to New York Methodist Hospital. He is expected to recover.*

The Ferraras took care of burial arrangements for Mike. He was laid to rest at Calvary Cemetery.

Beth held Joe's hand and in an agonizing whisper said, "Please leave everything to the police."

"I have a gut feeling. Something stinks," he said. His body was shaking. "I couldn't even be there to bury Pop. Somebody had to follow us to Rossi's. Whoever planned it and the son of a bitch who killed him needs to pay and pay big. I'll find him and . . . "

Mario, extremely distressed, leaned on the hospital bed railing and said somberly, "Instead of going bananas, listen to Beth. For once in your life, listen."

"Look who's talking," said Joe, forcing a slight grin.

Shaking his head, Mario grimaced and said, "Cheap shot. But unfortunately, I know you're right."

Hennessy's phone rang.

"James, good for you."
"What are you talking about?"
"You know . . . nice set-up."

Seconds later, Sam answered his phone.
"Sam, it's me, James. Barrett called. He's an idiot."

DECEMBER 5

A headline in the *New York Daily Mirror*
HORROR ON EAST SIXTY-NINTH AND PARK AVE

> *Richard Barrett, President of Gateway Bank, fell from his eighth-story balcony and was pronounced dead at the scene from massive head injuries.*
>
> *Last evening, Mr. Barrett, returning from a business trip to Rome, went directly from JFK International Airport to his high-rise suite. Witnesses heard a chilling scream, looked up, and watched him plunge to his death.*
>
> *A preliminary investigation revealed that a faulty railing caused his fall. The police ruled it an accident. His wife, on vacation on the French Riviera, could not be reached.*

1975

MAY 1

A headline in the *Daily Mirror*
VIETCONG IN SAIGON . . . A TRAGIC ENDING
SOUTH SURRENDERS UNCONDITIONALLY

> *Yesterday, in a failed war effort, Saigon fell into the hands of the Communists. The city was immediately renamed Ho Chi Minh City.*

Tony handed the newspaper back to Mario, flipped his right arm up and said in disgust, "Angelo died for what?"

"It's beyond that."

Tony, with tears welling up in his eyes, sadly said, "It's too late for anything—except to always remember Angelo's bright smile."

Mario hugged Tony as both men, heads lowered and backs turned to any customers that might catch a glimpse, shook with sorrow.

JULY 1

The day after reputed gangster Sam Giancana was gunned down in Chicago, Judge William Phillips retired from the bench.

On July 4, the power elite, including James Hennessy who recently had announced his candidacy for Congress, Sam Castellano, and some wannabes attended an outlandish luncheon given in the judge's honor. Cardinal Stanley gave the benediction and announced his own retirement and permanent relocation to Rome.

Leonard Knight, who was under indictment for criminal fraud and conspiracy, was in deep conversation with Judge Phillips.

The judge, flustered, wiped away perspiration from his brow and started to move away when Knight said furiously, "You're a rat bastard."

JULY 5

A headline in the *New York Journal American*
EIGHT-HOUR RETIREMENT TRAGICALLY ENDS
FOR THE JUDGE KNOWN AS "JUSTICE"

> *William Phillips left his retirement party and climbed into his classic automobile. He then headed to his New Paltz cabin in upstate New York.*
>
> *Along New York State Highway 84, he apparently fell asleep at the wheel and lost control. His '58 Corvette careened off a steep embankment, rolled a couple of times, and blew up.*

DECEMBER 18

A headline in the *Daily Mirror*
LEONARD KNIGHT, FINANCIER, CONVICTED

> *Knight, formerly a major shareholder of Gateway Bank, was convict-ed on all counts of criminal fraud and conspiracy. Hearing the verdict, he flipped over the defendant's table and had to be restrained by sheriff's deputies.*
>
> *Due to previous political campaign commitments, James Hennessy declined to prosecute the high-profile case. Leonard Knight was sentenced to 25 years in Attica State Prison.*

DECEMBER 20

"Mr. Solari, based on your excessive demands in favor of Vatican Bank, I have come to the conclusion that it's time for us to cease doing business."

"Mr. Castellano, don't be too sure."

"Mr. Solari, that is my final answer."

"Mr. Castellano, I repeat. Don't be too sure. We are, you might say, in the same rowboat with only one oar and no life preservers."

Sam curtly said, "Mr. Solari, it's time for me to go."

"Not too far, Mr. Castellano, not too far."

1976

On July 4, Tony stood proudly with *la famigha* and Frank Nunzi watching the hundreds of ships sail through New York Harbor in celebration of the nation's Bicentennial.

"*Papà*, we have to do it," said Mario light heartedly.

"Do what?"

"Go to the Statue of Liberty."

"How many times have I said *no*?"

"*No* is not acceptable anymore. We need to go."

"Tony, listen to him," Vincenza pleaded.

"To have you talk no more about it . . . OK," he said, grinning.

"You're making me crazy," she said and then she joined her family in laughter.

Two days later, Tony sat quietly on the ferry ride to Liberty Island to visit his beautiful friend Lady Liberty up close.

After touring the area, Tony stood in silence at the railing and stared across the harbor at the imposing structures on Ellis Island.

Tony said, "To me, it seems like not too many years ago when as a young man after work at the fish market, I would walk to the edge of the harbor and stare longingly across the Tyrrhenian Sea and dream dreams of America." He wrapped his arm around Mario, smiled, and said, "She has been good to us."

The pendulous swing of his emotions mirrored the fickle weather that flip-flopped with sun, clouds, and rain.

It was not until Mario took hold of his father's shoulders and hugged him that Tony let go of the railing and walked away with tears in his eyes. He said, "We can never repay God for what he did for *la famigha*."

"I agree. But maybe someday I can give it a shot."

Tony kissed his cheek and tenderly said, "I tell you, my son, God will let you know when it's time."

NOVEMBER 3

Jimmy Carter, a 52-year-old peanut farmer from Georgia, surprised the pollsters and beat incumbent President Gerald Ford in a close election.

James Hennessy barely squeaked out a victory and won his congressional seat. "This is only the beginning!" shouted the newly elected congressman, concluding his victory speech.

James found himself blinded in the frenzy of flashing cameras. He leaned over to his flashy date and whispered, "Power begets power and all in the name of liberty."

Chapter 63

December 14, 1976

Snow continued to fall, adding to the several inches already covering the sidewalk in front of Ferrara's Grocery and Bakery.

To the sound of windshields being scraped and wheels spinning on snow-packed streets, Tony strained against the blowing snow and finished shoveling the sidewalk. Satisfied with his work, he opened the store, turned on the lights, and took his last breath as he succumbed to a massive heart attack. Mario found him sprawled on the floor with one arm still in his overcoat. By time the city ambulance arrived, Tony was long gone.

Vincenza was hysterical. His last words that morning, *"T'amu innamurata,"* resonated in her mind. Sobbing, she kept repeating, "I love you too, sweetheart."

Mario, Catherine, John, and Carmela, though despondent, made the obligatory phone calls to family and friends who soon began arriving at the Ferrara household.

The following day the family, bringing with them the only suit Tony owned, met with the undertaker at Guidetti's Funeral Home on Spring Street. Choosing a casket that would hold the body of the man they loved and respected was an ordeal surpassed only by inspecting the gravesite at Calvary Cemetery in Queens.

Like many immigrants, Tony bought the cemetery plot as a young man. Life was difficult in those early years. Numerous families lost young children to diphtheria, whooping cough, and polio. Mortality became obvious.

Although his family had not been touched by death, the organized, prudent Tony insisted on buying a family plot, paying five dollars a month until the debt was paid off. Vincenza was very apprehensive and superstitiously fearful of tragedy besetting them if they were prepared to die. Yet, such prudent planning gave Tony a sense of security.

The three-day wake began with Vincenza, her children, and grand-children kneeling at the coffin praying. Sam, Rose, Joe, and Beth were openly weeping as they gathered behind the family, standing in support.

Fingering her rosary beads, Vincenza spoke softly to Tony, alterna-tively telling him of her love and praying for his soul.

Mario, looking intently at his father's face, couldn't believe this ashen, waxy-faced corpse with pink cheeks was Tony. "Why do they put make-up on a dead body?" he murmured to Catherine.

She shook her head sadly, took hold of Mario's hand, and tenderly held it to her face.

The funeral parlor was filled with the aroma of copious floral trib-utes that permeated the air with a sweet sickly scent. For weeks afterward, Mario recoiled at the smell of fresh flowers.

The wake was a grueling event. Taking only short breaks for meals, the family sat each day from 10:00 a.m. to 9:00 p.m. greeting those who came to show their respect. Memories and stories were shared—many happy and some sad.

"If I hear one more time that he never looked so good, I'm going to scream," said a tearful Carmela to Catherine.

Standing over the casket, Joe took a swipe at his watery eyes, bit down on his lower lip, and whispered, "I love you, Mr. Ferrara."

The family huddled around Vincenza. In agony she cried out, "How can you leave me? Please, God, help me. I love you, Tony."

Mario was most grateful to friends and neighbors who had come to help his family send Vincenza's beloved husband and their *papà* to the other side. However, by the third day his brain was saturated with chat-ter and small talk.

On the last evening, he spoke to those gathered in the funeral parlor. Taking a deep breath, Mario began, "My *papà* was my friend, my confidante." His body trembled as tears rolled down his cheeks. Placing his arms around his sister, he said, "*Siciliano* love drove him." Struggling, his voice cracking, he continued, "He had a wish for *la famigha* . . . to imagine . . . and believe the dream of liberty embodied in each and every one of us. In *Papà's* eighty-three years, he gave it his all and his spirit will always live and never die."

Frank Nunzi told his famous story, for the umpteenth time, of how Tony saved him from the jaws of death when they were young men.

In his gravelly voice, Frank said, light heartedly, "Antonio was a beautiful man. He saw goodness in everyone." Leaning on his cane in front of family and friends, he laughingly continued, "Except for those Irish bastards who beat the hell out of both of us. But later, we beat the hell out of them. Hey, he was a *Siciliano*! And so am I. He lived passionately. I loved him."

The services were held at Our Lady of Loreto's Church. A morose Father Carelli performed the funeral Mass and gave a moving eulogy. In closing he said, "Tony Ferrara was always available to his family and friends; he gave hope and light in times of darkness." Wiping away a tear, he said, "He was a man who lived life the way he saw fit; and now, in death, is born into eternal life."

It was a dreary, cold, and windy day as the funeral entourage moved in slow procession through the huge iron gates of Calvary Cemetery.

A number of four-door black sedans waited for the cortege to end so its occupants could discreetly photograph those in attendance.

Tony's *bocce paesani* were there; so were the police.

Family and friends pressed close to each other trying to keep warm as they gathered around the burial plot.

Mario tightly held on to his sister.
Catherine held on to Mario.

Carmela sniffling, her eyes red and wet, said, "Someone told me that *Papà's* gone forever, but that's not true: he will always be with us."

Sam and Rose came over to hug Mario. "I loved him," said Sam. "I'll never forget his smile."

John and Theresa were literally holding up Vincenza.

Tony's three grandchildren gathered round their *nonna*.

Joe Borelli was talking to an animated Frank Nunzi.

Beth Downing was hanging on to Joe's arm.

Father Carelli said a final prayer to conclude the services, "He lived what he believed and was never shy to say, *'T'amu.'* We love you too, Antonio. May you rest in peace. Amen."

Vincenza, with Mario's help, slowly approached the coffin and laid a branch of Tony's fig tree on top.

Mario placed a red tomato alongside.

Catherine became suddenly sick.

During the morning funeral services, a fickle sun played peek-a-boo in an overcast sky that ultimately gave way to more snow.

The quiet of the solemn ritual of lowering Tony Ferrara's flower-covered casket into the ground was shattered by Vincenza's mournful cry of anguish.

Frank Nunzi demanded the gravediggers stop the process until everyone departed. Mourners, ignoring snowflakes, sadly threw red roses into the open grave; afterward they began to sluggishly return to their automobiles. Walking by the huge headstones that dotted Calvary's landscape, several people gossiped about the strange number of black cars and their occupants.

The children took Vincenza by the hand and helped her to a waiting limousine for the long and lonely ride back to her home on Elizabeth Street that she had shared with Tony for forty-seven years. Once again, the Ferrara family was ready to greet friends and break bread.

While the last of the guests were leaving, a vibrant Frank Nunzi with his oversized arms around Vincenza said, "Whatever you need, please call me." He then made his way to the living room and said goodbye to old friends.

Mario slowly walked him to the open door.

Frank turned and cried out, "I love you all. You're *famigha*." He threw a kiss.

That was the last time the Ferrara's saw Frank Nunzi alive. That afternoon his private plane disappeared from radar off the coast. He and his pilot were killed as the plane broke apart when it plunged into Long Island Sound. Hearing the tragic news, the family again was thrust into sorrow.

Just south of Little Italy, the slow drag of wipers across the windshield of Hennessy's newly purchased BMW was representative of what had been for some an emotionally draining day.

It was about 4:00 p.m. when the snow finally stopped and clouds broke to let in glorious rays of an impatient sun.

Arriving at the designated parking stall at his New York City office, James noticed a white delivery van parked in the alley. Hurriedly, he left his car, glancing over his shoulder as the vehicle began moving in his direction. Heading toward the building's rear entrance, James picked up his pace. As the van pulled alongside, the driver lowered the window, temporarily blinding Hennessy with the bright sunlight that reflected off a pair of glasses.

He blew a kiss and entered the building.

1977

JANUARY

It was the day after the presidential inauguration. Catherine smiled and said in an uplifted tone, "It was so good to hear that President Carter held to his commitment and pardoned the thousands upon thousands who avoided the draft during an unjust Vietnam War. Maybe this will begin the healing process."

"I knew he was a good and decent man. This will not bring Angelo back though," said Vincenza, sipping coffee, her eyes roaming the kitchen searching for Tony.

One month later on a frigid day in February, Vincenza, yearning to be with her life-partner, passed away of influenza and a broken heart.

Once more, the Ferrara family fell into bottomless sorrow. First their *papà* and now their *mamma* . . . Life was changing.

She was buried next to her sweetheart, her husband Tony Ferrara.

MARCH 21

A headline in the *World Telegram*
THE GOLDEN CARE AWARDS HONORS LOCAL BUSINESSMAN

> *Sam Castellano, investment banker and philanthropist, was honored as "Man of the Year."*
>
> *In his acceptance speech, he took the opportunity to announce his long awaited engagement to defense attorney Rose Gramoli and congratulated James Hennessy, the recently elected congressman who stood smiling broadly and waved in acknowledgment.*

Leaving Lincoln Center, Sam leaned over to Rose, who was wearing her five-carat diamond engagement ring, and quietly said, "I have finally got Hennessy where I want him. He thinks he's power. I made him. He's my power. I've got him by the short hairs.".

"Don't you mean *we*?" Rose said with a huge grin.

JULY 14

The city stopped for a moment in silence before all hell broke loose. The blackout was a dichotomy. There were citizens helping one another and citizens maiming one another.

Mario said, "Hot or not, power or not, it was good to see people help one another whether they knew each other or not."

Joe shook his head and said, "I don't know about that. Beth got caught in the subway. No lights, no nothing. That's when I heard about the violence. In some cases the cops were helpless."

"Joe, just like during The Strike, there are those who always seek an excuse to loot and destroy whatever is in their path. Carmela told me, though, that in The Village, people took to the streets, not to loot, but to talk."

"I tell you, Mario, watching thousands run through the streets smashing store windows and setting buildings on fire brought back bad memories."

"It's over now. I can't help but wonder, though; every now and then I think there's got to be a way to—"

"Beth, why don't we treat these two to a pizza before I have to lock Mario up," interrupted Catherine, grinning.

AUGUST 24

A headline in the Italian daily *Buon Giorno*
JUSTICE AT LAST FOR SACCO AND VANZETTI

> *On August 23, 1977, fifty years to the day after the executions of Sacco and Vanzetti, Michael S. Dukakis, Governor of Massachusetts, issued a proclamation that concluded with the words:*

> *Therefore, I, Michael S. Dukakis, Governor of the Commonwealth of Massachusetts . . . hereby proclaim Tuesday, August 23, 1977, NICOLA SACCO AND BARTOLOMEO VANZETTI MEMORI-AL DAY; and declare, further, that any stigma and disgrace should be forever removed from the names of Nicola Sacco and Bartolomeo Vanzetti, from the names of their families and descendants, and so . . . call upon all the people of Massachusetts to pause in their daily endeavors to reflect upon these tragic events, and draw from their historic lessons the resolve to prevent the forces of intolerance, fear, and hatred from ever again uniting to overcome the rationality, wisdom, and fairness to which our legal system aspires.*

Mario handed Catherine the newspaper, cleared his throat, and said, "Too bad *Papà's* gone."

She held his hand while reading the article.

Over the next month, Mario, besides baking bread, reflected on past events. He pondered his encounter with Mrs. Roselli, the peddler's cart, and *Conte Alessandro*. In addition to writing *Me and Dante Down by the Inferno,* he also composed an exposé about Hennessy, Barrett, and the cardinal. After much thought, he chose not to seek a publisher.

One morning after baking bread, Mario, unable to let go of his vision quest, said, "John, I have a couple of ideas on how to spread the message of liberty."

John stared at Mario and bluntly said, "For the love of God, leave it be."

"Maybe that's exactly it—maybe *for the love of God* is why I can't leave it be."

Chapter 64

September 21, 1977

IT HAD BEEN THREE YEARS SINCE MARIO'S TRIAL ENDED.

They sat on the fire escape after dinner on a beautiful fall evening. Mario, filled with wonderment, said, "Catherine, it's unbelievable what happened today! You're not going to believe what I'm about to tell you. It's unbelievable!"

"You're always unbelievable." She chuckled, "With you, nothing phases me; go ahead and try me."

Looking upward at a moonlit sky, he exclaimed, "But it's unbelievable!"

She gave him a questioning look and said, "OK, *Signuro Unbelievable* . . . speak to me."

Mario gave a detailed account of what he witnessed in a place called Soul. He concluded, "When I stood up, I was dripping wet with sweat. I picked up a beautiful red tomato and wiped sawdust off of it. I looked around Mascotti's market thoroughly flustered and with my thinking disjointed—"

Interrupting, she laughingly said, "No comment."

Ignoring her, his eyes growing wider, he said, "At that point, my recall short-circuited. Maybe I was hallucinating, but what's interesting is that I clearly remember the eyes of the peoples of Soul. They had eyes of light. I really don't know how to describe it. They were warm, lovable, energetic."

He hesitated a moment, then, in celebration, cried out in amazement, "Children: that's it! They had the eyes of a child. Someway, somehow I was in Soul. It may have been reality or a figment of my imagination; I don't know—"

Interrupting again, she shook her head in acknowledgment and with a slight grin said, "It's OK; I know you're always confused."

"You're a real comedian," he said jokingly, and then turning serious he continued, "I'm not sure if Soul is a different plane running concurrently or a state of mind. What I do know is that it was a spiritual field of dreams that manifested itself in my heart. A place of being." Mario finally stopped his enthusiastic discourse and stared at her in anticipation, waiting for a response.

She leaned toward him, laid her head on his shoulder, and said, "I'm still listening."

"Soul offered me an enlightened learning process; the peoples there challenged our human side to move closer to the Divine."

Lifting her head, she kissed him and tenderly said, "That's beautiful, Mario."

"Please read what I wrote; this is what I wish to tell children about the Village of Soul."

Let me introduce myself: I am Mario Ferrara. To begin my tale, I can tell you with certainty that whenever I shop at Mascotti's Fruit and Vegetable Stand, I'm in heaven.

I love to walk the scent-filled aisles. It reminds me of *La Vucciria*, the colorful open air market in the heart of Palermo with each of its bins and baskets smothering the other, all filled with heaping displays of oranges, grapefruits, red and green grapes and peppers, rich purple eggplants as well as all the other fruits and vegetables imaginable.

Reaching into a bin to pluck out an apple, I spotted a huge crate of tomatoes two aisles down.

The market was crowded, forcing me to weave my way along the sawdust floor as I moved toward a beautiful red tomato beckoning to my taste buds.

In reckless haste, I accidentally dropped my choice tomato.

Kneeling to retrieve the elusive tomato that rolled onto the floor, I was staring straight at a pair of handcrafted black boots and what appeared to be the bottom of a black and red cloak.

Startled, my heart pounded rapidly, for that's how Mrs. Roselli had described the dress of Giuseppe the peddler to me years ago. Rising quickly, I smashed my head on the pinewood fruit stand.

The whole adventure was surreal.

In a complete state of bewilderment, I stood and surveyed the terrain, not of Mascotti's Fruit and Vegetable Stand, but of rugged snowcapped mountain ranges, one after another with no end in sight. I started to run, walk, and run again, and much to my chagrin I fell three times in the process.

At the end of a grueling up-down-and-up-again climb, I reached a towering mesa as wide and long as the eye could see. Totally discombobulated, I sat, took a deep breath, and wiped the beads of sweat off my face.

It didn't matter how seductive the sight in front of me, I knew enough to know I could not linger; I had to press on. To where? Who knew? But to somewhere I had to go. Rising to my feet, I began walking swiftly. When I had covered about two hundred yards, I started down a winding, narrowing path with an extreme vertical drop. Moments later, sucking in air, I barely squeezed between two five-hundred-foot-high boulders. Once I had passed them, my view became wider. I saw before me a vast canyon of multicolored granite walls touching the heavens.

Darkness began to fall and prudence took over. I chose a thick bed of purple daisies to rest my exhausted body. However, rest was not to be, as thunder and lightning rattled my nerves until a rising orange-blue sun appeared on the horizon. Finally, exiting the canyon, I found myself at a campfire occupied by two persons.

The white-haired man slowly turned, looking quite puzzled. He had fine features, light green eyes, and appeared to be somewhere in his eighties. When the woman turned, I saw that she was none other than Mrs. Roselli.

"What in the world are you doing here?" I cried out.

Mrs. Roselli answered with a huge smile.

The white-haired gentleman said, "Hello! My name is Michael. It's good that you are here."

"Hi, I'm Mario Ferrara. And I don't know where *here* is."

Without flinching, Mrs. Roselli cheerfully said, "Good morning, Mario. We're only half-a-day's walk to the village."

Stunned, yet managing a smile, I blurted, "What village?"

"The village of the Soul peoples . . . a land of liberty!"

I said nothing.

Mrs. Roselli without hesitation continued, "This is Michael, an old friend of mine."

Cutting through the small talk, I impatiently asked, "Who are the Soul peoples? And what are we all doing here? Better yet, how in the hell did I get here?"

Paying no attention to my rapid burst of questions or the frustration undoubtedly evident in my voice, Michael said, "Let us not keep them waiting."

"Are you ready, Mario?" asked Mrs. Roselli reaching for my hand.

I just nodded affirmatively.

On that extraordinarily beautiful morning—actually that's an oxymoron in this place—there every morning is extraordinary and beautiful. Anyway, in a matter of moments we entered one end of a mountain cave and exited the other end into the Village of Soul.

It was like magic. No, it was more than magic. I could sense the uplifting energy of love filling the air. Of course I cannot—nor has anyone ever been able to—adequately express the complete brilliance of Soul.

Over centuries, many travelers have asked many questions of its peoples.

"Was it on a different plane?"

"Was it conceived by a figment of someone's imagination?"

"Was Soul and the earth one in the same?"

"Was it, or is it an illusion or a reality within a reality?"

Questions without answers or answers without proof.

Soul was descript, yet nondescript: no government, no religion, no social class, no discrimination, no past, no present or future—just NOW. Maybe it's a different plane or maybe it's a state of mind.

As usual, the villagers graciously greeted their old friends, Mrs. Roselli and Michael, and instantly accepted me with an outpouring of their love without question or motive. They hear, see, and understand with love centered in their hearts. What a delight to meet these peoples filled with such a spirit of love and to see this spirit reflected in their smiles as in a magnificent, indescribable prism!

The village as it appeared to my eyes could be likened to a small New England town, or maybe it was more like rural Kansas or Colorado with its purple mountain majesties, or New York City with its concrete and steel forest. Or, did it really remind me of anything?

Actually, traveling through the Village of Soul could be likened to traveling through a three dimensional National Geographic viewfinder, looking at the entire earth at once; yet isolating nations and countries, while, at the same time, integrating its civilizations. Everything fit, all consistent with that part of the land where the peoples lived.

Instead of disorder, this was a land of order.

Soul was a village where peoples lived the life of the Divine.

A land of energy, imagination, and mysticism.

Yes, those elements were ever present, as was every human treasure to manifest the Divine within.

That's what is bestowed on Soul. They have it all. What a sight. Only if one could see it . . . or can we?

Soul is a village that manifests itself in one's wildest and most pleasant of dreams.

Soul is a village where peoples live a life of simplicity, a life devoid of complications or hidden agendas.

Now, how can all that be an illusion?

An elder engaged me in conversation concerning government and religion, both organized and unorganized. But most important were the conversations with a radiant, high-cheeked woman, conversations that centered on Soul's cornerstone—spiritual liberty.

"You talk about spiritual liberty, rooted in an all forgiving and loving God whom you call One. Isn't that what I call Christianity?" I asked while taking in the clean fresh air.

She smiled. "It is your choice what you wish to call the Deity. Some call One the ultimate mystery, the infinite, some Allah, and so on . . . and on . . . and on . . . And don't bother to ask *lo here or lo there*? The kingdom of the Deity, whatever you call Him or Her, *is* within you. Free the deity within.

"No, it doesn't matter what one calls a deity; what matters is how you *live* as a deity. What's important is to live a life of joy, which is love, in the Holy Spirit of One. When we understand love and the oneness of life, we are free from fear in all its disguises," she said ever so gently.

Later in the day, Mrs. Roselli and Michael took me on an unplanned expedition. Off we went through a maze like no other, a maze of woven caverns carved with outstanding images of life.

Mrs. Roselli happily said, "From the beginning, One is in all; everywhere, in solitude and in action, forever and ever."

Passing an engraving of a double arrow embedded into a granite wall, Michael said, "The white and black interwoven feathers symbolize light and dark, good and evil, each of which cannot be avoided. The dark side brings fear into the hearts of goodness. As humans, we're a self-contained entity complete with opposing forces. The Divine is light and always conquers the dark. So you see, the dark of evil is a mirage. "

I paused to look back at the etching and the black feathers were gone.

A moment later, out of nowhere, a wall of water engulfed us and tossed us about like rubber ducks until we found ourselves in a watercraft of flowers gently flowing down an underground river full of light.

Before I could ask any questions, Mrs. Roselli beamed and said, "Now you will witness a living story that has been told for eons. You see, no matter how one would try, no one has ever reached the end of this underground river or found the source of light. Legend has it that we are experiencing the light of eternal life."

Gently taking my arm she said, "The spirit always opens your mind to new and exciting thoughts and things you have not seen, heard, or understood. Destiny is your choice. Thus, in your daily struggles, the Holy Spirit of One clears the way.

In life's journey, when in deep waters, the spirit is your saving strength—strength to protect and provide refuge in days of distress. Gentleness, enthusiasm, courage, and persistence, interwoven with love, are the solid attributes that build a bridge across any river of adversity."

Disembarking our watercraft, Michael, leading the way, said, "Let's take this path. It will guide us to a lake, a sea of tranquility."

A short walk through an aspen grove led us to a pear-shaped lake—a sparkling crystal lake where slow ripples of water and harp-like sounds accompanied a flight of exotic birds that hovered overhead.

Mrs. Roselli sat on a perfectly smooth, round rock. She said, "Those who arrived thousands of years ago in the land of Soul named this body of water the Lake of the Divine Light. It's a glorious lake with an eternal flame of love bursting out of the burnt-orange water to reach the cosmos. A lake gifted with healing crystals that turned into water."

Her eyes shining brightly, she continued, "All roads in Soul lead to the Lake of the Divine Light." Holding Michael's hand, she explained, "The ancestors of Soul handed down a scroll of innate gifts of love in the I AM. They are the energy force behind the healing water, a legacy of pure light in the Holy Spirit of One."

"In a dream, or should I say nightmare, Dante mentioned the Scroll of the I AM," I said excitedly.

Sitting by water's edge, she held my hand and softly said, "Yes, I know."

Michael chimed in, "Believe, and when you believe, the crystal water of love heals."

Mrs. Roselli continued Michael's story, "Everyone who has come to the land of Soul to take up residence has chosen not to leave." She hesitated a second and, smiling, went on, "Except, there was a distant traveler who had a vision and left the comfort of Soul and decided to be reborn to a family who lived in the slums of Sicily. Ultimately, with the Scroll of the I AM and a handful of healing crystals, he wished to remind people of what they had forgotten in the evolution of humankind."

I excitedly blurted, "My *papà* told me about this man."

"Yes, it was Giuseppe Balsamo, later known as *Conte Alessandro di Cagliostro,* who discovered the Robe of Christ inside *Monte Etna* and who, without any hesitation whatsoever, began to spread a dream of reality: Pure Love!"

I continued to listen with astonishment and, being extremely curious about the healing waters, stepped closer to lake's edge. Losing my footing, I slipped and fell headfirst into the welcoming waters of the Lake of the Divine Light.

An instant later I found myself at Mascotti's Fruit and Vegetable Stand, picking up and wiping the sawdust off a beautiful red tomato.

"Mario, what a wonderful story," she said kissing him on the cheek.

He wrapped his arms around her and excitedly said, "This is the Scroll of the I AM."

THE SCROLL
OF THE I AM

available . . . accommodating . . .
accepting . . . accountable . . .
adventuresome . . . affectionate . . .
ambitious . . . attentive . . . aware . . .
active . . . analytical . . . adaptable . . .
bold . . . believable . . . blessed . . .
brave . . . benevolent . . . balanced . . .
candid . . . cautious . . . charitable . . .
cheerful . . . childlike . . . competent . . .
considerate . . . cooperative . . .
curious . . . calm . . . courteous . . .
caring . . . confident . . . creative . . .
consistent . . . courageous . . .
compassionate . . . credible . . . clear . . .
decisive . . . dependable . . . diligent . . .
dynamic . . . determined . . .
daring . . . discerning . . .
disciplined . . . dignified . . .
effective . . . empathetic . . .
enchanting . . . enterprising . . .
efficient . . . entrepreneurial . . .
enthusiastic . . . energetic . . .
ethical . . . enlightened . . . fair . . .
flexible . . . focused . . . fun . . .
faithful . . . forgiving . . . fruitful . . .
generous . . . giving . . . gentle . . .
good . . . gracious . . . genuine . . .
harmonious . . . healing . . .
healthful . . . honest . . . humorous . . .
helpful . . . humble . . . hopeful . . .
happy . . . independent . . .
imaginative . . . innovative . . .
inspirational . . . ingenious . . .

intuitive . . . just . . . joyful . . .
kind . . . knowledgeable . . . loyal . . .
meek . . . merciful . . . mindful . . .
moral . . . mystical . . . natural . . .
neighborly . . . nice . . . nurturing . . .
orderly . . . open . . . optimistic . . .
objective . . . positive . . .
productive . . . peaceful . . . patient . . .
persistent . . . passionate . . . polite . . .
practical . . . prepared . . . prudent . . .
pure . . . radiant . . . responsible . . .
responsive . . . respectful . . .
receptive . . . resilient . . . sensible . . .
sincere . . . stable . . . sensitive . . .
spiritual . . . successful . . .
supportive . . . strong . . . selfless . . .
sympathetic . . . tender . . .
thorough . . . tolerant . . .
trustworthy . . . unique . . .
understanding . . . vibrant ...
versatile . . . warm . . . wise . . . and
everything else that is love . . .
in the Holy Spirit of One . . .
in the Human and Divine
of who I AM

"Beautiful," she said warmly.

He looked into her enchanting eyes and tenderly said, "And this I wrote for you, my sweet Catherine, forevermore my White Rose of Love."

THE WHITE ROSE

From the beginning . . .

Our blessed fertile soil
Accepts without condition
A plethora of precious seeds
Tossed to and fro by fickle winds
Until they come to rest
To blossom and adorn the earth
With the magnificence and gracefulness
Of kaleidoscopic heavenly flowers

So, my dear Catherine,
You too are blessed
And accept without condition
The ever-changing seeds of life
Tossed to and fro by fickle winds
Until they come to rest
Upon your bosom

My precious, you have unraveled
The web of life
And adorn the earth
With the magnificence and gracefulness
Of your mystical being,
As the greatest flower seed of all
Returns again and again
To flourish in your heart,

The exotic enchanting and angelic
Pure White Rose of Unconditional Love.

Chapter 65

1978

<small>May</small> 10

A headline in the *New York Journal American*
ITALY'S PRIME MINISTER ALDO MORO DEAD

> *Moro's body was found riddled with bullets in the trunk of his car in Rome. Left-wing terrorists demanded the release of 13 Red Brigade members on trial in Turin. The Italian Government refused to negotiate with the kidnappers.*

"Catherine, his death will bring fear to the streets of Italy."
Watching his body language, she pleaded, "Please."
He snapped, "These terrorists are a bunch of lowly cowards."
"Please, Mario, pray. Only pray."

<small>September</small> 29

A headline in the *World Telegram*
POPE JOHN PAUL FOUND DEAD

The Holy Father was found dead in his bedroom only 33 days into his Pontificate. The Catholic Church mourns the man known as the smiling Pope.

ONE MONTH LATER

Sitting at the kitchen table with Catherine, Mario said irately, "The Vatican said the Pope died of a heart attack. You remember my friend Robert. We met in the park one day and still speak often when we run into each other there. Robert is still at the UN. He thinks the Pope was poisoned and they embalmed him quickly without an autopsy so there would be no evidence pointing either way."

"Oh my! He seemed to be a simple man with a wonderful heart."

"You're right. John Paul, besides shunning pomp and circumstance, was 100 percent ecumenical. But my friend said he made a fatal mistake when he began investigating the Vatican Bank headed up by Archbishop Paul Marcinkus."

Catherine gave him a questioning glance and said, "Mario, you're getting carried away with another conspiracy theory."

Unable to contain himself, he anxiously said, "Tim knew something was up with Gateway and Vatican Bank. And you know Barrett was a master at moving money in and out of risky and illegal operations."

"Was it speculation or fact?"

He let out a heavy sigh and said, "Tim told me that Barrett had flown to Milan to meet with Roberto Calvi, head of *Banco Ambrosiano*, who had ties to Vatican Bank. You never know how deep the network had gone. If only—"

She interrupted. "But you did! Please!"

"OK, I agree; back to writing *Me and Dante Down by the Inferno*."

"Shut your eyes," she said jokingly.

Mario, smiling, raised his hands to his eyes.

Catherine giggling said, "I'm Dante . . . I'm speaking to you and you are definitely *stunato*."

Laughing, he wrestled her to the couch . . . and there they stayed for a very long time.

Allegations that Vatican Bank led the international banking circle in laundering underworld cash sent shock waves throughout the financial community. Vatican involvement in a Mafia banking scam was unthinkable. However, the unlikely news started to spread and spread fast.

Mr. Solari of Vatican Bank was nowhere to be found. He was eagerly sought after for questioning by the Italian authorities.

DECEMBER 6

On their fortieth anniversary, Catherine and Mario, thanks to Joe Borelli, had tickets to Carnegie Hall where Frank Sinatra was performing.

1982

APRIL 29

Congressman James Hennessy received a subpoena from the Justice Department along with other power players throughout the United States, including members of the Masons, Opus Dei, reputed Mafia figures, and governmental intelligence agencies. Hennessy was certain that the Justice Department was investigating former transactions, money laundering, and political kickbacks between Vatican Bank and Gateway.

In the past, Hennessy was chief architect behind Barrett's negotiations with an Italian network of banks led by *Banco Ambrosiano* with Roberto Calvi at the helm.

In desperation, knowing that his career was on the cusp of destruction, he drove to Attica State Prison in upstate New York to talk to Leonard Knight.

The following morning, after a hearty breakfast of eggs, sausage, and a side of pancakes at a local restaurant, Hennessy left the town of Attica and headed back to the city. On the way, just outside of Dansville, he pulled his 1982 BMW off Interstate Highway 390 and into a rest area. He reached inside his glove compartment. His hand shook as he pulled out a .38 caliber pistol, closed his eyes, and blew his brains out.

Leonard Knight was found dead the same morning in his prison cell. The prison authorities said he committed suicide by poison.

Sam had left the evening before to visit Cardinal Stanley. When he landed at Rome's Leonardo Da Vinci Airport, he telephoned Rose, who told him the shocking news.

He cancelled his private limousine and took the next flight out to Palermo to visit his cousins in Polizzi Generosa, situated in the Madonie Mountains of Sicily.

Cardinal Stanley, since his retirement, had lived in the outskirts of Rome. The story of Roberto Calvi of *Banco Ambrosiano* and Vatican Bank was carried by every news organization in Italy. The following day the Rome newspapers reported that Cardinal Stanley was found dead in his Villa. He apparently had choked on a piece of hard-crusted Italian bread.

Sam returned in May and quickly liquidated Castellano Enterprises. Afterward, he and Rose retired and moved to Taormina, Sicily.

JUNE 19

A headline in the *World Telegram*
ROBERTO CALVI SWINGS FROM BLACKFRIARS BRIDGE
SUICIDE OR MURDER?

> *Roberto Calvi, known as "God's Banker," was recently convicted of fraud in the collapse of Banco Ambrosiano. Calvi subsequently fled to England, where yesterday he was found hanging from Blackfriars Bridge. The bridge spans the River Thames in London. An investigative source, speaking on the condition of anonymity, said, "He would have to have been a magician to have committed suicide." Pieces of bricks and rocks were stuffed in his pockets.*
>
> *So then, if Calvi was murdered, the question is, who was the murderer? Who knows? Maybe someone killed him to silence him in order to protect members of the Vatican hierarchy or other banking officials from accusations of involvement in fraud and a number of other criminal charges. If that's the case, you cannot rule out the Vatican Bank or the Mafia as suspects."*
>
> *Another conspirator in the scandal was an advisor to Pope Paul VI. This advisor, Michele Sindona, was convicted in the United States on 65 counts of fraud.*
>
> *Archbishop Paul Marcinkus still holds the office of President of Vatican bank.*

Mario shrugged and said with a smile, "I don't want to say I told you so; but, was I right or was I right?"

Catherine grinned and said, "So?"

BOOK VIII

Chapter 66

July 1982

Sitting on the fire escape, Mario, in a state of contentment, said, "It's wonderful to dream the dream of liberty under a beautiful sky."

"My dear Mario, . . . after all these years, does a dream satisfy your heart?" asked Catherine.

He smiled, reached for her hand, and said, "My heart still burns for the people who are poor in spirit and those whose hearts are broken by injustice." He paused, sighed, and continued sadly, "And I cannot forget those who are held captive in the prison of their mind."

"What else does your heart say?"

"It struggles; . . . then I remember the poet Dante, *Conte Alessandro*, and the peddler's cart. Catherine, my heart beckons."

She leaned her head against his chest.

SEPTEMBER

Mario rushed up the steps to his fourth-floor home, threw open the door, and said breathlessly, "I now understand the greater depth of love and the nagging call of what I should do."

Reaching for his hand, Catherine pleaded anxiously, "Take it easy. Tell me what happened."

Mario smiled and said, "Let's go out onto the fire escape."

The night sky was clear and the moon was full. They looked up and, at the same time, they both cried out, "*a bedda luna!*"

Her crystal blue eyes shone like stars. Snuggling close to him, in almost a whisper she caringly said, "Tell me what it is. You know that I listen carefully."

Mario put his arm around her shoulder and gently said, "This morning, for some unexplained reason I was filled with conflictive emotions. I kept asking myself why? Why injustice? Why civil unrest? Why war? There were so many *whys*. My feelings were knotted together in a state of bedlam, until I once again thought of the Poet Dante and the Count."

She nodded lovingly and kissed his forehead.

Holding her closer, he said, "So, I decided to go to Central Park to free my thoughts. While slowly walking toward the entrance at Sixty-second Street, all at once I saw it, I felt it, I sensed it, and I understood it. It was love, pure love."

Mario looked into her eyes and held her tighter. "The experience clearly manifested itself in the interconnectedness of not only each person, but of wildlife and plant life. Actually, everything was interlaced into an unbelievable experience. It was the reality of oneness in an expression of energy. All that was visible to my conscious and subconscious mind was energy."

He hesitated to collect his thoughts and then said, "During The Strike I spoke words of love and at my trial I spoke words of love. But today, for a few fleeting moments, I *was* love."

She smiled in response and said nothing.

Lying on the fire escape, they gazed at a starlit sky.

With a lilt in his voice, he added, "Someday while walking down any street, driving along a highway, strolling in a manicured park or hiking in the quiet of a forest, it could happen to anyone, much as it happened to me. In a split second and without any thought or effort on their part, they will be floating in a sea of soft snowflake-like particles of pulsating lights with all there is, in and on the earth, and throughout the cosmos.

The thin veil of obscurity will be removed from their eyes, and they will witness an illusion disappear into a reality of love. They will recognize one another and understand, without any doubt, that everything is one and everything is love. You see, we are the bristling leaf of a tree, the soft petal of a rose, the wings of a sparrow, and one with every living creature."

Catherine reached over, touched his face tenderly, and they kissed.

The following day, in a reflective mood, Mario went to the back of the store, unveiled, and began to clean the peddler's cart. In the process, much to his surprise, he discovered a false bottom that held trinkets of sorts.

Catherine walked in, gently took hold of his arm and smiled. They sat in silence on a vegetable crate. Gazing into her eyes, he tenderly said, "Are you thinking what I'm thinking?"

"I know what you're thinking. So, I'm thinking *so what?* This may be the time to follow your heart. Becoming a peddler can be a perfect outlet to spread the message of love wrapped in liberty."

"Yes! That's the way to take my life experiments to the street," Mario said, laughing. His face shone with a joy that overwhelmed him as he swept her off her feet. Holding her with her feet dangling in the air, he began singing "That's Amore."

At Caffe Reggio, Joe asked in disbelief, "Why would you want to peddle? It's time to rest."

"First of all, *Papà* was right when he said, I will know when it's time. Well, I know it's time. Especially after what happened in Central Park. It's clear to me that liberty, oneness, and love are more than just words. They are realities within all peoples, although, our thoughts, choices, decisions and actions can easily blur our vision of oneness."

Mario took a sip of espresso and full of enthusiasm continued, "So, now, I go and peddle and spread seeds of unity."

"Instead, why don't you go to Palermo and search out the fable of *Conte Alessandro di Cagliostro*?" Joe asked with his mouth full of bagel. "Do you think there's any truth to what your *papà* said about the Robe?"

Mario smiled.

Catherine excitedly chimed in, "Going to Sicily sounds like a great idea!"

Beth said, "Mario, you had an adventurous spirit before enlighten-ment. And now, after enlightenment, guess what. You still have an adventurous spirit." She chuckled and threw him a kiss.

Rolling his eyes and grinning, Joe said, "He's a dichotomy unto him-self . . . an enigma . . . a feisty rebel who can't let go in his pursuit of liberty and justice and a wannabe peddler simply espousing the ecstasy of love."

Not giving rise to his teasing, Mario excitedly said, "Sicily and the Count. Why not?"

A short three weeks later, Catherine and Mario left for his childhood home, the medieval city of Palermo.

NOVEMBER 4, 1982

After spending a month exploring the land Mario treasured, he and Catherine returned to Little Italy.

The very next evening, John and his family, Joe and Beth, and Carmela joined Mario and Catherine for a marathon dinner.

Mario held everyone captivated by his fascinating description of their trip beginning in Palermo and ending at Mount Etna; the tale of the Count; and of course, his aspiration to peddle.

John was the first to speak. "Wonderful! You just fired yourself. I expect you to follow your heart. It's time to peddle your trinkets of sorts and *Count Alessandro's Healing Tonic of Love*. The store will do just fine without you."

Mario, grinning broadly, jumped up and gave his brother a hug.

Joe enthusiastically said, "I'll come down tomorrow and help you get the cart ready. But whatever you do, please do me a favor and stay out of trouble."

Mario gave him a startled look, tapped his forehead, and said in a surprised tone, "What? Me? You can't be talking about me? Can you?"

Carmela and Beth were smiling. Catherine managed a smile as well, but blurted, "I stay awake nights wondering what's next?"

OCTOBER 1988

Six years later, on a fall day in Washington Square Park, a Greenwich Village reporter with his notebook in hand asked Mario: "Some of your *paesani* on the street said that after your trial you became more of an idealist, speaking of life freed of problems through love. Don't you think that's naiveté at its best?"

With a perplexed look Mario answered, "If they're really my *paesani* they know that I am full of faults and problems. And whatever I do, I try to do to the best of my abilities—by experiment. Sometimes I win. Sometimes I lose. In the end, who gives a damn?"

"You sound bitter."

"No, just realistic. We're all faced with diversions and temptations that are easy to fall prey to. I have, and continue to have, numerous failings, consciously and unconsciously, testing the patience of my *famigha, amici,* and society."

"Count me in," said the reporter. He was chuckling softly.

Mario paused and nodded, "Well, maybe I've pushed the edge a time too many, but when I immerse myself in the message of love I'm an immovable object. Nothing is going to shake me from this truth."

"How can you be so positive in your thoughts and actions? I know you have run the gauntlet. How can you be so sure?" he asked uneasily.

Mario smiled.

MINUTES LATER AT GARIBALDI'S STATUE

"The only way to salvation is through the pain of sacrifice," said a man apprehensively as he held his wife's hand.

The peddler shook his head sadly, "I'm sorry you interpret salvation as sacrifice, . . . when in fact, salvation is loving."

Straining to hear what the man said next, Mario looked astonished and replied, "You think I'm rewriting the Holy Scriptures as I see fit . . . and will be condemned to hell? So, you are the judge; nice to meet you, *Judge.*"

FEBRUARY 21, 1993

Mario continued to bare his heart and gained a greater understanding of humanity while keeping his vision of liberty and justice in sight. In an unorthodox manner and at the risk of appearing bizarre, he used as metaphors his trinkets of sorts, breaking up the soil of humanity in the hearts and minds of the peoples he encountered and planting there the seeds of change.

At Battery Park, Catherine would stroll, sit, and read. Sometimes her curiosity would take her to the peddler's cart to listen.

She was there the day a student reporter from New York University interviewed him.

The young lady questioned Mario about his past—courses of action that he had taken and their results. After an intense hour of inquiry, the peddler replied, "No, I wouldn't change anything."

Taken back, the reporter pushed further, asking him if he would change his actions that caused the volatile aftermath after the incident at Caffe Reggio and what his reaction was to his heart-stopping trial.

Mario, his eyes twinkling, answered, "My past trials are evidence to the peoples so they will see I'm an ordinary man; I did not despair; and I never, ever gave up. I didn't realize it at the time of my trial, but my *amicu* Tim Gallagher was right. The living God was my strength and my refuge in days of distress."

He paused, rubbed his forehead, smiled, and passionately continued, "So now in my old age, I have come to a simple conclusion. All my experiments in life, good or bad, happy or sad, have molded me into who I am today—a peddler!"

Catherine hugged him.

ONE WEEK LATER, FEBRUARY 27, 1993

A headline in the *New York Daily Mirror*
HIGH NOON ATTACK
TERRORIST BOMB RIPS WORLD TRADE CENTER
FIVE DEAD... HUNDREDS INJURED . . . THOUSANDS EVACUATED

Chapter 67

September 10, 2001

Eight years following the 1993 terrorist attack on the World Trade Center, Mario, then eighty-seven years old and still in the eye of the storm, step-by-step slowly made his way to Battery Park.

Just as the peddler crossed Centre Street, he glanced back at the Criminal Courts building and grimaced. In the midst of crisscrossing traffic he didn't notice a white delivery van parked alongside City Hall Park.

Soon afterward Mario entered Battery Park along with scads of people, most of whom were just milling about. He headed toward Castle Clinton, a jumping-off point for visitors to the Statue of Liberty or Ellis Island.

Every day he set up his peddler's cart at the very first series of steps to a winding promenade alongside the East River.

Always enthusiastic, despite jeers or ethnic slurs, Mario met and greeted all people of diversity: those of any color, race, language, social status, nationality, or religion.

Daily they rushed on or poured off a ferry from their tour of Liberty or Ellis Island.

This smiling old man opened his heart to anyone whose curiosity he could arouse. With arms flailing, he told intriguing tales that sparked the imagination and touched upon issues . . . problems . . . ailments . . . and solutions.

Before preparing his cart to hawk trinkets of sorts and *Count Alessandro's Healing Tonic of Love*, he retrieved from his cart a white rose with its tender petals perfectly in place. He strolled to the water's edge, knelt down, and gently tossed the fragile rose onto the rippling waters.

The peddler mindlessly removed his fedora, allowing the soft bay breeze to blow through his unruly gray hair as he whispered tenderly, "I can still see your beautiful blue eyes. *T'amu mia cara Catarina . . . my white rose of love.*"

In the breeze, he heard her soft and gentle whisper, "*I love you too. I will always be your white rose of love. Stay well . . . until we meet again.*"

Mario smiled, looked upward, and wiped away tears that flowed down his lined cheeks.

Back at the cart he recalled the words of his *papà*.

"*La famigha e´ sacra!* Family . . . all families everywhere are the paste, the glue that keeps the universe together. Family is first and last . . . Number one! That is the family."

The peddler thundered, "Be bold. Live love. Experiment in living life to the fullest and proclaim your liberty."

And so, Mario Ferrara, the peddler, began another day at Battery Park.

12:13 PM

While he greeted a ferryboat full of tourists disembarking from their tour of Liberty Island, Mario, his eyes brightening, excitedly bellowed, "Come . . . Come . . . take home a bottle of *Count Alessandro's Healing Tonic of Love*. It cures all your pain . . . and solves all your problems."

"How much?" asked a rosy-cheeked man reaching for his wallet.

"No . . . you don't need money; it's free. But for a small price, you can buy one of my wonderful trinkets."

Motioning to others to move toward him, Mario said, "Come a little closer so you can hear. Allow me to introduce myself; they call me Mario the Peddler. Over many roads I have traveled, near and far, to be here in this beautiful place."

Gesturing with his hands, he gently said, "Please . . . give me a moment in this timeless world . . . to help lift up your spirit . . . mend your broken heart . . . and free you from the chains that bind your mind."

"Hey, peddler, how do you expect to accomplish this unbelievable feat?" asked a young man unzipping his dark green windbreaker.

Enthusiastically, he replied, "With a bottle of *Count Alessandro's Healing Tonic of Love*. When you drink, it opens the window of your mind and you become love, pure unconditional love in the living God." Raising his arms high in the air, he continued, "Yes . . . transformation! Drink and believe; remove your uncertainty and take the plunge. Then, *in* and *through* love, your spirit will soar like an eagle, your heart will be healed, and your mind will be free to proclaim your liberty."

"Tell me about your success ratio with this snake oil," snickered a middle-aged man loaded down with rolls of blueprints.

With a disarming smile the peddler said, "There isn't any way you can measure success or failure—only progress. Measurement is done by those who think me drunk, a crazy man, but that's OK. I cannot control what people think, and they cannot control what I say. So say what you mean, mean what you say, but always speak your heart."

Mario reached into the cart, removed a trinket, held it high and, radiating enthusiasm, bellowed, "This is a NOW CLOCK, no batteries, no cord; it works on stardust, and the price is right. When I discovered it, it was the *right* time which was *no* time." Carefully holding it in his hands, he said, "The NOW CLOCK turns the pressure of time into the timeless so you can enjoy the paradise of God that is now. It is in us and among us. Nothing is excluded. And that's the truth."

A group of college students, hearing Mario, stopped long enough for the tall slender one in the group to ask, "*Truth*—what's that?"

He replied earnestly, "What's *truth*? One definition of *truth* is oneness." She smiled graciously and didn't ask any further questions.

Mario glanced back and with a glint in his eye said, "By the way young lady, if you place your hand over your Mickey Mouse watch, it will have the same results as the NOW CLOCK."

A retired lawyer in an icy tone inquired, "What makes you think you have a lock on truth?"

Mario shot back, "I didn't say I had a lock on truth. Every person has his or her definition of truth. Each person's individual truth is what they should follow."

"Then you have strife!"

"No, then you have order. Truth lives in the heart and the heart knows we are one."

"Dreamer!" exclaimed the lawyer walking away laughing.

At first, few people gathered on the field of grass and concrete at Battery Park, buying trinkets of sorts, while asking questions about their ailments and curiosities.

As ferry boats continued to load and unload, the crowd stopping to bargain with the peddler for his wares and words steadily increased in numbers.

Mario spun around to lend his ear to a man who was standing, glaring at him. Mario answered compassionately, "No, I am not here to undermine goodness and create havoc. It's your choice to think me a blatant heretic and sinner. That's OK."

"You should be chained and whipped," cried out the man as he tossed one of Mario's bottles into New York Bay.

"*Scusi?* Has the Inquisition returned?"

The peddler, squinting, reached into his bag and said, "Ah, that reminds me. I only have one TWISTED KEY left. This key was recovered from a rat-infested dungeon in Spain during the Inquisition. Which one will be bold enough to buy the TWISTED KEY and use it to unlock the shackles that bind your heart?" Scanning the group, with a lilt in his voice, he shouted, "When your heart is open, you will never be imprisoned in a moment of time. And then, all you have to do is love."

A skipper from one of the ferries came over and handed Mario his key.

"Eh . . . let me see; . . . yes, this key will work as well. But there was another key, one that Dante used. I'll tell you about it . . . later."

A woman with a radiant smile pushed her oversized sunglasses up to the top of her head, took hold of his hand, and gleefully said, "Everyone is different. That's what I enjoy about life."

Mario returned her smile and said, "Yes, everyone sees life differently. That's what makes us unique and special individuals, separate in our vision, one in our hearts. So, let your heart speak and act."

He turned and said, "Speaking of action, it reminds me of the time I was in the vestibule of the inferno."

Dante wanted to make a deal right there—right in the midst of the Uncommitted. A deal! Please, give me a break! I figured this could be another one of those so-called win-win situations: no doubt I knew about those good old win-wins. Win-win, which means more often than not, there's a "gotcha" involved with someone getting screwed in the process. Anyway, Dante wanted to make a deal . . . I thought, *How can I resist risk? Risk, that's part of my life.* So I said, "Go ahead, fire away."

Dante grinned and said, "OK . . . it's a simple plan. The first thing we need to do is travel through all the floors and sections of the inferno and then sneak into the pit of pits of hell itself . . . and that's assuming we can avoid the emperor . . . Satan. Once there, with this key of life that we all hold in our hearts, we can unlock the floor vault that secures the treasure map of human resources and technologies. They are all found in the Scroll of the I AM, . . . and voila! . . . that's our ticket to freedom."

Nervously, I began talking to myself. What does he mean, *if* we can sneak into the pit of pits, without Satan, the emperor of hell, spotting us? And *if* we can unlock a floor vault? Too many *ifs*, so the first choice was to tell him to get lost and try to find my own way out. This sounded—at the time—like a very dumb choice.

Kind of begging, he said, "Mario, you're my ticket to freedom. This may be my only chance to break out of Limbo and start all over again."

Trying to quickly process his words, I concluded that, in any event, he was taking a chance by agreeing to escort me through this God-forsaken place, so I said, "Why not."

"Wonderful, wonderful," said Dante. Smiling, he continued, "After we leave the vestibule for the Uncommitted we'll continue to an area reserved for the Covetous and Greedy."

Then I said to myself, why would I put myself through this misery?

He handed the woman a bottle of tonic and said, "After I catch my breath, I'll tell you more about Dante."

She shrugged and said, "No problem. I'll sit and wait."

A college professor, finishing her stroll along Battery Park, stopped to listen to Mario. She asked, "What is your opinion of new age theology?"

He shrugged and said, "*Sì, signura,* you ask about new age theology? Eh . . . new age . . . old age . . . Is there really anything new under the sun?"

"This guy never shows any distinction among people," said a middle-aged woman. She was holding on to her daughter's arm. The gleam in her eyes indicated her familiarity with his message and the value she placed on it.

Standing next to the cart, Mario compassionately said, "The spirit rests in the hearts of all peoples. It doesn't matter how they act, bad or good, or what they believe, whether they are atheists or religious purists. In everyone lives a God of love, as everyone lives in the God of love, the Holy Spirit of One."

Lifting a trinket out of the cart Mario exclaimed, "Look here. My feet still hurt from searching. But, direct from New Delhi, a special find. At least that's what the kind man who sold it to me said. MAHATMA GANDHI'S TEA CUP. Whatever you put in it to drink, it always tastes the same: try tea, coffee, hot chocolate . . . even wine. It all tastes like water . . . nothing tastes like you expect . . . except water will taste like water. So I say Gandhi's way of difference is no difference. Just unity."

"You look worried *signuro,*" said Mario to a man who was rushing off to work. He was sipping on a Starbucks coffee. "No need to worry, your coffee container can accomplish the same results."

He turned to those gathered and softly said, "Always remember. The sun of God shines and the rain of God falls on everyone . . . Nobody is left out. What's critical in today's society is that the equality and dignity of all peoples be preserved."

Looking to his left, he responded to a burly man in a tank-top shirt puffing on a cigar, "Eh? You're going to preserve me in a pickle jar? That's funny. That's OK!"

Tank-top man said angrily, "Peddler, you speak from both sides of your mouth. But your greatest offense is your snake-oil selling scheme."

Mario nodded in frustration and said, "Now, *signuro,* you say I'm a two-faced fraud, cheating peoples out of their money on some voodoo medicine. Yes, I do sell my trinkets and, may I add, all at a fair price. But, *Count Alessandro's Healing Tonic of Love* always finds it's way to those who need comfort in one form or another."

"That's it! Zip up your stupid mouth!"

"I'm sorry, you want me to be quiet?" Mario, shrugging his shoulders, asked in disbelief. "I don't think so."

Mario turned away for a moment, then turning back said, "What you say leads me to believe that you have a self-righteous attitude; a religious lockout mentality that contradicts and disowns any human being who does not believe as you. Because maybe you, sir, are afraid of the peoples who do not agree with you. Do you worry they may be right and you may be wrong? But no need to worry. In the end, it's all the same."

Chewing his cigar, the man snarled and said, "Go to hell!"

"You wish I go to hell? Sounds not too difficult and not too far, especially if I live in the society you wish to create," said Mario with a slight grin.

Standing face to face with the man, the peddler listened to the whispered words spewing out of his mouth and replied, "Now, you wish to burn me at the stake? That's not nice."

His eyes sparkled as he opened his peddler's bag and said breathlessly, "Unbelievable, it was extremely rough in the beginning, but now, after years of abrasive sand . . . the beauty of peace is reflected in this wondrous RADIANT PEARL, brought to the surface from the deepest of seas by none other than the Lady of Devotion. It was given to me when I was in Cefalù, Sicily. Reaching out, he softly said, "Here, hold the pearl in your hand and experience an experience beyond experience."

Smiling, he held the hand of a woman leaning on her walker equipped with a canvas carryall bag. "I did hear what you asked. Of course, rosary beads will accomplish the same results. Believe!"

"Hey peddler, you have not mentioned white-collar crooks. My brother-in-law's entire pension was destroyed," said an enormous man holding his bulging sack lunch. "Although, in a strange way, he was grateful to the whistle-blower."

"*Scusi*, you ask about corporate fraud and finagling? Ah, take some arrogance, add finagling, deception, and no conscience and you have it." Briefly hesitating, he tilted back his fedora, grimaced, and continued, "I remember what happened in Chicago. The commodity markets were hit hard after federal agents ended their two-year sting operation. End result: many indictments and convictions: yet, did it change anything?"

He shrugged and without waiting for an answer replied to his own question, "It is true. You may charge them, convict them, fine them, and jail them; still they will not change until love becomes their mission statement. And your brother-in-law is right. I give credit to those braveheart whistle-blowers in business as well as those in government who are willing to risk all by pointing out wrongdoings so that justice prevails and the manipulated can breathe a sigh of relief."

Mario started to pace and said with deep conviction, "Everyone who takes a risk for change is a braveheart. A perfect example was Frank Serpico, a courageous New York cop who, years ago, exposed corruption within the police department. Even a bullet to his face during a drug bust didn't stop him from testifying."

Raising his arms, he cried out, "When you drink *Count Alessandro's Healing Tonic of Love*, your mind and heart grows with love, and you become more human and more divine. And you will know what to do as words are planted in love and sprout into deeds."

The peddler sat on his crate and said, "This reminds me of an altercation in the inferno with Dante."

> After Dante raked me through the coals, I cried out, "I guess I'm asking too much for you to stop your tour of hell."
>
> "You're not as stupid as I thought you were," Dante answered, laughing. He adjusted his weird hat, and placing his hand on my back and pushing me forward, he said, "Onward to the Gluttonous with their inordinate capacity to receive and, of course, the Fanatics who need no description.
>
> "Is that it?" I meekly asked.
>
> "In your dreams!" he replied. His eyes lit up, "Then comes the exciting part. We'll travel Styx, one of the rivers of hell, the waterway of injustice. Along the left bank, we'll visit the Wrathful, wanderers who wished to inflict punishment in return for anything."
>
> "Don't tell me there's a right bank," I said, shaking my head.
>
> "Of course there's a right bank. That's where the Doomsayers reside."
>
> "Please . . . stop it," I cried out, "enough of injustice."

Addressing a group that had disembarked from the Ellis Island Ferry and had meandered over, he said, "Speaking of injustice, I ask the *signuro,* the one with the baseball hat. No, not you. I'm speaking to the one with a clenched fist. Is your job, your lifestyle, your every breath affected by acid rain; global warming; air, water and land pollution; tropical deforestation; power plant emissions; or toxic waste?" He paused to catch his breath, then added, "What about our forests and parks? Is *anybody* looking?"

The man with the clenched fist replied defiantly, "You're a trouble-maker."

"Before you say such a thing, give me a chance to express myself further. What about pesticides or emissions from automobiles? What are we eating? Is anybody looking? Does anybody care?" Then he held his hand up to stop any replies from his listeners. "Wait, I can answer that. Yes, there are a few people who care, but not near enough."

The man exhaled in frustration and irately said, "You know damn well the government has its watchdogs to protect our rivers, oceans, and wetlands and every other abuse to the environment."

Mario shook his head in disbelief and asked, "Are they looking under their desks? Or is it possible that certain corporations, industries, and special interests gain to the detriment of others?"

"You're definitely a troublemaker," he snapped. Then, he turned and slowly walked away.

A young man wearing a dark shirt with a history book under his arm joined the conversation. "Why do we rely on foreign oil?"

"Maybe the man with the baseball hat and clenched fist has an answer. My answer: It benefits the power elite. Every time someone is bold enough to change the system they get crushed. Explore the galaxies, no problem. Substitute fuels, big problem!"

Mario paused to take a drink of tonic, glanced at those gathered to his right and caringly said, "If you're concerned about life and death, then it's up to you—not just the *other* person—to act." He sat down on his crate and continued, "But be sure all understanding, solutions, and actions are entrenched in love. Bear in mind that the peoples have tried strikes, protests, boycotts, sit-ins, and civil disobedience."

He stood, and in a strong voice, said, "Whatever you name, it was probably tried. You see, change comes slowly. And lasting change only comes when love and no other motive whatsoever is the driving force behind every action. To those in business, take heed. There are ethics and then there is the ethic of unconditional love—the absolute blueprint for success."

The peddler tilted his head in the direction of a faint voice. He said, "I hear you *signuro,* but for those who did not, I'll repeat your question. 'Is the judicial system out of control?' My answer: Anymore, it's not what is right and what is fair. It's all about money. Without a sufficient amount of money, the peoples cannot defend or seek justice against deep pockets. The choice is money to pay lawyers or money to settle. If settlement is cheaper, you settle. It's called legal extortion. Where is love?"

Mario walked to the other side of the cart and sighed, "In litigation there's a process called discovery. That's a perfect word. Why not use the same word, the same process, to discover a legal system out of control. Now, you wish to know what I sell to change the situation."

With his head buried in the cart, the peddler, mumbling, removed a trinket, turned to his left, and said in a hopeful tone, "There is something special for a circumstance such as you described, a remarkable antique. It was found on a beach in Costa Rica. It is a MIRROR FROM ATLANTIS that reflects the mystery of life. Hold the mirror to the light and see that there are no opposites. It's all the same. Here, take it and go hang the mirror in the courthouse window."

The man who asked the question about the legal system held his briefcase between his legs, reached into his back pocket, pulled out his wallet, and asked, "How much?"

"Please, no need to pay me. It's my gift."

Turning to his right, the peddler acknowledged a policeman's question with a nod. Then, chuckling, he replied, "A bathroom mirror? you ask. Why not? *I* ask. It should work."

A man biting his fingernails said, "You haven't said a damn thing that makes sense. Do you leave crumbs to find your way home?"

"That's clever," laughed the peddler, and turning to the man's friend, he said, "and you, *signuro,* say I am an idiot who knows nothing about anything. That's OK. That thought is your choice."

"What about life?"

The peddler, responding to the parents of five children, said, "You ask about life. When it comes to life—yes, life—let me say this: You can read all the books in the world, from the motivational type to spiritual writings; or go to the finest universities; or be a great tradesman; or whatever your earthly vocation happens to be. But greatness without love is nothing. For without love, you have no foundation. So you see, life is love."

Leaning against the cart Mario said, "Then, when I think of a lack of love, my mind races back to the inferno."

Dante wiped away a pretend tear and said, "You wish I stop my tour of the inferno? You of all people have just hurt my feelings." He slapped his hands together and joyfully said, "Nonetheless, we will continue. Once we enter the WALL OF THE CITY OF DIS that leads to the underworld of hell itself, we'll be met by Mindless Zealots. Because they're mindless, our visit will be only for a short period of time—not a lot going on there. Then off we go into NETHER HELL."

"You are merciless!" I cried out.

"Me? Wait until I finish: then you can tell me what I am. You're so lucky to be able to meet the Tyrants who used an unjust exercise of power. And of course there are the Suicides. Simply said, they are violent against self."

"I give."

"I thank you, Mario, for your understanding. You will find it interesting visiting the Contemptuous, the Irreverent, the—"

I placed my hand on his shoulder and said, "Enough of *the* this and *the* that, please!"

"OK, I understand. Into the ABYSS OF LOWER HELL! We'll journey and meet the Pimp wanderers who used others for selfish purposes."

"You're kidding, right?"

"Absolutely not. At the next stop are the Arrogant. Wanderers convinced of their importance and devoted to self-interest and advancement. They're self-centered, pompous, egotistic:

you get the point."

"How could I miss it?"

"Oops, can't forget the Slothful or Flatterers who used the ass-kisser or brown-nose method, whichever term you prefer."

"I changed my mind. Stop the tour!"

Mario acknowledged a thin bald-headed man dressed in a yellow golf shirt whose mouth was hanging open. "Oh, you want to know what happens next? Not now . . . maybe later."

Chapter 68

·····································

1:20 p.m.

Reaching again inside his peddler's bag, he excitedly pulled out a purple drawstringed bag, carefully opened it, and said, "Yes, this prize possession is for sale. It looks and feels like a crystal ball. But, it's not like anything you have seen or experienced before. It was imported from Inner Earth. You don't gaze at it; you are transported into it. It's called IMAGINE. Just last night I tried it. Let me tell you what happened.

"I was at a party in North Carolina—a tobacco party. I looked. Next to me was Pietro, a *paesanu* who yelled, 'Let's do it now.' Without thinking I cried out in acknowledgment, 'Once and for all—it's time to shut down all the tobacco factories. No more should they benefit from disaster and death. Go with love and collect cigarettes, cigars, and chewing and pipe tobacco from your family, friends, and neighbors. Then drive to Market and Water Streets in Wilmington, North Carolina. Once there, walk, don't run to the edge of the pier. Remove the tobacco from its containers and dump the tobacco into the Cape Fear River.' Then, just like that, cars and truckloads full of cigarettes, cigars, and pipe tobacco from all over the country found their way to Wilmington to the North Carolina Tobacco Party. *Mamma Mia*—what a party! Tonight, maybe you try—IMAGINE!"

A bright-eyed, five-foot-eight-inch woman was cuddling her three-year-old, blond-haired granddaughter. She said, "Mario, taking your advice, I did try to imagine by using my crystal vase. What I imagined was amazing. It was love in action."

"I am most interested in hearing," he said enthusiastically.

In an uplifted voice, she said, "The international news services reported that at last gun control and arms control were working. No more pistols, assault weapons or nuclear weapons. All funds that were allocated to a war machine were being diverted to benefit humanity."

"That's wonderful," cried Mario joyously. "Then we would no longer have to worry about the crazies who kill or try to kill."

Waving his fedora he roared, "Imagine! Use your imagination to manifest your dream, and your dream will turn into reality—if you imagine with love."

A young Native American Indian sadly said, "Optimism only goes so far. History proves that."

The peddler's face lit up with anticipation as he responded, "I realize the government didn't listen to their heart in the treatment of your peoples. Promises meant nothing. Broken treaties meant something."

The young man said, "That's exactly what makes me angry. We got screwed, and we still are seeking justice."

Mario replied, "But no need to dwell in the past."

"Easy to say, difficult to do."

"Only if you think so. Take control of your birthright, look inward, use your sacred spirituality that flows through your peoples and understand that with each encounter comes an opportunity, an opportunity that's waiting to be taken with love. So observe, listen, and understand; use your intuition to choose for the benefit of all your peoples."

Mario smiled, reached out, arms extended, and said, "Here, for you, young man, a poem you may enjoy."

WINDOW

Let go of negative thoughts
And open the window of your mind
And watch the gentle wind of love
Blow away a veil of separation
And perceive unity in diversity.

The peddler, his face aglow in wonderment, said, "Now then, let me give you something to think about. I'll tell you a little secret; actually it's a mystery. There's an energy flowing through your body like streaks of lightning. It's so exciting! But, in order to see and feel the lightning you need to love God with all your heart, with all your soul, with all your strength, and with all your mind."

A student wearing an NYU sweatshirt couldn't restrain himself any longer and said to his friend, "This guy is wacko."

"What's this? You call me a wacko? I think that's a wisecrack. But that's OK," said Mario with a smile.

Holding up a jar he had removed from the top of the cart, the peddler cried out, "Maybe you should save your pennies and buy this jar of CRACKLIN' LIGHTNING bottled straight from high up in the Rocky Mountains of Colorado. Energize your being. Catch a bolt of positive thinking. In your personal experiences, when your attitude is positive, life changes to the positive. Then having done all, stand and surrender all to God."

He listened carefully to the question of a woman dressed in black whose gray hair was neatly combed in place. Then he answered her with a grin. "Yes, you are correct: crackling macaroni gives out the same positive energy."

Removing a beautiful multi-colored box from the peddler's cart, he held it high for all to see and declared. "From the rain forest in Brazil comes this marvelous dark *CIOCCOLATO* to clarify your thought process. A bargain and cheaper by the dozen. Absolutely delicious. So please, make sure you eat mindfully."

A woman munching on a bag of popcorn looked longingly at the chocolate. "Mario, do they sell this *cioccolato* in Georgia?" asked the woman in a deep southern drawl.

He shook his head sadly, "No, unfortunately they do not. But, the candy bar your little boy is eating accomplishes the same result. Actually any *cioccolato* will do."

After taking a bite from a *cioccolato*, his eyes lit up as he cheerfully continued, "Your thought process enables you to become who you are, and who you are constantly changes in the moment that you are. So bear in mind, you have to live with your thoughts, choices, decisions, and actions. Don't let them control you. With love, let them guide you to a better life for those around you. Always believe in yourself and trust your intuition."

Pointing a finger in Mario's face, a pudgy unshaven man barked, "You're full of crap."

Not the least bit taken back, he replied, "You say my head is full of *mierda*. Wow! But that's OK, that's your choice. That's life."

"Don't you ever worry?" asked a woman who was being dragged down by the worn leather portfolio that was slung over her shoulder.

"Worry gets you nowhere. My *papà* told me worry doesn't add a single benefit or a second more to your life."

She smiled graciously.

A frequent visitor to Battery Park opened the collar of his heavily starched midnight blue shirt and whispered to his friend, "That's the crazy bastard I told you about."

Mario heard him, chuckled, and kept on talking. "We have got to believe, believe in ourselves, believe in all peoples—no exceptions. Let me give each of you a bottle of *Count Alessandro's Healing Tonic of Love* and a question to ponder: When power becomes weak and dies, will it be because it's no longer fed with the sweat and blood of humanity?"

"I told you the guy is a crazy bastard," said the man, pulling his scratchy shirt collar away from his neck.

A thin, gray-haired woman holding two loaded-down shopping bags looked Mario over, giggled, and said, "For an old man you sure can dish it out. Don't you wonder if anybody is listening?"

With a wide grin Mario said, "I'll drink to your listening." He took a drink of tonic and then offered her a bottle.

"That reminds me how, once again, I begged Dante to stop his ramblings about the inferno. This is what happened."

He grimaced and said, "I, Dante, will do nothing of the kind. How dare I not expose the Charlatan wanderers who claim knowledge or skill, although they have none: or the Manipulators, or the Unscrupulous with whom anything goes if it's right for them."

"Now I know why some thought you *stunato.*"

"I pay no mind to what others think of me. Whether they consider me crazy or not, it makes no difference to me. Therefore, in spite of what you may think, I will continue."

"Please, don't!"

"I accept your apology. Let's continue." He paused and said, "Just so you know, those who really bug me are the Sowers of Discord. They enjoyed urging dissension or disunity, as their goal was to disrupt or separate. And of course, the Falsifiers who applied the *Book of 666 Ways To Be Intentionally Deceptive.*"

I glared at him and said, "Did anybody ever call you a vomit mouth?"

"Funny. Lastly . . ."

"Thank God."

"*That* you better do before we enter the WELL OF THE GIANTS, the watchful eyes of hell within a hell. It gets a little dicey when we enter the pit of pits. Don't worry: I'll be behind you the whole way," he said, chuckling.

His crazy eyes squinting, Dante continued. "This pit is filled with Traitors. These wanderers were against family, friend, neighbor, fellow workers, and the worst of the wors . . . in actuality, they were against The Divine . . . The Holy Spirit of One. This is Satan's den . . . where he keeps locked up the treasure of human resources and technologies spelled out in the Scroll of the I AM."

Mario gently reached into his bag and gave the woman a copy of the Scroll and said, "Actually when I think back, Dante's tour of the inferno was quite exciting. If you like, I'll tell you more later."

As the afternoon was wearing on, people still came and went, except for a man who never raised his head but finally found the courage to speak. "You don't seem to be specific. What's next?" pleaded the stoop-shouldered man with a distinct British accent.

Mario went to him, took his hand, leaned over to look him in the eye, and said, "Eh? . . . You ask, what's next? You already know the answer. Just do it. Remember, there's purpose—and then—there's purpose. The true purpose is first finding ourselves as one in a common thread of love."

Raising his voice a bit, he continued, "So don't place your hope on a social order designed by your human side. Place your hope on a spiritual order, a spiritual order already in place."

The man nodded in agreement and walked off.

A woman was standing at the back of the group gathered around the pushcart. She let go of her male friend's arm and covered her eyes with both hands, showing off her manicured nails that were painted a dark purple. She snapped, "Why don't you take a walk off the pier and disappear."

He said matter-of-factly, "You wish not to see me? That's OK."

A moment later, the peddler reached into his bag, pulled out a trinket, and enthusiastically announced, "A perfect keepsake of this gathering is a unique THORN REMOVER made from a fractured rock found in the Himalayas. This item, I only sell to those who absolutely need it. It removes an overload of knowledge for the sake of knowledge and fills the void with enlightenment for life's journey."

He held the THORN REMOVER high in the air and bellowed, "So, visualize your desires . . . love-laced. Imagine things the way you wish them to be. And above all, whatever the situation, hold on to your vision and never let go. If it's for the good of all peoples—and I repeat the word *all*—you will become the catalyst of your vision as it turns into reality. Think over what I have said, and if you listen carefully to the whispers of God, you will understand it all."

Acknowledging a young lady who looked troubled, he said, "*Sì, signura* you think I'm a simpleton. That's your choice. Simplicity is what confounds the intellect. Simplify your life: accept what has been given, poverty or riches, sickness or health. Forget yourself, give freely, turn the other cheek—and smile."

Her boyfriend, with his arms wrapped around her, gave him a piercing look and asked, "Isn't *knowledge* power?"

Mario laughed loudly. "Mass media, in its entire splendor and all encompassing networks, has contributed to an overload of knowledge. We know more than we'll ever need to know, sometimes all about nothing. Knowing 100 percent of nothing is still knowing nothing."

The young lady's frustrated expression spoke volumes as she glanced at her watch.

Reaching out, he said, "Let me give each of you a bottle of *Count Alessandro's Healing Tonic of Love* and a question to ponder. Have we short-circuited our brain so our intellect is fried to a dark brown crisp? My answer: Discernment is up to the receiver. The receiver is you. What you read, what you hear, and what you see should be linked to critical thinking and common sense. Your movement, past and present, is the continuum of a puzzle that shapes life. Now your answer."

The couple turned and swiftly walked away laughing uncomfortably.

Mario called out, "By the way, any rock will do."

Responding to a freelance writer for psychology magazines, the peddler said bluntly, "You say each person thinks and acts differently and they will never get on the same page?"

"Ah, they *are* on the same page. Everyone grows on a daily basis. We learn not only from our friends but also from our adversaries. Difference of opinion does not mean a break in a link of oneness. If the peoples listen to their hearts, and their hearts only, nothing will deter their actions. They will become bravehearts." With his arms flailing he cried out, "Acknowledge the Divine within. Then choose. Then act, always out of love. If you fall, pick yourself up and forge ahead."

"I'm sorry, Peddler; it's all still just words to me," said the man in a doubtful tone.

Mario quickly responded, "Words that should turn into action."

After a fairly long pause the man said, "You are an off-the-wall screwball and troublemaker," and then stomped off.

Turning to answer a gentleman with heavy jowls who moved behind the peddler's cart to heckle him close up, Mario said, "You must enjoy badgering me, but *I* don't think I'm seeking the impossible. What paralyzes life is a lack of faith and a lack of courage. I believe there's no need to be content with misery or mediocrity. Why not be radical? Throw caution to the wind. Believe. And go for it!"

Leaning into the peddler's cart, Mario started shuffling trinkets of sorts until he found what he was looking for. He said happily, "Look how it shines. It even glows in the dark. It's a FAITH BRACELET made from Saint Joan of Arc's steel breastplate."

A woman with carrot-red hair shrugged her shoulders and said, "It must be worth a fortune."

He shook his head and blurted, "No, it's magical, not expensive. A friend from the south of France gave it to me. The FAITH BRACELET rewinds your memory to the child within. Then once again, acceptance and believability take hold."

Listening carefully to a young man's murmur, Mario answered, "No, it's not just for girls and yes, a piece of rope will do nicely."

He tipped his fedora to those gathered and continued, "Everyone at birth was gifted with wonderful human treasures. And when you share those treasured gifts of love in whatever you are and whatever you do with one another, then the residual effect you have on society will be lasting."

The young man's lady friend gave him a questioning look and sarcastically said: "Tell me more. Tell me more."

Without hesitation Mario answered, "OK. It doesn't matter what the circumstance or how the odds are stacked against you; always believe there's a way out. And never, ever give up. Never, ever."

"What about mystics?" asked a smiling young woman. Strands of her chestnut brown hair partly covered her left eye.

He raised his arms and compassionately said, "Young lady, do you know that *you* are a mystic? Yes, indeed everyone is a mystic."

Chapter 69

2:00 p.m.

Mario turned and pointed to a young man at the back of a group of onlookers who was taking off his backpack. "I cannot hear you. You ask about this beautiful RED HAT? It's DANTE'S. Many years ago, when I took the inferno tour with him, he gave it to me."

A man whose tie was so tight around his neck that he could hardly breathe barked, "With who? The devil?"

Mario slapped the side of his head, grinned, and said, "Eh . . . see, now you think me a crazy man because I tell you about Dante, my old *amicu*. That's OK. I don't mind." As the wind picked up his voice got louder, "So I'll continue. I met Dante not too many years before I spoke my heart at Caffe Reggio in Greenwich Village. Maybe later I'll tell you about it. But for now, included with this hat is a special price and offer: a round-trip ticket into the inferno with Dante Alighieri as your personal guide. This is a tour you will never forget."

It begins in a stinking fog so thick you can hardly see your hand through the muck, and then slowly you see the inferno's tattered sign.

YOUR CHOICE . . . ENTER HERE . . . ABANDON HOPE

It has everything: the stagnant river of Styx, the ruined city of Dis, many floors with disgusting sights, sounds, and smells. The greater the transgression, the lower you go, at least in Dante's inferno.

I laugh because I remember it like it was yesterday. One time, during a wicked train ride, some guy named Merciless threw me off the train into the middle of nowhere. Dante called out, "Mario, take a deep breath. The Braggarts are so easy to locate; one whiff and you find them."

My nose almost fell off my face; my eyes burned. I looked, and what did I see? Just faces with bald heads. The rest of the Braggart's bodies were stuck in plain and simple *mierda*.

Excitedly, Dante, twisting his body, roared, "Look at those bald-headed wanderers who enlisted in the braggadocio club, trying to keep their mouths shut. They know every thirty seconds, keepers on speedboats come racing through the area."

"OK, I'll play along. How did you actually meet the poet Dante?" said a woman wearing a beige tailored suit and a Cheshire smile.

"You want to know how I met him? If you have the time, I'll tell you."

Moving closer, she snidely said, "You have my undivided attention."

"OK, here's how it happened."

Mario sat down on his crate, took a drink of tonic, and said, "Maybe not just yet. Every time I think about it, I shudder, and yet give thanks. I can tell you this: There was a time when people were made slaves by laws, and held together in chains, and dragged screaming into the inferno. Now, many times peoples become slaves to their position in life and are held together by fear."

The woman with the Cheshire smile mockingly pleaded, "Go ahead, tell us what happened next with Dante."

Mario smiled as he turned to another woman leaning on her wooden crutches. "*Sì signura?*" he asked, wanting to know her question.

Hearing her faint voice, he replied, "Eh? . . . You ask about religion with its dogma? To me, it's all just words and more words. Why confuse the peoples? More writing, more interpretation; all that does is lead to arguments and disagreements floating in the mumbo jumbo, the gibberish, of more words. Remember, in religion the letter of the law strangles and kills the life-giving spirit, the Holy Spirit of One that resides in all beings."

The peddler stopped, took off his fedora, and said, "Another thing, when I speak of Christ or the Holy Spirit of One, I speak of spirituality and not religion. Please don't confuse the two."

Mario slowly climbed up on his crate and said, "Get your bottle of *Count Alessandro's Healing Tonic of Love* and claim your liberty in the circle of life. Each morning when you awake, take a small drink and find yourself in serenity; then refuse to let anything push you one way or another. Indifference will keep you in a peaceful state of mind. Forget what is behind. Live in the moment. Seize the moment and strain to move forward—with love."

"Sir, I worship and follow my Lord and Savior Jesus Christ," said a young man with the sniffles who clutched a dog-eared copy of the Bible. The peddler cleared his throat and his eyes brightened as he said, "Oh, you say you are a Christian man and follow the teachings of the Bible and worship Christ. Yes, worship is good. But to live the Christ within is better."

The man began to fidget as his face turned red.

The peddler offered a bottle of tonic to the man and said sincerely, "So drink *Count Alessandro's Healing Tonic of Love,* believe in the ideal, and experiment with life. Make known the fact that Christ's message of love is not theory, but reality."

The man abruptly turned his back and began to weave his way through the group.

Mario called out, "Please, don't leave grumbling; express yourself." The man never turned or looked back. Mario sighed and called after him, "You wish not—that's OK."

"Your English is atrocious and your perception of religion is totally without foundation," said a young woman holding on to a man eating a hot dog.

Raising his eyebrows, Mario asked incredulously, "Do you really think religion matters?"

She answered in a haughty tone, "I most certainly do! Don't you think that what you believe matters on this earth and into the hereafter?" Without waiting for a response she continued, "My husband and I are devout Catholics and follow the teachings of the Church. Period."

Sitting back down on his crate, he took off his fedora, sighed and, in a nonconfrontational tone, said, "If I may answer your question *signura*: To me, no, of course it does not matter: Christ, Buddha, Mohammed. It does not matter whether one worships in the tradition of Judaism, Hinduism, studies the prophets, or searches and searches to find their spiritual home."

He put his fedora back on and quietly said, "I'm an old man and have come to the conclusion that there are many religions and ideologies, each protective of their respective domain, each going their separate way, many suspicious of each other's motive. But if they can meet in the light and choose to move in love, everyone will recognize that in diversity there is perfect unity. So, no need to judge or ridicule the faith of any person. That should not be your concern."

She turned her back to the peddler.

Mario reached out to her and in a tone of sincerity continued, "*Signura,* what does matter is your strength and faith in your circle of love. For when you reach its center you will discover the heart of every belief system, faith, and religion."

A heavyset woman holding on to the arm of her rather smallish husband timidly asked, "What about the Vatican and its authority?"

With his hands clasped prayer-like, the peddler said,

"What you ask about the Vatican is difficult to answer, but I'll try." Looking skyward, he continued, "Pope John Paul II has done much for the youth, poor, and oppressed; and he has done much, of course, in the struggle for liberty. Just ask the communists of Poland-Past. And of course there are countless, wonderful, dedicated holy people among all the religious orders and communities. But some, including some of his cardinals, are to the right of Attila the Hun and feed him words mired in muck."

He paused, tilted back his fedora, and said, "It's a delicate and difficult task to change things within the Church without destroying the very essence of it." He hesitated a moment, rubbed his forehead, and continued. "However, many times all good thoughts and work go astray when the business of structure takes hold. So, there are many things I disagree with."

"Like what?" asked her husband in a tone of indifference.

"First let me say, when I was in Rome I went to visit the Vatican Museum. Michelangelo's frescoes in the Sistine Chapel were magnificent." He paused and added, "It was interesting that my eyes saw no separation . . . just oneness."

"I cannot imagine it. It sounds unbelievable," said a teenager, holding on to the peddler's cart.

"There's more." He hesitated a moment to reflect back and continued. "Then there are the physical structures with pinpointed detail inside and out that only God-inspired laborers could have constructed as expressions of love. These temples are adorned with stunning stained glass creations and paintings to honor God. All are glorious and should be admired as such. Therefore, it's so easy to be drawn into the physical aspects of religion that sit within the walls of a building called a church. But in my opinion, the grandeur of art was created not to impress but to inspire. Homage should be paid through imitation, not edifices."

The heavyset woman said, "That doesn't tell me one thing about the Church."

Mario responded, "OK, here's more. At the very least, the Church of Rome should consistently examine its heart rather than its doctrine and go beyond being a maintenance church and lead the faithful to spiritual liberty."

The peddler raised his arms high and continued, "And yes, of course, it can change its archaic stance toward ordination of women to the priesthood, and celibacy for priests, and ah, never mind. I say too much already."

"You should be ashamed of yourself!" exclaimed the woman in a terse tone. She took hold of her husband, and they walked away shaking their heads in disgust.

Mario called out, "Wait, one more thing. Is it possible that the Roman Catholic Church from the outside looks pristine, but is slowly crumbling from the inside? Maybe it's time to rebuild."

The couple never looked back.

"My best friend tells me he is an atheist. Now what?" shouted out a man with a pencil-thin moustache. He looked to be somewhere in his early forties.

The peddler turned and smiled. "Yes, there are atheists. So what? Are they immune to love?"

Once again taking off his fedora, Mario wiped his forehead, shoved the hat back on, and said, "There are times that I wonder what some people are thinking. Why do ruthless pro-life groups torch abortion clinics? Why do environmental zealots set fire to ski lodges? Animal rights extremists destroy property. Why? Self-imposed inquisitors burn churches? White supremacists use violence in judgment? Terrorists run rampant? Why, why?" He hesitated a moment, squinted, slapped the side of his head, and said, "Eh, wait . . . now I remember why. They choose to exist in the bottomless pit of a living inferno!"

Mingling with those surrounding the cart, Mario was rudely interrupted and admonished for a lack of worldly knowledge by a visiting dignitary from the United Nations.

Mario forcefully countered, "Rather than think and study and analyze and rationalize, why don't we show our courage and make daily decisions based on love. The time is now; we need to stick our spear in the ground and say, no further—enough is enough!"

The dignitary, with his suit jacket draped over his arm, moved closer to the peddler's cart. He asked, "That's so abstract: do you have any specific suggestions?"

The peddler reached out to shake the man's hand and said earnestly, "I've been asked many times to share new concepts geared toward the goal of creating a better world. That's exactly what I haven't done. The problem, in my opinion, is that we have complicated the message of love, when, *in fact*, it's simple enough for all people, not only to understand, but to live."

"What you say in part is true. Still and all, we need systems, structures, and laws that translate into a sophisticated process for dialogue."

Mario gently countered, "The system is in place. We are family! There's a natural commonality of sisterhood and brotherhood among all of us. That's the system! And that's the reason there's no need for any dividing lines. We, and not God, have set up all structures, nations, and boundaries."

"Peddler, please understand that we live in diverse times, in diverse societies," said the dignitary. His words were almost drowned out by a commercial airliner on final approach to LaGuardia Airport.

Mario waited for the jet noise to dissipate before responding, "Maybe so; nonetheless, there's no difference between peoples, except what we choose to call different—the difference of color, the difference between friends and enemies, relatives and strangers, one nationality and another, and so on. They are all family. One family—*la famigha!*"

The dignitary listened with keen interest.

The peddler, his blue eyes getting wider, continued, "*Signuro*, we are all responsible—*we*, the billions upon billions of people that comprise all neighborhoods of planet earth. There isn't any law that divides us as a people except what we establish within our hearts."

The dignitary asked dejectedly, "How do you tell that to nations that are deaf to words of the heart?"

Mario looked directly into the delegate's dark eyes, placed his hands on the man's shoulders, and tenderly said, "It's possible. All things are possible. When words of love penetrate their hearts, it will bring back memories of the way it was and the way it should be."

Even after hearing Mario's stirring words, without emotion and with no communication, the Middle East delegation the man was with, except for one, left mumbling something unintelligible and in the process created quite a stir.

The delegate who stayed behind removed his suit jacket and asked halfheartedly, "What do you think is religion's greatest contribution to world peace?"

Mario scoffed and said, "I could answer better the question, what is religion's greatest contribution to *war*?" Waving a bottle of healing tonic, he explained, "There were times religions preached love, yet showed intolerance and closed their eyes to human rights rather than risk all for justice. So I ask you: Who are the criminals? Who are the leaders? Who are the hypocrites? And who are the servants?" Yanking on his fedora, he asked, "Isn't it true, some still use the mask of religion as a disguise of hate? Many times they declare war in the name of God. Maybe they do not understand. Religion is a means and God is an end. Together, we are the ultimate mystery; we are the reality embracing all reality."

The man, with a look of puzzlement, said, "I wish you could be more precise. I think you need to speak more to the point, to be more specific. However, let me ask, what about religion and truth?"

Mario paused to take a drink of tonic and said in a disheartened tone, "Some religions, specifically those that thrive on fundamentalism, claim to have the absolute truth. You tell me if that's foolish or not? To me the absolute truth resides deep within the heart and soul of each human being."

The delegate smiled as he moved aside for a woman who was making her way toward Mario. She said, "To what you just said, I somewhat agree; but let me ask, is fundamentalism and fanaticism one and the same? Or is fundamentalism only sometimes fanatical? Is it ever a path in the right direction?"

"The truth can be cruel. But if you wish, I will tell you what I hear and what I see." He paused to scratch his head. "Rather than reach out to create a common good, extreme fundamentalists *and* fanatics choose to follow a path created by cold hearts. In my opinion, that's the path that Robert Hanssen followed. Remember him? The FBI agent and well-respected member of the secretive and suspicious Opus Dei. What was his contribution to society? Fifteen years spying for Russia. Now *that's* what fundamentalism and fanaticism are all about!"

"Why pick on Opus Dei?" she asked.

Mario's eyes reflected a look of astonishment. "You're right. Let's don't pick on just Opus Dei! Remember what happened with Jim Jones and David Koresch, two men who took extremism to the maximum? They held their followers in a state of bondage camouflaged in righteousness of an unknown God. Nine hundred committed suicide with a cyanide cocktail in Jonestown in South America. And what about Koresch and his cult? After the FBI's armored vehicles and tear gas ended its siege at Waco, many of his followers chose to die in a blazing inferno." He leaned against the peddler's wagon and blurted, "That's two more sneak previews of what an extremely fundamentalist society could be like."

While handing out bottles of *Count Alessandro's Healing Tonic of Love*, the peddler continued. "There are times when fanatics in government or religion take society past the edge of sanity into the darkness of terrorism. They use whatever means are necessary to reach their goal of supreme domination over other belief systems—political, religious, or social. Those who partake in those loathsome acts should be inducted into Dante's hall of shame."

Soon after the United Nations group cleared the area, Senator Randolph Siegel from West Virginia approached the peddler. Even though he had been retired for ten years, he was still active in a quest of world peace. He introduced himself and with his hand resting on Mario's shoulder, shared his wisdom. "Permit me to tell you a short sea-story that you can pass on to others."

While offering the senator a bottle of *Count Alessandro's Healing Tonic of Love*, Mario replied, "I'd love to hear it."

Senator Siegel, always the statesman in his navy blue suit, shifted his slightly overweight body, leaned against the cart, and with a smile said, "It's a simple story about a captain and his ship. A skipper, no matter how hard he tries, never earns the respect from his crew until he navigates in the roughest of seas. Calm waters offer no challenge and prove no character. The same is true in the sea of life. It's inevitable your boat will be rocked by a crisis of some proportions. How you navigate through the storm of life will determine whether your peers will either respect or deny you."

The senator took a sip of tonic and continued, "Having said that, I would say to youth, chart your own course. Stay strong when waters get rough, for it's then, the ordinary becomes the extraordinary."

Mario wrapped his arms around the senator and hugged him.

The peddler turned and responded to a whispering gentleman. "OK, here's another thing I remember about the inferno."

Horror had kept my eyes shut tight, but a bit later, startled by a rumbling and rattling sound, I was shocked out of deep sleep. I slowly opened my eyes to focus on the grotesque surroundings. In disbelief, I watched a graffiti-decorated subway train come to a screeching halt within inches of my fetal-positioned body.

"*Scusame*, I must go to the other side of the wagon. I'll tell you more later."

The peddler, overhearing a huddled group of men's nasty murmurs, raised his hands in a gesture of surrender and responded in a passive tone. "You wish to get rid of me? Wishing, this is your right. And in due time your wish will come true. That's OK. And guess what? When all peoples live love, the military will go away, religious temples will go away, governments will go away. Everything that slows humanity's progress will go away."

The pudgy-faced man who was spitting and screaming at Mario earlier in the day had finally made his way from the financial district to Battery Park. The disgruntled man joined the huddled group of men who wished Mario harm.

He held his umbrella in a striking position and whispered, "That son of a bitch tried to tear down society years ago and still is at it. Maybe, just maybe, somebody will have the guts to take him out."

The man turned and started down the walkway as a white delivery van pulled up alongside the pier.

A young woman from Kansas approached Mario and laughingly said, "What else do you have in your bag of magic for goal setting?"

Looking up at her, he said, "Take a drink of *Count Alessandro's Healing Tonic of Love* just before bedtime and it will transport you into a learning state where you will be directed how to analyze and achieve your goals. Yet keep in mind, whatever you create and establish for society, if you create it without love, you have accomplished nothing. For without love, what you have created just can't last. And when you give money or talent to benefit churches, schools, and other institutions, you think good will come of it. But if the giving is without love, it simply has no effect on life."

The peddler turned to a well-groomed man who had just finished chastising him for his views on religion. Looking baffled, Mario said, "You say the Church teaches the way and declares only the fear of God can keep you on a straight path. But I say the living God removes fear. So, in liberty, you determine your own path. Have you not heard? Religion is contaminated with some *pazzi* clergy, teachers, and followers."

A voice shouted out, "Not them; it's you who is off the wall!"

Mario walked around the cart and continued, "So, do not be caught up in rules, regulations, and lessons that are memorized with no real meaning. With *Count Alessandro's Healing Tonic of Love*, your mind will open to absorb and understand the message of love that is written deep within your heart and the heart of your neighbor. So tolerance and friendship among all peoples will be commonplace. And—"

The man cut him off and curtly said, "Peddler, your voodoo words of love will fall on rocky soil. God seeks justice and righteousness and will punish those like you who stray."

Mario solemnly said, "Too bad you see a punishing God as the solution to sin rather than an all-forgiving God. Forgiveness is love in motion. The result is beautiful. That's life."

The man bristled, turned, and stomped off.

A man with a crew cut said forcefully, "Peddler, the man is right. The Church says that only the fear of God can remove the fear of death."

Mario gently said, "But again I say, the love of God removes fear of any kind, including death, for we live forever." He took a drink of healing tonic and continued, "Just look how organized religion has stifled, distorted, and created an obnoxious viewpoint of Christ and other spiritual icons."

The crew-cut man angrily screamed, "What?"

Lifting his arms, the peddler softly replied, "If you seek warmth and peace of mind, then you must buy the CANDLE OF ETNA made from volcanic ash. Just like the mystical mountain in Sicily, this candle will light the way to a sacred fire of love that burns within your soul this very moment. Come, take and hold. Feel the warm embers of an eternal flame as they simmer ever so gently in the collective consciousness of all peoples and manifest in the ecstasy of the Holy Spirit of One."

In response to a question posed by a woman wearing a white beret, he said, "You ask, can you make your own candle? Why not? My sister, Carmela, uses the ones she buys at Morelli's Novelty Store on Grand Street."

Giving out bottles of *Count Alessandro's Healing Tonic of Love,* the peddler passionately cried out: "Change now. Change your heart with love. And your thoughts, choices, decisions, and actions will change everything else. And you will find lasting happiness."

"I worry so much about the past," said a man whose drooped shoulders reflected his attitude.

With a voice of calmness Mario said, "For you, *signuro,* a poem."

PAST

The past is the past,
And there is nothing we can do
To change one second in time.

So recognize the moment
As a snow-white canvas
Ready to be painted anew.

To manifest your destiny
With mystical colors
Embedded in your soul.

Chapter 70

3:15 p.m.

By midafternoon, clouds lifted at Battery Park and rays of sun made their appearance. A policewoman noticed that the white delivery van that had pulled alongside the pier had not moved or unloaded any merchandise. She determinately approached the driver's side. After a few terse words, the driver turned the van around and slowly drove off.

Another ferry unloaded, and its occupants were joining the expanding group of people surrounding the peddler's cart. Greeting the group of ferry occupants, Mario asked excitedly, "Which one of you is the perfect person to buy this ENCHANTED CARPET once owned by none other than you know who? It will take you on the discovery ride of your life."

As he unbuttoned the top button on his crimson silk shirt, a man with a gold front tooth sneered, "I heard about you and your off-the-wall trinkets. Tell me where this rag is going to take me."

"It's not only this *rag* that will take you beyond your dreams; there is another way. If you read the poem "Brothers and Sisters" with any throw-rug, it will have the same result."

BROTHERS AND SISTERS

Let our thoughts run free
To let the subconscious be,
So we can discover and recognize
Our brothers and sisters
Throughout our sacred earth.

In towns, villages, and cities
And in plains of golden grains
And in grassy meadows of green
And in mystical timbered forests
And in purple mountain majesties
And in oceans and rippling waterways
And in endless skies of blue,

Lives humanity and wild beasts
And animals and mammals
And reptiles, critters, and creepy things
And fish, birds, and butterflies.

And if we believe, . . .
Even if for a moment
That we may be interconnected
In the mystery of life,
Then all we have to do is
Love . . . love . . . and . . . love
Our brothers and sisters.

A woman wearing Armani sunglasses inquired about a pair of eyeglasses he was holding.

Mario answered with enthusiasm. "Take a chance. Buy the EYE-GLASSES OF BENJAMIN FRANKLIN and see your unlimited possibilities unfold before your very eyes and choose in the perfect world in which you live. It's unbelievable, try it and you will like it. For Ben, it was in Philadelphia. That's where he found his unlimited possibilities and where I was given these glasses."

She said uneasily, "I don't know. I worry."

"You wish not to take a risk?" he asked solemnly. Then in a light-hearted tone, he said, "Risk is relative to a person's ability to stand the loss. Yet, there is nothing to lose because you *own* nothing. But you *have* everything. Another thing, don't struggle with a problem. The more you struggle, the bigger the problem gets."

Fear gripped her. "I'm struggling with *you*," she said, fussing with her sunglasses.

"Ah, you struggle with *my words*. That's OK." He reached for her hand and said, "One more thing, good news. The sunglasses you're wearing can also reveal your perfect world and unlimited possibilities. Of course, that's if you have faith."

She kissed his cheek.

Mario, with his arms outstretched, turned to those standing alongside the cart and optimistically asked, "Why not convert problems into opportunities? For it is when you are weak that you are strong. So abandon your will to God. Stay calm. Stay strong. Stay focused. Find the quiet time and pray for a solution. Prayer will carry you through anxieties, rejections, and misunderstandings."

"Save your breath. We live in a bizarre world that will never change," cried out a man. He was struggling with his overstuffed, scarred briefcase.

The peddler thought for a moment before taking hold of the man's shoulders and firmly said, "By now you should know negative thinking produces negative attitudes." Mario straightened himself and said boldly, "Avoid negatives, no matter how small or large. We must believe and have faith; that's what creates a positive attitude. Every time a pessimist speaks, I shut my eyes and close my ears rather than be dragged backward through a maze of shallow graves."

He held up a bottle and said, "Take a sip of *Count Alessandro's Healing Tonic of Love*. It will vaporize all your negative thoughts: frustration goes out the window and resentment down the drain. And disappointment—disappointment disappears on the wings of an owl!"

With this last statement Mario lifted his arms and moved them up and down as if in flight. The air seemed electric with Mario's enthusiasm.

He moved toward the peddler's cart, then back to the man again. "One more thing. Don't be afraid to burn bridges. Because sometimes in order to move forward, that's exactly what you may have to do—burn a bridge. Stand for what you are, for what you believe. And don't worry about the consequences. But don't let stubbornness walk you into a propeller blade."

The man, apparently moved to hope by Mario's words, but still looking disturbed, in frustration said, "How in this godforsaken land can you not worry about consequences? If you're not successful, you're a bum."

Smiling, Mario retorted in a lighthearted tone, "Life is not about winning or losing. It's about being, then doing. So be the amazing person that you are. Place your enlightened being into action and apply your skills in the marketplace of life. But do not be so preoccupied with everything that you concentrate on nothing. Listen to your inner voice— that small voice within."

The man said nervously, "Please, for the love of God, give it up." He tossed his briefcase to the ground, mumbling, "I don't want to be a hypocrite."

"*Signuro,* that reminds me, now is a good time to tell you another thing that happened with Dante in the inferno."

While we were on the floor of the Unscrupulous, some wise guys painted grease on the walls of the elevator. Dante was not a very happy wanderer. He called for a cleanup crew and in a New York minute the Hypocrites came and scrubbed it clean with garments of the Conspirators.

Dante, pulling his hat over his eyes, said: "Could you believe these hideous Two-faced wanderers? They would make Scarface look like Mona Lisa. What a wasted life. The Hypocrites are the maintenance crew of the Unscrupulous Pit. They come by every 666 seconds and listen with one ear of sympathy, before turning their deaf ear and throwing more grease into the pit."

I said, "It seems as though they have it pretty easy."

"They sure do . . . until they meet up with the pissed-off fire-breathing dragon on their way back from the tar pit," said Dante, chuckling.

"The thought of that still makes me laugh."

Listening carefully, the man, without thinking about his actions, picked up his briefcase from where he had tossed it and held it to his body with both hands, for it was full of *once-important* papers and quite heavy. He began fidgeting with its latch as he pleaded, "Please tell me more."

"Oh, you want to know what happens next?" Mario asked chuckling. "Not now, maybe later."

The man smiled and said, "Maybe tomorrow." He left his briefcase alongside the cart and strolled down the promenade.

Although not making eye contact with Mario, a young man with curly black hair said, "What you say is not easy to live. I don't have the confidence to go beyond my fear of failure."

The peddler, with a gentle smile, said, "Where you find yourself is not necessarily where God wants you to be, especially if you think little of yourself. Think good thoughts. The road to self-esteem begins with first accepting yourself the way you are. And above all, do not worry about what others say, think, or how they act: instead, love them!"

At the cart Mario turned to answer a gentlemen with slick red hair holding a book with a tattered cover. The peddler said earnestly, "*Signuro*, you are correct. There are many boundaries and laws. But, there is no mountain, ocean, or any natural boundary that separates or any law that divides, and there is no difference among peoples except what they choose to call different." The peddler smiled and pointed to a cluster of buildings dotting the lower downtown landscape and, with a gleam in his eye, said, "You see, there's only one of everything: one city . . . one building . . . and one street." He whirled around and pointed in the other direction and said in astonishment, "Look! One park . . . one waterway . . . and one peoples."

The man gave him a quizzical look, hesitated for a moment, grinned, and nodded knowingly.

A young woman greeted Mario with a handshake and asked hopefully, "Do you think we can ever obtain peace?"

He took a quick glance at those gathered and said, "First, let me ask this question: can a civilization without peace be a civilization?" He paused momentarily and declared in a firm tone, "No one is exempt from the responsibility of creating a world of peace—using a diplomacy of love. The solutions are there. With faith, we can do it." The peddler took a big drink of tonic, tipped his fedora, and softly said, "Faith. You cannot measure it, plant it, weigh it, buy it, sell it, trade it, see it, or taste it. But you know it's there."

He leaned against the cart and continued excitedly, "I believe when all peoples of all nations and countries accept, adopt, and live the simple message of love, then, and only then, can this earth have total joy and peace." Mario paused, took off his fedora, and softly said, "For those who think I know nothing—that's correct. I know nothing except for what I just said. For what I just said is truth. Thank you for listening."

Onlookers watched Mario remove a ring from deep inside a bag that was well worn with age and constant use. He held the ring up and announced, jubilantly, "This magnificent ring is for sale. It's called the BE RING. Everyone should own one. It took many years to find it in the Sahara Desert. Take it home and wear it daily on your middle finger. It will allow you to rise above the pressure of doing and change your reality to first BE who you are."

Bending down to greet a boy who was looking at his own finger, Mario said happily, "Yes, little man, your space-decoder ring also works and for you, *signura*, yes, your wedding band will do just fine. He reached into his pocket and pulled out a neatly folded piece of paper and simply said, "For you, a poem."

BE

Be not afraid . . . and do not hide
Be a braveheart and stand tall.

Be strong and not two-faced.
Say what you mean,
Yet, give thought to what you say
And when to say it.

And never cry out . . .
If only . . . I wish . . . I could have . . . or should have.

So go with love
Where there are no footprints in the sand,
And BE who you are
In the Holy Spirit of One.

Pausing, he shook his head sadly and sighed. "Unfortunately, some people choose to exist rather than be. They commit mental suicide. I shed tears for those who live life with a fatalistic philosophy."

Looking over a bottle of *Count Alessandro's Healing Tonic of Love,* a woman wearing black shorts and a white golf shirt said to the young couple accompanying her, "Mario warned me and my husband about being caught up in human commandments and lessons that are memorized with no real meaning. I'll never forget when he said, 'We need to approach God, not with our words, but with our hearts.' He handed me this note that I keep with me always. Here's what it says, 'To not think is a travesty. To stop people from thinking is a crime.'"

A person standing alongside her stood with a perplexed look, contemplating what she just said.

The peddler, mingling with those around the cart, said wholeheartedly, "No one should consider himself or herself superior or inferior to another human being. There is no measuring rod to determine a pecking order. No one less than the other. Human nature varies very little: our physical appearance may be different, but under the skin of all humanity is the same heart and soul that brings us together as a global family."

"Peddler, do you know what the hell you're doing?" asked a stocky man with a broad chest.

With a surprised look, the peddler replied, "If everyone only knew what they were doing—they were doing to themselves—life would be different. You see, one element of injustice is stereotypical thinking. Living proof of what I just said is that even though throughout history the Italian American has made his or her positive mark on all sectors of society, many times they get brushed with the tar of Mafia or organized crime innuendos—innuendos that are nothing more than filthy lies."

He turned to pick up his crate, stopped, and said, "One more thing. All peoples of every origin and color are tarred in some manner." Mario sighed and shook his head in disbelief.

Chapter 71

4:30 p.m.

Mario sat on his crate and kept rattling on. "Warped minds create warped thinking. My heart cries out for those captives entrapped in their self-ridden guilt and walking in the shadow of the unconscious: their pathetic plight will take them down a river of despair. Too bad they miss the harmony and enjoyment of life."

A woman standing alongside her husband and three-year-old son brushed a long strand of auburn hair behind her ear and asked Mario, "What irritates you the most?" He patted the little boy on his head, rolled his eyes, and said, "You ask what irritates me the most? I will tell you what irritates me the most. What irritates me the most is that I allow things to irritate me! That's what irritates me the most."

She and her husband laughed at Mario's frustration with himself while their little boy in his New York Yankee cap made a Herculean effort to climb into the cart and failed. He fell to the ground, and sitting there looking up at Mario, began giggling at his mom and dad's laughter.

Mario lifted the boy up onto the cart, kissed his forehead, and with a look of hope, said, "I pray this little one will not have to deal with all those rights—rights that are tossed about in the swirling wind: human rights, labor rights, gay and lesbian rights, animal rights, children's rights, minority rights, rights for those on death row, and rights for rights." He handed the child back to his mother and with a glimmer in his eye said, "We don't need no stinkin' *rights* with liberty. With liberty, love abounds, and the dysfunction of rights goes down the toilet as we live in love and light."

"Group hug!" shouted the father as he, the little boy, and his wife hugged a gleeful peddler.

Turning to a Wall Street broker whose face looked like it was chiseled out of stone, he answered, "I should be flushed down the toilet? That's nasty. But that's OK."

Taking a drink of tonic, the peddler listened for several minutes to a group of legislators who had arrived from Washington, DC for a tour of Liberty Island. He looked at them in astonishment and retorted, "Eh? You want even more power? Yes, power generates power. And it enjoys and thrives on mind games of wit—with one exception: losing is not an option. New power to control those who had the old power. But, have we not learned that power is short lived and fleeting? Just ask Caesar, Napoleon, Alexander the Great, and oh yes, the British Empire." He paused, then roared, "Don't we all know absolute power corrupts—absolutely!" In a calmer voice he added, "Please be a braveheart and take away the dark side of power."

A gentle-spoken woman from Iowa carrying a bag full of Liberty Island souvenirs said, "I overheard your statements about power. My question is, how can we change the situation?"

He took off his fedora, held it to his chest, and with a gentle smile responded, "*Sì, signura,* you ask how to eliminate the power of darkness? This is how I answer. Anyone who has been granted power or who has taken power needs to listen carefully. You have a greater responsibility than anyone else. So, who among the power structure will take a risk? Give up unrestrained power and lead with love?" Wiping perspiration from his forehead he continued, "Each person needs to take responsibility for himself or herself and change into love. Love transcends reason and is the most subtle and strongest force in the world."

A man with a bewildered look yelped, "You're a lunatic!" and he walked off pulling his oversized piece of luggage.

The peddler turned to face those standing in front of the cart and said, "To develop unique insights to life, drink *Count Alessandro's Healing Tonic of Love;* and if you do not doubt, but believe, you will find your way out of the labyrinth."

A woman with a look of depression on her young, angelic face called out, "What if we fail?"

In a confident tone, Mario said, "Discover success and failure and treat those impostors the same. Still and all, sometimes failure can be the greatest teacher of all."

She nodded, thankfully.

The peddler opened a bottle of tonic, took a slug, gave her a bottle, and declared, "It's important to understand that with success comes a myriad of responsibilities one must accept. Having said that, I ask you, is it fear of failure or fear of success that paralyzes?"

A distinguished-looking gentlemen asked specifically, "Don't we need to think before we act?"

The peddler hesitated slightly, then said, "Thinking is wonderful. But, action is doing; doing is experimenting; experimenting is reality; and reality is the path to real-world solutions and achievements."

Addressing a man spewing anger and hate, Mario cringed and said, "You cannot be concerned with what the next person is doing or what the politicians or religious are doing and so on until you concern yourself with what and who you are. So begin with self first and put on love."

The man's jaw tensed as he curtly replied, "Stick it."

"Please," Mario implored. He extended his hand.

The man slowly turned back and somewhat reluctantly shook the peddler's hand.

Mario said, "If you have another moment, permit me to tell you a story about Dante."

I remember after a three-hour journey in silence, we reached a huge black box that turned out to be a dilapidated mausoleum. Dante, swinging open the concrete door, walked into a dark caged elevator within the crypt.

Still standing outside, resisting going in, I said: "*Pathetic* is the right word to describe the vestibule of the inferno. I understand and feel for those who are stuck in relationships, jobs . . . or whatever, . . . afraid of the unknown and therefore uncommitted. They're better off making a decision—right or wrong—rather than making no decision."

"Corretto . . . you are absolutely right. But, if they make it with love, the decision is always right."

I nodded affirmatively.

"Anyway, we have to move along. Don't be a scaredy-cat: come on in to one of hell's super methods of transportation. This elevator is to the B floors of the inferno," said Dante with his cat-in-the-hat grin.

He adjusted his hat and shoved aside several wanderers who were sweeping away their ambition with rotting straw brooms. I entered the two-by-three-foot decrepit chamber. Dante closed the steel-grated door, turned the rusted crank, and down we . . .

"Enough for now. Maybe more later."

Mario blew a heavy layer of dust off a cardboard box that he removed from the bottom of the peddler's cart. He pried it open; standing on his crate he bellowed, "This beautiful RED CLOAK, once worn by Garibaldi, is a perfect gift for anyone. Whenever you wear it, fear turns to courage, frustration to contentment."

A short, spaghetti-thin black man in his twenties shrugged, cleared his throat, and said, "It's wonderful, though it will never fit."

"That's OK. I understand. You think the cloak is too big." The peddler's eyes widened. He slapped his forehead and said, "But, if I'm not mistaken, that faded Brooklyn Dodger sweatshirt you are wearing. It will do just fine."

The man with the Dodger sweatshirt helped Mario down off the crate. He returned Mario's smile as he reached out and hugged him.

The peddler tipped his fedora in thanks, turned to a gathering group of people, and with a strong and steady voice, said, "Let us together *awaken* from our apathy and challenge structured systems to uphold our birthright, match words with deeds, and shatter the illusion of exaggeration caused by *the lie*. Let us, together, melt away the tar of secrecy and eliminate the conspiracy of silence. Engage trust, understanding, and patience as stepping stones to peace."

He took another drink of tonic and added forcefully, "With strength and conviction, let us remain part of life's meandering vine and, together, acknowledge that our only method is love in our quest for truth and liberty and that nothing has been, or ever will be, manufactured or contrived that can conquer love."

His face showed determination as he declared in a steadfast voice:

> *So challenge your conscience. Become a nonconformist with clarity of thought. Challenge institutions. Challenge theologies. Think about what you hear and what you read. Challenge traditions. Claim your Liberty!*

Trying to ignore Mario's words, a man fighting his own frustrations was barely able to squeak out, "Change through love? It will never happen."

Startled by the man's statement, Mario's heart pounded, and with a look of astonishment, he said, "*Mi*, I should be called *Mario the Liar* if I ever stop believing that love is the one enduring solution to all our problems."

A reporter from the *Greenwich Village Looking Glass* walked up and stood in front of the peddler's cart. He said, "I'm conducting research for an article entitled, "Corruption in the '70s: an Upside-down Era." I tracked your trial, the outcome, and what happened to some of your old acquaintances and adversaries. My question is, what ever happened to Sam Castellano after he liquated Castellano Enterprises?"

Mario shook his head and sadly said, "He moved to Sicily. And since his wife Rose died, Sam has become a recluse and resides in a seaside villa in Taormina."

The reporter shook the peddler's hand, smiled, picked up a bottle of *Count Alessandro's Healing Tonic of Love,* and started to walk away. He stopped suddenly and asked, "Where's your sidekick?"

Mario paused, and with his voice breaking, said, "My dear Catherine passed away three long months ago, on June 10th. I miss her terribly and look forward to seeing her on the other side."

The reporter hugged him. Mario wiped away a tear.

A woman leaving Battery Park, walking with her family to the Staten Island Ferry, said, "I believe the peddler when he said, 'There's a oneness among all people and all living things. Nothing is separate from the other.'"

"That sums it up," said her husband in agreement. Their baby, sitting in a carrier on his dad's back, was starting to whimper because his dad had stopped and was standing still.

"Sweetie," the wife said half-jokingly to her husband as she shook a rattle in front of the child's face, "he means everyone is part of the family. If you take the peddler's statement to its true meaning, that means everyone, including our nosy neighbor."

"I'll go you one better," the husband countered. "How about those on death row?"

Ignoring some nasty comments from others in the crowd, Mario once again reached into his peddler's bag, pulled out a brown paper bag, opened it, looked inside, grinned, and said in wonderment, "Now some good news: in this bag are *PISTACCHIO* SEEDS OF DISCERNMENT from a garden in *Conca d'Oro,* Palermo, Sicily. They are very cheap. These seeds are like magic. After you eat them. Poof. You know what is right, what is wrong. Then, in liberty, it's always your choice."

He glanced over his shoulder and answered a young man who was without money. "Ah, don't worry. I'll give you a bag for free."

To a petite middle-aged woman, he happily replied, "*Sì, signura.* Sunflower seeds will work and maybe even better." Radiating enthusiasm he shouted, "Paradise is now. Here's a poem that speaks to paradise."

ALPHA AND OMEGA

All of life is embraced
In the Holy Spirit of One
Which is now.
It is in us
And among us,
The Alpha and Omega.

The curious group pushed closer to the peddler's cart as Mario removed with the care of a surgeon a strange looking oblong object from his peddler's bag. Holding it carefully, he said, "Found in a forest in Great Britain. For you who doubt, you must take with you MERLIN'S wonderful, mystical, magical KALEIDOSCOPE." With a hearty laugh and a huge grin he continued, "Here, see for yourself. Turn to the right and observe the gateway into an unseen world of energy, a world of light, constantly manifesting itself throughout the earth-plane as you become one in all in the eternity in which you live."

Those who stood around the cart listened intently.

Looking through the kaleidoscope, he hesitated, then merrily said, "Turn to the left and you will see how thoughts, choices, decisions, and actions create different results of the same situation when you apply love. MERLIN'S KALEIDOSCOPE will tease you to be bold and go where no one has dared to go."

Someone in a surprised tone simply asked, "How does that work?"

Mario shrugged and, with a smile, said, "Who knows? It's a mystery."

A couple of children, their eyes sparkling like precious gems, whispered to Mario, who in turn gleefully replied, "Of course, a glass jar will do as well, as long as you shut your eyes and believe."

The peddler walked around the cart and bellowed, "The past and the future *is* now; it's in the moment. So don't procrastinate. Begin tonight. First, take a drink of *Count Alessandro's Healing Tonic of Love*. Its mystical water will cause you to stay strong in faith so you can make choices in the light and transform the dream of *liberty* into reality. Then open your door, go outside into the middle of the street and shout out *liberty*. Open your window, stick your head and neck way out, and shout out *liberty*. Wherever you may be, shout out *liberty*."

Someone shouted, "Then what?"

Mario, getting more fired up by the moment, cried out, "Then go where you would rather not go. And go you will, for you know who you are. You are a person for others. So go with love!"

The peddler approached a man and woman who had a look of bewilderment plastered over their faces. He chuckled and said, "Would you like to try a bottle?"

Bending down to hear above the chatter and rush-hour horn-blowing, street-thumping-traffic hullabaloo of lower downtown, the peddler, with a kind and loving embrace, said, "Excuse me, little one; did you ask, can you do the same thing with water from your kitchen sink? Is that what I heard you ask?"

The child looked straight at Mario and, without hesitation, nodded his head excitedly in agreement.

The peddler knelt down on one knee and, with much affection, kissed the child's cheek. With a huge smile that only hinted at the profundity of the comment that followed, he said, "Of course you can! And not only can you do that; you can become a peddler too!"

With that said, Mario stuffed his belongings into his tattered leather bag, flung it over his shoulder, and began to push the peddler's cart north to Little Italy. He hesitated a moment, turning to those lingering, took a deep breath, tipped his fedora, and in an exuberant tone said, "How wonderful that we are planted with love in this glorious earthly garden to grow into the fullness of God. *Stare bene . . . Arrivedérci*."

Once again, he took hold of the peddler's cart, took two steps of his trek home, then stopped in his tracks, and with a look of admiration and a joyful smile, said, "One more thing . . . What I wish for you to remember is that I love you. And I do love you unconditionally."

BOOK IX

Chapter 72

....

5:30 p.m.

Evening traffic was horrendous. By the time Mario made his way back to 231 Elizabeth Street, darkness was descending on Little Italy.

Caught up in his thoughts, he never heard the whining sound of the stalled 1973 white delivery van with a dented right fender double parked across the street.

The peddler, exhausted from a long day of jousting, fumbled with his keys, picked the right one, and opened Ferrara's dusty, barren store.

He stored the peddler's cart, locked the store, and at a snail's pace, climbed the three flights of stairs to his fourth-floor home and pushed open the door. Once inside, Mario shuffled across the room to the kitchen, reached for the bowl of tomatoes on the table, and chose one. He cautiously opened the window, climbed outside to sit on the fire escape, and leaned his tired body against the open windowsill.

Mario stretched out his legs, stared at the heavens, sighed, and whispered, *"T'amu, Catarina,"* as the beautiful red tomato rolled out of his hand and came to rest on the open grate.

Heavy, dark rain clouds had gathered overhead as bursts of lightning caused the lights inside his home to flicker on and off.

The white delivery van slowly pulled away.

Later in the evening sheets of rain came down and came down hard, canceling the Yankee-Red Sox game.

According to the weather forecast, the quickly moving storm would give way to morning sunshine, lending itself to a glorious day for the residents and visitors of the Big Apple.

Chapter 73

6:30 a.m.
Tuesday, September 11, 2001
Little Italy, New York City

John arrived to have breakfast with his brother. Letting himself in, he shouted, "It's me." Moments later his heart jolted. Mario was sprawled out on the fire escape thoroughly drenched.

One of John's shaking hands grabbed for the railing to steady himself; the other reached for his cell phone and, leaning on the railing, he dialed 911.

Within minutes Carmela, Joe, and Beth were at his side. Police, fire, and other emergency vehicles arrived. Curious crowds gathered. Many prayed.

Before Mario was taken down the steps of 231 Elizabeth Street, the emergency medical technician handed John a crumpled piece of paper found in the peddler's pocket. John read it.

To all peoples of different languages
and nations and countries,
especially those who govern:

My dear, peace to you.

When the Holy Spirit spoke through the prophet Isaiah, He said:
    Go to this nation and say, you will hear and hear again but
not understand, see and see again but not perceive. For the heart of
this nation has grown coarse, their ears are dull of hearing, and
they have shut their eyes, for fear they should see with their eyes,
hear with their ears, understand with their heart, and be converted
and healed by me.

Isaiah wanted to know, "until when?" This is how I answer . . .

The time of waiting is over

Go now,
In the human and Divine of who you are
Hear with your ears the subtle whisper of God
See with your eyes the reality within reality
Understand with your heart
The interconnectedness of all living things
And proclaim your Liberty
In the Holy Spirit of One
In this very moment of life.

Mario Ferrara

The neighbors who had gathered slowly started to disperse as emergency vehicles pulled away on the rain-swept street.

Carmela and John, with arms entwined, their emotions ripping them apart, stood outside Ferrara's Grocery and Bakery with Joe and Beth.

It was about 8:45 a.m. when John handed Beth Mario's finished manuscript, *Me and Dante Down by the Inferno.*

Joe was just turning to hug John and Carmela goodbye, when his body suddenly buckled in fright as American Airlines Flight 11 out of Boston crashed into the North Tower of the World Trade Center.

Seemingly unaware of the terror in process, a lone figure making its way along Centre Street seemed to add a little bounce with each step it took as it passed the Brooklyn Bridge. Its frame gained a sense of posture, a bearing long forgotten, and with each step it moved with a stronger purpose toward some distant goal.

Alert passersby took note of the object in its hand and the intensity with which its eyes searched for something in the fog ahead. And had they not passed it so quickly, had they been able to hold in their vision its face a bit longer, they would have seen it transformed as the morning sun dispersed the mist and lifted the fog ahead, revealing that for which it searched.

Suddenly, a fedora went flying into the air as the figure cut into a run toward the finish line of a lifelong race.

As fire and smoke billowed from the North Tower, Carmela gave out a howling cry of grief and collapsed in her brother's arms.

The figure, oblivious to the sounds of screaming emergency vehicles, falling glass, crumbling buildings, people shouting and running to escape the horror, kept running itself. All it could hear were the loving whispers of God blowing through clouds of ash.

Beth, her eyes full of fright, held on tightly to Joe. The four friends with their arms around one another stood frozen in horror, only to be brought to their knees when, eighteen minutes later, a second hijacked airliner, United Airlines Flight 175, also from Boston, crashed into the South Tower.

The lone figure ran along Broadway until it reached Battery Park. No one recognized it, but some were struck with their own strong conviction as it ran past that its eyes saw and felt love . . . not hate . . . no good or bad . . . no right or wrong . . . no difference . . . no judgment.

At the water's edge, blissfully smiling, the figure knelt down and gently tossed the white rose in its hand into the rippling waters. Its spirit was soaring with the ecstasy of Divine Love.